OUR EVENINGS

BY ALAN HOLLINGHURST

The Sparsholt Affair

The Stranger's Child

The Line of Beauty

The Spell

The Folding Star

The Swimming-Pool Library

Our Evenings

OUR EVENINGS

A NOVEL

ALAN HOLLINGHURST

RANDOM HOUSE

NEW YORK

Published in the United States by Random House, an imprint and division of Penguin Random House LLC, New York.

RANDOM HOUSE and the HOUSE colophon are registered trademarks of Penguin Random House LLC.

Published in the United Kingdom by Picador, an imprint of Pan Macmillan, London.

Hardback ISBN 9780593243060
Ebook ISBN 9780593243077

Printed in the United States of America on acid-free paper

randomhousebooks.com

1st Printing

FIRST U.S. EDITION

E. L. H.

1919–2016

No rehearsal this morning, so we stayed in bed – I made tea, and we sat propped up, searching our phones for stories about Mark. Why we needed to read them I'm not sure: perhaps knowing a famous person makes you part of the story, and you want whoever is telling it to see the point and get it right. The segment last night at the end of the News had been earnest but perfunctory, forty-five seconds from a young correspondent with no first-hand knowledge of the subject. It was confounding to learn about a friend's death in this way. I muted the set, Richard put his arm round me, and we sat saying nothing as the cricket and then the weather came on.

Richard only met Mark once, at the ninetieth-birthday dinner at the Tate, where two hundred guests sat down in a room that was hung for the occasion with his own gifts. Mark looked and sounded frail when he made his speech, but we were all on his side, and he was modest and generous, toasting Cara too, who was one day older than him. I wasn't sure, when we spoke briefly with them later, if they were wounded or quietly relieved that Giles wasn't there.

In Mark Hadlow's story, from the press point of view, there has always been an irksome absence of scandal – an ethical businessman, a major philanthropist, married to one woman for seventy years; not a hermit, indeed 'a generous host', but with no taste for the limelight: he was said to have turned down both a knighthood and a peerage, and none of the galleries and halls he endowed bears his own name. He can only be got at, for invasive gossip, through his children. Nobody has much on Lydia, except that she once appeared topless in a Warhol movie, and died in a car-crash in France five years ago. But Giles, of course, is everywhere, and so fiercely opposed to all his father stood for that Mark's life-work is eclipsed by his son's destructive career. 'Mark Hadlow: Brexit Minister's millionaire father dies,' said the *Times*; while the *Mail* put Giles first in the sentence: 'Giles Hadlow's father dies at 94'. The photo of the two of them uneasily together dated from the 1980s. It would be mad to say Giles killed Mark, but I wondered what his feelings about him were now – continued defiance, or some kind of guilty grief?

'Will you ring Cara?' Richard said.

'I ought to, yes,' I said, but the question made me wonder: ours was a long and unshakable friendship, but I felt shy of ringing her up. 'Or perhaps I'll write her a letter' – then felt there would be almost too much to say. I looked across at the mirror that reflected the bed, and seemed to frame us in a larger and more beautiful space. 'To have money and do nothing but good with it – how rare is that?'

'Well, pretty much unheard-of,' said Richard.

I thought, inexactly, of everything Mark had done for me, even before our first meeting at Woolpeck in my early teens. I pictured myself on that sunny weekend, my anxiety dressed up as self-possession, my cleverness hidden by nerves from the people who were hoping to see it. 'The plain fact is,' I said, 'he changed my life.' I can cry at will, on camera or on stage, night after night; but now I surprised myself. 'I can't imagine where I'd be without him.'

'Oh, love . . .' said Richard, with a consoling rub. 'He was like the father you never had, I sometimes think.'

'We were never that close,' I said, wary of this idea. 'It was really just chance – if I hadn't won the Hadlow Exhibition I would never have gone to that school.'

'And you would never have met Giles.'

I thought of what Mum said, just before she died, when the campaign was launched: 'To think we could all be at the mercy of your terrible friend!'

'They won't win, Mum,' I'd said.

'Well, it won't affect me,' she said, 'I'll be gone, but you – and Richard . . .'

I looked again in the mirror, at the two old men in bed. Now Mum's gone, and Mark's gone, and here we are, with Giles all over the papers, all over the country, tearing up our future and our hopes.

In the evening I found a photo of Mark online that must have dated from about the time I met him; it's as sweetly breathtaking as seeing an unknown picture of myself as a young man: I'd forgotten that I'd known him like that. His mouth gives an impression of decisiveness, even impatience, that is qualified by the large, somehow humorous, brown eyes. His way of paying keen attention is at one with his need, once he's done so, to move on to something else. The attachment close to love that I felt for him as a child survives and comes back to me clearly through the steady fondness of the later years, when the habit of friendship became a more prominent part of its meaning.

In your fifties and sixties your father-figures drop away – the ones who had licensed, enabled and witnessed your life – and no one can replace them. Roland, Raymond, Mark all gone – and no chance of becoming a father-figure myself. My two godsons are grown and married and fathers themselves by now, and we barely know each other; our rare meetings have terrific cordiality, we hug fiercely and grin across the gulf between their lives as businessmen and mine as a queer old puzzle. Great respect is shown to me, and my obscure achievements are referred to in an encouraging way, rather as if I was their godchild. Otherwise, I do my bits of teaching, and when I'm in a show I regale the young actors with old theatre gossip, and rehearse them surreptitiously, sometimes, backstage. My warmth is comradely, more than paternal – or amorous: I registered the point, a few years back, when my flirting became more alarming than seductive.

Now I'm two weeks into rehearsals for *Bajazet* at the Anvil – we gather in a room just down the road, a battered blue door between a butcher's and an antique shop ('That's contemporary theatre for you,' says Richard). I'm playing old Acomat, the Grand Vizier, a gift of a part, and wonder when I first used the phrase, 'I'm playing *old* Someone': a while ago now. The man in the *Telegraph* said last year I was 'enjoying the golden autumn of my career', though it feels to me more like a lucky run of character parts that make a quick mark. Directors have decided they can use me, and Martin my agent has slipped into the role of a man who believed in me all along.

I would normally be off the book by now – never before rehearsals, something Ray taught me forty years ago: best to 'seal in' the lines in the first week or two as you'll speak them to these particular actors. I open the play and have six pages of blank verse in the first ten minutes – complicated stuff about plots, armies and empires which the audience, in their first eager ignorance, will take in intently, knowing their evening depends on it. It's just me and my confidant, Osmin, played by Keith Mackle, a young mixed-race actor (Glasgow, Ghana) who reminds me of Hector in his handsomeness and concentration; and he's absolutely patient when I call for a prompt (it's still early days) or jump by mistake into a later speech about the Babylonian troops. The fact is my famous memory's not quite what it was. I remember yesterday in detail, and fifty years ago with new and unexpected clarity, but a small mental floater blurs and half obscures last week. I leave my script on a chair at the start, then pick it up and carry it round like someone else.

I did send Cara a letter, and heard nothing, and then in the final week of the play she rang: she was frank, and told me she'd had cancer, an operation on her throat six weeks before Mark died. 'I sound different,' she said, 'I know.' 'Not to me,' I said with the sort of chivalry she'd never had much time for. 'Oh,' she said, 'it's nice of you to say so.' I thought her speech was very slightly altered, or obstructed, and with an elderly sense of effort to it. She said, 'Can you come for lunch tomorrow? – or any day, really,' an unexpected emptiness. I went round three days later, and by myself.

All my tender understandings about Mum in her last years were available to me, and the competence with very old people that I'd learned with her. But of course Cara wasn't Mum. With Cara there was candour, but not intimacy – with its indulgence of weakness; and besides she had people to look after her. I was let into the house by a quiet young woman who took my coat and showed me through to the drawing room, with its tall windows on to the garden and its large abstract paintings facing each other down across the white carpet. Cara was sitting by the fire with her glasses on her nose, apparently texting; she frowned at the phone as she poked the letters. I had a moment then to take in how she looked – the wide white brow, with a red turban wrapping her head, a silk scarf round her neck, her mouth on the right side slightly drawn back, the square well-known face both softer and gaunter. 'Hello!' she said, with touching warmth, not looking up, then pressed Send and reached her hand out to me. I went over, and kissed her on the cheek, and she gripped my arm for a second as I did so.

'You don't drink, I know,' she said.

'Well,' I said, 'I don't drink a lot.'

'I mean, do have something, I just can't at the moment.'

The girl was hovering. 'Perhaps just some water?' I said. So we both had that, and I sat down and we looked at each other. My look was sympathetic, I hoped, and humorous, hers somehow abstract – I couldn't tell where she would want to begin.

'Have you been able to work?' I said.

'Oh, I can't paint now,' she said, and raised her right hand diffidently, it seemed, the knuckles large and white and the fingers hard to straighten. 'I draw a little, but it's not up to much.'

'I'm sorry,' I said. 'I remember your work so well.'

'You were always nice about it,' she said.

'Well, not just me,' I said, aware though that I'd liked it mainly because I knew her.

I wanted to find out about Mark's funeral, from an odd knot of feelings – curiosity, and regret that I hadn't been there, and an awful inadmissible pique that I hadn't been invited. 'Oh, it was quite private,' Cara said, 'which was what Mark wanted.'

'I completely understand.'

'And I wasn't well, I couldn't have managed anything more. It was really just family – and three or four others.'

'Of course,' I said lightly.

'We had some Bach, and some Rameau, I think it was. Mark's old friend Mike Kidstow, do you know, gave the address.'

'Well, I know who you mean,' I said, 'I've never met him.'

'No hymns or anything, naturally. Giles gave a short reading.'

'Ah, I wondered . . .'

She looked at me. 'He speaks very well.'

'Yes, he does,' I said, and felt I could add, 'he's had plenty of practice!'

'Well, that was the thing, Dave, of course, we couldn't have crowds, and the press all over us.'

'No, I do see.'

'They kept all the photographers outside the gates at the crematorium.'

'Oh, that was good.'

'I mean, it wasn't Mark they were there for . . . We left in a blizzard of flashlights.' She raised her bent hand to shade her eyes.

We had lunch in the dining room, which I remembered as much gloomier, and with different pictures: there was that restless Hadlow sense that things could always be changed, and improved. Cara had a stick – I offered her an arm as we went through but she said quietly, 'I'm all right.' We sat down face to face at one end of the long and extendable table – a white plaster cast of some empty space, a carton or cupboard perhaps, by Rachel Whiteread was centred at the other end. I felt I might find this sequence of huge off-white rooms a bit chilly, with no husband around.

We were served by a young man called Rihaan, who murmured now and then in Cara's ear, and seemed to play a larger part in her care. I remembered Ashok here, decades ago, the smile of allegiance and the sense too that we all had our place. Cara wanted proper attention but no fuss; the meal was simple and digestible, sole, new potatoes, a green salad, a jug of water to drink. She might have been a very rich woman but she was also a farmer's daughter, who'd never lost the hatred of waste of all who had lived through the War.

I spoke warmly about the huge *New Painting from Europe* show at the Hayward, that Mark had been the invisible godfather to.

'I'm so glad you saw it, that was really his last great hurrah.'

'Oh, it was marvellous,' I said, in the committed tone of the Hadlows themselves around contemporary art. 'An amazing achievement.' There had been new work from all twenty-eight member states in the EU – the idea was exemplary, high-minded, even visionary, though as Richard said you couldn't help wishing about halfway through that several more countries had done a Brexit.

A little later she said, 'We've known each other a long time, Dave.'

'Fifty . . . -*four* years,' I said.

'I'm glad we've stayed in touch.'

'Oh, me too!' Like Mark, she'd always shushed away my words of gratitude, but I felt now some unaffected statement might console her. I glanced at her wide downturned face, lit strongly from the right by the large window. 'I always say how much I owe to you and Mark – meeting you really changed my life.' She scowled, just for a moment, at this, but I felt she allowed it too.

'You do know, Dave, Mark was always so proud of you, and interested by all you did. It was wonderful for us to see you make a success of things, not at all easy, I know, especially early on.'

'Well, thank you!' It wasn't the first time she'd said this, in almost the same words, but the repetition was none the less touching – I felt to her it still had the purpose and the warmth of something said for the first time. 'That means a great deal to me.'

'I feel awful to have missed this Racine play – you've had marvellous reviews.'

'Oh, you mustn't worry about that,' I said.

'Well . . .' and she smiled with a touching new note of uncertainty. 'I do sometimes wonder what you made of us all, back then.'

'Well, it was a great thing to stay at Woolpeck with you all.'

She blinked, perhaps trying to picture it. 'Did you enjoy it? I remember having to bandage you up, after one of the Minister's more violent episodes.'

'Oh, god . . .' I said, but glad of the unexpected joke.

'Before you knew us, I think, we had happier times there. But Giles and Lydia never saw eye to eye, and they were both difficult teenagers, in a way I'm fairly sure you weren't.'

'No, but I got difficult a bit later on . . .'

'You were very much closer to your mother,' Cara said. 'I think, in some way that I'll never understand, Mark and I were not good parents to our children.'

'Cara, you were dream parents!' I said.

She looked at me. 'Oh dear, what a melancholy conversation. I'm sorry.' I wondered again then if she had people to talk to, in the thin social air of her nineties.

The pudding was a large tart made with lemon curd. 'A favourite of yours, I remember,' Cara said, as Rihaan cut a thin slice for her, and set a good third of the remainder in front of me, with a dollop of white whipped cream on top.

'Amazing memory you have,' I said – better, really, than mine. I hadn't eaten lemon curd for at least thirty years, but I smiled and squared up to it, in a mime of my larger gratitude.

We had coffee after lunch in a sleek glass cube that projected into the garden. Cara sat down with a grunt, propped her stick beside her chair, and peered out abstractedly at the lawn as the coffee was poured. I saw we could easily part without discussing the Minister further, but both of us feeling perhaps that we'd missed a chance or dodged a responsibility.

'Do you ever go to Woolpeck now?' I said.

'Oh . . . not for some years,' said Cara, 'not since my brother Peter died. Thank you . . .' as the door was closed again. 'I can't, Dave, really . . . you know.'

'But it was your home,' I said.

'It was, long ago – well, I was born there, as you may know. But it's Giles's now.'

'I wonder if he's there very much?' I said. I was indignant about it, on her behalf, and also somehow on mine. I didn't know if Cara had seen him on *Newsnight*, in a piece about the impact of Brexit on agriculture, up by the Rings in a green Barbour and holding an ashplant, his hair whipped about by the wind. 'I farm all this land,' he said, 'as far as you can see.' 'Really?' said the interviewer – the camera panning slowly across the vast expanse of the Vale. 'In *that* direction,' Giles said, the stick now pointing to the long wood half a mile away.

'Laura doesn't care for it, I gather. He has a very good farm manager, of course.'

'To deal with all the EU subsidies . . .'

'Well, quite,' said Cara in a murmur. She was really beyond wondering at the madness of it all.

I felt she was opening the way to more talk about Giles. In my life he had come and gone and then alas come back, but there were whole years when I barely thought of him at all; Cara must have thought about him many times a day. 'But tell me, Dave' – and she looked up from her cup and held my eye – 'if you think back, years ago, to when we all first met, are you surprised by how Giles's career turned out?'

I laughed for half a second. Cara valued frankness, but she hardly hoped to hear that her son had been a swine all along. 'I think perhaps he always had a taste for power, yes, and punishing his fellow man.'

'He was an authoritarian, would you say, even then.'

'I remember he simply loved being a prefect. And he minded very much that he was never head boy.'

'Well, he's still not that,' said Cara, and we both made a face at the thought, the possibility. 'But he was intelligent, wasn't he?' It was as if she hadn't known him at all, or deeply doubted what she did know.

'I think so . . .' I said. 'I don't remember how he did at Oxford.'

She looked down. 'Well, he was very caught up in politics, wasn't he, the Union and so forth. But he scraped a Second, I think.'

'Right . . .' I said warily. I didn't have much faith in these simple searches for a key to Giles's behaviour – and I'm not sure they satisfied Cara, though talking things over perhaps eased her feelings, the long-term dismay beneath the later grief.

I

1

We were up at the Rings, racing about, playing war games without agreeing on the rules. Giles shouted something from the top of the bank and ran off, I ran the other way, tripped and slid down into a chalky hollow, and crouched there, while my heartbeat thumped in my ear and the wind poured over the grassy ramparts. Was I meant to hunt for Giles now, or was Giles already hunting for me? I pulled my watch round on my wrist and waited while the second hand made two circuits of the dial. No sound of footsteps, though now and again the clank of farm machinery came from a few fields away. I heard an awkward cry, and looked up – high above, dark against the cloudy blue, a buzzard sailed past, seemed to note our positions, flapped and circled twice before sliding away across the crest of the hill and out over the thousand-foot drop below. Then almost at once there was a light rhythmic sound, coming closer, the little giveaway jiggle of Giles's pedometer in his trouser pocket. He was coming from behind me, moving quite fast along the bank above, and I didn't risk looking up – I stayed hunched in my hollow while he paused, no more than ten feet away, savouring his advantage . . . but it seemed he hadn't seen me, he swore under his breath, and after ten seconds he jogged on. When I got up and crept on all fours to the top of the ditch, I saw him a hundred yards off, on the far side of the circle, strolling along in plain view against the sky. He had his hands in his pockets, as if to say the game was over, or that he'd never really been playing it.

We met at the trig point. Giles, with a scrambling of heels on its smooth concrete surface, pushed himself up and sat on it. In this bare, windswept landscape the little pillar of the trig point was a monument, as cryptic in its way as the prehistoric stones along the Downs. I examined the small brass benchmark buried in its side, an arrow and a number. The grooves for mounting a theodolite on the pillar's flat top made a three-pointed symbol, almost hidden now under Giles's thighs. 'You could fix a machine gun on here,' he said. 'Any Germans coming up from the farm wouldn't stand a chance.'

As far as I understood it, I'd been playing a Jap; so we were fighting on different fronts. I said, 'Is this all your land?'

He looked round, as if to be sure. 'This is all ours,' he said. 'Over there, of course, you get on to Denhams' land.'

Below the Rings the path that ran the whole length of the Downs vanished westwards in a fine white furrow, crossed a quarter of a mile off by the track that led down to Woolpeck. A Land-Rover was making its slow way along it now, rocking and tilting over the deep ruts. The farm buildings themselves lay far below, the long L of the barns and the three gables of the house showing tiny but distinct, the tennis court marked out in white on the left. A small figure, a mere speck of chaff, was crossing the yard and disappeared behind the house, where I imagined the bell on its rope being rung for tea, the sound carried off in the glitter of wind and distance. I looked at my watch again, then squinted up at Giles on his pillar, handsome with the sun behind him. He was only three months older than me but growing faster, and impressively big. 'Should we go down now?' I said. He sat staring at the view as if to say I was missing the point of being here and perhaps of the whole walk.

Mrs Hadlow had told me at breakfast that on a day like today you could see for fifty miles from the Rings, but I asked Giles anyway.

'From here? You can see for eighty miles,' he said.

'Eighty miles is a very long way, isn't it,' I said. It was all the way to London, or Birmingham.

'On a clear day,' said Giles, 'you can see five counties, though I don't expect you to know what they are. They're Berkshire, Oxfordshire, of course . . . ' – he gazed out.

'Gloucestershire,' I said, 'Wiltshire.'

'*Wiltshire*,' said Giles, half turning round, and frowning as though something had caught his eye.

'And Buckinghamshire!'

He stared at me, with a hint of mockery, or even doubt, as I peered in the general direction of Gloucestershire. Where the boundaries divided one county from another was impossible to guess on the gleaming expanse of the plain below, where details were soon lost in the wash of the April light. I shivered, goose-flesh under my shirt in spite of the sun; though now and then there was a quiet lull, ten seconds of scented warmth tucked up in the cold wind that flowed endlessly over England. I ran off a few yards and gazed at the featureless circle behind us, the scruffy grass dotted with sheep droppings, though no sheep could be seen or heard. When I looked back, Giles had sprung down from the trig point and set off towards the track, shouting something I couldn't make out.

I went scrabbling and jumping down after him, nearly out of control in the steep chalky channel of the track, Giles far ahead, and then out of view, so that I stopped chasing; it was a relief to let him go. I felt the start of a stitch, and waited for a minute with my hands on my hips, catching my breath. From here, halfway down, I picked up the bleat of the lambs and ewes in the lower fields, and when I looked back, the bare mass of the hill behind me had risen against the sky. I was happier by myself. These games with Giles were undermined from the start by a feeling that we were too old to be playing them. And his violence when he caught me, his Chinese burns, and bending my fingers back, made me dread them too. I stood listening to the birdsong, and then carried on down, skirting long slimy puddles in the ruts of the lower track; by now the bright distances were hidden from view and the places that ten minutes earlier had lain below us like objects on a tray had slipped back behind woods and hedgerow trees into the everyday mystery of the landscape.

Near the bottom of the hill a gate stood open into a field on the right and when I went in through the rough grass and looked over the bushes I could see a thin stretch of the empty lane below and the main entrance to the farm; but there was no sign of Giles. The house itself stood back from the road beyond a meadow and the square dark hedge of its front garden. It was built of red brick, and you could see, from a slight change of colour, that the left-hand end, with the third gable, had been added on later. The house stared out at the hill from ten square windows. The farmyard with all its noise and business lay behind the house, but it was the vast primeval fact of the hill in front of it that seemed to place it and define it and almost to mesmerize it.

There was the country sound of a dozen miscellaneous things unself-consciously happening, and under it the sigh, like a gathering wave, of a car approaching – from round the corner a red Citroën DS swung into view, and sped along the lane just below me; the sun flashed from its windscreen as it slowed and turned into the driveway of the farm. I'd never seen the cabriolet before, with its soft black roof – and the other thing, glimpsed for a second, was that the driver was on the left-hand side. I knew at once it was Giles's father, he was expected and now he was here: as the brake lights came on and the car turned into the yard behind the house I found myself running through the scene, in the hall or the kitchen, where at last we would meet, and I would have the chance to thank him. My pulse raced at the thought, but the rehearsal reassured me. I was anxious for a moment, almost guilty, after a whole day messing about here without him, but also relieved he had turned up to take charge. It was an inroads of order and purpose, a touch of discipline brought into the holidays, and for me perhaps some protection from Giles himself. Now the breeze rose behind me and rustled the hedge, there was a jiggle and a grunt, he said nothing and I barely saw him, just an eye and teeth, I was flat on my front in the stony grass, the wind knocked out of me, a burning pain in my left arm, and Giles on top of me, fumbling for my right arm and pulling it back. 'Got you, you dirty mongrel,' he said. 'Got you! Bloody half-nelson!'

2

The red-tiled hallway ran straight through the house, from the rarely used front door, which had a window in it, to the muddy obscurity of the back door, where everyone went in and out, prising off their wellingtons on a rough old boot-jack and flinging them down under a row of hung-up coats. The kitchen was on the right, the lavatory and a cheerless little office on the left, and to move down the hall, past the stairs and the dining-room door towards the sitting room at the front, was to step into the light. Giles's father came out of the dining room now, a silhouette before he saw us and smiled.

'Dad,' said Giles, 'this squalid individual is Dave. As you will no doubt have realized.'

'Dave, very good to meet you,' Mark Hadlow said, shaking hands and nodding slowly as he held my eye for a long five seconds, a warm and searching look. I felt he was entirely reassured by what he saw there, and also somehow shy of looking at the rest of me. 'We're all so delighted you were able to join us.'

'What else would he doing, Dad, honestly?' said Giles.

'Well, thank you very much for having me, sir,' I said, taking him in – hair silky brown, mouth thin and decisive but his brown eyes large and kindly. I had my own feeling for fathers, their looks and atmospheres, what they allowed to their children, and to other people's, the quality of their attention. You only ever saw part of them, of course, they had jobs you only partly understood, but they were a proof of family life, and the whole thing working. Fathers had characters, like masters, heavy or funny or remote, but their power was of a different kind. As a rule they were very nice to you, and treated you more considerately than their own child, who was your friend. In that first moment, Mark Hadlow gave off something specially reassuring, a sense of fairness.

'Give me a hand, old chap?' he said to Giles, and swept us back out with him into the yard. The DS19 was drawn up next to Mrs Hadlow's Riley – it loomed and gleamed there, sunk on its special suspension close to the ground. Mark opened the boot while I drifted round, peering in at the black and chrome of the dashboard, the empty hoop of the steering wheel, the unexpected absence of walnut and poshness. The bonnet was still warm after the run from London, and the importance of London seemed to radiate off it. 'Sit in, if you like, Dave,' Mark said, but I said, 'Oh, it's all right, sir,' and then, 'Can I help?' Giles showed he was able to carry a box of French wine bottles, and his father balanced a second box on his raised knee as he slammed the boot shut. I had never known anyone buy a whole case of wine before. I trotted in after them, feeling futile, but excused.

The boxes were stowed in the cold pantry and we stood for a minute in the kitchen. 'So has Giles been looking after you?' Mark said, and I sensed that perhaps it was more than a routine question.

'I just took him up to the Rings,' Giles said, and tugged out his pedometer. 'Six and three-quarter miles, Dad.'

'You do know you have to adjust that contraption, don't you, Giles, to your own pace,' and he gave me a look that was nearly a wink. 'Anyway, it's a decent walk, you must be dying for tea – I know I am' – going back towards the door. 'Audrey not in yet?'

'Not till six, Dad.'

'Put the kettle on, old chap, would you,' said Mark. 'Now, where's your mother?' – and he went out down the hall calling 'Cara . . . Cara . . .', almost chanting it, like a line from a song, and I didn't know at first, as I followed after, that it was Mrs Hadlow's name, though I knew, of course, what it meant. They ran into each other in the doorway of the sitting room, and when they came back towards me she seemed changed from the stern Mrs Hadlow of lunchtime by the fact of her husband coming home and calling out her name. In this moment of enlightenment I saw the next stage of our meeting starting before I'd made my little speech, which to me was the crucial part of the first stage. I said,

'I just wanted to thank you, very much, Mr Hadlow . . .' but Mrs Hadlow, Cara, saw straight away the thing Mark had missed, the ripped and filthy left sleeve of my shirt.

'It looks as though you've taken a bit of a tumble, Dave.'

'Oh, lord,' said Mark. 'What happened there?' Giles hovered inhibitingly in my mind as I held out my arm with the torn shirt and the long jewelled graze underneath.

'I'm so sorry, Mrs Hadlow,' I said. There was a narrow opening for clarity and justice which I heard myself decline. 'We were just playing a game, up on the hill.'

'Hmm.' She pushed back the torn sleeve, examined the scratch and the graze with the suspended judgement of a schoolfriend's mother. 'Giles's games can be fairly boisterous affairs, I'm afraid. Let's get that cleaned up' – and she took me back to the kitchen, where Giles was eating a biscuit as the kettle creaked into life on top of the Rayburn. She fetched out a black tin from under the dresser; I was torn between noble silence and making a thing of the sting of the TCP. 'It'll heal up best without a dressing,' she said.

Now Giles hovered in person, coolly intrigued. 'He's fine, aren't you, Dave,' he said, and once both his parents had turned away he smiled and punched me on the shoulder.

'We like to meet the Exhibitioners,' Mark Hadlow said as we sat down to tea in the dining room, 'but we don't believe we own them, you know. We think of you as ours, but not ours.'

'Well, yes, quite,' I said, as though used to this kind of frankness.

'That's why we don't suggest meeting you until some way into the first year. We feel you should find your feet. Then we hope to become good friends.'

'Doesn't always work,' said Lydia.

'Julian Donnington,' said Giles, and rolled his eyes.

'We haven't given up hope on Julian Donnington,' his mother said.

'You've met Andrew Ward,' Mark said, 'and Peter Sealy-ham?'

'Yes, sir. Well, Mr Yule introduced us.' The thing was it went against the norm to talk to seniors unless you were a fag or a tart, and I couldn't really be friends with the Hadlow Exhibitioners from earlier years. The next time we'd met in Top Washrooms, Ward had looked straight through me.

'And you've settled in all right, I have the feeling?'

'Yes, I've settled in very well, sir,' I said, and glimpsed the dark dormitory under the phrase. The pressing thing I knew I couldn't say to him or, worse, to Giles was that I was home-sick, at night especially, after lights out, and it could lead to another worry, that they might think I was homesick here, at Woolpeck.

'Bampton's a friendly school,' Mark went on, 'and a civilized one, that's half the point of it.'

'Oh, yes,' I said, interested by this view of the place.

'It's not a bear pit, like some of the older public schools. And of course it's much smaller than most of them. You haven't had any trouble . . . you know?' – and again he looked me in the eye, very warmly and firmly. 'No, I wouldn't expect it.'

Giles winced and shifted. 'Anyway, there's lots of, um . . .' and cleared his throat in an unnecessary way.

'Well . . .' I said, unsure of myself. I glanced across the table, at Cara, and her silent brother Peter, whose farm this was, and at Lydia, with her bored way of leaning back in her chair and occasionally shaking her head. The still-unpoisoned mood of my four years at Bishop Alfred's hadn't prepared me for the day-and-night sneers and jokes and random violence at Bampton.

'And your mother's managing all right?' said Mark, pressing on.

'Really, Dad . . .' said Lydia.

'It must be hard for her, sweetheart, being on her own, and with Dave away. You hadn't boarded before, I think?'

This was almost too understanding. 'No, sir . . . I think she was more upset than me at the start.'

'Well, I can imagine,' looking at Cara now, but she merely raised her eyebrows, as if to say it had never bothered her. My mother in term time was the image called up by her Wednesday letters – the handwriting itself was her presence, more vivid than the few things the letter described, with many exclamation marks, work, a visit to Wantage, small ordinary events that covered four sides of blue Basildon Bond in a brave avoidance of the real subject: not only that she missed me, but that she knew how much more I missed her.

'We think rather well of the Art man – Gregson,' Cara said.

'Oh, yes, he's very nice,' I said.

'And there's a new English teacher, Hudson?' Mark said – 'whom we hear good things of.'

'Yes, I haven't had him yet,' I said.

'Hudson's a ruddy ponce,' said Giles.

'Do watch your language, Giles,' Mark said, and I blushed though I wasn't sure which bit of language it was he was objecting to.

'Have another sandwich, Dave,' Cara said. 'Jam, or paste . . . ? Or both!' – and she gave me one of her rare smiles as she pushed the plate towards me.

I was helping to take out the tea-things when a young man called Roly appeared at the back door – he had driven over from Challow to play tennis with Lydia, and was wearing a tracksuit. 'Do you know the area at all?' he said, when she introduced me.

'He lives in Foxleigh,' said Lydia, 'he's known it all his life.'

'In Foxleigh, really? – golly . . .' and he nodded and stared at me pleasantly enough. 'I always think Foxleigh's a nice little town.'

'Let's get out and play while it's still light,' said Lydia.

I went back to see if there was anything else to carry, I wasn't sure what was happening next, but Mark said, 'I'm just going to look round the garden, Dave, if you're not too tired out from your six and three-quarter miles earlier.'

'Oh, thank you, sir,' I said, and we giggled at each other.

'You might want your jacket.'

I ran back with it, and Mark unbolted the front door, with the bordered glass panel in it, and ushered me out onto the front path. We walked along, past the playroom window, and across a strip of lawn to inspect the pond. Mark had a look of London about him still, in his brown suede shoes, grey flannels and sports jacket, and red silk tie.

We stood side by side and leaned forward to peer into the water, Mark's face, half shadow, half reflection, filling the pale stripe above my own. It seemed a good time to try again, if it wasn't already too late: 'I just wanted to thank you very much, sir, for all your support – ' though the words came out stiffly, and Mark shushed them away before I had finished.

'No, no, Dave, don't thank me. My father was the one who endowed the Exhibitions, I just keep them ticking over.'

'Oh, I see . . .' I said, not sure if Mark's father was still alive to be thanked.

'The best thanks you could give us is to enjoy your time at Bampton.'

'Thank you, sir,' I said anyway.

'Get the most out of all it has to offer. If you round it off with a scholarship to Oxford, we'll be delighted. But we won't mind in the least if you want to do something different.' He put his hand on my shoulder, and gazed down at me, practical but kindly. 'Ah, darling,' he said, but he was looking past me now – Cara had come out to join us. 'Hello, there!' she said, as if she'd hadn't been with him five minutes before. We went on across the lawn talking, with me in between them, at a daw-dling pace that made the walk itself seem as important as getting to the far side – and then up the bank to the rustic shelter at the end of the tennis court, to watch Roly and Lydia knocking up.

That night I went first in the bathroom, shut my bedroom door in a mood of fragile security, then got undressed and put on my pyjamas determinedly deaf to what I knew was waiting, when I turned off the light and curled up facing the window in the chilly darkness: the inward surge of the feeling, the shaming and engulfing emotion, a grip on the heart and in the throat, unsayable. Then I heard the click of the door-handle, a glimpse of light over my shoulder, and a voice cooing, 'Winny?'

3

After breakfast I sat for some time in the downstairs lavatory, half listening for voices as my eye traced squares in the pattern of the lino. In the window a little plastic fan span round intermittently and let in a cold raw smell from the farmyard beyond. I wasn't sure what was happening next, and the desire to get out of another walk or game was mixed with a dread of causing trouble; I felt I would stand out just as much in my absence as I did when I tagged along. There was a basket on the floor with old copies of *The Field* and *Berkshire Life*, the glossy paper weirdly softened by damp; at the bottom of the pile the damp had gone further and fused the pages in a stiff swollen wad, which creaked and scrunched when I bent it. So the minutes passed.

I came out into the hall just as Cara's Uncle George was cautiously descending the stairs. He'd nodded at me amiably yesterday when I arrived, but it seemed that he took all his meals in his room, and I hadn't set eyes on him since. 'You haven't seen my stick, I suppose,' he said.

I gazed up at his shadowy bulk framed in the narrow space of the staircase, walled on both sides. 'Is it the one with a silver knob, sir?' I ran off to where I'd seen it propped, in the corner of the sitting room.

'Don't need the damn thing,' said George, when I handed it over, 'but Cara says I have to have it.' He moved off holding it in front of him, without it touching the floor, like something purely ceremonial. I found myself following, then watching as George reached up for his cap and the brown mac that hung under it. 'So how are you getting on?' he said, handing the stick back to me for a moment.

'Oh, very well, thank you, sir,' I said.

He gave me a kindly but doubting look, as he shrugged on the coat. 'You've met Ernest already, I expect?'

'Ernest . . .' I said. 'I'm not entirely sure.'

'Come and have a word with him, then,' said George, turning towards the back door.

'Should I tell Giles?' I said. 'I think we were supposed . . .' but the dilemma had solved itself, and after a moment I followed him, relieved to be under the old man's protection, and putting off any thoughts of Giles's revenge, and the forms it might take tonight. I was still holding the dark stick with its silver knob as we crossed the weedy expanse behind the house; I tried using it myself for a step or two.

When we reached the gate into the farmyard, George said, 'I'm not absolutely clear where you're from.'

'Well, I'm at school with Giles, sir,' I said.

He cleared his throat and glanced down at me. 'Giles must be older than you.'

'Yes, I'll be fourteen later in the month.'

'But I happen to know you're in the class above him. So you're cleverer than him.'

'Well, I'm not sure,' I said delicately. I felt what I said might somehow get back to Giles.

We made our way past the big open-sided barn that housed the dwindling cliff of last year's straw. The baler stood dusty but dangerous at the far end, and the broad canvas belt of the elevator angled up towards the roof. 'But your parents,' George said. 'Not English.'

Again the answer required some tact. 'My mum's English, I live with her.'

'Yes, I see . . .' said George, tactful in his turn, but not giving up. 'She's separated from your father, perhaps.'

It was a decision to be taken, each time, and the fact was I only knew what I knew. I twisted the stick round in my hands and said, 'The thing is, you see,' as if I were an old man explaining to a child, 'my father was from Burma, but I'm afraid he's dead now.'

'So you're half-Burman,' said George, without any fuss. 'You should probably give that to me.' I handed back the stick and found myself blushing. 'Now, watch this muck here, we haven't got our wellies on.' We were passing the open gates of the large cow-shed where a thick slew of straw and cow shit spread into the yard. Inside, barely visible in the gloom, a man raised his pitchfork in reply to George's greeting. I was glad the cows were out, not because they frightened me at all, but because I wouldn't be asked to prove it. I thought perhaps the man with the fork was Ernest, but George said, 'That's Stanley, by the way, he's worked here all his life.'

'Yes, I think Giles mentioned him,' I said. Stanley was a bastard, who never let Giles and his friends climb on the tractors or make camps out of bales.

Along the far side of the barn was a ridged concrete track leading off towards the fields where the cows grazed; George turned down here now. It was interesting, in its way, but not pretty. 'I've got *this* walk, you see,' he said, 'which takes about eighteen minutes, unless I get nattering to one of the men. If it's a longer hike I'm after I head over towards Denhams', which can take an hour or more. Have you been up the hill yet?'

'Yes, sir, we went there yesterday. The Rings, you mean.'

'I don't get up there much now. Was it fun?'

'Yes,' I said, 'it was quite windy.'

'Well I know what you mean,' said George with a frown, focusing already on what lay beyond the end of the main barn. As we turned the corner I took a moment to see what it was, a breeze-block wall about as high as myself, and beyond it a rough mass of something, a coal-heap covered in a brown tarpaulin, which twitched and then slid sideways – it was only a second's confusion, but I seemed to slip too, as if the earth had moved. 'Now, now, Ernest,' said George, going up to the pen while I hung back. The wall reached to his chest, and he leant over it and scratched Ernest's shoulder with the silver knob of his stick. Ernest moved, with a delayed shudder and stamp, but he couldn't move far, because of the narrow space he was in. All I could see from five yards away was an immense brown back, with the thick root of a tail at one end and the high broad hump of the neck at the other, patched with dirty white, like melting snow on a ploughed field. So this was a bull, a great story-book terror, physically stronger than anything outside a zoo. The bull's head hung out of view, under the massive muscular yoke of its neck and shoulders. 'I've brought someone to see you,' said George; and to me, 'Go round and say hello.'

The end of the pen was a five-bar steel gate, its everyday latch reinforced by a heavy chain and a knotted red nylon rope. Ernest's furry white face loomed behind the bars. I wasn't sure if he could see me or not – if I was an irritant or an irrelevance; his small brown eyes under white lashes seemed worryingly inadequate, fixed on the stultifying sameness of his pen but perhaps on some larger scheme of violence. His wet pink nose was stuck with wisps of the straw that his forelegs were planted in, up to his bulging knees. But his ears stood out alertly, the left ear with a bright yellow tag stapled to it, and he twitched his head now and then as if determined to shake the tag off. When he did this, the fold of white wattles that hung like a gathered curtain from his chin to his knees swung heavily from side to side.

'Does he live here all the time?' I said.

'What's that? No, no,' said George. 'He'll be out when he's got his next job to do. Won't you, Ernest?' I nodded responsibly. 'Give him a scratch, he likes that.' I smiled tensely, and stayed where I was. This left it up to George himself to show how well the two of them got on. 'He's been polled, you see,' he said. 'No horns to worry about.' Behind the ears I could see two overgrown lumps – which way the horns had grown, and how long they had been, I could only imagine. I felt that when Ernest lowered his head he assumed they were still there.

He was close to the wall of the pen, with about enough space for one more creature the same size to stand beside him. George started smacking his rump, quite hard but with a pally expression, so that in a minute Ernest shifted round, thrust up his head with a fierce bellow, lifted his tail and dropped a heavy heap of dung into the straw. He almost stumbled as he backed away, his shoulder crashed against the gate as he tried to turn round, and the gate sang and rattled in its place. I saw that if Ernest did put his head down and flatten the gate I would be right in his path. We'd had a film about bullfighting at school and a bull, like a ship, took a while to turn round. So I came back and stood beside Uncle George in the shelter of the wall. 'What would he weigh, sir, I wonder?' I said.

'Ernest? Ooh, by now he'd be a good fifteen hundredweight.'

'Really, sir . . .' – I took this in doubtingly, three-quarters of a ton, as we stood and looked at him. In a minute George leant over and Ernest let the old man stroke his muzzle once or twice before he twitched his ears and stamped again. The little silence fell when neither guest nor host knows if a matter has run its course.

'Goodness, though,' George said, 'Burma. Have you spent any time there?'

'Oh . . . no, sir, I haven't,' I said, and peered closely at Ernest in the blur of feelings that the place, the mere name of the place, set working in me.

'You've read about this latest business?'

'Well, a bit, yes, at school, in fact. The *coup d'état*, you mean, sir?'

'The *coup d'état*,' said George slowly, 'exactly so.' He scratched Ernest's head between his vanished horns, and at this the bull twitched again and staggered sideways away from us. 'All very terrible.'

'Yes, indeed,' I said, with a tingle of inadequacy that passed down my arms into my unoccupied hands. George rested his own consoling hand on my shoulder, and I gazed in a kind of compound embarrassment at the unreachable subject of Burma and at Ernest's under-parts, the large hanging triangle of flesh that carried and concealed his thing, and behind his thing, and hard to get my mind round, the vast shape, heavy as dumbbells, purple as liver, swinging and knocking against his knees as he moved. George took his hand away, I said, 'Well, thank you very much, sir,' and we set off back past the barns. We might have been there for two minutes or much longer – and I had a peculiar feeling of having failed a test with Uncle George, or not understood what was expected of me.

'The thing is, Mr Pollitt,' I said, 'I'm the Hadlow Exhibitioner.'

'Are you now? Yes, I think I knew that. Well, I said you were clever' – genially, but as if his own cleverness had briefly been doubted. 'What are your favourite subjects?'

It was a standard adult question, but he asked it without the usual condescension. 'Well, English,' I said.

'Oh, English, yes.'

'And French too.'

'Have you been in France?'

'Not yet, sir, no . . . And also, I'd have to say, History.'

'What are you doing in History?'

'Well, at the moment we're doing the Civil War.'

'Ah, yes, awful business,' he said, and shook his head, rather as if he remembered it personally, and regretted his part in it. 'Now, are you a Roundhead or a Cavalier?'

I weighed it up. 'I think a Cavalier,' I said, and looked solemn because of the other meaning the words had at school. 'What about you, sir, if you don't mind my asking?'

'Oh I was a Cavalier too, at your age. You may well become a Roundhead, at least for a while, later on. I know I did.' I thought this was unlikely, but I noted what the old man was saying. 'How long are you stopping with us?' he asked, as we came back across the yard. I said I was going home on Monday. 'And you live in Foxleigh? Well, that's not far away. Perhaps you'll come back and see us in the summer.'

'Thank you, sir,' I said, not sure if this was an invitation.

'Do you play tennis?'

'Not really,' I said.

'Peter's a good tennis-player. As, in fact, is Lydia. She's got the reach for it.'

We'd stopped again briefly a few yards from the back door. The lower wing, jutting out from the rear of the house, closed off the yard, with the broad open porch below, where the bell, like a school bell, hung with a rough cord dangling from its clapper. George raised his stick and pointed to a window on the floor above. 'That's my room,' he said. 'I'm out of people's way up there, but of course I can see who's coming and going.' The thin ellipse of light from a tilted Anglepoise glowed in the glass but showed little of the room. 'It means I can get on with my work,' he said, and smiled in a way that made me think I must be keeping him from it. 'It may not be up your street . . . you know . . . but feel free to knock on my door any time if you're at a loose end. We might have another little chat before you leave.' He smiled thoughtfully, not at me, but at a space just over my left shoulder. Then, with a shake of his stick, as if chasing off a dog, he turned and went back indoors.

4

I stood there, under the bell, for a minute, thinking that if I lifted my hand to the rope and rang it, Giles would probably appear – then just in time I thought I could say that I'd searched for him and couldn't find him. I opened the door of the boot room, which was dusty and cobwebbed, dried mud on the stone floor, a smell of motor oil and fertilizer, and I poked round in there for a while, among the buckets and boxes. Overhead I heard slow footsteps, that must have been Uncle George back in his room, a chair being dragged, then the faint voice of a wireless. I tugged open the heavy door on the far side, and went down a few steps onto a brick path under apple trees where hens were pecking about. This was another part of the farm I hadn't seen before. Along one side of it ran the high bulging yew hedge which screened the near end of the tennis court – a bright desert of sunshine ten yards away which I pictured with a kind of awe as I dawdled in the gloom among the hens. The hens had a couple of chicken-wire runs, with a rough little carpentered kennel at one end and a gate like a guillotine at the other, to shut them in at night. Now they were randomly out and about, eyeing and pecking up scattered seed, bits of grit and grass, clucking fretful objections as I moved among them; one strutting past me in a devious preoccupied way and five seconds later hopping up the steps into the boot room behind me – I leapt back myself, only panicked it more by shouting and flapping, it squawked and leapt up onto the table, knocked over some canes, pecked wildly at the window for five seconds before darting back out through the door into the orchard, with a run of ruffled clucks that seemed to say *oh for god's sake*, and left me with a sense of a small unobserved misdemeanour, that might soon have turned into a scene and a telling-off. I closed the door firmly and went back down through the trees.

At the far end of the orchard there was a red-brick wall, a mossy slate roof, an old outbuilding adrift from the house and as hidden from the farmyard as it was from anyone serving and volleying on the far side of the hedge. There was something I very much wanted to do, by myself, and I thought this might be a good place to do it; then hid the thought when I heard voices. I followed the path round the corner of the shed – which had a window, flung open at right angles, the single large pane containing the image of a small teenage boy, transparently reflected against the green, his face hard to read among the shadows of the trees.

There was a grunt of laughter from inside the shed – 'Well, please don't jump to conclusions!', a voice which I took a weird two or three seconds to know was Lydia's: I stood watching myself, now doubly unsure what to do. 'I'm not jumping anywhere, love,' said a deeper voice, Cara, of course, but in a patient, humorous tone. 'I mean . . . you can jump wherever you like.' A rustle and scrape, a throat-clearing. 'Mm, well . . .' My mind had them engaged in some task together, some routine of work that this outhouse was kept for, and which filled the gaps in their talk with small scratchings and shufflings. The talk was alert, but its pace sedated. 'You know,' said Cara, 'Daddy's quite prepared to pay for Roly too.' After a further short pause they both spoke together, 'Well, thanks, Mum / We just want you to be careful . . .' The fear of being caught had me scuffling on past the window as if on my way to somewhere else.

'Exploring?' – this was Cara, much brighter and louder, so that I turned round. She was standing at the open door of the shed in shabby blue trousers, with a paintbrush raised in one hand and a rag bunched up in the other; she cocked her head as if to hear my answer. Was exploring a good thing, or was she seizing my likely excuse for being there and turning it on me? The three bright syllables were a lesson in ambiguity. 'I rather fear Giles has abandoned you.'

'Well, I'm not absolutely sure,' I said.

'Typical, Mum,' said Lydia. I came closer. Through the door I could see her in profile, sitting on a kitchen chair, with her right hand, nearer me, raised to her right shoulder. In contrast to Cara, she looked formal for the place and the time, in a red dress and dangling earrings, her wavy fair hair swept up and back, but she had kicked off her shoes. I could only see the canvas at an oblique angle but I understood now that Cara was painting her portrait.

'Let's take a break,' she said. At which Lydia got up, chased her toes into her shoes, and made off to the house, red evening dress sweeping the young nettles. Cara stayed on the step, weighing things up. 'Are you interested in painting?' she said.

'I am quite, in fact,' I said.

'Are you? Whom do you like?'

'Well, last term I got rather keen on Sir Lawrence Alma-Tadema,' I said.

'Oh, I see . . .'

'We did him with Mr Gregson.'

'I'm starting to wonder about Mr Gregson.'

'And Francis Bacon I also quite like.'

She turned her laugh into a clearing of the throat. 'Well, you'd better come in.'

'Oh, if you're sure. I didn't know this was here, Mrs Hadlow,' I said, stepping into the room with a cautious feeling – the whitewashed brick walls and open rafters made it twice the size you expected. There was a chemical tang, paints and turps, a table with tubes and jars of brushes, and in the set-up of easel and chair and a jug of tulips something new in my experience, but recognized at once, an artist at work.

Cara had her cigarettes in her cardigan pocket, and lit one with a lighter and stood back as I walked round. I had the feeling the cigarette set the limit for the time I should spend there, and her tolerance of my visit. 'I mostly work here. In London there's just too much going on.'

'Oh, yes, I suppose,' I said. I examined the portrait of Lydia, still a swirl of red lines with only the face done in detail, and not that much like Lydia, at least as I knew her; but I'd never seen a proper painting at this early stage. Then I gazed at a couple of pictures leaning against the wall, still-lifes of broken brown pots, a trowel and an old trug, which must be things from the boot room where I'd just been poking around, offered in quite a new light.

'You don't have to say anything,' Cara said. 'The young can be lethal critics.'

'No,' I said, 'it's very interesting.'

'Most of these things aren't finished, and one doesn't want premature criticism, you know?'

'No, quite,' I said.

'Wait and see the finished picture before you put your oar in.'

I smiled nervously. 'Well, thank you for letting me look,' I said.

She blew out a jet of smoke, and squashed the rest of the cigarette beside others in a saucer. 'Is Giles being foul to you? I rather suspect he is.'

'Oh!' I said, embarrassed and annoyed and relieved, all at once. Life here seemed to have these invitations to disloyalty, perhaps standard in full-size families, which I wasn't used to. I chose a phrase of Mum's, 'I think sometimes, Mrs Hadlow, he doesn't know his own strength!'

'Hmm, I wonder about that . . .' she said, and looked at me as if he was a problem for both of us. 'Does he bully you at school?'

'No, not really,' I said quickly, and it seemed worth explaining, 'we don't actually see much of each other at school, you know, being in different forms.'

'No, I suppose,' she said.

I stood looking for a moment at Lydia's pinkish face on the canvas, which seemed to me a mystery of family as well as art. The eyes were what Cara had worked on most, and they stared back disconcertingly. She started cleaning a brush on a rag, plunged it in a jar of turps, the pink clouding to grey. She said,

'Of course, Giles is at a difficult age.'

'Yes,' I said, absorbing this confidence uncertainly.

'I have the feeling he's quite popular at school?'

I shook my head. 'Oh, I think so,' I said. There were things you couldn't talk about with parents, such as how certain people fancied Giles, and how he fancied himself.

'But I mustn't cross-examine you!'

'No, that's all right,' I said.

'We keep doing it.'

'Not really,' I said.

'Well, I'll see you at lunch.'

'Oh . . . yes,' I said, colouring as I took in the instruction. 'Goodbye!' – and I stepped out of the shed, and went back briskly towards the house, the hens murmuring ominously as I came through. 'Pay no attention to me . . .' I said, when I stopped and looked around. Cara had gone back into her studio, I was alone, and a compulsion I'd felt the day before, on the tennis court, to get into the yew hedge, rose up in me again now I was on its other side. I'd had a glimpse of gloomy tunnels there, beneath the lowest branches, that a dog might get through, and perhaps a boy of my size. On this side, bendy strips of chickenwire kept the hens from going through. It looked dry when I knelt down, and in a minute, though the pressure was painful on my wounded left arm, I had crawled in and wriggled through the needly dust to the centre of the hedge. I lay there with my knees pulled up and a low bright view of the court beyond, the net hanging slack between the posts, and two magpies patrolling the far base line.

5

At breakfast that morning I'd heard Cara reminding Uncle Peter that Elise liked Irish whiskey, and later telling Mrs Over, 'You know Elise won't touch pudding'; but it wasn't till just before lunch that I found out who Elise was. 'Your mother gets in at five to four, remember,' Cara said. It was part of the adventure of being here that the Hadlows explained nothing about themselves.

Mark looked rather critically at his watch, and then squared his shoulders. 'Want to go and meet Gran at the station?' he said. Giles sounded reasonably keen, and I saw the chance for a first ride in the DS; though under the imagined excitement of the moment when it rose on its hydropneumatic suspension I saw a new challenge shaping in the unexpected presence of another guest. There was an hour to kill after lunch, and we drifted round outside, ending up at the tennis court, where Giles got me to crank the net up as high as I could, and then did some work on his serve. 'Don't worry if you can't get to them,' he said, as I trudged back and forth to retrieve the balls.

At half past three we presented ourselves in the yard, where Mark was getting the car ready. Its black roof folded down into a surprising space behind the rear seats; a red leather cover fitted over it, and buttoned like a glove.

'I pronounce this car,' said Giles, 'a UFO.'

'The car of the future,' said Mark, and smiled at him sweetly, a shared happiness I hadn't seen till then.

'An ugly foreign object,' Giles said.

I threw up my hands and stared, I was pretty sure of myself. 'I don't know how he can say such a thing, sir,' I said.

'Well . . .' said Mark, with an intake of breath.

'It's the most beautiful car I've ever seen.'

'Yes, thank you, Dave, very much for that,' said Mark. 'It pains me to say it, but my son has no sense of beauty.' Giles smirked at his own provocation, and I felt he was secretly absorbing the praise of his father's car. 'Just get a Jag, Dad,' he said, as he tipped the seat forward for me to climb into the back, then took the passenger seat himself. Mark himself of course got in on the left. 'You comfortable back there?' he said, and pressed the ignition, and it was the moment I'd been waiting for when the body of the whole car rose like a hovercraft and settled itself comfortably off the ground. Giles turned and grinned at me, in spite of himself, and Mark said smoothly over his shoulder, 'That's all there is to it, Dave.' We floated off at once across the potholes of the yard and along the chalky roughness of the drive.

The floating sensation was only part of the novelty. I had never been in an open-top car before – there was the surprise of moving off, the air stirring already around us, and once we were out in the lane the absence of anything between us and the trees and gateways and swiftly reorganizing landscape as we picked up speed, while the trees and the gateways set up their own rhythmic bluster, fast irregular patterns of whooshes and thumps: I felt full of air, almost stifled by it. It was a day with a stealthy almost summery warmth, though once we had climbed and turned onto the main road I was shivering – I grinned back at Mark as our eyes met again in the rear-view mirror. Then we slowed at a cross-roads and it was warm, and the smell of the engine mixed for a second or two with the complicated scent of the hawthorn in the hedges. It seemed the sloping windscreen and the raised side windows wrapped Giles and his father in a cockpit of quiet while funnelling the fierce draught into the rear seat, sleeking and riffling my hair. We passed along the road that ran under the Downs, with the great bare flank of the hill reaching upwards on the right, and the sweep of the Vale stretching far away to the left. The road itself plunged up and down, with solid white lines on the blind crests and hidden dips which Mark just about observed. He had to wander out wide to see past the van or the tractor and trailer in front, Giles acting as lookout. 'Take him, Dad, take him!' he shouted, as we closed in fast on a struggling Morris Oxford and I braked hard in the back. After ten minutes Mark indicated, slowed and swung into a side road with a narrow bridge over the railway line and a view down the empty track. In thirty seconds we'd pulled up in the forecourt of Challow station.

The train wasn't signalled yet, and we drifted down the platform. A couple waiting with a cat in a box gave Mark an unassuming smile that admitted they didn't know him personally but knew who he was. Mark smiled blandly back as he passed. I felt the reflected glory of being with him, and the waiting couple's curiosity about me as well. I stooped and looked in at the cat and felt rather sorry for it. Giles walked along the very edge of the platform with his arms out for balance. There was a country stillness, with birdsong and bleating of lambs again on the air, and then round a bend half a mile down the line the flat-faced locomotive came into view and three or four carriages shivered into place behind it. My heart was racing, I didn't know why. 'Don't you miss the romance of steam, Dave?' said Mark. 'Yes, sir!' I said, though I could only recall being in a steam train once, years before, when Mum and I went up to Maidenhead for the day. The train pulled in, powerful and grimy, and romantic enough for me. The engine's roar as it crawled past us to a stop was inhuman, but in the light that gleamed through the carriages three or four figures were standing and moving towards the doors. 'There's Gran!' shouted Giles. She had already lowered the window to reach for the handle when Giles jerked the door open – a man behind her caught hold of her arm. She stepped down, small but impressive, with swept-back auburn hair and prominent dark eyes; in her short dark coat and black court shoes she brought an unignorable note of elegance to the little country station. Mark came up and kissed her, on both cheeks, as she handed her suitcase to Giles. When I was brought forward and Mark said, 'Mummy, this is Dave Win, a friend of Giles's from Bampton,' she gave me a quick doubting look, as if I was another example of her grandson's mischief. I put out my hand and said, 'How do you do, Mrs Hadlow,' and she wrinkled her nose and said, 'Not Hadlow, but still,' in a soft rasping voice. She shook my hand in one jerk, up-and-down, as if trying to shake it off, and I felt for a split second the ridges of rings under her thin leather gloves.

When she saw the car waiting with the roof down she cocked her head, as if torn between the glamour and the discomfort. 'My hair!' she said.

'You'll be all right, will you, Mummy?' said Mark.

'I've just had it done,' she said, in a quietly difficult way.

'You'll be OK in the front, Gran,' said Giles. 'I'll go in the back with Winny.' It was the first time he'd used my school nickname with the family, and his grandmother gave me another odd look. She found a fine blue mist of a scarf in her coat pocket and tied it lightly over her hairdo before we started off. And she seemed to enjoy the ride, which Mark took more sedately going back. There was just one moment when he went too fast over a crest in the road and we all gave a sickened shout. She half turned and stared at me – 'All very thrilling!' she said, and it was then that I realized, from the way she said it, that she must be French.

We all came together for drinks before dinner, when she changed the mood very notably – the tone was heightened but inhibited;

she was the centre of attention, pretending unnervingly that she was at home. She wore black high heels, and what Mum would have called a cocktail dress, dark red, with a star-like silver brooch. Mark passed her a whiskey with a lot of ice in it and we all watched her as she tried it. 'Ah, that's better,' she said, and her little shiver and secretive smile somehow helped us to picture the strong cold drink slipping down inside her.

'We don't have to stand. Mummy, you take that comfortable chair.' In the hovering scramble that followed I found my place last, and next to her, on the black-leather pouffe which broke wind softly as I sat on it.

'Really, Dave . . .' said Giles.

'Oh, darling, could I try one of yours?' Elise said, and watched as Cara got up to offer her a cigarette. 'Thanks,' she said, blowing out the first smoke with a quick repeated nod, as if settling to her theme. 'Well, it is charming to be here again,' she said, beaming around, 'after so long.'

'It's been too long,' said Mark, and Cara said, 'I know, ages,' but as if it couldn't be helped. 'We've not been here ourselves all that much in the past year, as Mark's been so busy.'

'And will Peter be joining us?' said Elise.

'Pete's been over at Denhams' all day,' said Cara, 'you may catch him later on.'

'Ah, yes,' said Elise – any further explanation deflected by the arrival of Uncle George, who took her in with his pleasant nod and smile, as though not quite sure if he'd greeted her already. There was a mild gleam of chivalry in the air between these two senior figures, as well as a tacit insistence, in Elise's playful glances, that she was, even so, a good ten years younger than him. I was caught up barely consciously in family resemblances, Mark as father and now as son, the round jaw and wide mouth of Elise carried over undeniably into Giles.

'So what news of the play, Gran?' said Lydia, who didn't look like her at all.

'Oh, I don't know,' said Elise, shaking the subject away, which only made us more interested in it.

'It would be great if you did it,' said Mark.

Crouching there, sipping at my small glass of cider, I was an extra, but conspicuous by being next to her. I watched the ash on her Kensitas lengthen, wondered whether to act, but when she tapped it abstractedly above the ashtray I saw how she was in control. 'Oh, they want me, you know, but is it the sort of thing I should be doing?'

'What is it, again?' said Giles.

His grandmother stared as if fascinated at a spot on the carpet, and we sat watching her with a sudden anxious interest in the answer. 'Well, it's S. Keel,' she said, 'though of course very much updated.'

'Updated to when?' said Cara.

'What is it?' said Giles again.

Mark translated. 'Eschyle,' he said quietly, 'Aeschylus – *Agamemnon*, isn't it, you said, Mummy?'

'Very much the present,' Elise said. 'Modern dress, you know,' with a simple gesture, a turn of her right hand, as if she might wear what she had on now.

Uncle George said, 'And you of course will be Electra . . .'

Elise laughed dryly at this. 'Dear George . . . The director seems to see me as Clytemnestra.'

'A great part, Gran,' said Lydia.

Elise looked at her with teasing sharpness. 'You see me wielding an axe, do you?' she said.

'I do!' said Lydia, and I peeped up at Elise, unsure how much she herself could be teased. It felt risky to me, but she went on in a reasonable tone,

'It's true there are precious few *rôles* these days for women over fifty.'

Cara said, 'There's Queen Margaret, isn't there,' in a reasonable tone of her own. 'And what's she called, Volumnia?'

'One day no doubt I will come to those parts,' Elise said.

'I mean, how old *is* Clytemnestra?' said Lydia.

'*Well* . . .' – Mark raised his eyebrows as if trying to work it out exactly. If she turned out to be younger than Elise surely that would be all right – or would it only draw attention to the fact that Elise was already too old to be playing her?

'Personally, I'm still hoping for your Portia,' said Uncle George.

'Vroom, vroom!' said Giles.

'Not Porsche, you idiot,' said Lydia, though everyone found this joke, which had been really stale at school last term, quite funny.

At dinner there was wine for the adults on top of the whiskey and gin, and soon a rising noise of conversation. Mrs Over served us all from the sideboard, and I jumped up to carry the plates, out of good manners and a tingly disconnection and excitement from the cider. 'Thank you,' she said, but I felt she resented it too. I put a flourish into it, Mark and Cara played along, Elise said it was far too much and sent it back, and Lydia said, 'Why on earth is Dave waiting on us?' 'I don't mind!' I said, with a bow as I set down her plate. I served Giles next, and he looked at me quite nicely and said, 'You make an excellent skivvy, Winny. Well done!' Mrs Over switched off the overhead light as she went out and we were lost for a minute in the near-darkness of candlelight before details softly reappeared, eyes widened and glittered, the shadows beyond filled with dim hints of colour, and the talk, that had faltered for a moment, picked up again. We'd just started eating when Uncle Peter came in, paused outside the circle to get his bearings, answered Uncle George's questions about where he'd been with a phrase and a grunt, and took his place opposite me. I beamed at him, to put him at his ease, and he seemed for a second to acknowledge me as his gaze ran round the table. Mrs Over came back in – 'This plate's hot, mind,' she said, and helped him to the vegetables and gravy, and he took a kind of mothering from her without seeming to notice it. I hardly remembered, none of us seemed to, that it was Peter's own table we were all sitting down at.

I was next to Lydia, who'd more or less ignored me so far, as a friend of Giles's, but who now said cosily, 'Mum says Giles has been beating you up.'

'Oh . . . I wouldn't say beating me up, exactly,' I said, not looking at Giles, but listening to see if he'd heard; he was talking, almost arguing, after his own glass of cider, with his father about politics.

'You must try not to mind it,' Lydia said, 'it's just jealousy.'

Now I looked at him quickly, handsome and already grown-up tonight in the candlelight, and with his monthly allowance, and everything else that was waiting in the shadows behind him – 'I don't think it can be jealousy, really,' I said.

'It's . . . well, it's various things, isn't it,' said Lydia. 'It's always so funny when the new Exhibitioners come for their weekend, and now he's at the school himself – and you being obviously much cleverer than him . . .'

'Oh, Giles is quite clever,' I said – and I half understood that I meant Giles knew about the London Underground and the Common Market, and was in the Debating Society already, which I was still shy of going to.

'And then you went straight into the Fourth Form while Giles is stuck in the Remove – I know all about it!' She had the firmness, the lack of sentiment, of all the Hadlows, and she had something else, a way of laughing about them. Still, I felt I couldn't mention the main reason Giles wanted to hurt me, though I looked in her face and wondered if it was as obvious to her.

*

45

As we came through afterwards, Elise seemed much friendlier. I tried to slip past her but she beamed at me warmly. 'What fine silky hair you have,' she said, and ran her long fingers through my fringe as if I'd been her own child. I beamed anxiously back. 'Lydia tells me you're from *Burma*,' she said, and the hint of a guttural *r* seemed to colour the country with her own unknown assumptions about it.

'Well . . .' I said, 'I'm not *from* Burma, really . . . you see, my father was,' and I went straight on, 'we're doing *Twelfth Night* next term.' The presence of a famous actress had had a sort of alcoholic effect on me, over dinner, as she talked about films and directors; the fact that I'd never heard of the great Elise Pleynet made this sudden exposure to her fame all the more convincing.

'Doing . . .' she said.

'I mean we're putting it on. You know, in the theatre at school.'

'Ah, the famous school play. What fun!'

'Well, it's just the Junior School play—'

'And Giles will be in it – am I right?'

'Yes, I expect.'

'Well, Orsino . . . yes. Can't you see it?' – and she made one of her slight hand gestures, seemed to mock Giles but still believe in him. 'Mark, you know,' she said confidentially, 'was once in the school play at Bampton.' She looked across at him, to see if he could hear. 'He was the Duke of somewhere or other, in *Henry the Fifth*, I think it was, and he looked simply marvellous in his robes, everybody said so, but it was clear from the moment he stepped on the stage that he simply wasn't an actor.' She shook her head as she reached for her handbag, and took out her cigarette case. 'He didn't have to open his mouth, one simply knew. He was just . . . Mark!'

'Oh,' I said, 'I see . . .', and again felt a little disloyal.

She flicked a silver lighter, sent out a first focused jet of smoke. 'Well, I must come and see whether Giles has got the knack!'

'If you can,' I said, feeling this raised the stakes for my own first appearance on stage.

'Somehow I think he'll be better at it than his father . . .' She smiled at me. 'And it will be so useful for you. You will learn about lighting . . . or costumes perhaps . . .' – she shrugged happily at the possibilities.

'Mr Clark's put me down as Fabian,' I said, 'but really I'd like to play Antonio.'

She looked at me consideringly. 'Well, no one remembers Fabian . . .' And then, 'Have you acted before?'

'Not really,' I said, 'not real acting'; at school I'd won myself some unlikely friends and even a first magic taste of popularity by mimicking people – the masters mainly, rather than other boys. A lot of people did it, but I did it better, with a secret feeling that I had a gift that was quite different in kind from being good at French and History and having an Exhibition.

'I wonder . . .' she said. There was something sad, but resourceful, about her. 'Well, why not?' She glanced round. 'Let's sit . . .', folding herself downwards with quick stiff elegance onto the settee, where I perched beside her, excited but hoping to be rescued in a minute or two. The others were still standing by the door, Uncle George explaining something on the framed county map which hung there. 'If you have the gift,' she said, 'you can do anything. But it will be difficult for you.' She gave me the pondering stare of someone needing to be frank as well as supportive. 'Not because of your talent, but because of how people see you. I can tell you, I have worked with . . . I've worked with all sorts of people, Algerians, for instance, and with the most fascinating Indian actors. It's not easy for them. Well, in India, of course, they make their own films, but in France, and in England, these actors by and large have to play what we call the *mauvais rôles* . . . you understand?'

'Yes, I think so.'

'Or of course you can do radio.'

'Yes . . .' I said, feeling we were getting rather ahead of ourselves.

'No one can see you then!'

'Well . . .' I said, staring for a moment at her pale powdered face, her auburn crown, not entirely following what she was so confidently saying, the scale of this unthought-of problem.

'At school it may well be different, I expect you all have to *muck in*. Why not have a coloured Romeo! At my school in Grenoble we had a beautiful girl from Sénégal who acted all the time – Molière, Rostand . . .' – she seemed to see her just beside me. 'She dreamt of a life on the stage, poor thing, but the only parts she ever got were as a coloured maid, you know, or a slave-girl or something. It was only at our little *lycée* that she could be Bérénice.'

'Or Clytemnestra,' I said.

Elise gazed at me, I thought I'd tripped myself up, but she laughed and said, 'She was *made* for Clytemnestra,' so that I felt she had probably decided we were friends and, more than that, that I'd seen the wisdom of her advice. Mark came over, and I sensed he was pleased we were getting on, and I was pleased myself by her attention, and the privilege of it, something always to remember. I got up and made space for him, and it was only in the moment I turned away that I let myself feel what had happened.

I was in bed, with the light still on, when Giles came to my room again – a stealthy turn of the handle and he was in, and closed the door behind him. 'Ah, Winny!' he said, and smiled at me with his head on one side. Tonight he was wearing the red pyjamas with black piping that I knew from school, tight on him now, the jacket unbuttoned.

I said, 'I saw you stealing that glass of port after dinner.'

'You can't steal things in your own home, Winny, for heaven's sake. Now budge up . . .'

'Anyway, it's not your home,' I said.

He was pulling up the bedclothes as I tried to hold them down. 'Well, it will be my home, as a matter of fact, if my uncle Peter dies without issue. It will all be left to me, now shove up,' and after a five-second struggle he was more or less in there beside me. 'You're quite strong, aren't you, for a . . .' – he looked in my face as if to find the word.

'Buzz off, Hadlow!' I said. I wondered about shouting it, though his warm hard pressure against me in bed was different from the roughness of him in our fights out of doors. I had to make space for him, or fall off the bed on the other side, so I clung on. He had the smell of the day on him still, but toothpaste breath. 'Ow!' I said, 'my arm!' – again I just hissed it, still being a decent sport. I was tense for the rabbit punch, the Chinese burn, and pretended with a racing heart that I was bored and annoyed, and not frightened, and all at sea with conjecture that Giles knew something about me and was leading me on.

'This *is* cosy,' he said.

'Hmm,' I said, tense with the novelty of being in bed with another boy. The nylony shininess of his pyjamas might have been beautiful if Giles had been somebody else, such as Morgan or Roberts.

'I'm sorry about your arm, Winny,' he said, and ran his fingers up and down it almost gently. I shifted away again, though he was heavier and bigger than me, there was a furtive fight that must have made a bit of noise, and then he was half out of bed. 'You really are a tart, Winny,' he said, panting and laughing sourly, and I said, 'I'm not, you're the tart,' and then he got on top of me and kissed me, pushed and slithered his lips over mine as I tried to twist my head away – somehow I struggled out from under him and half fell out of bed, onto the thin bedside rug. After this he was abruptly on his dignity. He stood up and buttoned his pyjama jacket. 'I've had it with you, Winny, I really have,' he said, and went out without properly closing the door.

6

The next evening I was the first person into the sitting room, and though it was still quite light outside I closed the curtains and turned on the lamps, feeling by now that I knew how things were done here. It was a room with a different atmosphere from the rest of the house, red-and-white striped wallpaper, framed hunting prints, a glass-fronted cabinet with plates and china figurines displayed. Above the fireplace there was a broad mirror which in daytime reflected the hedge and the rise of the Downs outside, but now, with the curtains closed, made the large room feel oddly claustrophobic. The fire had been laid but not lit, and I sat down next to it, in a provisional way, and opened my copy of *Le Grand Meaulnes*, though I wasn't really taking it in. In a minute or two there were footsteps in the hall, and Elise entered, wearing her red evening frock, with black handbag and a black shawl round her shoulders. I jumped up and said, 'Bonsoir, madame,' and she nodded and crossed the room with a thin smile as if deferring her reply until she'd got a drink. As she squinted at the bottles she shivered, and pulled her shawl tighter.

'No fire?' she said.

'Oh, I'm sorry,' I said, 'do you want me to light it?'

She shot me a look. 'Normally I think the woman does it'

– and in fact Mrs Over knocked and came in at that moment, knelt down and touched a match to the crumpled-up paper, and sat back on her heels to watch it take. We looked on as she set the mesh guard in front of the fire, then she nodded and went out without saying a word. The first smell of burnt paper and pine twigs in the room seemed to mix with her evident feeling that we could have lit the thing ourselves.

Elise came round the sofa clutching her thick tumbler of whiskey and we stood together watching the first crackle and hiss, little streams of smoke pulled upward, flames sauntering the length of a twig, the slither and soft crash of the fire falling in on itself as the kindling burned up. Then she looked round, with a moment's indecision about where we would each sit. 'You were there,' she said.

'Oh – I don't mind,' I said, picking up my book to clear a space for her nearest to the fire. She shook her head and smiled graciously, but in the air, with the encouraging scent of the fire, there was a strange embarrassment. For a moment she moved towards a small hard chair further off, then turned back, with a shrug, and sat down in the armchair facing me, as if it couldn't matter less. I smiled at her, wanting to ask her more about what she had said last night, and at the same time hoping to avoid the subject altogether.

'What are you reading?' she said.

'Oh, it's *Le Grand Meaulnes*,' I said, and sat forward to hand it to her. It had struck me last night that she might know something useful about it, that I couldn't have got from an English person. She held it at arm's length, with a mocking smile, as if calling up very distant memories, then handed it back with a quick shake of the head. Of course she didn't have her glasses on.

'Et il vous plaît, monsieur, ce roman?'

'Ah . . . ! Oui, beaucoup, madame!' I said, not sure if the *monsieur* was flattering or mocking. 'Et à vous aussi?'

'En France, il est très connu, tout le monde l'a lu,' which didn't answer my question, but then I felt it would be rude to press her. 'Vous l'étudiez à l'école, j'imagine?'

'Oui, oui, absolument,' I said, with the worldly new personality that came over me when speaking French. 'Nous avons étudié la première partie pendant le trimestre passé, et il nous faudra avoir lu le reste avant que nous ne retournions à l'école à la fin des vacances.' This was a sentence that ran through a set of points and I hoped I'd come out of it on the right subjunctive; Elise's look was somewhere between amusement and mild offence. But just then everyone else came in together, and my suave new persona slipped into hiding.

'Did I hear you practising your French, Dave?' Mark said.

'He speaks French well,' said Elise.

'Ah . . . merci, madame,' I said, and Giles sniggered and said, 'Oui, oui, sacrebleu.'

She looked at me, blinked as she chose her words. 'The grammar,' she said, 'is . . . *remarkable*. But he must work, work, work on his accent.'

'I don't suppose they get much chance to speak French at school, Mummy,' Mark said.

'Not really, sir,' I said.

'It's all just vocab,' said Giles. 'And verbs.'

'Do try to remember, Giles,' said Elise, 'that you are a quarter French yourself.' I wanted to explain that she was the first completely French person I'd ever met, but I was too ashamed by what she'd said about my accent.

As we sat down to dinner, Cara said, 'We should really have a game of something later.'

'We haven't had a game for ages,' said Mark. I pictured the boxes waiting in the window seat and felt the mixture of dread and anxious resolve that gripped me whenever a game I didn't know was suggested, or one pack of cards was shuffled briskly with another.

Lydia said, 'Not pontoon, though, please, Dad.'

'Not likely,' said Cara, 'we don't want to bankrupt poor old Dave!'

'Or me!' said Elise, 'thanks very much,' so that the far more serious threat of playing cards for money seemed already to be in the room.

'Giles cleaned us all out the last time we played pontoon,' Cara explained: 'what was it, you beast, twenty-five pounds you took off us by the end?'

'Twenty-six pounds ten, Mum.' I grinned at this and Giles, enjoying my discomfort, went on pleasantly, 'Dave could do just the same to all of us tonight.'

'I'm sure he would be very embarrassed if he did,' said Elise, and at the mere suggestion I found myself blushing.

'I've never played it at all,' I said, just in case pontoon might still be an option.

'And I don't think your mum would like it if you did, do you,' said Mark.

I winced and said, 'I'm afraid she wouldn't, sir,' childishly grateful to him for thinking of her, despite Giles's mocking stare across the table. If I lost my entire £4 to the Hadlows, who effectively paid my school fees, she would see it as a small social disaster, though to *clean them all out* would surely be even more embarrassing.

I thought perhaps they would forget about it, but at the end of dinner Mark said, 'Is it Plutocracy?' with a grin that showed he at least was up for it, and I found myself clearing the place mats and sweeping the crumbs off the table as if eager for a game. Lydia went to the playroom to get the box, Uncle

George waved at us, and went back upstairs, and Cara in one of her brisk stage directions said, 'Are you seeing to those ewes, then, Pete?' 'I'm going to look at the ewes now,' Peter said, as if it had been his own idea. He got up and went out and a minute later I heard him in the passage saying goodnight to Mrs Over.

Plutocracy was clearly a family favourite: the corners of the box had been mended more than once with Sellotape, and inside, with the board and the cards and counters and money, was a list of the many times they'd played it before, and who had won. Mark had given way, over the past year or so, to Giles, though Cara had won it last Christmas ('Fluke' in brackets after her name, in Giles's writing). Now Lydia was dealing out cards with pictures on them, sacks, picture frames, gold bars. 'I won't try to explain the rules in full,' Cara said, 'you'll just have to pick it up as we go along.'

'It's really quite simple, Dave,' said Mark. 'You need to build up your reserves in the strongest currency you can.'

'Yes, right,' I said, with a shake of the head, and thinking I would probably work it out, just by mimicking the others.

'You ought to explain about the exchange rates, though,' said Lydia, who had finished setting out the board on the table between us, and was standing red, white and black chips in columns between her fingers. It looked a bit like Monopoly, which I did know the rules of, but rather than Monopoly's right-angled struggle from hardship to affluence through districts of London, the board for Plutocracy showed a map of the whole world. All the borders of the countries were drawn in, though some were left unnamed; my eye slid quickly over the blank of Burma to examine Japan, where Tokyo was marked with a red circle ringed in blue.

'The red circles are the major stock exchanges,' said Mark. 'Tokyo opens first, obviously.'

'And also closes first,' said Lydia meaningfully.

'Oh . . . yes, of course,' I said, 'absolutely,' and Giles looked at me for a moment with the smile of a competitor for whom all claims of friendship or remorse are as nothing.

Lydia stared at her watch. 'Eight forty-five,' she said.

'I hope we won't be too late,' said Elise, pulling her shawl round her.

'Just let me win, Gran,' said Giles, 'and you can all go to bed.'

'I should warn you, Dave,' said Mark, 'that this game may take some time. Indeed it has been known to run on over three days. But since you're leaving us in the morning, we'll try and get you in bed by midnight.'

'Oh, thanks very much, sir,' I said, and peeped round at them all, with their competent secretive expressions, their look of boredom, almost, at the merely preliminary business of the game.

'So, Mum, you're starting,' said Giles. Cara promptly discarded a sack and a barrel, shook the die briskly in the plastic cup and rolled it out across Russia. It was a 4.

'Aha!' she said, taking a pull on her cigarette and surveying the board through the smoke. She gave Lydia £1,000 and received a tiny railway engine, like a bracelet charm, in return. With a pleasant but self-absorbed expression she jumped it from London to Dover to Calais to Paris to Frankfurt.

Lydia said quietly, 'Well played,' and then nodded at me: 'so – your turn, Dave.'

'So . . .' I said, 'you have to, um' – and I threw the die and with a little bit of muttered coaching from Cara, set out into the unknown.

Afterwards, I couldn't remember the game in any coherent way, and though I ended up winning I spent most of the time taking pointless chances, breaking unexplained rules and paying enormous forfeits. 'Dave's playing for high stakes here,' Mark said at one point, an hour or so in, when I had a brief climax of lightning advance and accumulation, jetting at dawn from one stock exchange to another – just for a moment I thought perhaps this was all there was to it, just for a moment I looked at the world from behind a great rampart of art and gold bars, and stood up trembling to pour myself a glass of squash. 'Oh, bad luck, Winny!' said Giles, and I turned to see all my money and my chips being incomprehensibly swept away from me and into the little compound in front of him. It was almost a relief. Half an hour later, he did something much worse to his mother, I couldn't understand it, and Lydia had to look in the rules, but it seemed it was just about allowable. Cara thrust her entire possessions across the table with a set look, as if reminding herself she was playing with children – she sat back, lit a fresh cigarette, then got up and went to the drinks tray, almost as if abandoning the game: 'If at first you don't succeed,' she said, and all the Hadlows joined in loudly: '*try a gin.*' I laughed and watched her squinting through the smoke as she plucked up the bottle.

By eleven o'clock Elise was yawning behind her cards, and I sensed that her act of being a good sport for the sake of the family was wearing thin: she took her turns very decisively, but I wasn't sure she had much more grasp of the rules than I did. I felt invested in the game with a strange beetling politeness which I hoped disguised my bewilderment, and as the night extended, a kind of distress. The others marched cheerily on, as if I was learning from my mistakes. I was the Hadlow Exhibitioner, after all, and I guessed they were taking my clueless deals and doomed mergers as a maverick boldness. The tone of their play was an increasingly fraught kind of fun, of emerging triumphs and gripping dilemmas; there were strange fading shouts of horror and joy, and a further little traffic in muttered side-remarks which showed their complete absorption in the game, to a pitch where the world of the not-game almost ceased to exist. I was grinning but on the brink of tears when I said I had to go to the lavatory, and in that chilly room with its bare lightbulb and smell of the nearby farmyard I stood for a minute and pulled myself together.

When I came back in I found the game had continued without me – I didn't know if I was wounded or quietly pleased. A minute later Elise was destroyed – all at once she had nothing left. 'I'm out,' she said, lifting her hands as if at some unimagined horror, while Mark with a murmured 'Sorry, Mummy,' absorbed her last chips and cards and carried straight on. She gave me a shrewd little look as she got up to fix herself a last drink – I envied her freedom as my turn came back round, and I did something blindly and I hoped suicidally: there was a great intake of breath. 'That was bold,' said Cara. I threw the die again. 'Ah, well done though,' said Mark, with a competitive smile. By now perhaps I really was into my part – my six took me nimbly eastwards over green Thailand and black Burma: I landed on Tokyo unsure if I'd done something clever or better still made the stupidest mistake of my life. 'Oh dear, oh dear . . .' said Giles, which could have meant anything. 'I very much think you've got him,' said Cara.

I smiled at my holdings as if calmly assessing my options. I don't believe Cara or Lydia told me to, I just found myself shouting, 'Capital!' and then staring round at them all to see the effect.

'Hang on a minute,' said Giles, outraged, but the others slumped back, blinking in the effort of mental arithmetic, and after five seconds broke into a staggered laugh. 'Well, well – well done, Dave,' said Mark, in quiet admiration. And then the three of them leant forward and in a slow collective gesture pushed all their heaps of chips and money into one great jumbled wall just in front of me. It was a victory too accidental to relish, and my main feeling was relief that the game was over at last, just coloured by an unexpected sense of shame that I'd deprived them all – even Giles – of the pleasure of winning themselves.

As Giles and I were saying goodnight, Elise smiled narrowly at me. 'Vous partez quand?' she said.

'Oh . . . demain matin, madame, à dix heures,' I said, almost reluctant to remind Mark.

'Ah – moi aussi . . . If you have a moment we might run through a scene together in the morning, before we go our separate ways? "You that way, we this way", as the play says.'

'Oh, yes . . . thank you,' I said, 'merci, madame!' – I looked up at Mark, who was smiling at this happy outcome, and I thought perhaps the great Mme Pleynet truly did want to help me, in her impatient and alarming way.

In a china box on the dressing table I found three old keys, and when I tried the second one in the bedroom door the lock turned at once with a nice oiled snap and I gasped with a fairy-tale sense of security and an inrush of regret about the previous nights. I came back from the bathroom and locked the door as quietly as I could, and the feeling that I'd dreaded, alone, was held off, so it seemed, by the awkward glow of my victory downstairs and the gift of the key.

I got out my school copy of *Twelfth Night*, and climbed into bed. The text had been heavily marked up all the way through by the boy who'd played Malvolio in an earlier production, his speeches underlined in red biro, and rubbed-out pencil notes in the margin still half-readable. Fabian's lines lay unmarked between them, like mere filler for Malvolio's part. They were almost all prose, until just before the end, where I had fourteen lines of verse, which I'd already learned by heart, explaining to Olivia about the baiting of Malvolio. 'Good Madam, hear me speak' – from those first words the verse seemed to tell me how to deliver it; but the prose bit that followed was more difficult to remember and to know how to say. I felt Elise had been a bit vague about *Twelfth Night*, but the thought of being rehearsed by her next morning made it hard for me to get to sleep.

7

At half-past nine we went into the sitting room and the door was pushed to. The room looked very different in the morning, sunlight angled across one wall, Mme Pleynet in her dark blue suit, ready for the journey, hair gleaming in the morning light, the view of the Downs reflected in the mirror, and the clock ticking. 'Now, we do not have long,' she said, rather severely.

'Oh, that's all right,' I said, 'it's very kind of you to help me like this.' My speech took less than a minute to say, but I knew she might have detailed criticisms and advice, and the short time that was left probably wouldn't be enough to get to the bottom of it, and get it right.

'I have the script here . . .'

'Oh, you have . . .'

'You must give the first cue' – and she passed me a tatty sheaf of paper, slipping free of a large paper clip, with a long column of verse down the top sheet. 'Or read the Chorus, why not,' she said, 'it will be good practice for you,' half snatching it back and looking at it again before plucking off her glasses and staring over my head with an impressive new remoteness from the room and from the other chorus we must both have been aware of, the cows massing and jostling in the yard behind the house. 'Line?'

'Oh! . . . Um,' and I pitched in, wrong-footed but quick-witted, I felt, and loudly, being the whole Chorus,

'In time, O Queen, to the great gods I'll pray;
But in amaze I first would hear you tell
Once more of these great matters —'

'No, no, no,' she said, 'you're too close. Never *crowd* the star' – with a blink of a smile and a tiny gesture of her right hand. I edged backwards past the sofa and stood between the TV and the table with the drinks tray. She stared, then nodded, and I declaimed my three lines again: I was ashamed but even so I felt I made a better fist of them the second time. There was a pause in which she seemed to be thinking of multiple objections to what I'd said, but then her eyes swept round the room, she threw up an arm, and she was off:

'The Greeks this very day prevail in Troy,
Do you not hear their shouting in the streets,
Far other than the wailing of the vanquished,
As oil with vinegar poured in one jar,
Combined and shaken, never to be mixed,
Such are the cries of triumph and defeat,
Fates co-existent, never to be shared.'

It was such a new voice, fast, swooping, almost growling at times, then running up the scale as if running out of breath, that I stood smiling and terrified, unable to take in a thing she was saying, although noting she'd got several words wrong.

'The howling Trojans fall upon the ground . . . Upon the —' she darted a look at me —

'*Um* . . . The Trojans howling,' I said, 'fall upon their dead, / Whose corpses —'

'— fall upon their dead, / Whose corpses, husbands, brothers, grandsires old . . . *yes?*'

'They mourn —'

'They *mourn* . . .' – she wailed it – 'They *mourn* from throats enslaved . . .'

I turned the page, where Clytemnestra's speech went on for a good thirty lines more, and I started to adjust, felt the madness and excitement of ranting about Troy in the sitting room after breakfast, and then quite soon after all I came in again, my heart speeding up with my new sense of what acting required: 'Well have you spoken, though a woman!' – I stared at her, and flinched just a little as she stared back – 'And shrewdly, with the wisdom of a man!'

Her shoulders slumped, her head dropped with a sigh: 'Yes, yes. But do try to remember,' she said, 'you're not a character – you're the Chorus. I'm the one who's acting.'

She held out her hand for the script and searched forward for her next big speech, while I glanced at my watch, knowing Mark would come in soon to get me. I hoped she would never glimpse my little fantasy of doing Fabian's speech, and hearing her advice. 'I think we have time,' she said, passing back the papers, and taking off her glasses, which I guessed turned me and the whole room back into a blur: she wasn't going to spot the dog-eared *Twelfth Night* in my jacket pocket. 'Now here,' she said, 'you'll have to help me again. Read the Messenger there, do you see?'

I found the place, and cleared my throat, unsure now if being the Messenger was 'acting' or not: 'Great Queen, to Argos in the night —'

'I think *kneel*,' she said.

'Oh . . .'

'It's better for me. Yes, that's right' – she glanced down and then lifted her head again.

'Great Queen, to Argos in the —' There was a gentle knock, and I looked over my shoulder to see Mark peering round the door.

'So sorry, Mummy . . .' – and she stared at him, with a tight little smile that seemed to me to have a long history in it. I stayed on my knees, looking from mother to son, though for me of course Mark still had all the presence and authority of a father. 'I was just hoping to hear Dave do Fabian's speech before he goes.'

She looked down at me with sudden concern. 'No, no, he *must* do that,' as if shocked at being kept in the dark about this plan.

'Oh ... well ... if you like ...' I said. 'It's only a *short* speech,' getting to my feet and thinking this sounded cheeky. Mark came and perched on the window seat, and I handed back *Agamemnon*, found the place in *Twelfth Night* and passed the book to Elise. She held it mistrustfully at arm's length, head back, then quickly put her glasses on again. I wasn't sure now if *she* was acting, I tried to think of her as Olivia, and not just the famous Elise Pleynet, which I'd started to see was quite a role in itself.

I began, 'Good Madam, hear me speak,' and I thought, from the way she pursed her lips, that she heard the humble protest in the words – 'And let no quarrel, nor no brawl to come, / Taint the condition of this present hour, / Which I have wondered at' – I smiled and spread my right arm in answer to the lift and the neatness of this little phrase, and felt without looking Mark's focused attention on me: for a second his attention was a challenge, my mind emptying, and then at once it was a prompt and a motive, a need for the words that flowed steadily out of me, about Toby and Maria, and the plot against Malvolio; the belief that I could do it ran over the fear that I couldn't. 'Maria writ / The letter at Sir Toby's great importance, / In recompense whereof ... he hath married her!' Elise herself looked surprised at this, and Mark grinned. 'How with a sportful malice it was followed / May rather pluck on laughter than revenge, / If that the injuries be justly weighed / That have on both sides passed.' Now there was a nervous moment, nothing was planned, but I gazed at Elise, and she said magically, without looking at the text, 'Alas, poor fool! How have they baffled thee!' And in that moment, not just of acting but of being acted with, I felt something fizz inside me, a certainty that went beyond acting, as I entered the difficult prose bit, mimicking phrases from the fake letter, 'Some are born great, some achieve greatness, and some have greatness thrown upon them' – words everyone knew anyway, which I chanted out in a very ironical tone. 'And thus', I wound up, with a big circling gesture, 'the whirligig of time brings in his revenges.' Elise and I both for some reason looked at Mark, who sat forward, raised his forefinger, and said, 'I'll be revenged on the whole pack of you!', so that Elise too was smiling when she said, with another shake of the head, 'He hath been most notoriously abused.'

I stood not knowing what to do, it had happened so quickly, and my pulse raced on though the scene was over. 'Well, jolly good, I'd say, wouldn't you, Mummy?' said Mark. And I remembered her comments last night on my French, that I knew the words, but not how to say them, and I felt sure that this time I'd proved her wrong. At the back of my mind I knew I'd have to take any criticisms she made. She put her head on one side, then the other, made her little moue, little frown, that seemed to teeter between indifference and a reasonable failure to find anything wrong.

'You speak well,' she said. 'Of course, a very short speech.'

'But one with a lot of different moods in it,' said Mark encouragingly.

'And a lot of information,' said Elise. 'But, as I say, you put it across very clearly. He knows how to project,' she said to Mark, 'which few children of his age do.'

'Indeed,' said Mark.

She ran her eye over the lines again, 'You say, "Sir Toby's great importance",' swelling the phrase. 'You could make more of that,' and I said, feeling a tiny correction was praise of everything else, 'Sir Toby's *great importance*', overdoing it, and knowing too that she was wrong, 'importance' here meant something else, meant urging or in fact *importuning* – we'd been over it in class. But I let this go.

'We will need your Hamlet, to truly judge!' she said.

'Well, thank you . . .' I said, glowing for a moment before I realized this was a part she was confident I would never, and could never, play.

'Well, you'd better get your things, Dave,' said Mark, 'you're all packed?'

'Yes, sir.' I waited and took back my book. 'Thank you, Madame Pleynet' – and she smiled and touched my cheek, as if 'seeing' me suddenly, and all my potential. As I went out down the hall I heard her say, 'Dear solemn little face he has – like a little brown cat,' and Mark said, 'Are your things ready, Mummy? Cara wants to make sure you catch the ten thirty-five.'

Giles came out into the yard to see me off. He had his hands in his pockets, and a look of already reclaiming his life here, after the imposition of my stay. 'See you next term, Winny,' he said, and smiled, no doubt picturing the horrible things he was hoping to do to me then. For now, the annual ritual was over, and next spring the new Exhibitioner would be a year younger than Giles, and very likely of a more acceptable appearance. Elise's case was stowed in Cara's Riley, and Cara came out and shook hands and we all said goodbye. 'Good luck with the play!' said Elise. 'Thank you very much,' I said, 'the same to you,' and she looked slightly taken aback. I opened the right-hand door of the Citroën, I got all that right, and Mark threw his soft leather briefcase onto the back seat beside my over-night bag. It was too cold this morning to have the roof down, and no one would see who we were as we raced through the lanes; but I had a more magical sense, when the button was pressed, the car rose on its suspension and we floated off across the yard and down the drive, of having Mark all to myself, for the fifteen minutes, or more, of the journey home.

8

We drove, pretty fast, into the market square. 'Tell me where, Dave,' Mark said.

'Oh, anywhere here, sir,' I said, and glanced up at my bedroom window on the top floor. On the pavement outside, some children were staring through the much bigger window of Harding's below, at the wirelesses and gramophones and three blank-faced television sets.

'My compliments to your mother,' Mark said as I climbed out of the car. I thought I should really invite him in to meet Mum, but I sensed from his pleasant fixed smile that he was keen to get on. When I turned at the front door the DS had already slipped off down the long slope of the square; a couple of men outside the Bull turned and stared at it, and as it swung round the corner into London Street it was traced for a vanishing second in Morleys' window, red lost in grey. Watched by the other children, I searched for my key and let myself in; then stood quite still with my bag in the narrow hall, where the light of the outside world came in only obliquely, through the square pane of glass above the door.

The first thing I heard as I came up the stairs was the sharp squeaks and moans of the ironing board under pressure, and the hiss of steam. Through the dining-room door I saw Mavis, in her housecoat, pressing a skirt, running the nose of the iron in under each narrow pleat in sequence, and then across the top of it. 'You're back then,' she said. There was a smell of fresh hot cotton and stale sweat. 'Your mother's with a customer.' I went on, past the nearly closed door of the sitting room where Mum (on her knees, no doubt, with pins in her mouth) was murmuring and another woman grunting and laughing, and upstairs again to my room and closed the door. I dropped my bag on the bed and stared round at my things as if I was a guest here too – the rag rug, the shiny blue eiderdown, the pagoda repeating in diagonals up the wall, the map of Middle-earth and the more detailed one of Mordor and Gondor taped up above the desk: everything small and clear. Then in four or five seconds these facts of the room lost their strangeness, and I opened my bag and took out my books and my shoes and my bundled-up mud-stained and blood-stained clothes.

At lunch Mum went on about her new customer, Mrs Croft: 'From Hertfordshire originally. A very stylish woman, and with quite a sense of humour.'

Mavis had an advantage in gossip about her. 'I've lived in this town all my life,' she said. 'She lives in Marlborough Close, or used to.'

'Crackanthorpe Lodge,' said Mum, la-di-dah. 'And what do you know about Mr Croft?'

'I don't know that there is one,' said Mavis, and looked down with a frown at her soup, in which she had floated three or four bits of bread.

'Esme Croft,' said Mum, sailing on.

'Esme 'at on straight?' said Mavis, with a cackle.

Mum half smiled at this and turned to me. 'Did Mrs Hadlow feed you well, dear?'

'Yes, thanks, Mum, she did,' I said, and then, with a dull sense of boasting, 'though there's a cook, too, in fact.'

'Oh, is there indeed . . .'

'Mrs Over,' I said.

'Good God, Audrey Over,' said Mavis. 'I knew her in the War.'

'You certainly ought to eat well on a farm,' Mum said.

'What's the set-up there, these days?' said Mavis. 'These posh friends of yours don't live there, do they?'

'No, no, Mr Hadlow's a very important businessman. They live in London – though actually,' I went on, 'he does a lot of his business in France.' I held back the fact that Mark was half-French himself. 'They just stay at Woolpeck sometimes in the holidays. It's Mr Pollitt's farm.'

'He's a bachelor, of course, Pete Pollitt,' said Mavis.

'Hence the need for Mrs Over, no doubt,' said Mum.

'Mrs Hadlow's Mr Pollitt's sister,' I said. 'Their uncle George lives there too.'

'Is he a bachelor too? Or a widower, perhaps . . .'

This was beyond me, and even Mavis shook her head. 'He's writing a history of Berkshire,' I said.

'They're all a bit odd, the Pollitts,' said Mavis.

'He's nice,' I said. I wanted to tell them about my interesting discussion on the First World War up in Uncle George's room, and my triumph at Plutocracy, and rehearsing *Agamemnon* with a famous French actress, and I wanted even more to keep these things to myself, unbruised by anything Mavis, or even Mum, might find to say.

I met Esme Croft myself a week later. She came in for the suit she'd had made, and she was 'closeted' with Mum for the final fitting. My French book was in the sitting room, but I wasn't let in while the women's business was going on. Again I heard muffled laughter, and then bits of louder, relieved-sounding talk that suggested the business was nearly over. The door was plucked open and Mum came out and went past me to the kitchen. Almost under her breath she said, 'Mrs Croft's going to have a cup of tea.'

I didn't know if Mrs Croft was decent, and I waited for a minute once the tray had been carried through before I went into the room. Mum was standing beside her at the big sash window, looking down into the square, Mrs Croft taller and stouter than her, with wavy brown hair kept short and the hasp of her pearls on the bare white gap between collar and perm. She was laughing, in a mild, mocking way. The view outside, of the square and the raised market hall, the bus stop, the butchers' and the chemists', the Crown and the Bull, and the day-long coming and going of people and cars and vans, was a routine part of our lives; but to Mrs Croft it seemed the angle and the interest were all new. She held her cup and saucer in one hand as she followed someone on the pavement opposite. 'Poor thing, she doesn't know what she's doing . . . now she's going back again . . . oh dear! Women look so foolish, sometimes, and lost, don't you think?'

I slipped in behind them to pick up my book from the chair where I always sat, across the fireplace from Mum's. Mrs Croft must have heard, she turned and saw me, raised her chin, and said, 'Ah . . . !', as if detecting a small problem and knowing almost at once how to deal with it. Mum turned too, and said, 'Oh, Mrs Croft, this is my son David.'

Mrs Croft smiled narrowly, as if suspecting a joke. I said hello, and we shook hands. 'So what have you got there?' she said. I gave her *Le Grand Meaulnes*, which she held at arm's length for a moment and then passed back to me.

'I expect it's your prep, isn't it?' Mum said. 'David's in his first year at Bampton School.' Our unspoken tactic was to assume that any person thrown by my appearance was puzzled by something else, and to solve that other puzzle for them; there was nothing they could say then. Mrs Croft's tack was rather original.

'He has a lot of his mother in him,' she said warmly.

'Mm, I think so,' said Mum.

'Your mother's very much in my good books,' Mrs Croft said.

'Well, thank you,' said Mum.

'No, no, Mrs Win, I had no idea we had a dressmaker of your calibre in our dreary little town.'

Mum coloured slightly, and said, 'Oh, it's not such a bad place, is it?'

Mrs Croft looked at her then, with an air of humorous calculation. 'Mm? Well, maybe you're right, my dear,' she said.

We hardly had friends in the town, and seemed not to feel the lack. Mrs Wiley, at Stimpson's, had snubbed Mum more than once – I knew that, and that some of the other parents at Bishop Alfred's had avoided her, looked down or crossed the road, in the early days at least. For a while I'd walked home after school with Sally Pike, who wanted to marry me, but Mrs Pike was strongly against the idea, and frosty to Mum when she came to collect me after tea. 'David has been a popular and much-valued member of his year,' Miss Bird said, in her final report, 'and I know he will thrive in the bigger pond of Bampton School. We all wish him well!' I can still see Mum reading this proudly, then searching in her sleeve for a handkerchief and leaving the room.

All that first year at Bampton, when I pictured Mum she was at home in the flat, I saw her over and over, her face out of focus but her actions familiar and clear as she sewed by the fire, steered a hem through the sewing machine or fetched out the two hot round tins of a chocolate sponge from the oven. At midday she still had Mavis to feed, and we both knew the sense of relief about five, the sigh and the firm smile, when the boom of Mavis slamming the front door behind her echoed back up the stairs. I didn't think much about Mum's evenings, the hundreds of suppers that by now she had sat down to eat alone.

In the holidays she was still working, and our evenings were the time we had together. Even then she might be hand-stitching as she sat across from me, or in the next room with the sewing machine, set up semi-permanently on the dining table. But mainly I see her by the fire, head tilted over her work under the bright lamp, and now and then catching my eye when she tied off a thread or looked round for her needle-case or scissors. I see her dark hair and high forehead but still not really her face, more familiar to me than anyone's; and I see her hands, as familiar, too, in their way, strong, broad-knuckled and nervously revealing.

The teak sewing box was open beside her, plump pads of velvet bristling with pins, the upper layer a tray that lifted out to reveal a store of coloured threads on spools and cards beneath. The box was one of the few things she'd brought back from Burma, and the sharp far-off odour when you lifted the lid was air from Burma stored and never fading. On the outside the lid was inlaid with two black elephants flanking a palm tree, and the sides were scored with geometrical patterns. Years ago Mum had seen twenty elephants together being washed in a river, with a boy on each one sitting up behind its ears. I longed to see that myself, and to be one of the boys.

The other Burmese treasures were clothes that you made as you put them on, lengths of bright cloth laid up in the chest of drawers, but on special occasions unfolded and furled round her, the skirt called a longyi, and the six-foot-long gaung-baung wrapped round her head clockwise, with the end jutting out like a tongue or a drooping petal. Unlike English clothes, these were worn in Burma by both men and women – once or twice Mum fixed me up in the gaung-baung and sat me at her dressing table, me in love with this beautiful self, like a brother, in the mirror, Mum tensely admiring me too for a minute, and then quickly undoing it.

Apart from that there were two white cotton hand-towels with GOOD MORNING worked into them in red, a gold bracelet, a couple of large rings and a necklace – 'probably worthless,' Mum always said, 'I've never had it valued' – light-weight, eye-catching and wonderfully different from what other mothers wore. And then there was 'A Tragic Gesture', a colour print of a painting of a dancer, seen from the side, with her left arm extended and her hand strangely bent. The tropical purple and pink of the woman's dress had faded pale blue in the English sun; in small sloping type just inside the mount it said, 'From the Original Painting in Oils by Sir Gerald Kelly PRA'. When I was eight or nine Mum got tickets as a treat for me, and we drove to Oxford for an 'Evening of Burmese Dance' – which turned out to be not just dance but opera, with slapstick and puppets too, and a group called the hsaing-waing, drums and cymbals hit with a stick, and one shrieking oboe, play-ing loudly all the way through. Mum said she'd been to such evenings in Rangoon, it was like a variety show, but all the excite-ment I'd been feeling for weeks about going was crushed within minutes by the baffling monotony of the thing. We didn't have the language, we couldn't stand the hsaing-waing, Mum stared for-bearingly ahead, while I sat up and slumped back in waves of fierce attention and half-insane boredom. A man called a mintha, in white make-up, high headdress, huge earrings and necklace, came on time and again to keep the thing going just when we thought it must be the interval, and a chance to escape. The women who were dancing swivelled and kicked back the thick trains of their dresses, signalled love and despair with arms angled or flowing, and on and off through my yawns I looked out for a Tragic Gesture – the stretched arm, and the hand, palm down, fingers flexed, the gold-ringed thumb turned fatally floorwards.

By the last week of the spring holidays it was light until nine, and I could perch in the window seat watching men passing and chatting below, while Mum was bent over her sewing and absorbed in her own feelings. 'I never have liked the spring,' she said. 'It's never agreed with me, I don't know why.' There were noises in the square, car doors, conversations rising and falling just within earshot as I worked on my translation of set passages from *Le Grand Meaulnes*: 'We left the country nearly fifteen years ago / It will soon be fifteen years since we left the country / since we left the area, and we will certainly never come back there / we will never go back there.' The difference between *to go back* and *to come back* hung somewhere beyond me as the late sun broke through down the length of the square, burned like a cool spotlight on the slate roof of the market hall, the white-lettered panels of the war memorial in the arcade beneath, where three or four boys sat smoking and waiting for the Swindon bus. I longed to be down there, looking at them as we strolled by in the fading warmth of the streets. 'Well, we'd better get out,' Mum said tersely, 'before it's too late,' and put down her things and stood up, in an obscure effort of self-control. And so for me the sudden getting-ready, jacket and change of shoes and going downstairs, was shot through with the awkwardness, close to guilt, of having a favour performed for me.

'Now, which way?' she said briskly, once she'd slammed the door. I thought of Uncle George, with his three walks, exactly timed. We had nine or ten, a dozen, spreading out from the ends of the four main roads from the square in branches and loops, the church path, the goods station, the reservoir with its bench in a shelter, where there might be boys playing a transistor radio or a courting couple who carried on snogging as we turned our backs and stared for a stilted ten seconds at the view across the Vale. On our side you were out of the town in five minutes and onto farm tracks, and soon after that, if you turned towards the sunset, onto paths through hazel woods that by now were green overhead and all around, the floor of the wood greening densely too with spring saplings and young nettles; sometimes voices heard, figures half-seen through the fresh undergrowth, a man and a girl on the path ahead, separating for a moment as they came towards us, her arm round his waist again and stifled laughter when I glanced back.

Tonight Mum decided on Ansell's Farm, which meant a longer march up through the town. We stopped as usual outside the Regal, where I looked sternly at the stills of Alan Bates in *A Kind of Loving* while Mum inspected those for the forthcoming feature displayed on the other side: *Flower Drum Song*, starring Nancy Kwan. 'I believe that's meant to be very delightful,' she said. 'We might even go and see that.' Together we peered at the small colour picture of Nancy Kwan, with a tense swimming feeling of a subject being almost touched on. She was described in the caption as 'That Petite Delightful Ball of Fire'. 'Is she Chinese?' I said. 'English mother, I think I read,' said Mum. Just then the doors opened and the audience for *A Kind of Loving* came out, not a lot of them, several men by themselves, young couples still taking it in, and I looked at their faces for a clue about what they'd just been through, that the black-and-white photos obviously couldn't show. Just after the others Mr Rodgerson came out with his face almost hidden in his wife's fur collar as he nibbled at her neck and squeezed her waist while no one was looking. Then he spotted me, and a second after, making sense of me, saw Mum, gave us an uncertain and pitying look before nodding sharply and steering Mrs Rodgerson off across the street – she said something to him and looked back over her shoulder. 'I don't know why they have to run X films in the school holidays,' Mum said, as we walked on – past Jennifer's Pantry, and the two glass-eyed petrol-pumps in Lynalls' forecourt, and a little further on Bishop Alfred's, where we slowed our pace to acknowledge the recent past, the silent playground, the large clean windows of the upstairs classrooms reflecting the late sun.

We crossed the main road at the top and climbed the gate into the footpath through Ansell's Farm. 'It's a public right of way,' we usually said, as if expecting a challenge. The path, sown over and tramped flat again each year, cut the corner off a field on its way to a gap in the hedge and a stile into the next field. The tender green growth was shoe-high each side of us, barley or wheat, it was too soon to tell, though by now I remembered this field and the next one in August, in the weeks before harvest, when the wheat came up to my chest and jostled where it stood under sudden gusts of wind. Mum talked cautiously about the summer term, four days away, and the cricket whites she had made me, to save money – 'I hope they'll be all right,' she said. 'They're perfect, Mum,' I said, and they were beautiful, they fitted me, unlike the uniform blazer, bought to grow into, and I couldn't admit to my worry that the light sheeny flannel was too fine and showy for school. Though perhaps, when you stood out already, it did no harm to stand out some more – I wasn't sure about this. In the next field we saw there was a woman by herself approaching on the narrow path, and a strange social pressure seemed to pause our talk and stiffen our faces as we readied ourselves to smile and say hello. I didn't think I knew her, a lady as old as Miss Bird but much thinner, in a headscarf and belted brown mac. There was something in Mum's face, when I peeped at her, that I knew already and was almost embarrassed by, a shutting-up, a pinching of the mouth. The woman herself looked astonished by my smile as I stood aside for her – it was as if I'd made a joke at her expense, and when Mum said 'Good evening,' she gasped, very quietly, took two or three steps herself off the path as she skirted us, with a frosty nod that acknowledged and dismissed the courtesy at the same time. 'Old trout, Mum,' I said as we carried on, and for the first time ever I took her arm – my heart was thumping at the insult to both of us, and also at my pained attempt to feel the insult as Mum felt it, her own hurt quickly concealed to protect me.

At the lane beyond the next field, we turned back towards the edge of the town. The air here was creamy and bitter with the hawthorn, white along the hedgerows. 'That smell,' said Mum, and shuddered, and I felt that the smell that she hated was mixed up now with the sting of the memory of the woman on the path. 'Oh, I love it,' I said, and thought of myself this time next week, already in bed, the sun still bright through the unlined curtains of the dorm.

Soon we came up to the council houses, where Mavis lived, in the last of the red-brick semis staring out towards the Downs; then some bigger houses, Dr Grahame's with his old grey Rover 90 in the drive, the entrances, dusty or tarmacked, different moods of the fences and glimpses of gardens, half-remembered interest of a garage or fishpond, and a secret knowledge, more Mum's than mine, but shared now and then, of women she'd made clothes for, who lived in certain houses that we passed. In bedrooms there, vacated, as we walked along, by the last touch of the sun, dresses and blouses by Avril Win hung waiting in wardrobes, or lay perhaps where they'd been thrown on a chair. At the junction with the main road she said, 'Go a bit further?' and turned right, and I fell in with her, not sure what she had in mind; we went single-file because of the traffic, with a sense of talk deferred.

Soon a narrow footpath led off to the left between tall larch-lap fences, and we emerged at the end into the turning-space of a gloomy cul-de-sac. 'I thought there was a way through,' Mum said; I had no idea, for a minute, where we were. The houses here were newish, large, and set back, one with lions on the gateposts, the outside verges mown. There was a feeling their owners had paid a lot of money not to be looked at, and even

between the houses there were tall thick hedges. Mum sauntered along with an odd half-anxious, half-mischievous
expression, not finding quite what she wanted – she stopped,
just for a moment, before the last house but one on the right.
The front gate was open onto the wide gravel sweep, and the
empty garage with its open doors made me tense with a feeling
that whoever lived there was about to come back and catch us
looking. It was a large plain red-brick house with white metal
windows and a porch with white pillars, and a view through at
the side to a lawn closed off by a tall hedge of fir-trees. I de-
ciphered the wrought-iron name on the wrought-iron gate:
Crackanthorpe Lodge.

'Oh . . .' I said. 'Oh, it's Mrs . . . um . . .'

'I was just curious,' Mum said.

When we got in I made cocoa, and Mum worked late, with a
frock to finish for a girl's birthday party – Mandy Wiseman,
who'd been at Bishop Alfred's the year above me. 'She's a big
lass,' Mum said, checking again that the measurements were
right. 'She always was,' I said. Mandy's famous bosom felt awkwardly present in the twinned satin cups that jumped in Mum's
lap as she sewed a crimson flower to the shoulder. She held it
up to see how it hung. 'Time was,' she said, 'you'd have tried
this on for me.'

'But not now, Mum . . .' and my weary smile at that childhood self couldn't quite keep a blush from coming through.
'That was a long time ago!'

'Do you remember at Auntie Susan's?' Mum said, so that I
could see where she was going, but not yet how far.

'Oh, Mum . . .' I said.

'The moment we got to the house you were off upstairs,
you knew exactly where she kept those black velvet evening
shoes.'

'Well, she's got tiny feet,' I said, 'only size three.'

'The sight of you when you came clattering down again, in that red skirt of hers, which on you of course came down to the ground.' Mum's faint smile, as she shifted and shook out Mandy's frock, was mainly nostalgic, but the batting of her eyelashes seemed to fend off some reawoken annoyance, or shame. 'Ah, you were a dear little boy.'

'Thanks very much,' I said, and stuck out my tongue at her. It seemed she wasn't going to repeat what Uncle Brian had said, in his stony unamusement at the sight of his six-year-old nephew in his wife's best clothes: *Ruddy hell, Avril, we're not in flaming Rangoon now.*

'It's no good dwelling on the past', was Mum's firm position, often stated. But just sometimes on those evenings the atmosphere yielded – there was a brief fireside lapse into reminiscence. Her memories of Rangoon were generally things I'd heard about before, the elephants, the Governor's limousine, the Burmese women smoking huge cigars, but sometimes she said something new, which in turn gave me a sense of further matters she was holding back; and sometimes, very rarely, she would mention my father, in a quite straightforward way, as if we talked about him all the time. When I won the Hadlow Exhibition, she said, 'Well, you take after your father, of course, he was a clever man.'

'Oh, was he?' I said.

'I don't know what he saw in me.'

'You're clever too, Mum,' I said, and meant it, and saw that I partly meant she was clever at keeping things to herself.

'He knew all about politics, the whole situation in the country after the War, which I really didn't understand very well – well, I didn't have to, I was just a humble typist!'

'You must have learned about it, though,' I said.

'I had my list of all the frequently used names, the Burmese officials and politicians, pinned up by my desk, to make sure I spelled them right. I suppose I picked up a bit about who was who from Sir Hubert, you know, and Lady Rance was also completely on top of it, she had to be, because of entertaining people all the time, and knowing how to address them. Burmese names can be very confusing.'

I smiled almost anxiously at Mum in the circle of light and felt perhaps I could press her, ask some easy and general question and this time get a more detailed answer than 'I wish there was more I could tell you, my love.'

The one thing we both had for sure on my father was the photograph, framed but kept in the drawer of Mum's dressing table, beneath handkerchiefs and scarves. I got it out secretly sometimes when she wasn't home. An unsmiling young man, dark-skinned, a sheen on his round spectacles: unknowable, but looking just a little like me in the mirror of the silent bedroom. Then on rare occasions he would be downstairs in the sitting room, beside a small vase of freesias or carnations. Then he was gone again – I see now that he slid to and fro between being useful and unmentionable. Some of Mum's regular customers expressed an interest in her story and were touched to be shown her husband's image; most found the whole subject too difficult, there was no need at all to go into it, and they took their lead from her own fierce discretion.

'I need to take some samples up to Mrs Croft,' Mum said two days after the fitting.

'OK,' I said – the visit as I saw it had the drabness of all adult social life then, of things gone through because you more or less had to, with eager politeness and a rolling prickle of boredom. 'Are we going in the car?'

'You might as well stay here, love. Get on with your translations!'

Now that I was being let off I felt I was missing something with an unexplained interest. 'I don't mind,' I said, meaning I didn't mind going with her, but I let the wheel settle where it would.

'Esme Croft has got it into her head that I'd like to make her some loose covers.'

'Oh Mum, you hate doing loose covers.'

'It will be exceedingly boring . . .' – she pursed her lips. 'But I'll make her pay.'

'Good,' I said. 'Is she quite rich?'

'I get that feeling . . . don't you?' She looked at me. 'Do you like her?'

I shrugged, and then grinned. I only had our two minutes' talk to go on, something physical and emphatic about her. 'She's all right,' I said.

'Mm, hard to know yet, isn't it? I'll just go and change.'

'You look fine, Mum.'

'I can look a bit finer,' she said.

I sat in the window seat, heard the bump of the front door slamming below and watched her as she walked off down the marketplace, swinging the cloth bag with the swatch-books in it – someone spoke to her but she didn't see them, she went on smartly, with the toss of the head, half-nervous, half-resolved, that I knew so well.

When she'd been gone about ten minutes the phone rang. Or rather it made a small buzzing click, like an instantly stifled urge to ring. I went out into the hall and stood watching it for a minute; and then, very carefully, lifted the receiver. 'Oh this keeps happening, I'm sorry, the line is busy,' said a man's voice. 'Oh, sorry,' I said. 'Try later, will you?' said the man – 'we'll be on the line for the next half-hour.' I put my finger on the bar and after fifteen seconds, and even more carefully and slowly, lifted it again, the receiver still close to my ear. (The danger here was of my breath, or some remoter sound in the flat or even outside, a shout or car horn, being audible; but then a dry hand pressed over the black cup of the mouthpiece risked making a suspicious little noise of its own.) The other man was speaking now, 'Well, we could do that, lovey, if you think Jill won't mind.' 'We'll get off into the woods, won't we, most of the time. We can easily lose Jill. Then we can do what the hell we like.' 'Ooh, can't wait . . . we probably shouldn't talk about it on the phone.' 'It should be all right for a bit. You know I've found out who they are.' 'The Post Office don't tell you, do they.' 'No, no, it's all confidential, for obvious reasons.' 'I don't know why they can't just make more lines, if that's what the problem is.' 'Anyway, it's some trying little woman in the town who seems to be a dressmaker – a woman and her son, I think it is.' I stood blank-faced, denying everything, as my heart raced. 'There isn't a husband, you mean?' 'He's probably out at work – not that I've the remotest interest in listening in. She tends to come on after lunch, measurements and things, when I was trying to ring Desmond, actually, about our naughty weekend. That's how I learned her name – Mrs Avril Win.' 'You *have* been snooping!' 'I just happened to hear it,' said the first man, with a giggle, '*kindly make the cheque out to Mrs Avril Win.*' 'What a name . . .' 'I know . . .' 'So was that the son just now, do you suppose?' 'Yes, he's a teenager – *young* teenager, Jeffrey! before you get any wicked ideas – well, you can tell, his voice sounds as though it's just broken . . .' 'Give him a few years, lovey,' said Jeffrey, I hung up – did I trigger a tinkle at the very last moment, make them freeze with suspicion? I ran upstairs to my room, pulse thumping with confusion and excitement from the guilt and the daring of listening in, as well as the things the men seemed to be saying to each other, in such cheerful and confident tones. Probably I'd seen them, down below, in the square, or at the cinema, perhaps, smoking in the dark. I heard them more than saw them in the woods where we walked, in the green thickets and the evening light, getting away from Jill.

It was nearly dark when Mum got back, and as soon as she'd taken her coat off she put on her apron. 'Egg and chips?' she said, briskly, but giving me a treat.

I set our places at the kitchen table, the dining room unusable. 'Well,' I said, 'did you meet Mr Croft?' I didn't care much one way or the other, but I needed a distraction from my thoughts about the men, about Jeffrey and the other one, Lovey. I felt I'd woken up but the dream was still going on.

Mum had put on the chip pan, and the speckled grey disc of old lard grew steadily gold and translucent over the flame. She patted the thick chips dry in a tea-towel, and dropped one in – no sizzle yet – and looked sideways at me as if I'd said something wrong. Then I saw she was merely thinking how to put something probably comical in words. '*Well*,' she said, 'I didn't like to ask, obviously, but after five minutes she just came out with it.'

'What did she say?'

Again she seemed to find some delicacy in the matter. 'She said of course she had been married, but she's not any more. I get the impression Mr Croft wasn't altogether the marrying kind,' and she looked at me almost shyly.

'He made a strange mistake, then,' I said.

'Yes . . . or she did, I don't know . . . Anyway, Mrs Croft says she got a divorce some years ago. I have the feeling she did pretty well out of it.'

'And has she got any children?'

'No, I'm sure she hasn't,' said Mum, with a little shake of the head.

I didn't think I'd ever met a divorced woman, and now that it turned out I had, my initial sensation of being bored and somehow challenged by Mrs Croft seemed to find a proper focus.

'And what's the house like inside?' I said.

Mum thought for a moment, tried another chip, the fat was ready. 'Oh, it's nice, you know – very comfortable, anyway. I can't say I care for the material she's chosen, but still.'

'Which is it?' I said. 'Not Sunningdale?'

'Worse,' she said, tumbling the chips into the pan. 'Ladies in Waiting.'

'Oh, Mum . . .' I said.

9

Manji asked me, 'What's your earliest memory?' and I said straight away, 'What's yours?', guessing this was why he'd asked the question. He seemed to keep, clear and intact, a system of images, characters, stories from his life in Bombay – people I now felt half-familiar with myself and pictured loyally, and laughed about as if I knew them, but was secretly bored and a little oppressed by, not having met them or being likely to do so. I knew all about the house, about the aunts who lived with them and the aunts in other parts of the city, about the bicycle rickshaws that got in the way of his father's Lagonda when he was driven to the office, about his uncle in the country who had elephants, with a mahout in charge of them who sometimes took Manji for a ride. All this I pictured for myself, I had never been shown photographs of any of these people or places.

'Oh, it's just a tiny thing,' Manji said, 'when I was three or four years old, I've told you about the Maidan in Bombay, the great Maidan where cricket is played.'

'Yes, you have,' I said.

'My grandfather, it must have been, my father's father, took me with him to see a cricket match. That's all – I don't know who was playing, or anything like that, just a picture I have of the grass, very brown grass, not like here in England, and the palm trees and the cricket players who seemed to be a long way away.'

We had reached the far side of our own green cricket field

83

now, where Mr de Pury was carefully decanting more white-wash into the well of the line-marker; after a minute he trundled on, stooped forward with his eye on the wheel as it laid out the final arc of the boundary. It was the bright hour after prep when we all did what we liked, but the Fathers' Match tomorrow gave it an uneasy feeling.

'So, your turn, Win,' Manji said.

'Let me think . . .' I said. I stopped and looked back at the house, the dark asymmetrical cedar on the lawn to the right, the famous wellingtonia topping the woods on the left. Sash windows up and down were gleams and depths across the great plain face of the building; in front of it, small senior figures in white could be seen running up at the nets. They blocked out my own frail images, first newsreel flicker of faces. There was the shiver, before the swirl of a skirt like a ball gown around my bare legs, of something not in fact a skirt, a longyi for a child, in pink and blue tartan, wrapped round and tied, and a door being opened in front of me; but the room I entered was a brown blur, not the present-day flat but somewhere we had lived before. I had a sense, even more obscure, that it had not been a success, the surprise and the costume, and the blur of the room was also a murmur of resistance. 'I suppose it would just be something boring like Christmas,' I said, 'you know, at my aunt and uncle's place,' which made Susie and Brian sound almost the equal of the well-to-do Manjis. 'Like you, it's just an image, though.'

Manji nodded at this, he expected no more, and we walked on round the boundary, me hardly listening now as Manji chattered on, with his marvellous grown-up fluency that was mocked and mimicked by everyone else but not by me, the other brown boy in the house and his grateful but even so slightly reluctant friend.

✳

The Fathers' Match came on like one of my dreams where I was naked at lunch among the fully clothed masters and boys. No one noticed while I was sitting down, then I was told to fetch something from the hatch and I swung round, pulled up my knees to get out of my place on the bench, and walked out through the dining hall unsure if I was laughed at or pitied or simply not seen. The relief, like a dream in itself, was that the end of the match marked the start of half-term, when the parents could take their sons away with them. In my letter home that week I wrote out the rules with a first-year's respect for the detail. It is hoped as many parents as possible will watch the match first; no boy may leave the school until the match is over. In her reply Mum said she would get there as early as she could, 'and I might just bring a friend!' – which I felt showed she was as anxious about the day as I was. I had no idea who the friend could be.

On the Monday before, I was hanging about by the notice-boards when the teams went up, and I read them and considered them in a pained but fair-minded way. A small number of boys were in the funny position of having a father playing. Pinsent's dad was captain of the Fathers' XI, and Randall and Hamilton-Martin, who were both in the School 1st XI, had the chance to bowl out their own dads. Pinsent looked proud about his father being captain but also a bit shifty. 'I wonder who you will be cheering for, Penis?' Harris said.

'*Whom*,' said Pinsent. 'Whom do you think?'

'I really wouldn't know,' said Harris, 'with someone as greasy as you.'

Pinsent said, 'Oh, get knotted, Harris!' and sloped off, but it seemed to me quite an interesting question. I felt if I'd had a father I'd have prayed all week for him to take five wickets and smash the school's bowling into the trees. I coloured up in confusion at the sight of M. A. Hadlow on the fathers' team '(School House 1939)', though I hadn't heard from Giles's parents at all this term, and Giles was so caught up with Harris himself that he didn't have all that much time left for bullying me. I understood, from something Harper said, that Giles had been ragged when it came out he'd had me to stay in the holidays, he'd 'lost face' with a number of people, and that was why he carried on now as if he barely knew me, even in Mr Clark's rehearsals for *Twelfth Night*, where he'd been cast as the Sea Captain. I did wonder if Harris had also asked Giles which team he'd be cheering for.

I seemed to be the only boy with no father at all, though there were those whose whole families were out of reach. Manji would be staying with the Holmeses in Worcester over half-term, and Cox, whose parents were in Ottawa, had to spend the five days alone with the Headmaster and his wife. He had a Family Assortment he'd been working his way through, blank-faced, by himself; now he offered us the nearly empty tin. 'Thanks a lot, Cox,' I said, leaving the last fruit crème, with its tacky core of jam, and picking out the broken Garibaldi. There was a cautious solidarity, and part of me felt I should have asked Cox to stay with Mum and me, until I reasoned that he wasn't really a friend.

'Does your dad play cricket?' Cox asked me, and at once I felt the air tingle.

Manji frowned at him. 'Of course he doesn't,' he said.

'Well, he might do,' said Cox.

'He doesn't have a father, Cox,' said Manji.

'Oh, yes, he does,' said Cox.

'I don't, actually,' I said, and something blurred the room around my performance.

'Win's father was *assassinated*, for goodness' sake,' Manji said. It was a thrilling word, but I wished he'd kept it to himself.

'Yeah, my dad was killed, I'm afraid,' I said.

'Oh, I didn't know that,' said Cox. He stared at me with a

frozen grin for a moment. 'This was in Australia,' he said, to make sense of it.

'It was in Burma,' said Manji. 'Years ago now.'

'He was a government official,' I said, 'a secretary. Not like an ordinary secretary, obviously.'

'More like the Home Secretary,' said Manji.

'I thought you said he was a fighter pilot,' Cox said, 'in Australia—'

'I know, I know,' I said, 'sometimes I have to say something like that, because I don't want people knowing the truth.'

'It's too painful,' said Manji.

Cox clearly felt both excited and cheated. 'Well, sorry, Winny,' he said, and patted me on the shoulder, perhaps still thinking the pilot story was more likely. His sudden air of discretion let a hint of mistrust gleam through, but he didn't ask anything more. 'Why don't you have that fruit crème?' he said.

'If you're sure,' I said, 'thanks a lot,' and I searched his face as if he really was a friend. 'But please don't tell anyone, will you?'

'Assassinated,' he said, and I saw the word at work in him, and the need to spread it that he was already feeling.

All the upper forms knew the drill, and I fell in with it alertly, as if I'd done it before. By eleven, I was out in the fields with everyone else, waiting for the first cars to appear through the gap in the woods. The big iron gates by the Buckley lodge had been opened, and parents could come up the old back drive and straight onto the ground. There was an area marked off as a car park on Tadmoors, but it was clear the best places to park and set up camp were round the boundary. I hung back as the first boys who recognized their parents' Wolseleys and Jaguars flagged them down and climbed in and were chauffeured off round the circuit of the ground to find a spot. My lurking shame about the blue Morris Minor was eclipsed by my longing to see it come out shining from under the trees. This waiting about in a large loose crowd was like a game in itself, though it wasn't quite clear if the parents or the boys were the competitors. Boxwell ran up to a Riley and then curved aside as the Pierce brothers strolled over and climbed in – he ambled off then by himself for a minute, too mortified to re-join the rest of us waiting. Soon the wide ring of the boundary was filling up, tailgates of estates were raised, folding chairs and picnic baskets lifted out. These parents did it every year, knew when to get here, where the best places were. Hanging back now, as if not bothered after all about seeing my mother, I watched as the Hadlows' DS came out into the sunlight, the roof down, Mark and Cara like royalty on show as they floated round the boundary and came to a stop on the far side of the field, facing the pavilion, central but still somehow aloof. Quickly Triumphs and Daimlers and an Alfa Romeo drew up beside them, a party, random-seeming but possibly planned, was unpacking and mingling – I glanced across now and then, Mark was moving round in whites and looking like a very senior schoolboy himself in a white cap. Then I saw Giles bringing Harris over to meet his parents.

Still no sign of the Morris when the match started, and I sat cross-legged on the grass for a while, gazing at the pitch. I was afraid Mum hadn't understood about the Buckley gate, and had tried to come in the other way, through Main Gate. I ran over my letter, certain I'd made it clear. The boys had won the toss and gone in first, and there was a tall grey-haired father fielding quite close to me, almost in smiling distance as he roamed about after each delivery. I picked up the drama of the cricket match, the noise abrupt and absorbed, the red-faced father with his short lazy run-up and lethal spin, the low delayed knock of Knapton's returns, but I couldn't concentrate. When people clapped, I took notice and clapped too and

looked across at Taylor who was already hooking and unhook-
ing the white-stencilled numbers on the scoreboard – the
numbers, on their double-sided slates, spread round in a
half-circle on the grass. I thought one year it would be wonderful to get that job, everyone relying on your quickness and
accuracy.

To my left, beside a large black Wolseley, Roberts was sitting on a picnic rug with his knees drawn up, and now Morgan
came over, a shimmer in the air as he shook hands and chatted
with Roberts's parents and then sat down next to Roberts on
the rug; in a minute he'd rolled up his blazer into a pillow, and
stretched out beside him with his arms behind his head.
Morgan's parents lived in Malaya, and we'd once had a completely unexpected and never-repeated chat by the Fives Courts
about where I came from; now he must be going home with
Roberts for half-term – they were in their last year, their last
term, and whenever I saw them they were together. Morgan's
shirt had ridden up and uncovered the dip of his stomach – each
time I craned round at the late cars arriving I stared for two
seconds at the gap between his shirt-hem and his belt, the
downy hairs silvery in the sun. Morgan turned his head to look
up at Roberts and at the same time, I felt sure, he saw me, and
knew who I was, and though he didn't acknowledge me he
seemed not to mind in the least that I was there. I felt conspicuous as always and also, today, sitting low on the grass beneath
the towering trees, very nearly invisible.

Four or five overs into the match the sun winked sharply on
a moving rear window – a large green Humber had emerged
from the woods and was trundling its way in a wide circle
round the boundary, slowing down now and then as if spot-
ting a space. People watched it as it passed and then carried on
talking. The car swung at last into a narrow slot beside the

sight screen, reversed, nosed forward again, came to a halt. Heavy but rakish, dark green bodywork and glinting chrome, it made its presence felt. The driver's door opened first and a woman climbed out who resembled and then unmistakably was Mrs Croft – nodding to the unknown parents next to her, then standing hands on hips to survey the scene. In the car, a mere shifting gleam behind the windscreen, reaching for something on the back seat, was a second figure, who even before she got out, far off, was intensely my mother. She had pulled on a small white sun hat, a bit like Mr Clark's, who was umpiring. I stood up and set off round the boundary towards her, nearly in a panic as I marched, head down, past the other families, only dimly aware of the different ways they looked at me, noting, or staring, or smiling indulgently ... The bowler was just picking up speed as Mrs Croft, with her look of sizing the place up, strolled across in front of the sight-screen. Jackson who was facing the ball blocked it boringly and stared and shook his head at her as I came trotting towards them – my embarrassment blinding me somehow to Mum's own intense self-consciousness: that she'd got here late, she knew next to no one in the great watching circle of her fellow-parents, had no husband of her own to show off and share with them, and thought perhaps, as she shaded her eyes with her hand to look at the game, that she would never have been here at all if it hadn't been for her son's Exhibition. She came to meet me with a touch of play-acting in her smile and tilt of the head, but her hug, and the arm she kept round me as we turned back to the car, had all her fierce warmth. 'I've brought Mrs Croft,' she said, 'or rather, she's brought me!' For a moment I ignored the other woman, manners lost in the spasm of love and bewilderment. 'She's very keen to see where you live, of course,' Mum went on, 'and what you get up to.' I was sorry and thrown, but Mrs Croft kept a tactful distance at first, and once she had laid out a tartan rug in front of the car and made me fetch the picnic basket from the boot a strange but not unknown mood of acquiescence overcame me. I was hungry too.

'I'm sorry we were late, David,' Mrs Croft said, kneeling by the basket and starting to unpack, 'it's entirely my fault. I insisted on going into Hubbards' for some lemon curd, which your mother tells me is your favourite.' Mum's smile mixed apology and vindication. 'And Hubbards' were completely out of it, so it turned into quite a chase round the town.'

'Thank you very much,' I said.

'I refused to give in,' Mrs Croft said, smiling severely. Now she set out boxes and beakers, and passed heavy china plates and chequered napkins round. 'I expect you'd like a glass of Lucozade.' It was rather as if she was my parent, and Mum a shy friend she'd brought along. 'I don't know about you, Avril, but I'm going to have a proper drink' – a suggestion Mum seemed surprisingly keen on. 'I've *pre-mixed* it,' Mrs Croft said, unscrewing the lid of a Thermos, 'but you must tell me if it's too strong.'

'I've not had this before,' Mum said, and prepared to take a sip.

'It's a good summer drink,' Mrs Croft said.

'My word!' – her head went back at the jolt of it.

'What is it, Mum?' I said.

She swallowed again, spread her hand on her chest as if absorbing flattery. 'So this is Pimm's, is it?'

'Some people drown it in lemonade,' Mrs Croft said, 'but for the life of me I can't see the point of that. Good, so we've all got a drink.' She lay across the rug, propped up on her right elbow, and peered tolerantly towards the wicket – it dawned on me then that she was wearing the suit Mum had made for her. 'Now who's batting, David?' she said.

So I told her – Jackson and Van Oss, facing – with a muddled sense of falseness and relief, of being in two places, the school with all its important and complicated laws, and the outside world of a middle-aged woman completely unaware and unafraid of them.

'You should run round,' Mum said, as the first fielders jogged out after lunch, 'and say hello to Mr and Mrs Hadlow' – but just then I saw Mark himself strolling across the outfield, pads on, the bat in his right hand set to the ground now and then like Uncle George's stick. 'Go on,' she said, so I scrambled up and went towards him. 'Dave, excellent!' said Mark, shaking my hand and coming over to be introduced to Mum, who stood up smartly, while Mrs Croft squinted at him from the rug, shading her eyes with her hand. I was beamingly aware of Mum's urge to heap thanks on Mark, and of Mark's own wish to dodge all displays of gratitude – he almost over-played it, as if they were no more than random parents. 'You can bowl, Dave, can't you?' he said after a minute. 'Yes, sir.' 'Well, come along with me, help me to warm up . . . If you can spare him for ten minutes, Mrs Win' – smiling back and touching his cap to her as we moved off.

And now the day was over-charged, dazzling to the mind, hot sun and shadow, the outfield hazed with flowers and floating pollen, at the centre the match, about to resume – Mum and Mrs Croft camped out somewhere behind us by the Super Snipe – the casual privacy everywhere of parents with their sons – and Mark, all in white, both practical and elegant, filling me abruptly with his own sense of the occasion as he swept me off with him to the nets. We walked along quickly, past picnicking families, Mark nodding or lifting his bat to one or two but not stopping to speak. 'When are you in, sir?' I said.

'Number five,' he said, 'so we should have a bit of time, and Newsome and Pinsent are famous stickers.' It was funny to hear them named like schoolboys. 'I've told Giles to call me when two wickets fall. If, indeed, they do, Dave!' I closed my eyes as though accepting the challenge, but already the match had a dreamlike remoteness.

Mason was just leaving the left-hand net, and Mark walked into it, set the bails on the stumps, and knocked a few balls that were lying there back to me along the ground. 'Just dollies, Dave, to get my hand in.' He took up his stance, smiled at me, his almost handsome, forward-looking face in the suddenly impersonal focus that I remembered from playing Plutocracy against him at Woolpeck. My first fast inswinging ball sent the leg stump flying. 'Hmm . . . !' Mark said, stretching his neck as he put back the bails and readied himself for the next one; which was out of control, he leapt back to dodge the chin-level bouncer. He called out, 'As I say, just a warm-up, Dave . . .'

'Sorry, sir!' I said, excited and alarmed at my own performance.

After that, I settled down a bit, and there was something lovely in the situation, the two of us facing each other, Mark with his games face still, which I did my best to match, and in the to-and-fro rhythm of the play almost nothing needing to be said.

Then, after what might have been ten minutes or twenty-five, Giles was calling out from some way off, 'Dad, Newsome's father's out!'

'Right you are,' Mark shouted, and nodded at me for one last ball – perhaps it was Giles watching, it was a wide, Mark reached for it with a grunt and then came back down the net. 'Well, I'm thoroughly warmed up!' he said. 'Thanks so much, Dave,' and pulling off his glove he shook my hand again. Giles had already turned and was loping off under the trees towards the bright field beyond.

We walked back with Mark's hand for ten seconds on my shoulder, and his pads chafing quietly together. 'Good luck, sir,' I said.

'I'm not sure you're meant to say that!' said Mark, and went off with a quick laugh after Giles.

When I got back to the car the picnic had all been packed away and Mum was standing by herself staring with abstracted intensity at Hamilton-Martin's long lolloping run-up which started almost at the boundary – a no-ball and he had to do it all over again. 'Hello, love,' she said, and stood with her arm round me in a way that, unlike Mark's embrace, I half hoped no one saw. 'Well,' she said, 'he seems very nice!'

'Oh, Mark, you mean, yes, he's awfully nice,' I said.

'You don't call him that, I hope.'

'No, Mum, of course not.' I looked around. 'Where's Mrs Croft got to?'

'She's just talking to some friends she spotted, with the swish red car over there. I said I'd wait for you.'

'What, the Lancia Flaminia?'

'Is it . . . ? Yes . . .'

'That's Leatherby,' I said. I could see Mrs Croft talking to Leatherby's parents, who were laughing politely but keeping an eye on the match.

'I think she's a bit bored by the cricket,' Mum said.

'Why did she come, then?' I said, as lightly as I could. Her tight clutch made it hard for me to look up at her. She seemed not to know the answer. 'She just wants to be kind, I think,' she said. 'And she wanted to see you! That's what she said.'

'I can't wait to get home,' I said, and cleared my throat at the feeling the words had released.

By about half-past four the last pair were in, and here and there on the boundary a clumsily discreet process of packing up and driving almost reluctantly, as if still savouring the game, out of the ground and onto the school drive had begun. 'Are we off, then?' Mrs Croft said.

'We'll have to pick up David's things from his house first,'

Mum said. There was a murmur from the pitch and applause round the boundary – it took me a moment to see that the Fathers had won, and then explain it to the women, and the fact that the school had lost laid a sort of flatness over the ground as the captains shook hands and Mr Clark untied round his middle the jerseys the batsmen had handed him.

'Well, better luck next time,' Mrs Croft said. 'I can't say I think it's fair, grown men against boys, but there you are.'

We all got into the green Humber Snipe, Mum in front and me behind, where just on the four-hundred-yard journey to Main Buildings I began to feel sick. I rolled down the window and tried to look relaxed when other boys ran past or looked out from the back of their own cars, the Leatherbys' Lancia, the Stapleford twins in their father's maroon Singer Vogue. 'Good game!' shouted someone behind us at a passing MG. I had a feeling that I'd more or less missed the game, what with one thing and another, and all that mattered now was that it was over.

Mrs Croft was a no-nonsense driver, and we sped back to Foxleigh with the air rushing round us, and the joy of release overriding the low-level nausea. 'I think you're happy at Bampton, David,' she said over her shoulder. 'Joan Leatherby tells me you're going to be in the school play – I think her boy's in it too?'

'I've only got a very small part,' I said, but I was pleased she knew. 'Leatherby's playing Sebastian.'

'Aha!' Mrs Croft said warmly, braking as she signalled with her arm thrust out of the window that she was turning right. And now here was the pillbox perched above the road, the long descent into the town, the crossroads and steep London Street, with its shops shut and their blinds down, and three or four people I looked at to see if I knew them. 'Now this is you,' she said, as she pulled up in the square, and she was right: it was all there, just as I'd left it six weeks before, and it was us. Mum sat looking at her, head on one side, as if grateful for some far bigger favour than a lift and a picnic.

'Thank you, Esme,' she said.

'Yes, thanks so much, Mrs Croft,' I said, climbing out with my bag, sort of slamming the door and going round in mock-courtesy to open Mum's door. Some little joke had passed between them in those seconds, Mum freed her hand and then quickly got out.

Back at school some weeks later, in a lesson about rainfall, the figures from Burma came up, and one or two people looked at me sideways, turned round for a moment – somehow I felt proud and also uneasy at the record-breaking wetness of the country. We took a brief look at the physical geography, it was the coastal regions that got two hundred inches a year – which Collishaw worked out was sixteen point six-recurring feet, more than five times the annual rainfall we recorded with our own pluviometer behind the gym. Mr Halls didn't mention the people of Burma at all, and I wondered if I was the only person present who knew there were many different peoples, mixed up, and muddled in my head too, from various things Mum had told me. We moved on to tropical rainforests in Brazil and Ecuador, with an unvoiced feeling that Burma was too freakish, and my own connection with the country too tricky for me, and for the class as a whole, to cope with.

Years before, at Bishop Alfred's, I'd done a project on Burma, at Miss Bird's request. 'I'm only a half-caste, miss,' I'd said, half hoping to be let off. Mum steered me towards clothes and fabrics, which were her own way of managing the presence of Burma in her life, and I brought in the gaung-baung, which most of the class tried on, instructed by me: pale country faces topped for a minute by a red and gold turban. They looked one by one in a hand-held mirror and blushed and laughed, and a sense of discrimination, ridicule, absent until now, seemed subtly, perhaps immovably, to enter the room. 'Now you try, David,' Miss Bird said, 'show us how it should really be worn'; so I wound the thing round and tied it at the side and stood up in front of them feeling foolish in a way that I knew none of them had done. 'Beautiful!' Miss Bird said, but somehow I'd spoilt it, for them and for myself, by showing them up and showing them (what they generally forgot) how different I was.

Later, at Bampton, in an undecided mixture of hurry and reluctance, I read books from the Library about Burma, written by British travellers, or former colonial officials. The Library was empty, or nearly, in the hour between prep and bed, and I put them in among other books I had piled up, for History and English. I didn't want anyone to know that my smug-looking silence on the subject was ignorance, or that I cared enough to put it right – both things were embarrassing. When someone came in, I pulled my collected Yeats or my Gerard Manley Hopkins on top of the still-open pages on Burmese culture and trade. If it was a friend we might talk for a minute in whispers about this week's essay, gazing round at the white marble fireplace, the view through the tall sash windows of the lawn in the evening, the Balustrade and the trees of the park beyond. Then I would be alone again, my left arm shielding a volume whose stamped card showed it hadn't been borrowed for ten or fifteen years.

The school had most of the series called 'Peeps at Many Lands' – Belgium, Wales, British North Borneo, the one on Burma published in 1909. It was written by R. Talbot Kelly, 'Commander of the Medjidieh' – was the Medjidieh a ship, a regiment, a province, a fortress? I had no idea. It had wishy-washy colour plates of temples, 'dainty ladies', a bungalow on stilts called a dak. The Burmans, said R. Talbot Kelly, were a charming but lazy race, no wonder they were known as the 'Irish of the East'. I wondered if the Burmans themselves wrote books about their country and their fellow-Burmans – not in English, probably. It was only later I wondered whether R. Talbot Kelly might not have been a little bit Irish himself.

Sometimes when the Library was more or less deserted I pulled out the heavy *Times Atlas of the World* and leafed my way crabwise through 'India', 'India South', 'East Pakistan and Bhutan', to 'Burma', split in two, the long tapering tail of the country three pages ahead with 'Thailand and Indo-China'. There was Rangoon, the capital in capitals, Mandalay way to the north, and between and beyond them in differing sizes and weights of type, three or four hundred more places that nobody using this atlas had ever heard of, or ever would. It was meaningless detail, impossible to take in, and I trekked east again in an unseeing stupor over China, Mongolia, Japan, until at last heaving a wodge of the large gleaming pages back I sank into England, laid out in everyday detail and depth. There was London, Maidenhead, Swindon, Foxleigh itself, with a large friendless capital B that floated half-registered next to the Oxford road, and turned out to be BERKSHIRE beginning its widely spaced arc across fifty miles of the page.

10

On the first day of the summer holidays I lay in bed extra-late, and when I drifted down in my pyjamas and dressing gown Mum was on the phone in the hall – she widened her eyes at me as she listened, then turned her back: 'Oh, well, yes,' she was saying, 'that would be very nice.' In the kitchen my breakfast was laid beside a heap of runner beans she was stringing and slicing for lunch. I shook out my cereals and soon the roar of the kettle obscured what Mum was saying on the phone until the dead jingle when she rang off. She waited a moment, perhaps writing something down, then rushed in saying, 'Good morning – still – just about!' and kissed me and hugged me. 'Well, this is nice!' she said.

'Mum!' I said, struggling but not minding.

'Eight whole weeks!' she said. It was as though she was the one on holiday and I saw for a confusing few seconds how much she must have missed me.

'Who were you talking to?' I said.

'Oh . . .' – she let me go: 'it was Esme – Mrs Croft – going on, as usual!'

'How is she?' I said.

'She sounds fine.' She looked round for her apron. 'Anyway, she's coming to tea tomorrow, so you can ask her yourself.'

The next day I heard Mrs Croft come up the stairs, quiet talk in the hall, and ten minutes later Mum called up to me. I dawdled down in a fractional sulk of compliance. 'Ah, Dave, good afternoon!' Mrs Croft said when I came into the sitting room. 'How nice to see you again.'

'Hello, Mrs Croft,' I said – I'd been David to her before. She was wearing a blue sleeveless blouse and white linen trousers, tight round her hips when she started to stand up.

'Look, I've taken your place, Dave . . .'

'He can change places,' Mum said, in strange high spirits; she poured a cup of tea for me, and then went out to get more hot water.

I sat down on the Windsor chair. 'How are your new loose covers, Mrs Croft?' I said.

She stared for a moment. 'Well, of course I'm jolly pleased with them. No, they're marvellous. You must come and see for yourself – come and sit on them!'

'Ladies in Waiting, I think, wasn't it,' I said. I saw the dining room overrun with their hoop skirts and bonnets.

'I think you're right,' she said. 'A touch of Regency elegance!'

When Mum came back into the room a brief silence fell, while we watched her refilling the pot, and Mrs Croft said, 'Do you know, I was thinking, Avril, we should go away somewhere,' in the capable tone I'd already come to know.

'Oh, goodness,' said Mum, 'what, all of us, you mean?'

'You deserve a holiday,' Mrs Croft said. 'Doesn't she, Dave?'

I agreed she did, flustered at the idea of sharing it with someone we barely knew. 'I think we're going to Clevedon with Uncle Brian,' I said.

Mrs Croft smiled and blinked in a brief show of respect for this plan. 'I was thinking more of Devon. Sidmouth? Budleigh? What do you think?'

'Devon! Gosh, well . . .' said Mum, with a hesitant smile at me. 'It's a thought, isn't it, love? I mean, Susan and Brian . . .'

'I've just had my dividend,' Mrs Croft said, 'so you don't need to worry about that.'

'Oh, we couldn't let you pay for us,' Mum said, and looked across at me again.

'Or, of course, there's *North* Devon,' Mrs Croft said.

'Well,' I said, caught, as I now saw I was, between the two women.

North Devon it was. At the start of August we drove down for ten days at Friscombe Sands: the Cliff Hotel, dinner, bed and breakfast, twelve guineas a head, as Mum let me know. In the Morris I seemed to have grown out of my carsickness, but in the back of the smooth stifling Snipe I rolled down the window and took in deep breaths against the tightening of my gut and spreading numbness in my fingers. 'You should come in the front, Dave,' Mrs Croft said, but there was martyrdom in my sickness too, and I stayed where I was. My half-useful trick was to think in great detail about something so private and absorbing that for minutes at a time I would forget to feel ill. Now, as the green drains and hedges of the Somerset Levels rolled past, I worked my way back to the dim basement changing room, and the time I'd been sitting there whitening my cricket boots when Roberts and Morgan came in – the incredible chance of being there unnoticed and watching them change into their white shirts and trousers, long glimpses, while I ran the soaked sponge round the heel and then trickily over the tongue of each boot, of Morgan's legs and downy stomach and Roberts's broad beautiful back. And then when they'd gone clattering up the stone stairs together in their studs, removing my own shoes and socks and slipping my feet into Roberts's worn-down old slip-ons and dragging round the room to look at my changed image in the full-length mirror.

*

I'd pictured the hotel perched high up, but it turned out the cliff was behind it, a crumbling stretch of sandstone that loomed over the car park at the back. The hotel itself was painted white, with its windows and one or two fancy details royal blue. Mum and Mrs Croft had a twin-bedded room with a balcony overlooking the Bristol Channel; I was in a room that Mum agreed, when she knocked on my door, was very small but seemed almost to envy ('so much quieter'), up on the top floor, with a window that looked out at the side wall of the pub next door. 'You're in a world of your own up here,' she said, and closed the door behind her and went back downstairs. In fact I would be sharing the bathroom and lavatory with the two other rooms on this floor, and as I unpacked and tried to make the place my own I had a trapped and still nauseated feeling. The basin with its glass shelf and mirror was jammed in next to the door, the wardrobe swung open noiselessly ten seconds after it was closed. I sat, and then lay full length, on the bed, under the sloping ceiling, and wished we had stuck to our usual plans, or just gone to Weston by ourselves, as we sometimes had before. Then I got up and went down and knocked at the women's door.

'Hello, love,' Mum said, 'feeling a bit better?' She was hanging up her skirts and her evening frock, and I saw I had to make a go of it for her. 'The water here's lovely and soft.' She seemed tired, but refreshed by a wash, and the prospect of ten days without work of any kind. Mrs Croft could be heard in the bathroom having a wash herself – this was one of three rooms in the hotel with 'en-suite' arrangements, 'Which I really insist on,' she said. I went out onto the balcony and just then the clench of the carsickness lightened and I found myself squinting and almost grinning in the dazzle of arrival, of being here, sunlight and voices, breeze off the sea and the yacking of gulls. I took in the view, I felt excited and oddly conspicuous to the people in the street below, who had settled in days ago and all knew their way round. The hotel seemed to be at a point where things changed, where the long open road above the beach on the right turned a narrow corner to enter the old town on the left, with the harbour glimpsed from here over roofs of the buildings between. The beach was half a mile of silver and gold, bare now at low tide, the sea brilliant but far off; steps in the wall just opposite led down to the sand, which stretched away to a tumble of rocks and the reddish-brown cliffs that closed off the view to the north. Active swimmers and paddlers were distant silhouettes against the sheen of the wet sand; though all across the beach up to the low seawall a few yards away there were people with towels and umbrellas, stripy wind-breaks taut in the breeze, small children digging and screaming, the loose threatening knots of other families, and among them the dozens, I couldn't start to count them, of almost naked boys and men. There were two men getting changed just below me at the top of the beach, easing wet trunks down under towels, and both of them looking out and then shouting, 'Ollie! Oi!' to a third man who jogged up towards them from the water, thick fair hair pushed back, a wide grin on his face, odd overlaid areas of sunburn and suntan on his arms and shoulders, and blue square-cut trunks that the sea had half succeeded in tugging off. It was as if Ollie sensed my helpless stare, he looked up as he reached for a towel, drew it round him and shivered and stamped as he talked to his friends, and I went quickly back into the room.

When I went down to fetch the ladies for dinner, Mrs Croft was still in the bathroom, getting ready. Mum was sitting in the little round armchair, changed and made-up, with her handbag beside her. The long window was open to the noise of the sea and the gulls and families trailing in from the beach. I slipped out onto the balcony again and under a broad show of drinking in the view I scanned the boys still playing on the sand;

when I leaned out there were others coming up the pavement below, some I'd seen already this afternoon, in the street or in the tea-shop with their families, or quickly getting dressed behind the rocks. I heard Mrs Croft saying, 'I don't altogether trust that balcony . . .', but Mum stepped out and leant beside me on the narrow iron rail. In the thick evening sunshine she looked like an actress, pale powder and strong red lipstick. 'You look pretty, Mum,' I said. 'Hm, thank you,' she said, and peered out at the beach. The tide was the obvious interest, everything unguessably covered as the waves pushed late sun-bathers up and up towards the seawall. The sun itself was a dull glare, baffled in haze as it dropped towards the Bristol Channel. We watched in our usual freedom from having to say much. Sometimes the boys, the families they were with, looked up from the street, or from the beach below, and half took in the puzzle that we always represented. I felt the tidal move-ments of holidaymakers towards hotel lounges and guest house dinners, the rough unanimous rhythms of an English seaside resort, flow beneath us and catch us up too.

'Are you happy with your room?' I said.

'Oh, yes,' she said. 'Yes, it's a nice room.'

'I thought you'd have your own room, Mum.'

'Well . . .' – she made a little grimace – 'Esme's paying, you know . . . By the way, she says she'd like you to call her Esme.'

'Does she . . . oh, all right, then . . .'

'She feels Mrs Croft's a bit formal, now we're all getting to know each other better.' I'd never called an adult by their first name, even Mavis I called Mrs Watchfield. When we shuffled back into the room I called out, 'Good evening, Esme!' but the swagger of adult equality was undermined by the feeling of cheek. Hunting round for her handbag, Esme merely said, 'Ah, Dave,' and then we went down for dinner.

*

In the dining room we had a table in the window, something else it seemed Esme insisted on. That first night on holiday I felt a prey to waiters, all settled into their parts in a way I wasn't; it was raw contact dressed up with rigmarole and an allowance of charm they could easily withhold. As new arrivals we were greeted by Terence the head waiter, a tall lean-faced Yorkshireman in a black jacket who clearly enjoyed the unexpected effect of his voice and his humour in the soft Devon setting. We watched him at work on the next table, telling an elderly couple what to order and writing it down left-handed, his paw curled round the pad. In a minute he was back, at the window table.

'Good evening, ladies!' he said, in a carrying tone.

'Ah, yes, good evening,' said Esme, 'now, I'd like—'

'Welcome to Friscombe, welcome to the Cliff Hotel' – passing them small blue-bound menus, and smiling thinly at them. The third menu was tucked under his arm, and it was only after Esme had asked for a gin and tonic that his head jerked back and with a quick glance at the women, as if they were all in on the joke, 'And who do we have here?'

Mum looked up with a frown, but also, in the forcefield of a joker, a quick regretted laugh. 'This is my son, David.'

Terence's head went back a fraction further. His shock was disguised in a quick-thinking silence of four or five seconds, as he stared out of the window. Then he leant in confidentially – 'Let me know if he gives you any trouble, madam, won't you,' he said, and grinned at his own mischief and pinched the smooth back of my neck quite hard.

'And I'll have a gin and tonic too,' Mum said.

When he'd gone Esme sat gazing round at the room with a complicated expression, as the one who had picked this hotel, and wasn't yet ready to confront its failings.

*

Besides Terence, who barely spoke to us again, there were two staff, a waiter and a waitress, who over the week and a half of our stay came to colour and unsettle our lives, and not only at mealtimes.

There was the Irish girl, Maureen, in a self-absorbed daze about doing things right, who made a dozen shy journeys from the sideboard to the tables, each time bearing a single item – a fish knife, a forgotten napkin, a pat of butter. Her procedure seemed to match the tempo of the kitchen, a semi-deliberate way of filling the long gap between ordering and serving. The wait for the starter felt the longest, measured out by Maureen's well-meaning walks back and forth across the room and questions about who was having the soup. At last there came a point when the setting was complete, we had all the right cutlery, our bread roll and our water, in fact we'd eaten our bread roll some time ago and Esme was on to a second gin and tonic, and Maureen would stand in hesitant triumph by the table and enumerate the things she'd amassed on it. 'You've got your knife, you've got your fork, you've got your other knife . . .' until her climactic phrase, 'You've got everything except your meal!' At which Esme, with unusual sweetness, would say, 'You're absolutely right, dear.'

Esme said Maureen was a 'sweet little homesick thing', and followed her movements indulgently when the melon and two bowls of cream of celery soup were finally brought to the table. The evening sun streamed through the big window, and while Maureen was serving I gazed at the figure who passed from the shadow through its horizontal brilliance as he moved round the tables on the far side of the room. This was Marco, 'from Bari', 'nineteen', 'first time in England' – I picked up the facts from just-heard questions at other tables. Marco, here in the room, in and out of the shadows, back and forth through the swing doors of the kitchen, working in the section furthest from us, though sometimes he came over if called to a nearby table, or helped Maureen with the plates for a large serving. The food wasn't at all what Marco was used to, and I noted the ways in which he wasn't quite as charming as the guests expected. He answered pleasantly each time he was asked where he came from and how long he was here for, but he didn't lay it on. Esme liked a stroll after dinner, just to clear the head, and when we came back to the hotel the dining room could be seen through the large seaward window, empty and brightly lit, and Marco, tie off and sleeves rolled up, setting places for breakfast, while Maureen ran the hoover in and out under the tables and got in his way. There was something illusionless in the scene, stage-hands at work now the audience had left. Once when we came in from behind the hotel, Marco was standing by the lattice fence that screened the kitchen door, smoking a cigarette, I nodded bravely to him, he raised his head and half smiled as he blew out smoke, and the question of what he did and where he went when he wasn't working seemed to hang in the night air. By the third day at the Cliff I could tell if Marco was present, even with my back to the room. The pitch of his voice, glancing light of his accent on English words, wove itself through the air, and the air itself had the shimmer of his presence as he moved behind us – then a neutral feeling, of interest removed, till the waft of the kitchen door and his tart little laugh brought him back in range.

For a long stretch of every day we were on the beach, with the two light folding chairs, in different stripes, and the useful groundsheet that Esme had brought. Esme was fair-skinned, and got Mum to rub cream methodically into her shoulders and the white scoop of her back left bare by her swimsuit. Sometimes I saw to Mum myself, sometimes Esme said, 'Let me do that.' Mum was a strong swimmer, quick as a knife, and was soon off past the rocks and out of sight. Esme strolled into the sea as if looking for something else, fell forward and shoved around with her head held up high. When I swam by myself I left them in their chairs, or Mum stretched out perhaps at Esme's feet, and ran off towards the waves in the lick of windy sunlight embracing and exploring my bare body. On the beach in high summer with the light behind me I was nearly a copper-tanned white boy – I felt less exposed wearing next to nothing, just my cherry-red trunks with white stripes down the hips. One day we went to Combe Martin, another to Croyde, with its hard ribs of sand at low tide, and breeze-ruffled ribbons of clear water waiting between them. There were beaches all around, each with its promise of new men to look at and the pang of missing Ollie and the others at the beach we already knew. Did the women catch even a hint of this? I dissembled by instinct.

When I swam by myself and came back up the beach, panting, heart racing with a new sense of power, I kicked past other nearly naked boys and men, in their family groups, glimpses keen and keepable as snapshots, and sometimes they glanced round too, unthinkingly curious as to who I was with, how I fitted in. I jogged up to Mum and Esme, in their low chairs. Mum shaded her eyes to look at me, and we chatted, all three, as I wrapped a towel round me and looked down on them, Esme large, white and firm in her red-skirted bathing-suit, Mum more exposed in her black one-piece, a smaller and leaner woman. There was scope for embarrassment for a teenage boy at the sight of their unsupported bosoms and bare thighs – something I sensed that I ought to feel and, fleetingly, did. They weren't unlike other holidaymakers, several women in pairs or trios paddling together or sharing a table in the hotel dining room, but the difference was that these two had a foreign-looking child. I wondered sometimes what those others made of us – I was a refugee, perhaps, an orphan being taken to the seaside for a special treat.

Esme brought the *Telegraph* to the beach, and worked at the crossword, clicking her biro while she thought. Sometimes Mum leaned over with a dim smile, and Esme let her see the corner she was stuck with. After some hesitation Mum would say, 'Not WOMBAT . . . ? No . . .' and Esme would stare and then write it in. Each day one of the clues was a quotation with a word missing, and these Esme read out loudly and slowly, as if speaking to a Frenchman. ' "In the south suburbs at the _____ is best to lodge" (*Twelfth Night*). Eight.' 'At the Elephant!' I said, and she raised an eyebrow and wrote it in. The next day I was keyed up about the quotation – but it turned out to be from *Paradise Lost*, which we hadn't done yet, and I let us all down.

When the puzzle was finished, more or less, she turned to the share prices listed in tiny print at the back of the paper. 'How are my Town and Country doing today?' she would say, and pull a face when she found the entry and its plus or minus figure. She also had shares in something called Malahide, which were on the up and up. 'They seem very strong, Dave,' she said, 'but it was a tip from Gilbert, so I don't wholly trust them.'

'You could always sell them,' said Mum, bored by Esme moaning about money when she seemed to have so much of it.

'Well, I could,' said Esme, and gazed forgivingly towards the sea. A minute later, 'A pretty little thing,' she said, with a nod to draw Mum's attention to a woman settling further down the beach.

'Mm . . .' said Mum, in the bland screened tone she had at times with Esme.

'Though the husband looks rather a brute.' It was the beautiful husband I'd been watching already, as he changed under a towel, very deftly, just a glimpse of bare bum, and then knotting the drawstring of his tight blue trunks, and now I peered at him strictly, as if weighing up what Esme had said. The man trotted down to the water's edge while the pretty wife folded his clothes and put on a hat.

There was an odd sharing or not sharing of talk between the three of us on the beach – me and Mum, Mum and Esme, sometimes Esme and me, rarely all three of us. I lay sunbathing, on my back then on my front, with *Washington Square*, which I wasn't really taking in. Esme chatted, in her forthright fashion, and Mum, sitting back in a stupor with her eyes closed, smiled distantly, and murmured in a way that seemed both intimate and evasive, as if conscious that I could hear. 'Did I say I had a letter from Bobs?' Esme said. 'Mm . . . no, you didn't,' said Mum, with a pinch of a smile on her upturned face: 'how is she?' Esme sighed. 'Well, I don't think it's been easy for the old sausage. That house in Fulham takes a great deal of work.' 'Yes, it's a large house, isn't it.' 'And you remember Betty Matthews, dark little thing, reminds me just a tiny bit of you.' 'Did I meet her?' 'She was at Bobs's party that night.' 'There were so many people there, weren't there . . .' Mum said, and then, 'Oh, yes, *of course!*' in a tone of such certainty that I knew she couldn't remember this woman at all, but didn't want Esme to describe her further: 'Yes, *Betty*.' At which point, turning over, I said, 'I didn't know you'd been up to London, Mum' – and she opened her eyes and looked at me with a slight concern. 'I'm sure I told you,' she said. I was teasing her, wounded a little by the fact she'd kept it secret. Esme had a disconcerted frown, as if sensing she'd put her foot in it but not exactly knowing how. 'Well, it was some time ago, wasn't it,' she said, 'I mean when was it, back in May probably.' 'No, you didn't tell me,' I said, 'I'd have remembered.' Mum sat up then and smiled at me in a private way that seemed to call on some family understanding, and need for tact. Esme said, 'Do you care for London, Dave?' 'Well, I've only been a couple of times,' I said; 'we went to the National Gallery.' This set Esme off. 'Do you remember what Betty said that time –

when she got back from London and Derek said, "Well, where did you go? Harrods? Or the National Gallery?" And she said, "Oh, Derek . . . you can't expect me to remember things like that!"' 'Anyway,' Mum said, teasing me in turn, sitting back and closing her eyes again, 'I don't have to tell you everything I do.' 'Of course,' said Esme, 'we all knew where she *had* been. Poor Derek . . .'

A little later, when Mum had gone into the sea, I said, 'Do you have a party line, Esme?'

'For the telephone, you mean? Oh, no, Dave, no – can't stand the things. The number of times I've tried to ring your mother and there's been these other people on the line – I don't know how she puts up with it.'

'Do you know who they are, then?' I said.

'Some man in the town, isn't it – I think your mother knows. He seems to spend half his life blathering on the phone. Probably someone we see all the time without realizing it.'

'Yes, I wonder if it is,' I said, and rolled over and gazed out to sea, with the bright floating thought that I could find out who Lovey was, and beyond it the other, not really surprising, disclosure that Esme was always on the phone to Mum.

'You still haven't told me about Burma,' said Esme, at dinner that night, 'not really.' It was about halfway through the holiday.

Mum shook her head and looked down, 'No . . . well,' she said.

'I suppose you weren't there all that long.'

'No, I wasn't.'

'Sort of how long?' said Esme, distracted briefly by signalling to Maureen with her wine glass.

Mum sighed, reluctance half-disguised as thought. 'Well, less than a year, you see.'

'You were a secretary, I think you said . . . or perhaps something more?' Esme narrowed her eyes at me, as if we were colluding in dragging secrets out of her; though to me, to Mum as well, it was one of those alarming occasions when an outsider saunters unawares into a subject very rarely mentioned at home. At passing moments Burma was allowed to be beauty and adventure, but mostly it was an avoided subject. 'Do you think your mother was a spy?' Esme said.

'Mm, I expect so,' I said.

Mum sniffed at this. 'Nothing so exciting,' she said. 'No, I was just a typist really, in the governor's office, though he liked me and, you know, sort of took me under his wing.'

'Indeed,' said Esme.

'He was a nice old boy.'

'Who was he?' said Esme.

'Well he wasn't the governor for very long, of course – he was the one who handed over to the Burmese. Sir Hubert Rance.'

'Rance . . . right,' said Esme, and nodded knowingly at me.

'He didn't enjoy very good health,' Mum said, in an oddly rehearsed tone. 'The climate really didn't agree with him. Horribly hot and humid, Burma!' She looked round and smiled with relief at the sight of Marco approaching – and for me the air thickened and tingled.

'It must have been exciting, though, for you, Av,' said Esme. 'Quite dangerous, too, I expect.'

'Well it was – thank you so much,' nodding gratefully at Marco as he set down her tomato juice. I caught the quick closeness of his sweat, the curve of his thigh as he turned away to the next task.

'So glamorous!' said Esme. 'And there was I, stuck in the Pay Corps at Kidder . . .'

'Mm, this was after the War, of course,' Mum said, drawn into explaining things after all.

'Yes, but still . . .'

'In the War I was stuck in a typing pool in London, also quite boring, though probably more frightening.'

'I don't really see why you went to Burma, in that case?'

'I went to Burma to get away from home.'

'You'd already done that by going to London,' said Esme. 'Well, you clearly had a great sense of adventure.'

I thought for a moment Mum was going to snap, but her exasperation seemed as much at herself. 'It was a foolish adventure,' she said. 'I was glad to come home.'

'Despite leaving . . . ?' – but Esme glanced at me, and saw she couldn't ask more about the man Mum had left behind.

'There were lovely materials, of course,' Mum said with a hurried smile. 'The famous Mandalay silks.'

'You'll have liked those,' said Esme.

'Stiff silks, you know, and the colours . . .'

'I sometimes feel there's a touch of Burma in the things you make here,' said Esme, in an encouraging tone. 'What do you think, Dave? Am I right?'

Mum looked out, almost shyly, at the lawn beyond the window and the sea below. 'I'm not sure,' she said. 'I find most English women don't really care for bright colours and patterns.'

'I fear you're right,' said Esme robustly, sitting back as our melon arrived. 'Well, you must tell me more about it all another time,' and as we picked up our cutlery I had the troubling idea again of the talk they had had and could keep on having when I wasn't there.

Later that night a heart-racing panic, the light suddenly on and the smash of the tooth-mug into the basin. He was very sorry, once he'd worked out that he was the intruder, not me. In a minute we found ourselves searching for bits of broken glass on the carpet, me in my pyjamas, the man in a cap and a light rain-coat – which was when he introduced himself, Tim, down from Welshpool, which I hadn't heard of but which was indeed Welsh, as was Tim. I stood and peered down as Tim knelt in front of me, talking on pleasantly now as he made sure there was no glass left to cut my feet. There was a smell of drink around him, confusion more than threat. He stood up and looked about. 'It's not a bad little room you've got here,' he said, which I felt was moving us on to a new phase of conversation.

'Well, thank you,' I said stiffly, and then relented a little: 'though I'm afraid I don't have a sea view.'

'Well, nor do I, David, nor do I. Estelle's the only one with a sea view up here, have you met her, Estelle van der Hooper?' He said the name carefully, almost satirically.

'No, I haven't.'

'Oh, a lovely girl, you'd like her. From Cheshire, as a matter of fact, though her family's Dutch, of course, with a name like that.'

'Well, yes, so I imagined,' I said.

'And where are you from, David, if you don't mind me asking?'

'Oh, from Berkshire,' I said.

Tim looked at me a bit comically for a moment. 'That's a good one,' he said, 'I like that.' And then, 'Well, I mustn't keep you.'

And with that he withdrew.

The following evening it was celery soup again. 'As Gilbert once remarked,' said Esme, 'the food here's inevitable. He could be amusing. Mind you, that was on our honeymoon.'

'Did you come here then, Esme . . . ?' I said.

'No, no, love. We had our honeymoon in Bude. I wasn't

sure why, but then it turned out Gilbert was a close friend of the man who owned the hotel – a very close friend, as a matter of fact. They'd been in the air force together. Of course it was still rationing then, it wasn't easy.' She looked around, raised her empty wine glass, and tried to catch Maureen's eye.

'What does Gilbert do, Esme?' I said, going all out for first names; over the holiday she'd made Gilbert a presence – an irritant, an off-colour joke – in our lives, and questions about him seemed to be acceptable to her, in fact she quite enjoyed them.

'Gilbert Croft?' – she shook her head: 'Mainly, these days, I suppose, he keeps the wine and spirits business going.'

I saw him, for a second, across a counter, wrapping bottles in white paper. 'Oh . . .' I said then, and smiled, and felt a little unsure, since Esme herself had admitted she looked forward to her twelve o'clock sherry from a moment not long after break-fast. I sensed there was something else about Gilbert, an essential fact, sat on with a murmuring half-amused censorious-ness by Esme herself, and acknowledged by Mum with no more than a blink and a sigh.

'Oh, I was well shot of Gilbert,' Esme said.

'He sounds rather . . .' Mum said.

Esme spoke to me as a man of the world. 'You know, Dave, he said most of the marriage vows he had no objection to at all, it was just the "forsaking all others" bit that never quite worked for him.'

'Oh, I see,' I said, and laughed, appalled that I'd been told this.

'I have to admit he was *bloody* good-looking, but boy! did he know it.'

That night I came up with them to their room after the late walk round the harbour and drifted out again onto the balcony, with an anxious luxurious certainty that Ollie would be coming out of the pub next door and sitting with his mates on the sea-wall. But the street lamp below showed only a man and a woman leaning at the top of the stone steps, his arm round her waist, their words muffled by the thump and sizzle of the waves on the beach below. I thought they were only in their early twenties but they were adult and private, unlike the lads who shouted to each other the length of the street. I glanced back into the room, which cast its light across the shadow of the balcony, and I had a strange feeling of spying not only on the men but on Mum and Esme, now clear, now blurred as the breeze stirred the thin net curtain at the open window.

There was a knock at the door, and a distinctive voice it still took me a second to recognize – it was Maureen, and she smiled anxiously at me as I slipped back into the room. She was closer in age to me than to the grown-ups, and she looked between us with an uncertain sense of allegiance. She held a tray, with three very full cups on it, jogged a little into the saucers. 'Lovely, just put it there, dear,' said Esme. Maureen slid the tray onto the low coffee table and stood staring down at it, as if to say 'You've got your cups, you've got your hot drink,' until Esme opened her purse and drew out a ten-shilling note.

'That's too much, Esme,' Mum said. 'I've got some change.'

'Well . . .' said Esme. 'She's bending the rules for us, aren't you, my dear?'

'Still, you're spoiling her.' Mum peered in her own purse and pulled out a two-shilling piece. 'There you are, thank you, goodnight,' she said, and Maureen, caught between the two tips, was dumbstruck for a minute, then pocketed the coin and shot out of the room.

Esme opened the drawer in the bedside table where a bottle fitted neatly beside the Gideon Bible. 'Not much left, I'm afraid,' she said, holding up the familiar Martini Rosso and winking at me.

'Oh, you finish it off,' Mum said almost crossly, but Esme gave her a humorous look as she took a gulp from her cup and then filled it to the brim from the bottle. 'I can tell what you're thinking, Dave,' she said. 'I call it my "Ovaltini" – not to everyone's taste, I dare say, but it sends you off a treat.' Mum raised her eyebrows, but smiled, no point in protesting. Esme lifted the cup again with both hands and drew off a long sip. 'It's pretty disgusting to start with,' she said, 'but then like anchovies or something you get to like it. Straight Ovaltine tastes awfully sweet to me now.'

'I don't mind sweet,' Mum said, and I said airily, 'Perhaps I'll try it, Esme, if there's any left'; Mum made a funny face but again said nothing as Esme held the bottle upside down over my cup to shake the final drops into the chocolatey froth. I perched on the end of Mum's bed, the sheet turned down by the maid during dinner and her red striped pyjamas laid out ready. Esme it seemed used a nightgown, pale blue with a frilly collar, somehow unexpected. She watched me as I sipped – it was like nothing I'd tasted before and I didn't know what I thought of it, a dark contradictory taste that as Esme said might well take a while to get used to. 'Mm, not at all bad,' I said judiciously.

'Well, there you are,' said Esme. 'Your son's a sophisticate, Avril.'

'Well, I know *that*,' Mum said.

'Ollie-Ollie-Ollie!' came a loud drunk voice from outside, almost singing.

'Trevor . . . you old poof!' – very loud, laughing, the words sinking and warming inside me like the Martini Rosso and rising at once in a blush.

'These Friscombe lads are really too noisy,' said Esme, crossing to close the door onto the balcony, though sound still came in through the half-open sash window. 'I imagine you two are more used to this kind of thing, living in the middle of town.'

'Oh . . . ? I don't know, really . . .' I said, unable to concentrate, looking down and sipping intently at my disgusting drink. The word 'poof' seemed to float, unfading and undiscussable, in the mirrored shrine of the dressing table, where Mum's cream and powder were grouped on the left and Esme's things, rather different, spread about on the other side. I knew of course Ollie didn't really think Trevor was a poof, it was only the certainty he wasn't one that made him able to shout the word out in the street, on a warm August night. But I also had a strange intuition that Ollie was voicing a secret wish and revealing, by accusing Trevor, that he was that sort of person himself.

'So what are we doing tomorrow?' Mum said.

'There's that old historic house, was it? you said you wanted to see, Dave,' said Esme.

'Oh, I really don't care,' I said, 'perhaps if it's wet.' All I wanted to do was to be here, on the beach, in the shifting parade of the known and unknown men. I could still just hear Ollie and Trevor down below, with a third voice now, not their words much but their rambling rhythm, the glinting and disappearing thread of their sound among the other sounds of the night.

'I just don't want you to be bored, Dave, that's all,' said Esme.

'I think he's quite happy just mucking about here,' Mum said, loyal but oddly remote.

'Yes, I suppose I am,' I said.

'Well, fine,' said Esme, slightly bewildered that the boring excursion she'd been ready to go on for my sake had now been turned down. 'It didn't sound particularly thrilling.'

'Let's see what the weather's like,' I said. And then, as soon as I could, and gripped by need, 'Well, I'm going to bed.'

'You must be tired, love,' Mum said, 'after all that swimming,' in a quick bland tone I knew very well; it was the tone of my first morning in school kit, and the day, just as bad, when she closed the car door on the gravel at Bampton, turned the ignition, and a shaming, asphyxiating sob rose up in my throat as she drove away. It would have been worse if we'd made more of it. I stooped down and kissed her – I never kissed Esme, who went into the bathroom with a yawn and called back, 'I'll see you at breakfast.' I went out, pulled the door shut with a click, and was halfway down the landing when I heard the key turned in the lock and the handle tested from the inside.

In the hall I walked frowningly past the reception desk and out through the glass-paned front door into the street. It was cooler already than when we'd come in from our walk, and the night had slipped into a new phase. The sea was closer and louder on the rocks, and the people out and about, men mostly, were louder too. I went round the corner, into the view of the harbour, widely spaced street lamps and black drop to the water. The Admiral in the crowded half-hour before closing was a dimly lit hubbub inside, other figures in or out of the shadows on the pavement and over the road on the harbour wall. I was crossing a stage, now spotlit, now hidden, finding the right pace to go by the lads – headed somewhere but with time to stare, though a stare might last only a second. My magic was the fusing of images, the way I'd captured Ollie, though Ollie himself had no idea of this – how I knew him as the loud doggy-paddler, sea sucking at his trunks when he emerged from the waves, and as the after-lunch sunbather, lips parted, blinded and aroused by dreams, and now as the slicked-back beauty out at night, drunk, jeering, leaning on the wall with his mates in his loose blue jeans and short-sleeved shirt open to the furry navel. He caught my eye as I passed, caught it and let it go, as if I wasn't even there, though the murmur and laugh among the lads a few seconds later undermined me like the locking of the bedroom door. I walked on to the end of the front, where the road turned abruptly inland, and when I came back past the Admiral five minutes later the wall was deserted, and Ollie and Trevor and friends had moved on into the next stage of their night.

The next morning the tide was coming in again by the time we found our corner, in the loose scruffy sand towards the top of the beach. It was the last full day of the holiday, and I peered round for Ollie as I helped Esme spread out the groundsheet and pin it down with the two deckchairs. 'We should get another chair for you, Dave,' Esme said, 'it's not at all fair.' But I didn't mind – I liked being free to sprawl at the women's feet or to run off. I needed to be in the sea at once today, I had my trunks on under my shorts, and in a minute I'd peeled off and snaked through between the other couples, kids and parents, and into the first grim shock of the Bristol Channel – ankle-high, knee-high, over my head. I surfaced and spluttered and turned over to look back at the beach I'd just left. Then I swam on out, past the end of the concrete jetty, and with a memory, when I stopped and hung in the light swell and looked back at the land, of the long brown ribs and stacks of rock that I had clambered over yesterday, now covered to a not quite calcul-able depth underneath me. I waved at Esme and Mum, but they were huddled together, over the crossword perhaps, and a man I didn't know waved back. I trod water there, between solitude and something colder. Then I came in again, a fast crawl, hoisted up and carried forward on the waves, I touched bottom, stumbled, knocked forward by the next wave – waded then strolled out over the shining sand and beyond it the warm and slipping sand towards the women, with the sea breeze shivering my back and the sun hot at once on my face and chest. I saw, coming up across the beach, how people took me in, brief smiles, the undecided welcome. Mum's eyes were hidden by black lenses, but her mouth was amused and reassuring. 'What's it like?' she said. 'My turn next.'

There was a bottle of squash made up, out of the sun under a towel in the basket. I needed to do what I'd meant to have done in the sea – perhaps now behind the rocks, but I was, as Mum often said, so very fastidious. 'There's a public loo up there,' she said, 'I don't know what it's like.'

'Yes, I know there is,' I said. It felt a long way off, up on the main road in my damp trunks.

'Just run up like you are,' she said, practical as usual in the face of my reluctance. I felt annoyed by this and by the childishness of the situation. I buckled on my sandals and strode off and up the steps onto the road, cars parked all along and the blue and white guest houses on the other side staring seawards over their hydrangeas. The toilets were two hundred yards off, built in against the bottom of the cliff, the Gents' entrance round the far side, screened by a wall. After the glare of the sun, the room was like twilight, but I could see an old man leaning at the urinal, and feeling next to naked I pushed the locked door of one cubicle, but the one beside it was free and I went in and slid the flimsy bolt.

I lifted the seat to pee, and as I got going my eyes were adjusting and I saw that the white words EVERTON F C and BRISTOL ROVERS with FUCK on top of it on the wall beside me were dimly surrounded by other writing, scribbled, overlapping, in felt-tip or biro on dirty grey plaster where earlier writing must have been scrubbed off. My eyes were still adjusting, and the words seemed to sink into shadow, or rise out of it. Little pleasantries they seemed at first, Fun Times, mutual fun, and then under them and further up, over my head, amazing words that were lurking there swam forward, will suck off . . . BIG COCK, 10 inches . . . meet here . . . 16-years guy, well-endowed, always ready . . . suck-off, with a crude enormous picture – my mind wouldn't take it all in, but my body did, with a suffocating heat as I finished peeing and turned round in search of something less alarming, more alarming. There was my own shock and at the same time an anxious embarrassment at the thought of all the nice people, the uncles, the dads, who came in here for ordinary reasons and had to see all this, notice it, block it out in their own way. The men who wrote these things were nearby, you might not know them in the street, or on the beach right now, but at 6.45 p.m., 9 p.m. Tuesdays, the times scratched up here, they met in this small filthy cubicle and did things that I'd heard about, thought about, as well as others I simply couldn't understand. And then I had a further more disorienting feeling that the uncles and dads, men of all kinds who'd been in the army and travelled the world, knew all about these things men got up to in secret, and took them for granted. In the two minutes, three minutes that I stood there and worked on myself, then sat down on the damp seat to finish myself off, it was the words themselves that went through me, drove me on with their overlapping humourless intensity, and the twitch of light, shadow, light again nonplussed me till I saw the round hole where some former fitting had been torn out and sitting forward lowered my eye guiltily to the hole and found an unblinking blue eye six inches away on the other side. Even when I tugged up my trunks and knotted the string in a panic I felt, as I was, almost naked and defenceless; it was worse, with the little delay, five seconds perhaps, as my ear picked up and my mind understood the hard click-click-click of a belt-buckle tapping the wall, and the fact that I'd been caught without knowing it in something so dreadful had me snatching the door open and striding very fast in my sandals down the esplanade without looking round till I was back on the beach. 'Was it all right?' said Mum, and Esme in her chair woke up and looked around. The children ran about in front of them, the experimental sandcastle was a little bit larger and fancier than it had been when I'd marched off five minutes earlier. There was a cavernous normality to everything, the absolute ignorance of everyone here about the world I'd just entered and escaped from.

'I'm going in again!' I said, and discarded my sandals and jogged off at once, ran down the last slope of damp sand into the waves, where I would be hidden from the man with the eye when he emerged from his stall and strolled with his terrible knowledge and purpose onto the beach.

At dinner that last night, Mum and Esme both seemed tired, and bothered perhaps about the packing and the journey the next day. Mum had a way of making remarks, comments on people in the room, too quietly, and when Esme said, 'What's that, Avril?' saying in a louder voice, 'Oh, nothing . . . It doesn't matter,' so that a dissatisfied mood built up. I tried to jolly them along, though the knowledge that after breakfast tomorrow I would never see Marco again squeezed my heart and almost made me ask for a drink, a proper drink, myself. 'So have you enjoyed yourself, Dave?' said Esme, and Mum seemed secretly to wait on my answer too.

'Oh, I've had a wonderful time, thank you very much, Esme,' I said, with a feeling, like treading water, of all the things underneath my sentence that Mum and Esme had no idea of, things more gripping and shocking than mere enjoyment. Then for the first time I wondered if Marco himself ever went to the Gents under the cliff.

In the lounge after dinner Esme asked Maureen to bring her a brandy with her coffee, and left a pound note tucked under the sugar bowl for her when we got up to go for our walk. 'I believe in tipping good service,' Esme explained.

'Good service, I agree,' said Mum, which I saw in a moment

could mean two things, but again she said it quietly and it was hard to tell.

On the walk I had a horrible sense of excitement and constraint, as we passed along the harbour, the rising tide washing at the steps below, lights in ripples on the water, and the lads by now getting louder as they went from one pub to the next. I fell behind so that I could look for them without the women noticing. Thirty yards away a figure I thought couldn't be Marco went from the street into the porch of the Britannia, suddenly bright as the inner door opened, and it was him, without a doubt.

No Ovaltini tonight, and I went up to my room in the grip of the urge that I knew would bring me straight down again ten minutes later. There was a party in the bar breaking up, but no one on reception at this hour, and I dodged out onto the road among the red-faced people leaving. A couple who'd seen me with Esme and Mum just before broke off and looked at me as I turned down to the harbour. I heard the man say, 'Hard to tell, probably older than he looks.' On a bench halfway along, outside the Britannia, where Ollie and his friends had gone the other night, Marco himself was sitting alone with a pint and a cigarette. His face was in shadow from the lights strung up outside the pub, but he nodded at me in a friendly enough way as he blew out smoke.

When I crossed the road and said, 'Hello, there, Marco!' I seemed to be observing the person I'd become, and wondering what he'd do next. The night walk, this second time, felt something like a habit, though the habit perhaps of someone else. 'You're having a drink, then, I see.'

Marco didn't find this worth answering, but as I stood smiling at him he smiled very slightly back, and after another drag on his cigarette said, 'You havin' a drink?'

'Oh, I'm not allowed to go into pubs yet, I'm afraid,' I said.

'How old you are?' said Marco.

'I'm fourteen.'

Marco laughed at this in a disconcerting way. 'Why you out here now?' I thought for a second that he knew the answer, then wondered if I knew what it was myself. I wanted to be with Marco, that was all, to be the friend of someone so beautiful and not just his customer.

'Oh, I always like to get some air before I go to bed, I find it helps me sleep.'

'Yeah? I never know your name,' he said.

'Oh,' I said, 'I'm David – Dave,' and mastered the awful fact of Marco not knowing as swiftly as I could. His little tilt of the head was a signal perhaps that I should sit down beside him. It was like being all alone with Morgan or Roberts but wilder, with no rules I was aware of.

'Have some of this?'

'Oh! . . . thanks a lot, Marco,' I said, and leant against him as I took the pint glass, warm from his hand and the length of time he'd been nursing it. The liquid was bitter with a chemical aftertaste like a mild electric shock – I couldn't imagine ever liking it, looking forward to the pub and a pint of it, and I handed the glass back to Marco with a nod, as if it had been just what I needed. 'So you're from Bari,' I said, in my role, which Marco perhaps thought odd, as he looked at me, of the welcoming Englishman.

'*Yeah*, I from *Bari*,' he said, with a weary little laugh, not at Bari, but at the question and the answer, so that I sympathized – with each week's new set of arrivals Marco went through what I went through all my life.

'Marco,' I said, 'I couldn't help wondering, you know, if you ever get homesick?' Marco took a last pull on his cigarette, then flicked it towards the water, though it lay and glowed for five or ten seconds on the granite-like edge of the harbour.

'I'm not sick,' he said, with his sour little laugh.

'No – good!' I said, 'good.' It was too hard, and too obscure, to explain: I saw that. We sat forward, side by side, in the posture of friends talking over something private, our knees lightly pressing, Marco's warm forearm brushing mine when he raised his glass. He smelt of the long day's work in the dining room, and there was beer on his breath, two not very nice things fused and confounding.

'So you goin' on your holidays with two ladies,' Marco said.

'Oh, yes . . .' I said. 'Well, my mother, and . . . a friend of ours.'

Marco stared at the water. 'An' which one your mother, the little one or the big one?'

I laughed and hoped very much he was joking. 'Well, the smaller one!'

Now Marco had a smile of enlightenment. 'So the little lady is your mother, and the lady with' – he made a weighing gesture at chest level – 'is her friend.'

'Yes, that's absolutely right,' I said.

Marco looked at me regretfully. 'Cos you don't look like neither of them.'

'Actually, I do look quite like my mother,' I said – ready for the perpetual question about my father, but Marco seemed unfussed by that, wiser, I somehow felt, but maybe just not interested. It was the two women who preoccupied him.

'So they avin' the same room?'

'Yes, they are,' I said, 'well, it's cheaper, isn't it. And also it has the bathroom en-suite.'

Marco turned his head slowly, smiled at me, steadily, for four or five seconds, said nothing, then gazed out to sea again.

Back in my room I locked the door, cleaned my teeth and got into my pyjamas and into my narrow bed, and turned the lamp off. In a minute or two the wavy-edged stripe of light above the curtains grew bolder, and the locked door was outlined by the weak all-night light from the landing outside. I heard passing voices and footsteps in the side street, a car waiting with the engine running, a bit of singing cut short, clunk of doors, then a random silence, it was like at home, but with the square taken over by the vast slow breath of the sea. Then a door slammed loudly on the floor below, and slammed again a few moments later, disturbing Esme and Mum, no doubt; I heard a woman's voice raised, but not what she said. I lay on my back, closed my eyes, slipped away for an hour, Morgan and Roberts, Ollie and Trevor, and Marco at last, in wave over wave like a rising tide till the end, and then I fell asleep. At first I thought Tim had tried my door again but the thud and the murmur of voices was in the next room, just through the wall beside my bed. I'd had a glimpse of the room when the chambermaid was in, the door propped open by the hoover – it was like my room but confusingly bigger, with a sea view and a view in the mirror of Miss van der Hooper's things strewn round, and the girl in the middle of it, pulling the bed apart. Miss van der Hooper herself, Estelle, I still hadn't seen, and in the dining room Mum and Esme and I each had different ideas about which one she was. Now she'd got herself a visitor. The talk came in patches, on the verge of making sense, giggles and grumbles, just loud enough to keep me awake. I knew they were drunk from the gappy rhythm, voices rising then hushing, and a more secret sense of things being done in between without words.

It grew quiet and I slipped into the pillow zone of other lights and voices, the instant busy logic of the first dream where after a bit a dull thumping was going on and I opened my eyes again to the thinned hotel darkness and listened to the knocking of the unseen bed against the wall beside me, slow and stopping, starting again and as it got faster the voices were louder, sounds of laughter and pain, 'No . . . no . . . !' Estelle was yelping, but she seemed to be breathless with laughter too, and the man was making the dull stifled sounds of the one doing most of the work. In a minute the rhythm got faster still and squeakier and then for a long time there was silence, as worrying in its way as the noise. I found I was standing beside my bed, motionless, my hand in my fly, heart beating fast with excitement and shock. Then they started up again and I knelt carefully on the bed and put my tooth-glass to the wall, and at once I seemed to be inside the room, though the actors themselves were still garbled and wavering. I felt that Estelle had been anxious at first about the noise, but she didn't care now, and the gripping thing was the thoughtless abandon of these two unseen adults, and above all, since I knew more or less what the man did, the effect of it on the woman, too carried away to care.

I didn't sleep then for an hour or more, until I heard her door open, and then the man trying to be quiet as he unlocked the door across the landing.

I went downstairs to collect Mum and Esme, and the holiday routine that had gone on for so long had a strange new tension, on this last morning, in the light of departure, and of the old routines, out of mind for ten days . . . restarting the milk and the paper, Mavis coming in at 9 a.m. . . . . that were waiting to reclaim us at home. I tapped at their door and said in a high-pitched Irish accent, 'Good morning to you, ladies, I've got yer early morning tea,' and when Mum opened the door, barely glancing at me, I went in with my imaginary tray, 'You've got your cups, you've got your saucers—'

'Not now, love,' Mum said.

I lowered my arms and dropped the joke. 'Morning!' I said. The door to the bathroom was closed, Mum looking round quickly for her handbag.

'Let's go down,' she said.

'Are we waiting for Esme?'

She seemed not to have heard, then said, 'Esme's going to skip breakfast today.'

'Is she all right?' I said.

'Well . . .' said Mum, and I followed her out with an anxious look at the bathroom door. On the landing she tidied it up a bit: 'Shall we just say, too much hooch last night.'

In the dining room Marco was scowlingly busy, Terence shorter than ever with the elderly guests, and Maureen was nowhere to be seen. Marco treated me and Mum like strangers, said nothing about Esme's absence, never looked at me at all until a blink and a nod in the half-second when he turned away. I was awed and instructed by his act, his way of keeping our secret. When we'd finished, Mum looked in her purse, and tucked a half-crown under her saucer; we both seemed to picture for a second the week and a half we might have had here by ourselves. At once when we stood up Marco homed in to clear the table, and I was pleased to think of him getting the tip, I half turned round as we crossed the room for my last ever view of him.

I went up to bring down my bag, and then knocked again at the women's door. Esme was busily checking the wardrobe and chest of drawers. 'We have to be out by ten, I believe,' she said. The airy artificial tone of her remarks made it difficult to ask how she was. I lugged the three suitcases out to the car, and when I came back into the hall Mum was studying the barometer with awkward interest while Esme at the counter paid our bill. It was done in a quick almost wordless way, the cheque glanced at, shaken for a second and tucked into the till, no farewell chit-chat.

In the car park, Mum said, 'You'd better go in the front, love.' I climbed in obediently and wound down the window and watched while Esme opened her handbag and gave her the car keys.

'I'm perfectly fine,' Esme said, tugging open the door behind me and sliding heavily into the back seat.

I said, 'Are you driving, then, Mum?', with a sense of adventure at odds with the unsmiling mood. I giggled at her little jolts and starts as we moved off, though of course I wanted her to make a success of driving this huge car for the first time. She looked so small and determined, feet stretched out to reach the pedals. She had written down the route on a crumpled piece of paper, and I kept an eye out for the road signs and hardly thought of being sick.

I didn't know what had happened, I had a horror of atmospheres and an unhappy feeling it was up to me to make things all right. I thought perhaps Esme had got Maureen into trouble, with her special favours and tips. The mood between the women fused murkily with my own guilt about going out in the town at night, I wondered if someone from the hotel had seen me and word had got back.

But once we'd passed the Somerset sign and left Devon behind us the holiday too seemed to fold itself away in the quickly receding past. The traffic was heavy on the A303, Esme in the back had slid sideways, asleep, and it was Mum, with a thoughtful stare in the mirror, who started up the singing, with our old journey favourite 'Tea for Two'. Esme woke up with a rumbling cough of surprise more than disapproval. She indulged us, but she didn't join in, and perhaps didn't know the words beyond the first lines; there were changes of rhythm from one verse to the next, which gave the song a shape in my mind like connecting rooms. 'I'm so discontented – With homes that I've rented – That I have invented – My own!'

'You both sing well,' said Esme, perhaps hoping that was the end of it, before we peaked on the couplet, 'We won't have it known, dear, / We own a telephone, dear!' – smiling at each other for a moment with the collusion of duettists who had sung the song dozens of times together and loved it as a ritual as much as a song. Funnily enough it was when we were singing the jingling last lines – 'I'm contented / Cos you've consented / To marry me!' – and Mum slowed and swung the heavy wheel round to pull into a petrol station, that I noticed the pale ridge on her sun-browned finger where her wedding ring had always been before.

After we'd stretched our legs and had a sandwich, Esme declared herself fit to take over, and we reconfigured, with Mum now in the back for the final stretch home. That put paid, really, to the singing. Soon we were in country we all knew, Esme took the high road over the Downs, 'Avoid Swindon, don't you think?' she said. I was wondering how to tell the story of this holiday next term to Manji, who'd been home to Bombay, and Giles, who had spent a month with his parents at their house in France, and had Harris and Blanchard to stay with them too for a couple of weeks.

There was something glaring, when we came into the town, about the car and the holiday it had been on, and the new set of relations the holiday seemed to have confirmed. But actually nobody noticed us, or seemed to, people went into shops or crossed the road with the busily bland look of extras in a film. Esme drew up in the square, outside Harding's Electrical, and we all got out. She stood by the deep-set boot as I lifted out our bags and set them down to shake her hand, and then for the first time she kissed me, a quick forceful dart at a spot just under my right eye. Mum, standing on the pavement, gave a screwed-up grin and turned away to search in her purse for her front-door key.

11

'Look who it is!' said Uncle Brian. 'You made it then!' I had a momentary, almost musical sense of how the two phrases could have been spoken, with warmth and relief. He seemed to block the front door that he'd opened to let us in.

'We did!' Mum said, insisting on a happy tone.

He looked down at me and I said, 'Happy Christmas, Uncle Brian,' holding on, for now, to the basket with our presents in it.

'Roads all right, then?'

'Oh, fine,' Mum said, 'they're saying snow later perhaps.' She blinked at him and shivered.

'Well, come in,' he said, 'come in!'

Mum went into the kitchen to hug Auntie Susan and her sister Auntie Linda, and I followed after and was hugged in turn. 'Don't you look smart!' Auntie Linda said. 'Thank you,' I said, loved always by the aunties and with a note of flirting now. I was wearing my worsted school suit with a red paisley tie, and Mum revealed her new red and green frock as she shook off her coat. 'Wow!' said Auntie Susan, making her turn round. 'Well, go through and join the others, if you can face it!' The sherry bottle was open on the table among the sprout leaves and peelings, and a humorous mood of defiance of Brian was building but not completely taking hold.

In the sitting room was a mild-looking bald man in a dark suit and tie, Mr Holland, a friend of Uncle Brian's from work. 'I was sorry to hear about your sister,' Mum said, with unexpected knowledge, and he said, 'Oh, thank you – I'm so grateful to Brian and Susan for asking me this year. And this must be your son,' he went on, in the welcoming tone Uncle Brian had failed to find. The table was laid for lunch behind the sofa, with a tree in the corner hung with Christmas balls and tinsel, a red glittery star at the top. Malcolm and Shirley appeared in the doorway. 'You lot going upstairs?' Uncle Brian said. 'All right, then, go on.'

'Ooh, open a window!' Shirley said as we went into Malcolm's bedroom. 'I do apologize, David . . .' – flapping a hand under her nose. There was a poster of a red E-type Jaguar on one wall, and a white wardrobe and chest of drawers. A bursting old armchair had been brought upstairs for Malcolm and he sprawled there now, one leg over the arm, while Shirley cleared a space for us to sit on the bed. The smell was like some of the senior studies at school, socks and stiff hankies and the fart competitions. Last Christmas when Shirley'd gone out of the room Malcolm had groped under the mattress and shown me a copy of *Health & Efficiency* he'd stolen from W. H. Smith's, completely naked families, beautiful Roundhead fathers and Cavalier teenage sons playing volleyball and crazy golf together. 'Look at those lovely titties,' he said, watching me, and I said, 'Oh . . . Oh, yes, I see . . . !' before he quickly hid them away. 'Comfortable?' he said now, and winked at me unnervingly. He had the bulk and the menace of someone three years older, and both of us must have remembered his ambushes last year under the pier at Clevedon, in the wet rocks, where no one could see us. Still, it was Christmas, and he made an effort to be pleasant.

'So what did you get?' he said.

'My mother made me a new jersey,' I said.

'Oh, nice. What colour?'

'It is nice,' I said, 'it's dark green, with a boat neck, you know? and cable-stitch panels on the front and sleeves. And I got some money from . . . my other aunt, in Scotland, who's not an actual aunt . . . and otherwise really just a book that I asked for.'

'Which one was it?' said Shirley, as if picturing the titles available.

'Um, *Poems and Fables*?' I said, 'you know, by John Dryden.'

'Ooh, after you with that, Dave!' said Malcolm.

'What about you?' I said.

'Mum and Dad gave me a beautiful bracelet,' said Shirley. 'And Auntie Linda gave me this ring.' She extended her right hand. 'Do you like it?'

'It's really rather lovely,' I said.

'I've seen them in Wooly's,' said Malcolm. 'I can tell you how much.'

'All right, Malcolm,' said Shirley, warning but wounded too. 'Malcolm got a tape recorder,' she said.

'Gosh,' I said, 'what will you use it for?'

'Gosh,' said Malcolm. 'All sorts of things.'

'When you work out *how* to use it, Malcolm,' said Shirley.

Malcolm shifted in his chair. 'It's easy,' he said. 'Even you could work it out.' He had the bluff deflecting manner of his father already, his air of not needing to bother with us.

'You just have to make sure the tape doesn't come unspooled,' I said, 'I can show you how to do it if you like.'

'You haven't got one, have you?' Malcolm said.

'No, no . . .' I said, 'there's one we use at school, for recording, oh, operas and things off the radio.'

I wondered if they would ask me about the summer holidays, but nothing was said, and I couldn't be sure if this was troubled dignity on their part or total indifference, and even relief, that Mum and I had gone off somewhere else without them.

*

'Well, give them their presents, Malcolm,' Uncle Brian said when we went back down. I got a five-shilling book token, the card from Brian and Susan but written as always by her. Mum gave everyone hot-water-bottle covers that she'd knitted. 'Oh, lovely, Av, thank you!' said Auntie Susan. 'Aren't they lovely. Look, Shirley' – wisely not looking for praise from Brian or Malcolm; Shirley herself was non-committal.

'You don't need a hot-water bottle,' said Brian, 'when you've got a missus like mine,' and he grinned rather meanly at Mr Holland.

'I'm sorry, Mike,' Mum said, 'I didn't know you would be here, I'd have made you one too.'

'Oh, not at all, Avril,' said Mr Holland.

'I think we're all going to need our hotties this winter!' said Linda, nodding towards the window and the purposeful grey of the sky above the front hedge. Mum turned anxiously, and I stared out too, half hoping to see the first wandering snow-flakes make their appearance.

'You may not know I make things, myself, Mike,' Uncle Brian said. 'That hearth rug's one of my productions.' Mr Holland smiled uncertainly at it, green and white, singed brown in places by the spitting fire. 'You'll see another example of my work upstairs, which I think you'll enjoy.' This was the smaller black and white mat in the toilet that said PLEASE AIM STRAIGHT, a source of weary embarrassment to Auntie Susan. 'I find it brings out my artistic side.' The mats were made up from kits, no artistry involved beyond tugging bits of wool through holes in a canvas pattern, and knotting them in place. It was done with a wooden-handled hook and in a spirit of mockery of his sister's work, as if to show anyone could do it.

'I think it must be a very restful hobby,' Mr Holland said.

Uncle Brian smiled pleasantly. 'So how's business going, Av?'

'Not too bad, thanks,' Mum said, with a smug look meant to ward off further questions.

'Getting plenty of work?'

'Too much, really, isn't it, love?' she said, bringing me in.

'Get some more help, then, Av. Take on staff.'

'Well, I may have to,' she said, in an unconcerned tone.

Susan said rather anxiously, 'And what about your new investor, was it, you were saying?'

'Oh, yes?' said Brian.

Mum did something never seen, a blush rose up her neck, glowed in her cheeks through the face-cream and powder, and dropped away slowly through the long thirty seconds she took to outline her business plan. Brian enjoyed her discomfiture, eyes narrowed as he turned it round mentally, looking for purchase.

'Mrs Croft, you say. I think I heard someone talking about her,' and his gaze was suddenly distant and offended. 'That's the woman you went on holiday with, isn't it? We never heard much about that.'

'No, well,' Mum said.

'We had a lovely card,' said Susan, 'Friscombe Sands . . .' She had a nostalgic look, as if she wished she'd been there too.

'As a matter of fact I remember now what it was. Your friend Mrs Croft, she was married to some well-off fruit, I believe,' Brian said.

Fruit was new, and I saw it absorbed and deflected, as mantalk, by Susan and by Mum too, and Malc said, 'Oh God,' in a world-weary way, and then blushed as well. 'Anyway,' Mum said, 'she got a divorce from him, several years ago now.'

'Did she,' said Brian, 'a divorce,' with a wintry nod as if that was almost as bad. 'A rich divorced woman in Foxleigh. God help her. Well, perhaps she'll find herself a nice new husband.' He looked round the room as a new idea struck him. 'Bless me! Of course. Introduce her to Mike, why not!'

Mike raised his hand modestly, Shirley giggled, and Linda looked on the edge of saying several things, little sighs, head on one side then the other. 'I think I've had too much of that Allontimado,' she said.

'You could do with a man in your life, too, Av,' said Brian.

'I'm fine as I am, thanks very much,' she said; and, 'we manage very well, don't we, love,' quickly rubbing my knee in deflected embarrassment. Brian looked at the two of us, his chin down, eyebrows raised as he thought how to put it. He said solicitously,

'I suppose, when there's a kid involved . . .'

'Brian!' said Susan.

'Well – be fair, not everyone, you know—'

'He's a very good kid,' said Susan, 'anyone would be lucky to have him as . . . well, you know . . .'

'I know, love, I know,' said Brian, breaking off on a magnanimous note but leaving the thought he'd stopped short of expressing somehow visible in the air. 'Doesn't worry me. I'd be happy to take David anywhere.'

'So I should blooming well hope!' said Susan.

Shirley and I had Tizer with lunch, and Malcolm was allowed a glass of red wine. He sat eating his turkey and roast potatoes in a self-absorbed daze, for the most part, while the talk hopped around. I had my usual experience of being ignored by Brian, who never spoke to me directly, and picked on in a well-meaning way by Susan and Linda and Mr Holland when a silence had fallen or they wanted to change the subject. 'Another glass of claret, Michael?' Brian said in a posh voice, with a quick mocking look in my direction.

Mr Holland didn't seem quite ready for the role Uncle Brian had cast him in. 'So your aunt tells me you're boarding at Bampton School,' he said, with a respectful smile at Susan. I felt warily vindicated, in the spotlight.

'Well, he's been there a while now, hasn't he,' Brian said.

'This is my second year,' I said.

'How are you finding it?' said Mr Holland.

'Yeah . . .' said Malcolm.

'It's a very good school, actually,' I said.

'So is it dormitories you sleep in, your mother said?' said Linda, glancing round as if they all thought this rather fascinating.

'Yes, that's right,' I said, politely, but with a fed-up feeling we'd had this conversation the previous Christmas.

'Don't you get homesick?' Linda went on. 'I know I would!'

'Not any more, do you, love,' Mum said.

'Are there any other, you know, coloured boys?' said Shirley.

'Yes, of course,' I said.

'How many would that be, then?' said Malcolm.

'About twelve?' I said.

'Oh,' Malcolm nodded, 'that's unusual,' and Mum looked at me a bit oddly, but didn't let me down.

'Yes, it's quite an unusual school,' I said.

'They could have their own cricket team, Mike,' said Brian genially. 'What would they call it?'

'Well . . .' said Mike, and glanced round.

'I don't think we want to know, thank you, Brian,' said Auntie Susie. 'Mike, have some more?'

'That was lovely, ladies,' Mr Holland said, sitting back in his chair.

'Go on, have a bit more of that bird, Mike,' said Uncle Brian.

'Really, I couldn't,' said Mike.

Uncle Brian let his eyes slide over me in his general festive survey of the table – I smiled back for a moment and then looked down. 'Shirley, find out if David wants some more,' he said.

'I've had enough, thank you,' I said.

'He says he's had enough, Dad,' said Shirley.

'Saving space for his next course, I expect!' said Susie, and shot Brian a look before starting to clear the plates.

We had Christmas pudding, which was in fact my favourite part – I struck a match to light the brandy in the kitchen, and it was Shirley who carried it in. There was custard to go with it, and more sugar, and only after that the crackers, stacked up like a pyre in the middle of the table, were passed round, and arms crossed, and we shouted the countdown to the haphazard pattern of bangs, shrieks and grunts, Malcolm suddenly with two and Linda with nothing, and then the silly game of admiring the novelties and groaning at riddles and seeing by laughing at the others how daft we must each look ourselves in our paper hats. Part of me loved the strangeness of being in the hat, everyone in hats, as if they'd all agreed at last to be someone else.

After we'd sat around like that for a few minutes, Uncle Brian set out tiny glasses for the port, and Malcolm went behind the tree and seemed to turn on the radio. 'Is it the Queen already?' Mike Holland said, pushing back his chair. There was an echoey noise of voices, some very near, some further off, scraping and rustling, with murmured thank-yous and louder questions about salt and gravy from someone who sounded like an unkind imitation of Auntie Susan. A painfully posh-sounding young man said, 'May I have some bread sauce, please?' and there was convincing rustling and tapping and Mr Holland said, 'Susan, shall I say grace?' Already there were gasps and shrieks and talking over what we were trying to listen to, the adults much drunker now than they had been at the time.

Uncle Brian speared a date from the white-frilled box and chewed as he listened to his own loud contributions. He seemed to decide he liked the trick that Malcolm had played on him – he smiled admiringly at him, and in his mind the expensive present he'd given him had promptly paid off. I found myself anxiously listening for things I had said that had made me feel somewhat embarrassed the first time round. There was a terrible silence just before I said, 'In fact I'd have to say I prefer Shakespeare's comedies to the tragedies and histories, in general,' and Mike Holland said, 'Do you really, David . . . ? Yes, yes . . .' I didn't know if I was more thrilled or appalled by what I sounded like, though I knew now what I sounded like to the others, and I laughed and held up my red paper napkin in front of my face. 'You ought to be on the wireless, love,' Linda said, 'oughtn't he, Av?' 'Well, I don't know about that,' I said. We'd started listening now for the things we hadn't heard at the time, in the general busy chat as the meal had got going . . . a brief little murmured exchange between Linda and Mr Holland that I had hardly been barely aware of – 'Yes, a nice-looking young lad,' Mr Holland had agreed. 'Oh, I've heard enough of this, Malcolm!' Susie said. 'No, really. It's Christmas,' she said, 'turn it off,' and Malcolm got up and went back behind the tree with a smirk of vindication and after some fumbling switched the tape recorder off. More port was poured out but for two or three minutes a new conversation struggled to get going. Auntie Susan said, 'It makes you think, though, Linda. I wouldn't want everything you and I said about Brian being recorded!'

'You'll have to watch your words, then, won't you, my love,' said Uncle Brian.

Mum kept glancing out of the window, for telltale flakes against the darkening sky. She dreaded them and she longed for them too, as an absolute reason to leave. Then I went to the lavatory and from the window on the stairs I saw the cars crawling past, headlights on, over the first gleaming slush, the hedge of the garden opposite silvered in the three-thirty dusk. Mum said we must set off immediately, she found her handbag, our coats, Brian saying he never saw her, and she was going already. Susan and Linda hugged us, and we made do with a hasty wave at the rest of the party; only Mike Holland stood up. In the hall Mum said, 'I haven't had much to drink,' a sherry and a glass of red, but enough to add to her worry; Brian put on his coat to see us off. 'Go Chippenham way, will you?' he said.

'Oh, I'm not going over the Downs in this,' Mum said.

'You'll be fine. Take care, then, Av,' Brian almost sentimental as she got into the car. 'And you, young feller,' with a hard groping tickle I wriggled out of.

And at once in the car, with the doors shut, headlights on, heater blowing ice-cold air as I swiped my cuff across the fogged-up windscreen, we were ourselves again, in grateful silence where the whole day waited to be talked about – or not. 'Are you all right, love?' was all Mum said as she moved off, eyes on the road and in the mirror in the first apprehensive few minutes. 'Oh, it's not too bad,' she said, when we got onto the main road, where the traffic kept the surface clear.

Not that there was a lot of traffic. I had the sense as we drove through Westbury and out towards Melksham of everyone else in the cheerful stupor of Christmas, all England behind small lighted windows collapsing and snoozing in front of the special from Billy Smart's Circus which we would be home too late to catch. The few other drivers out on the roads seemed to share an air of purpose, or crisis. The heater hotted up, and a reassuring burning smell filled the car. 'Now I mustn't make a mistake here,' Mum said, as we came into Chippenham, turned right and passed slowly through the streets, a few people walking in snowed-on hats, and a Christmas tree lit up in the empty square. 'I should know, I've driven it dozens of times' – and I knew the way myself, in the passive, subjective way of the child who is driven and notes things the concentrating driver doesn't see. 'Left here, isn't it?' Mum said, and I said yes it was. When the town fell behind, it was properly night, dashboard lights reflected in the windscreen among the thousands of wet snowflakes rushing towards us, head-lamps dipped against the white reflecting swirl. I started us off on 'Tea for Two', but Mum wasn't really trying – she smiled and said sorry, and I knew how intensely glad she would be to get home.

It was the next day the great snowfall came, and all day the day after that, day after day into the unimagined January, the coldest since 1814. We wondered more and more about how I would get to school; then when term began Peter Pollitt came over in his Land-Rover with chains, with Eastman and Du Cane already on board, and carried the three of us with our trunks and our tuck boxes through the wind-whipped snow-drifts and glittering woods to school. The drive had been cleared and then half disappeared under the following fall. Other parents' cars slithered along in low gear, and I was proud of the chains, and the way Mr Pollitt waited capably for the worried Wolseleys and Rovers to creep past. The whole situation was thrilling and also, as Mr Pollitt quietly mentioned, a very big problem. The school buildings came into view beyond the plantation, lights beaming out across the snow in uncurtained welcome. The great cedar on Hawkers was shelved deep in white, the branches tilting but the frozen snow holding in place.

12

I was last in any alphabetical list, but when the Field Day squads went up it took me a second or two to find myself – there I was, in Morris, under Craven and Manji and half a dozen others, including Hadlow. 'Oh, god,' said Giles, when he'd pushed in to the crowd around the noticeboard, 'I've got all the fucking wogs.'

'You've got all the fucking brains, actually, Hadlow, I think is what you mean,' said Manji. 'I wonder if you've ever considered how it makes me feel?'

'What, being a wog?' said Giles.

'Having such a moronic colleague as you, Hadlow?'

'Anyway,' I said, not attacking Giles directly, 'it's not Hadlow's squad. Pinsent's the captain.'

'Pinsent . . . !' said Giles, with a despairing laugh. 'Anyone feel a mutiny coming on?'

Fascist Harris came through, signalling smaller boys out of his way, and stared disdainfully at the lists. I watched his blue eyes and blond forelock reflected in the glass beside me, his look of outrage when he saw he was in Kent and his vengeful grin as he turned away. Last week he had made a much-quoted speech explaining how he saw his role as House Captain: 'I have the power. You don't.' He must have been hoping he and Giles would get out of school together, as they had last summer, but the master who drew up the squads had more power still, and had sensibly kept them apart.

That evening after prep I did another Jeeves in Blue

Commons. *The World of Wooster* was on TV, and my famous readings were mostly imitations of Dennis Price, and of Ian Carmichael as Bertie. The stories were funny in themselves, and my mimicry tightened the grip of the comedy when I perched on a desk and read 'The Aunt and the Sluggard' or 'Jeeves in the Springtime' to ten, later fifteen or twenty boys – each time the number went up, the first uncanny proof of success: there was a demand for it. All week, on and off, I was slightly Bertie, with the daft little stammer that Ian Carmichael had added to the role; but it was my Jeeves people wanted to hear, my highly ironical 'Indeed, sir . . .' and other phrases I cooked up, 'Most felicitous, sir', 'I think you'll find it was Shakespeare, sir' – things like that. Boys I barely knew became Bertie themselves, as we queued for lunch, or got changed for a run. 'I say, Jeeves,' they would say, and stand back expectantly as I slipped into character: just three or four words would be enough to set them off. I also had the invaluable knack of raising my left eyebrow all by itself. Bit by bit this gained in significance, until just a hint of it was enough to bring the house down. Perhaps that was the lesson – not just to give something it turned out they liked, but to have them hungry for something I'd given them before: it was stardom.

Tonight for the first time Harris came along, to see what the fuss was about, and stage a kind of passive protest just by being there. He sat in the front row, next to Giles, and stared blankly at me while people were coming in and finding a place. But after half a page of 'Sir Roderick Comes to Lunch' he was wriggling and looking round, and soon he was as red as a tomato with laughing. There was something coercive about the looking round, to make sure everyone was laughing as much as he was; he almost stopped it being funny. I thought, 'I have the power, and you don't' – it was an unexpected battle of wills for five minutes, but I held my nerve, and when Harris guffawed I raised my left eyebrow, just a fraction, which made everyone else laugh even more. At the end he hung back, with a devious expression, while people gathered round and talked to me. Then he nodded at me amiably and said, 'You're really the perfect little English gentleman, aren't you, Winny?' And Giles said, seizing his moment, 'Well, the perfect little English gentleman's gentleman, anyway.'

Next morning I woke with a lovely sense of lingering celebrity, and a further half-pleasurable tension about the task just ahead, whatever it was going to be. After breakfast Pinsent, in his premature performance of a weathered old sergeant looking out for his men, embarrassing but reassuring too, got our squad in a huddle by the fives courts and nodded his freshly shaved chin over the list of tasks as he pondered how to split us up. It was one of those moments when leadership is asserted, and personal authority meets natural obedience, and it was specially irksome for Giles. 'Oh, get on with it, Charlie!' he said, but appealing to him too, by using his first name, mutiny mixed with sucking up. The Field Day missions were challenging and sometimes surreal. Last year, also with Manji, I'd hitch-hiked to a marmalade factory in Bicester and come back with free samples and a letter from the managing director. Hadlow and Harris had tried unsuccessfully to board an American bomber at Brize Norton aerodrome. Now Pinsent broke us up into three groups, and did the very thing I was counting on him not to do, and partnered me with Giles. We had to team up with Kissing Cousins, in the year below, a sleek little blond who'd been Jessica in *The Merchant of Venice* last summer, so he and I had that in common, but Giles I think had never spoken to Cousins, except possibly to call him a greasy tart. He nodded amiably at him now, and gave me a strange long look, a half-surprised hint of a smile in which the suspended fiction of our friendship seemed to be reviewed, and assessed for present usefulness.

Pinsent gave me the instructions sheet. It was a carbon copy in blue ink, some letters ghosts, others blotted and blocked in.

There was the general rubric, *Initiative and boldness will be rewarded, but squad members must bear in mind at all times that they are Ambassadors for the School.* I read out our specific task, in the voice of Kenneth More in *Reach for the Sky. Your group must report to M.H.S. in the Gym by 1800 hours, and present to him a tape-recorded interview with someone describing incidents in the First World War from their own experience, with a signed letter from the interviewee confirming that the interview took place today.* 'Let's have a look at that,' said Giles, and read it out again as if expecting it to say something quite different.

At first I felt weightless – I knew no one. Vaguely I pictured us hanging round outside Woolworth's in Foxleigh, stopping anyone over seventy and asking them questions. Then Cousins said his grandfather had been in the trenches – 'Well, there you are,' said Giles; but it turned out he lived in Shepton Mallet. The signed letter was the catch – otherwise we could just have rung Cousins's grandfather up, recorded what he said over the phone, and had the rest of the day off. 'I don't suppose you've got anyone, Winny?' said Giles, irritation disguised by a sympathetic sigh. My idea then was very simple.

'Well,' I said, 'what about Uncle George?' I remembered our talk about the War, three years earlier, the privileged mood of the occasion itself more than what he had said to me. I thought it was odd Giles hadn't thought of him himself.

'Where does he live?' he said.

'I mean your Uncle George, if he's still alive.'

'Of course he's still alive,' said Giles, with a puzzled smile, and as if I'd been too familiar in calling him Uncle. Then the smile shifted, he let us see the idea working in him, and responsibility, to our odd trio and to the whole squad, unignorably emerge. 'We'll do it,' he said, 'this is excellent,' rewarding me with a canny stare but mainly applauding himself. 'Old George will talk till the cows come home.'

'Quite literally,' I said.

This was lost on Cousins. 'So where does he live?' he said. All around us, as we walked back to the house, small groups of boys were talking intently under trees, or running off to hunt for the unexpected items they suddenly needed. Harris was snapping at the boy in his group whom he'd picked on to do all the work. 'No need to run,' said Giles to us under his breath. 'We've got all day.' He gave Harris a cunning look, competition as ever more powerful than loyalty in Giles's make-up. 'Let them see we're quietly confident.' In the back passage teams were bent over Ordnance Survey maps, and in the changing room and upstairs in the dorm there was a lot of indecisive activity. We wore mufti for Field Day, but the boys who were drawing the portrait of an Oxford don would need different outfits from the ones who were felling a pine tree and sawing it into eighteen-inch pieces. Manji and Craven had got the Oxford job, which I liked the idea of, but the vision of going back to Woolpeck on a warm May morning had a deeper hold on me. I felt I could get something private, almost secret, out of our team effort. Giles went up smoothly to Teagarden to borrow his cassette recorder, but found he'd already loaned it to Harris for ten shillings deposit; so presumably Harris was doing for Kent what we were doing for Morris. 'Isn't there a tape recorder at the farm?' I said, but it was the heavy old thing in the sitting room I pictured, and Teagarden's Philips 3302 set the standard for ease and desirability. Giles looked briefly stumped, and it was only then that Cousins, with a slow smile and sideways glance, as if offering something much more personal, said, 'We can use my machine if you like.'

'Bless you,' said Giles, and stroked Cousins's glossy hair.

'And how are we going to get there?' I said, giving Cousins a quick rub myself – he raised an eyebrow, smiled at me, mocking or inviting, I wasn't sure.

'Where is it?' he said again.

A queue had formed for the phone, in its small indoor kiosk, where we made our occasional contact with the outside world, reversing the charges. 'I was thinking,' said Giles, as we strolled past, 'that your mother could easily drive us there. It can't be more than ten miles away?'

'She hasn't really got a car,' I said.

'Well either she has or she hasn't,' said Giles.

'She has a van,' I said reluctantly.

'Right, I see . . .' said Giles.

'Can't we just get the bus?' said Cousins.

'Really, Andrew?' said Giles, personalizing his disappointment. He looked at me. 'I mean, I can drive, if your mother can lend us the vehicle.' And it was true, he'd passed his test within weeks of his seventeenth birthday. But still the idea was so risky and worrying that I could only say no.

A minute later I was in the queue for the phone. It was something unaccountable about Giles, about not wanting to disappoint him, in fact wanting to please him as Cousins had done. He made it seem no more than fair – Cousins after all was lending a valuable cassette recorder, he himself was supplying a real live uncle, and it was my duty to contribute the third key ingredient. Giles had emerged in five minutes as the leader of our trio and Cousins and I had submitted. It was just what I didn't want to happen, and it was already too late to resist. Now I was next in line for the phone, nerving myself for the very tricky call. What I hadn't expected, as I stood in the stale-smelling booth and dialled 100, was the way Mum too would come round to Giles's idea. I heard her note of alarm when the operator asked her to accept the call, I seemed to see her before I could speak to her, in the second's hesitation before her puzzled 'Yes, of course . . .' Whatever disaster she imagined in those few moments made the actual request, once I'd steered my way awkwardly round to it, seem so trivial and beside the point that she immediately said no. But then it was also such an odd thing to ask that maybe it merited a second half-humorous look. For her it was part of a pattern of surprises and adjustments, now I was seventeen myself, with needs that she had to face up to. Mum's reluctance was instinctive, but short-lived: she was a realist. So she ran over what I was saying, and then she was thinking out loud how on earth it could be done, while I stood smiling her onwards and doing my best to ignore Du-Plessis and Milsom pulling slit-eyed faces at me through the glass. 'I'm sure Giles will be careful,' she said, voicing her anxiety but revealing too her constant awareness of the thing that I often forgot, our unrepayable debt to Giles's family.

We ambled down the drive and out past the lodge onto the main road with the quietly shocking sensation of slipping the rules and protections of school. We met Mum in the lay-by on the Radstow road, a five-minute walk from the school gates. The van looked terribly small and homely, and I don't think Giles had expected it to have *Wincroft, Dressmaker* in red and gold cursive script along both sides. 'Ah, an Austin!' he said, warmly shaking Mum's hand.

I had a sense – perhaps no one else did – of Mum being over-keen to play her part. 'We must make sure your team wins!'

'That's the spirit!' said Giles. He was six inches taller than her, and was conjuring up rather loosely an adult manner, beaming courtesy with an edge of condescension. I looked at Cousins, who rolled his eyes, and smirked again.

'I don't know about the insurance, though,' Mum said, with a flinch: 'that might be a problem.'

Giles was already shaking his head, 'No, no, I'm insured to drive other people's cars,' he said, 'you don't need to worry about that.' And somehow, it seemed, she didn't. He took the keys from her with a tolerant smile.

He drove her back with us to Foxleigh, hand-signals and checking the mirror all the way, while Cousins sat facing me on the floor behind the seats, holding the tape recorder on his drawn-up knees. The light clean smell of new fabric in the van, the sharper notes of chemical dyes, were parts of the air I'd grown up in, a backstage or dressing-room smell I'd never thought I would share with other boys from school. When we all climbed out in the town square, Cousins's jeans were dotted with lint and bits of thread. I slipped past the threat of a hug and into the front seat, as Mum said goodbye to us. She stood on the edge of the pavement and waved us off as if it had all been her idea.

'So what's this Wincroft?' said Cousins, as we roared up Chalk Street in low gear, me now in the passenger seat, with a tense undisguisable feeling the van had been hijacked.

'My mum's business partner's called Mrs Croft,' I said, glancing over my shoulder at him.

'Oh, I *see*,' said Cousins: 'Win . . . Croft!' There was something very cheeky about him. 'Yes, I heard someone talking about your mum.'

'Now, now, there's no call for that,' said Giles.

'She must get a bit lonely, that's all,' said Cousins.

'Does she, Dave, do you think?' said Giles, protecting me, not sounding like himself. 'She ought to get married again.'

'She's fine as she is,' I said.

'She's got you,' said Cousins.

'That's right.'

'And she's got Mrs Croft, her business partner.'

Once we'd left the town and turned off into the narrower lanes towards the Downs, Giles showed he'd got the measure of the vehicle, and put his foot down. 'Steady on, old chap . . .' I said, Kenneth More again, doing my best to smile. Giles turned his head and gave me an almost friendly look, and I nodded and glanced forward to show he should follow the road. He did a tight double swerve where a fallen branch of a tree jutted out from the verge; Cousins, on the floor behind, was thrown about. 'Not a bad little motor,' Giles said, irony dissolving in simple excitement. My anxiety about the van was hopelessly mixed up with embarrassment, my sense of the sort of car Giles was used to. 'What does your old man drive?' he said over his shoulder to Cousins. 'We've got a new Rover 3000,' Cousins said, with a grunt as the van rode another big bump in the lane. I didn't look round, I heard his comic note of nostalgia for the Rover, and something else typical of him, a refusal to be impressed, even by his own well-off parents.

'I suppose Uncle George will be there?' I said, as we drew nearer the village. 'Oh, he's always there,' said Giles. Ahead of us the hill rose up and stirred its flanks, the Rings two notches in its crown against the sky. I very much wanted Cousins to like Woolpeck, to feel the atmosphere and situation. 'You get amazing views up there,' I said, 'on a clear day you can see five counties.' But Cousins had turned round, his back against the front bench seat, his view the disappearing lane seen through the small rear windows. Now we were in the village, the old pub, the shop, the sharp turn and then the brief open straight before the entrance to the farm. It was the beeches planted out along the drive that marked the difference now. The pale staked saplings of three years ago, with green leaves pressing through protective mesh, had risen and thickened into free-standing trees.

We parked in the yard and I went round to let Cousins out from the back of the van, like a dog. He stretched and slipped me one of his ironical looks, sweet or sharp, I just didn't know where I was with him. Giles strode towards the house, gave the bell on the porch a quick clang to announce our presence, and then opened the back door, rather cautiously, peering into the hall and then calling out, 'Hello . . . ?' I think he'd rushed ahead so that Cousins and I wouldn't see this moment – it wasn't his house, after all, but his Uncle Peter's, however much the Hadlows had made it a home. We came in behind him, stood and gazed down the shadowy length of the hall, all just as it was, forgotten and remembered. The sound of a hoover came from a room at the front. The kitchen door was ajar, and we went in and stood there uncertainly; there was something about the heavy pan left to simmer on the Rayburn that gave me a nerve-racking sense we were trespassers. Giles said, 'Wait here, chaps,' and went off down the hall. Cousins set the tape recorder on the table, and we stood looking at it abstractedly. We heard Giles calling, 'Hello! . . . Mrs Over,' a little shout and the raw downward scale of the hoover being turned off. Cousins made a funny face at me, and we went out.

As she came along the hall Mrs Over had her old look of exasperated competence, but slightly adjusted to Giles's new size and maturity. 'You should have told us you were coming,' she said, glancing at Cousins and me.

'I tried ringing,' said Giles, 'but I couldn't get through.' He looked to us, to confirm this fiction, and Cousins smiled at her so broadly that she briefly smiled back. 'Is he in from his walk?' Giles said.

She stopped at the foot of the steep narrow stairs. 'I don't know that he's even been out. It's his hip, as you know.'

'Poor old Uncle George,' said Giles.

'He's eighty-two,' said Mrs Over, with a hint of a reproach. 'Are you all going to talk to him?'

Giles was politic. 'Well, if we can . . .', looking at us again and then glancing upstairs. 'Shall I just run up and see . . .'

As he climbed the stairs his manner was respectful, his impatience held in. We stayed, gazing upwards at where he had been, until we heard his voice, raised but cheerful, startling and reassuring George at the same time.

'Well, I'll get on,' said Mrs Over, and went back down the

hall with no sign that she remembered me, though I knew of course that she did.

In a minute Giles reappeared. 'Come on up,' he said quietly. 'Bring the machine.' I went first, with a former guest's sense of showing Cousins the way and being to some tiny degree a host myself, in this house that I'd so often thought of, and dreamt of too. Just before the first-floor landing, the stairs branched off to the right, into the passage of the lower side-wing of the house. There was a bathroom and, opposite, a door with a china sign saying LYDIA in a ring of forget-me-nots. The door at the end was open into old George Pollitt's room.

We sidled in and stood by the single bed, and it closed about me, very softly, the hour in this room after tea when I'd looked at confusing old maps of the neighbouring farms with George's arm round my shoulder and the kind unfamiliar smell of his Harris tweed jacket and hair oil confirming the privilege. Now he was moving around, shaking his head out of mild bewilderment and the sudden need to concentrate. 'You'll have to excuse me,' he said. He was in shirtsleeves, brown braces crossed between his shoulder blades, and when he turned round, the red tie with its frayed knot half-covered by his chin.

'Uncle George,' said Giles, 'these are my colleagues, Andrew Cousins and David Win.'

'Colleagues you have now, do you,' said George as we leant forward to shake his hand. 'We know each other,' he said, keeping hold of my hand as he looked into my face, breathing through his mouth.

I said, 'Yes, sir, I stayed here . . . a few years ago now.'

'We talked about Burma,' he said. 'You'd never been.'

'Still haven't, sir,' I said.

He patted my hand with his other one before he let me go. 'Well, this is unexpected,' he said, and looked rather searchingly at Cousins over the top of his glasses.

'Well, as I was saying, Uncle, we want to talk to you,' said

Giles, and went on to explain the whole thing to him again. George seemed hardly to be listening, but I think he was taking it in as he shifted files about on his desk, lifting them up to read the words written in ink on the cardboard wallets. 'So we needed someone with first-hand memories of the Great War, and of course the first person I thought of was you.'

'Well, I can tell you things,' said George, 'though as you know I had a very unusual war. I may not be quite what you want.' There was something in the way he said this, a little tremor of punctilio, an old man's slight loss of confidence and fear of a misunderstanding, through deafness or debility, that showed me George had aged since my first visit to Woolpeck.

Cousins said, 'We'll be really grateful for anything you can tell us, sir,' in a rather smarmy way.

And so we settled down, George turned his desk chair round, Giles and Cousins sat side by side on the narrow bed facing him, and I perched on the desk to George's left, holding the microphone in front of him, but strangely abstracted by performing this task, my eyes running over the tall bookcase on the end wall, the framed photograph of men in uniform that hung beside it, and now and then checking the noiseless rotation of the spool of tape inside the machine. When there was a sound of voices outside I could turn my head and see Peter Pollitt in the yard down below, asking Mrs Over about the Wincroft van.

It started out unpromisingly, as it seemed Uncle George hadn't served in the First World War at all. 'I was already thirty when war broke out, and your grandfather of course was three years older, but as we were running the farm we knew we couldn't volunteer: we were needed back here, you see.' He spoke mainly to Giles, but smiled now and then at Cousins, who sat blinking back at him through his fringe. 'I've been doing a lot of work on this whole subject, as it happens,' he said, glancing round at the folders as if undecided whether to go into them. 'I'm writing a history of this side of the county, the western end, it's been quite a thing of mine.' He looked up at me and I nodded encouragingly.

'So what did you do? Something funny happened, didn't it?' said Giles, like a barrister with a nervous witness.

'Well . . .' said George, perhaps not quite liking his tone, 'I don't know about funny. But within a week or two it was decided Bob could run the farm by himself and I was appointed the local HPO – quite a tricky job, I don't mind telling you. I remember feeling I'd rather have been sent to the Front.'

'What was it, then?' said Cousins.

'HPO? That stands for Horse Procurement Officer. I'm sure it's hard for you youngsters to imagine how important horses were. But of course we used them everywhere, in town and country alike, and now they were urgently needed for the war effort. In the first two weeks of the war, I've been looking into it, how many horses do you think were requisitioned?' Cousins shook his head, Giles sat with a narrow stare as if working it out, and I made a helpless grimace. 'Well, I'll tell you: one hundred and sixty-five thousand. A hundred and sixty-five thousand horses secured in two weeks.'

'Gosh, sir,' said Cousins.

'And that was just the beginning.'

'So why were you chosen, Uncle?' said Giles.

George sighed and slumped, and I wasn't sure if he was irritated or if he thought it such a good question that it needed careful answering. 'Well, I was here, I knew the country, we were pretty well-known ourselves, respected, I mean, we weren't landed gentry exactly, in fact for over twenty years my brother Bob rented Woolpeck off old Darcy Denham – that went on until '29, when the Denhams got into a hell of a lot of trouble and he bought it off him. Now, of course,' said George, looking up at me and shaking his head, 'it's the Denhams who are the big shots again. They've even got their own plane, you

know, little two-seater Cessna. But there you are!' – and he sat
nodding as if he'd wound up the subject rather than gone off
on a tangent.

I smiled back and said, 'So you were in a good position to
be the . . . er . . . HPO?'

'Oh, ideal – from the Ministry's point of view. Absolute
hell, of course, for me. I had to requisition some of my own
brother's horses, your grandmother's hunter,' – he nodded at
Giles – 'that had to go too. We needed to keep some horses, of
course, to work the farm, but we couldn't be seen to be fudging
it, in any way. The most difficult days of my life.' He panted a
bit as he thought of it, then looked abashed. 'Nothing compared to what the boys at the Front were going through, of
course. But still . . .' He looked stricken, for a moment, that his
duty had put him in the role of an enemy, almost, to his own
friends and neighbours – but I said, 'This is all really marvellous, Mr Pollitt,' and he said apologetically, 'Oh, will it do?' I
couldn't imagine Fascist Harris, or anyone in the other squads,
getting anything as good.

I went out to the bathroom next door, which had George's kit
on the shelf over the basin, his hair oil, razor, old badger-hair
shaving brush frizzed up at the ends, white china shaving mug
– things never seen at home when I was growing up, until early
this year, when I'd slipped into Baxter's for a razor and a beautiful badger-hair brush of my own. In the cabinet, with its
sickroom smell of old medicines and cosmetics, there were
packets of soap, Coty talc, a bare-faced box of Tampax, which
must be Lydia's things, left from long ago, like her name on the
bedroom door – Lydia herself, according to Giles, had been
working in New York for the past two years: she'd done what
I always knew she wanted to do, and got away. I pulled back the
net curtain and looked down into the orchard where the hens

used to peck about, none there now, and the runs and wooden coops overgrown. On the left the high yew hedge screened off the tennis court. I came out and went very quietly along the passage and up into the main part of the house, the square open landing with sunlight through bedroom doors to the front and the shadowy room at the back where I'd slept three years ago. A further narrow staircase led up to the attic floor. I think I'd sensed then it was a big house for two bachelors and a house-keeper, in its ordinary weeks and months, when the Hadlows and their friends weren't here to liven it up and fill up the beds. Today we had caught it in its unobserved morning, the sunlight fading now across the floorboards and the square of carpet, then brightening for a moment as the cloud moved on. It had an indoor silence like a far-off hum in the ear, outlasting the brief interruptions from outside, crows in the field, fading rumble of a lorry on the hill out of the village. I stood and listened for the missing thing, the quick, incongruous atmosphere of Mark and Cara, gin and Kensitas, talk of Paris and painters, even Elise, in all her difficult glamour. Then I nipped back to join the others.

When I came into the room, Cousins had lowered the microphone inattentively as George hunted through a folder looking for photographs. 'Don't worry, Uncle,' said Giles, 'it's really just the tape we need, you know.'

'You see I thought,' said George, 'as you're so interested . . .'

'Well . . .' said Giles, and stooped over him for a minute or so as though he was. I thought Cousins was smiling tartily at Giles, then I realized he was trying to look in the mirror behind Giles's head.

As we packed up, I said to George, 'Could you very kindly sign a note, sir, saying you spoke to us today,' and after a bit more searching round a statement was written on the farm's headed notepaper in George's beautiful grown-up hand. 'Perfect,' I said, 'I'll look after it.'

'Will you, Dave, thanks,' said Giles.

I folded it twice and put it in my jacket pocket. The writing had an inexplicable effect on me, in its fluency and competence, its air of decades of professional life I knew nothing about. This was the signature he'd written on the documents taking his friends' and neighbours' horses away from them, fifty years ago – 'All for the greater good, of course, though we knew damn well what their end would be.' I felt we'd rather used and hurried Uncle George, and that he was panicked and disappointed by us, though he smiled at us now with a touch of gratitude, that he'd been useful, and we of course were sweet and grateful to him as we shook hands and said goodbye.

I hoped we might hang around longer at the farm, perhaps climb up to the Rings, but we'd got what we came for, and Giles and Cousins were in no mood for anything strenuous. George said, 'Are you boys staying for lunch?' though not exactly as an invitation. I thought he'd probably had enough of us, and Giles himself seemed keen to press on. He persuaded Mrs Over to wrap up some bread and cheese and fill a bottle with orange squash, and we took this off with us when we left. It was still only half-past one when Giles braked without warning and pulled into a gateway a mile down the road. Of course we were hungry, and the dryish bread and Cheddar had the difference close to luxury of non-school food eaten in term time. 'The thing is,' said Giles after a minute or two, chewing and staring ahead through the windscreen, 'I really have to see Fiona.'

'Oh, God,' I said.

'Who's Fiona?' said Cousins.

I said, 'She's Harris's sister. Giles met her in the Easter holidays, and now he keeps getting letters from her.'

'And sometimes, Winny,' said Giles, 'I write back.'

'Anyway, isn't she at school?' I said.

'School?' said Giles. 'She left school last year, for God's sake.'

'Pardon me,' I said, 'so what's she doing now?'

'She's just lying round at home while she looks for a job.'

'Not looking very hard, then,' I said.

'Where is home?' said Cousins.

'The Harrises have a place near Highworth,' said Giles.

Cousins and I both hooted at this.

'What . . . ?' said Giles. 'Well, they do!' and his irritable frown gave way to a smirk and a slight blush, very rare in him, as he heard what he sounded like. He said, 'I say that because they also have a flat in London.'

'Whereabouts in London?' said Cousins.

'I believe it's in Tooting,' said Giles, in a reasonable tone. This meant nothing to me, and Cousins himself seemed undecided about it – he gave his pursed little smile and left it at that. Like Paine and Van Oss and Casserley they both 'knew' London, and I didn't. 'Look, teammates,' said Giles, 'we've finished early, we've got the ruddy tape recording and the letter, and we don't have to be back till six.'

'Let's go to the pub,' said Cousins.

Giles gave him a commiserating glance. 'I doubt they'd serve you, old chap,' he said. 'Or you, Winny, actually. I'm the only one of us who could get away with it. No,' he went on, 'what I propose is a little diversion via Highworth on the way back. That would really be best for me.'

'Oh yes?' said Cousins. 'And what are Winny and me supposed to do while you're snogging Harris's sister?'

Giles made it up ably, as always. 'You won't want to be bothered with all that, Andrew,' he said. 'I'll drop you two on the main road – you can easily hitch a lift back to school.' He turned to me. 'Dave, your mother trusts me – quite rightly,' and he gave a little smile, self-mocking and somehow seductive, that was soon to be dropped from his repertoire.

*

'So how do we do this?' I said, as Giles pulled out into the road with a toot on the horn that seemed to sum up all that was worrying about the situation. 'It's easy,' said Cousins, 'haven't you hitched a lift before?' 'What? – of course,' I said. It was a straight half-mile of open road, and I watched the van grow smaller as it picked up speed, the indicator came on and then Giles had turned onto the Highworth road and disappeared. I knew just where we were, but it was eerily different to be standing abandoned on a spot that we normally whizzed past, seizing the chance to overtake. Now the intermittent buzz of traffic shook the hedge and dust lifted in the air in the wake of a lorry and settled on the buffeted grass. It was a broad verge, flat but lumpy to walk across, bright bits of rubbish blown under the hedge, pages of a *Penthouse* with two blonde women kissing on a bed, then a red-haired woman on all fours, glossy boobs pitted by rain. Cousins turned down the corners of his mouth. 'Go on, have a wank if you like,' he said, and I looked through it gingerly, feeling he was saying it wasn't his sort of thing, and trying perhaps to find out if it was mine. 'Nah,' I said and flicked it over the hedge with a snort and a feeling I was overdoing it. Cousins looked at me as if he knew everything.

Very soon, the odd rhythms of the roadside were making little cycles of anxious attention, the lull as a slow truck or trundling tractor and load of silage kept back a line of cars edging out, once the straight began, to overtake. Of course we weren't in uniform, and no one speeding past would have known us as ambassadors for Bampton School. Someone taking us in as they approached might have wondered, even so, why we weren't in school, since we both looked young for our age, and a blond boy standing with a brownish one suggested some further complication it was better not to get involved with. 'It'll be best if I do the hitching,' said Cousins, walking up ahead and standing just off the bank, in the gritty margin of the road. 'Remember to say something nice about their car, when they've picked us up.' As the first car came into view he cocked his head, flung out his hip, and raised his arm. I couldn't see if he was smiling or not.

After ten minutes or more, a van appeared round the bend, approached very slowly, and came to a complete halt a few yards short of him. There were two men already in front, and the one on the passenger side rolled down the window. 'Where you off to?' he said, narrowing his eyes at the little conundrum of Cousins. The man was dark-haired, round-faced, very young himself, but the question from inside the van seemed to hang in the curious gap between sixteen and twenty-three, between humorous suspicion and level acceptance. A scruffy black dog pushed up panting behind his ear, and whined as I came over.

'We're going to Bampton,' Cousins said smoothly, as if he'd flagged down a taxi.

'We can't take two of you, we've got the dog an' all,' said the man, and the shadowy driver beyond said, 'Can't fit two.'

'Oh, well, never mind,' I said, 'thank you, anyway.'

'That's fine,' said Cousins, 'my colleague can get a lift by himself.'

So the man got out, much taller than I'd thought in stained jeans and a black T-shirt – a rich sweetish smell of oil, apples and dog on the air as Cousins clambered in.

'You be all right there?' said the man.

'We're not really supposed to hitch-hike by ourselves,' I said, but as if I didn't care about the rules.

'For God's sake, it's Field Day,' said Cousins, squeezing in between the men in the middle of the bench seat, smiling at the driver, and rearing back a bit from the slobbering of the dog.

'Dorothy, get down, calm down,' said the man. He gave me a sideways look, friendly enough. 'You with the Yanks?' he said.

'Oh . . .' I said, searching for his meaning, and shook my head.

'Be someone along in a minute, anyway,' he said, and climbed back into his seat.

When the van moved off I almost ran after it, as it lumbered its way up into second gear, and then third, with a tearing noise that grew fainter with distance, till a huge pantechnicon swept past, buffeting me back across the low verge, and blocking my last view of the van; though I pictured Cousins inside it very clearly, wedged snugly between the two working men, in that atmosphere that had nothing whatever to do with school. I felt shockingly alone, and a half-forgotten hatred for Giles, mixed with gnawing regret that I'd let him get away, took hold of me like a panic. I knew where I was, just a few miles from home, but something else had darkened the place, like the mood of a bad dream. I squeezed through a thin bit of the hedge into the field and thought about walking back, cross-country, arriving after lights-out and losing the squad all the valuable points we'd won with Uncle George's interview. The *Penthouse* was lying there reproachfully, and I turned the pages with a flinching foot.

Then something changed, I went back to the roadside, a drop or two of the remembered power flowed into my legs, into my raised arm, as I stood with one foot on the verge, and tried out a sequence of faces on the briefly empty stretch of the highway. A smile seemed the obvious thing, and a sign I was pleasant company, but then pressed into a grin it turned somehow presumptuous, even slightly alarming; I thought a tilt of the head, with left eyebrow raised a fraction in polite uncertainty, could do the trick. An unsmiling gaze at driver after driver seemed businesslike, but might also suggest I'd been there a long time, and had low expectations of anyone stopping at all.

No one did stop at all, for the first ten minutes. I saw that on a main road every driver knew another car was just behind, ready to make good their own failure to stop; and one or two of the kinder non-stoppers pulled apologetic faces, or showed they were soon to turn off. Some shook their heads in unspecific rejection. Some seemed to go past without seeing me at all. But then there was a black Austin Cambridge with a couple in front, the woman driving, and someone, a young girl, in the back, turning and gaping as they went past and slowed, and stopped fifty yards further on. I saw myself already in the back of the car with the girl, and heard the friendly conversation as they found out who I was and the interesting things I'd been doing. The car waited there and I ran, nearly laughing with relief, along the rough verge, other big traffic now pounding past and pulling out suddenly to avoid the stationary car. The passenger door opened and the man got out onto the verge, dark suit and tie, a hand smoothing his hair. 'What are you doing?' he said, as I came up.

I said, 'Thank you very much for stopping, sir, I'm trying —'

'Why are you here?' he said. 'What are you doing here?' There was something troubled in his face, not dissolving but hardening at the touch of my good manners.

'I'm trying to get to Bampton,' I said. I wasn't in uniform, I was somehow undercover, but still pretty obviously a schoolboy. I smiled firmly in the face of what seemed to be anger. Through the car's rear window the girl, a bit younger than me, gazed at me, as though to see if something she'd been told was true. I assumed the man was her father.

The rage, if that's what it was, that had forced him from the car seemed to have blocked his speech. He waved me away from him, pointed back the way I'd come. 'Go home,' he said. 'Go back to wherever the hell you come from.'

On the far side of the car the wife, anxious against the traffic, half opened her door, called out to him. The girl seemed torn between them. I turned aside, with a sense of floors giving way, sudden blackness on a clear May afternoon in the heart of the country – I stepped away through the rough grass, heart pounding, heard the woman call a second time, the slam of his door, but he must have opened it again, as the car moved off, to shout something else, that was swallowed up by the thunder of traffic.

I didn't know what had happened; I sat down on the grass, breathing heavily, and started telling myself the story. For a second as he got out of the car he was a master, unrecognized, looming, who had caught me thumbing a lift by myself . . . but most simply of course he was a man who'd decided to be kind to a total stranger. Then he started shouting and pointing. His aggression had the air of a joke I was slow to get – not a good joke but one I would have to pretend to enjoy. It was Cousins I was telling all this to, and blaming him. Then it was the rest of the squad, back at school, and Giles, of course, and I was turning the events in my mind for some glint of hilarity in them, my brush with a bloody nutter, a story worth wider acclaim in the final accounts of the day. The fear of the attack, the quick sense, in those few seconds, that there were witnesses, passing drivers with a three- or four-second exposure to what was happening on the verge, the grip of crisis: all these instantaneous things could be shopped into the school's own currency of jokes and gossip. It was only as the story settled and took shape that my own anger came, a kind of delayed revelation. And part of the revelation was that it had taken so long to come. All my life I'd been ambushed, and slow, every time, to stand up for myself.

I got up and went back to the roadside. Then I saw that if I went the obvious way, got a lift to Foxleigh, then another one to school, I might well see people I knew in the town, or even Mum herself, who would want to know straight away where Giles was. So I worked out another route, picturing the road ahead as I knew it, passively but watchfully, from trips with

Mum in the van, or in the back of Esme's Super Snipe. If I went in the other direction, to Buckley, I could take the pretty country lane over to Bampton, and just hope someone stopped for me. It was a longer way and a quieter road. I saw the day running out, and the culpable damage I would do to the squad's score by coming back late with Uncle George's letter. All these worries formed a shield round the deeper worry of the Wincroft van, which I saw in unguarded moments buzzing along between distant hedgerows, or parked under trees with Giles and Fiona snogging, or worse, Fiona on all fours on the back seat, like the woman in the magazine.

I crossed the road and stuck my arm out and perhaps the anger and half-defused fear of the raving man still showed in my face when after no more than a minute a blue and white Ford Anglia put on its indicator and came to a halt just beyond me – for five seconds the two things were linked in my mind, the man had reported me to the police, or in a simultaneous story he himself had been reported, and the police were hunting him, not me. The blame hovered, undecidedly. The blue light wasn't on, but to anyone driving past we looked like an incident; a mute spasm of loyalty made me glad after all that I wasn't in school uniform. No one got out, and then the policeman on the passenger side half opened his door and called back, 'Where you going, young feller?' – I walked up to him, blinking in the gleam of that friendly, contemptuous phrase.

'I'm trying to get to Buckley,' I said.

'Been waiting long, have you?'

I was beside him now, looking down at him as he said something to his mate. 'Yeah, a bit,' I said.

'We'll take you,' he said. The Anglia only had two doors, so he had to climb out to let me in to the back. It was an offer with the look of an arrest, and there was no resisting it. He held the door wide, and jerked his head sideways. 'Get in,' he said. 'We're going that way.' As I slid into the cramped little space behind, the officer driving barely glanced at me. We moved off, and there I was, on the road, in the unimagined air, the male smells and the radio crackle, of the policemen's afternoon; there was a folder of papers on the seat next to me, and their head-gear, a helmet upright and a hard peaked hat upside down, with an apple in it. I had an awkward outsider's sense of work-time, the men at a certain familiar point in their shift, and a feeling of listening in on their silence as much as their talk.

'Where are you from, son?' said my friend, barely turning, raising his voice.

I thought it best to be clear. 'I'm at Bampton School,' I said. 'It's our mad day today.'

'What's that, then?'

'Oh, it's Field Day, when we all have to go out of school and perform . . . certain tasks.'

'That again, eh,' said the one driving. 'They kept us pretty busy last year, picking up the waifs and strays.'

'Oh, yes,' I said. 'Well, it's very kind of you, sir.' I saw they probably didn't know about the shouting man, they'd picked me up out of the strange English thing I knew so well, mistrust shot through with cautious hospitality. I knew as soon as I thought about it that I wasn't going to tell them what had happened.

'How old are you, then?' said my friend.

'I'm seventeen,' I said.

Now he did turn and look at me. 'Date of birth?'

'April the twenty-third, 1948.'

I watched him work it out, nod grudgingly. 'You don't look it,' he said. 'You're not Indian, are you.'

A message came through on the radio, and I stared through the window as if not listening. It was something none of us mentioned, but the Anglia wasn't a car to inspire much respect or fear, not like the old black Wolseleys or the swanky Zephyrs the police were using now. It was a pert English midget with a Lincoln or a Studebaker somewhere on its mind, one of those high-finned miracles as wide as haycarts with US airmen smiling at the wheel, even once or twice saluting as they floated down this very road when I was ten years younger, outdoing everyone in needless scale and glitter . . . Whereas the Anglia, with its anxious little grille and back-to-front back window, seemed eager to be smaller, and fold itself away. A policeman with a solemn or dramatic idea of his job might have hoped for a car with a bit more authority.

On the roadside up ahead a small group appeared, teenage refugees, trudging along, one with his thumb out, another struggling to refold a map – it took me a moment to see the third person walking in front was Harris, followed of course by Priestman, clutching Teagarden's tape recorder, and Stallybrass the navigator. 'Some more of yours?' said the driver.

'I rather fear they *are*, sir,' I said, Jeeves for a moment. 'Oh, don't stop!' And then, 'I mean, we couldn't fit them all in, could we.' We slowed to pull out round them, and I loved the swift sequence of alarm, self-righteousness, and disbelief on Harris's face at the sight of the police car and then the glimpse of me in it. I smiled kindly, as if at bowing subjects; and turned round, just before the next bend, for a snapshot of them staring after us. I knew what Harris, at least, must have made of it. And I could already hear the laugh of the others when I reached that part in my story.

At Buckley the car stopped to put me out. 'You can get back from here, then?' the officer said, when he'd climbed back in. Perhaps they would have taken me the whole way, but an incoherent sense of being set free without charge made me say, 'I'll be fine, thank you very much, officer' – understanding from TV that this was how you addressed a policeman.

It was hot on the long country lane, dead straight for hundreds of yards, then making a small angle and hiding where I'd come from. Now and then hedgerow ashes made lonely patches of shade. I had a new sense of the depth and duration of the day, of the minutes and hours away from school, the astonishing openness of the world outside carrying on as it always did in complete unawareness of our rules and routines. I realized I'd never been all by myself like this before – it was as if I'd run away, and the wide fields and woods didn't notice or care, whatever ruckus might be caused at school when my absence was discovered. A long unmade driveway led off to the right to a farm that was hidden by trees, and in the field in front a race-horse in a coat was grazing with two donkeys – the horse trotted forward, curved round by the fence in a brief flash of energy and my feeling it was interested in me was followed in five seconds by my sense of its absolute indifference.

I carried on, tramped along, looking round now and then in case a vehicle was coming, but the undisturbed calm persisted for a mile or more; once a tractor and trailer came rumbling and bouncing the other way, and I climbed onto the verge to let them pass. Then I heard a noise behind me, and a shiny red Riley, a One-Point-Five, came round the bend fifty yards back and I flung out my arm, then ran up to the car when it braked quite sharply and stopped. A small dark-haired man leaned across and opened the passenger door, peering out at me and panting slightly, as if he'd been searching for me all afternoon. 'Well, hop in!' he said.

The Riley's dashboard was glossy walnut, reddish brown, with grey forms in it like clouds. It set the tone, somehow, as we moved off. 'You've got a nice car,' I said.

'Thanks very much,' said the man, with a quizzical smile at me as he changed gear and then glanced in the mirror. 'How long were you waiting there?'

'Oh, not very long,' I said.

'You're lucky I stopped for you. There's not much traffic on this road.' He shifted slightly towards me, as we picked up speed, with his left hand, once he'd changed into fourth, loosely covering the black knob of the gearstick, and his steering arm cocked against the windowsill. His smile, at the road ahead and occasionally at me, grew more friendly. He said, 'I'm guessing you're still at school?'

'Yes . . . I'm at Bampton,' I said, though glimpsing the chance not to be, to be someone else entirely. 'I'm going back there now, in fact.'

'Well, that's a marvellous school,' he said. 'I had a great pal at Bampton, Roger Hamilton.'

'Was he one of the masters?'

'Oh, this was years ago,' he said. 'Of course, if you live nearby, you're always aware of a school like Bampton. I should explain' – an odd courteous tone from a man of forty to a teen-age boy: 'I live at Radstow.'

'Oh, do you, yes,' I said.

He gazed ahead as he thought about it. 'Yes, I've got a little cottage there, just over the bridge – thatched roof, you've probably been past it dozens of times. People often say how darling it is.'

That was a word to save up for my story. And I knew the cottage – Mum and I used to say, as we waited to cross the long single-file bridge, how we'd like to live there, though the car lights searching through the windows at night might be a nuisance. 'I'm not sure,' I said.

'I know you'd like it – if you like those sort of quaint, old-fashioned English things.' He flashed a grin at me.

'Well . . .' I said.

'My name's Jeffrey,' he said, as if the time for full disclosure had come; 'you can call me Jeff.' I nodded and looked out blandly at the lane uncurling ahead of us. 'Are you going to tell me your name, I wonder?'

'Oh, John,' I said, as the thought and the voice started working in me.

'And where are you from, John?'

'Well, I'm originally from Melksham, but we live in Fox-leigh now.' He gave me an almost teasing look. 'My dad was Burmese,' I said, and something went through me at the phrase, the *dad* and the *was*.

'Is that right,' said Jeff. 'Well, I think you're my first Burmese.'

'What do you mean?' I said.

'I mean that I've picked up,' said Jeff.

We rode on in silence after this – I soon saw we were nearly there. From time to time he glanced across at me, and when I glanced enquiringly back he smiled as if reassured. It was years since I'd heard him on the phone, before we lost the precious party line, though I'd thought of him often, and I knew, with a feeling both logical and magical, that it must be him. The beauty of it falling into place was as great as the terrible novelty, the squeeze of danger, of being in his car. Now here was the green, the shop, the Willett Arms, with their heightened inde-scribable presence of places in the free world just outside school. We went through, and onto the Witney road. 'I won't actually go into the school,' Jeff said, 'if that's OK.'

'That's fine,' I said. I could already see the spire of the wel-lingtonia above the school woods, and the entrance lodge was round the next bend in the road. Jeff slowed and pulled into a gateway, then switched off the engine and sat smiling at me again. He looked a year or two older than Mr Hudson, darker, thinner-lipped, not sweating exactly but glowing in the warmth of the day, shirtsleeves folded up tight above the elbow, diver's watch. Suit trousers, lap hidden by the wheel and his right hand resting there.

'What sort of things do you like getting up to, I wonder, John?' he said. 'You know, when you can.'

I saw myself floating above possibilities I only half under-stood. 'I like acting,' I said, 'and poetry. I've started a poetry society at school.'

'Well, that's nice.' His smile had a kind of tactical patience. 'You've probably got a girlfriend or two in tow, haven't you?'

'Oh, not really,' I said, with a feeling I was ahead of him now – but grateful too for this little detour.

'Good-looking young chap like you.' I couldn't help smiling back at him. 'Is that where you've been today, I expect?'

'God, no,' I said, startled by my own tone. 'I've been over . . . on the other side of Framley, at a friend's farm.' And I told him a bit about Field Day, without mentioning any names.

'Look, I'll give you my number, John, in case you ever feel like meeting up. I think there's a phone, isn't there, that the boys can use.'

'Oh . . . all right,' I said, and waited as he found an envelope in his jacket on the back seat and tore off the pale blue triangle of the flap to write on. I knew he was being extremely reckless, though what threw me, watching tensely as he wrote his number, with no name, was his intuition that with me he might get away with it, it might very well come off.

'You know where I am now, and obviously I've got the motor,' and he patted the wheel and swivelled his hand round speculatively once again on the knob of the gear shift.

'Well, thanks for the lift, Jeff,' I said, and got out and shut the door, then opened it and shut it again properly. I started off down the quarter-mile to the gates, expecting him to come past me, already almost hoping he would stop as he did so and pick me up again, but he stayed where he was – I looked back once and he was sitting watching me, as if wanting to see me safe home. Down the road from beyond the school entrance I saw a knot of three or four boys approaching, and a sense of solidarity overwhelmed me for a second, though I hardly knew who they were. I still had the triangle of paper in my hand, and I stuffed it in my pocket with the all-important letter before I joined them. In the long tree-lined drive there was a sense of gathering, the collective return, rivalry and exhaustion. Of course what I wanted to hear was that Giles had delivered the van safely to Mum, and was even now on his way back to school. 'Weren't you with Hadlow?' someone said, and I said, 'Yes, he's coming with the tape,' in a show of confidence I found myself almost believing.

13

His door at the top of the stairs had a frosted-glass pane like a detective's office and a glow late at night that felt like a welcome and sometimes, if you were creeping about, a warning. You knocked, and you waited for his slow-voiced 'Come in', which conveyed both the depth of his concentration and a reasonable interest in why you were disturbing it. Then there was the little shift of values, of atmospheric pressure, as you stepped into a master's space.

The study held a peculiar surplus of chairs for play-readings and the Record Club evenings; there was a gas fire, and a gas ring on the hearth in front of it, and above the mantelpiece a John Piper print in blue, white and black of King's College, Cambridge, seen from Trinity College, which was where Mr Hudson had been. It was almost an aerial view, roofs, chimneys and pinnacles, with scribbles that looked like TV antennas but can't have been. In the bookcase were books signed by writers he knew – some of them, such as Thom Gunn and Ted Hughes, had been his friends at Cambridge. We only ever had glimpses through the door of the room beyond, the wardrobe and the bed.

Now the pinky-yellow glow of the gas fire was reflected in the glass front of the bookcase. The chairs had been stacked and pushed back when the Record Club left, but the small red light of the stereogram burned on, and the speakers gave a crackle once or twice to ask us to use it or turn it off. It was our quiet routine – the others gone, the eight or nine coffee mugs stacked on the tray, and a new sweetly sedative drink being made, the milk no more than whispering when it rose in the pan on the hearth. It wasn't precisely an Ovaltini, Mr Hudson liked cocoa, and with an added shot (for me just a drop) of Bell's whisky – quick illegality we shouldered and shared, the slim half-bottle back in the desk drawer, nothing needing to be said. Mr Hudson's black BA gown and fur-trimmed hood hung on the back of the door and half covered the frosted-glass pane, but the door itself was never locked: any boy, any fellow master could tap and come in. I wondered from time to time if the bedroom door had a lock.

'I have a feeling you liked the Sixth, David?' – jacket off now, and first names.

I nodded, narrowed my eyes as I thought back to it. 'Mmm, very much, sir. I found it quite moving, in fact. In a very different way from the Fifth – as you said.'

'That big E-major tune at the end of the first movement.'

'I know, sir . . .'

He sat down opposite me. 'We must listen to it again, of course that theme's been there all the time, half-hidden, hurried along, so that you can't see its potential. And then . . .' – he sang it to me in his unembarrassed baritone, though the fact of being sung to brought the blood to my face, and I grinned as I looked at him.

'Yes,' I said.

'Great tunes, sparingly used: that's the secret.'

'Yes, sir.'

'Not like that Shostakovich symphony last week: commonplace tunes repeated hundreds of times.'

'Perhaps not hundreds, sir,' I said. I'd been knocked out by the ruthless repetitions of the Shostakovich, but Mr Hudson liked to challenge my reactions.

'Now I'm just going to try something else on you' – crossing to the low teak cupboard under the record deck, and squatting down with his back to me. I played the game, closed my eyes when he stood up, and I knew he was tilting the sleeve to slide out the record, the rustle of cellophane, the tap as the disc met the mat, and the click as the lifted arm set the turntable going round. A crisp crackle, a piano, right beside me – he turned it down at once, it was quiet time, night time: again we acknowledged the rule as we broke it. He put the sleeve out of view.

He sat down again in his desk chair, moved some papers, slurped his cocoa – he wasn't precious, he liked attention but not reverence, and anyway he'd heard this music lots of times before: a deep scratch butted in, across four or five turns of the record, then wandered off. I stared at the pink glowing pipes of the gas fire, which made their own little sucking and fluttering noise. The piece seemed simple and songlike, but the modulations in it made you wonder, and an agitated figure broke in higher up and then, like the scratch on the record, disappeared and left you with the song in a further change of mood, which didn't quite replace the first one but seemed to cast the shadow of experience over it – what, I couldn't say, but I felt it. I had no idea what we were listening to or how long it was going on – there was a very quiet passage when the agitated figure came back, but subdued and dreamlike, a trance of sadness and beauty, and soon after that the piece ended without any fuss. I glanced at Mr Hudson, but he was staring at the fire too, and then he jumped up and said, 'Shall we hear it again?'

Going back to my study-bedroom warm and swimming in the night-lit corridors from the mere drop of whisky in my system. Footsteps ahead, unavoidable. 'Good evening, Win' – it was Hoppy, on a malign late-night trawl.

'I've been seeing Mr Hudson, sir – Record Club business.'

'Ah – I thought the Record Club packed up at eight.'

'It does, sir, but I'm the secretary – Mr Hudson likes to try out some other records with me, before the next meeting.'

He looked at me, in all his mastered ambiguity, the frozen fraction of a smile that might usher in relief at a cleared-up mis-understanding, but might just as well be a sarcasm shaping, or a wigging you were stupid to think you could ever have avoided. The superior air of the Upper Sixth, our unwritten freedom from most school rules, was a challenge to him too. It meant acting like a friend towards boys he had bullied for years, a humorous disowning of his natural cruelty. And then music, besides, he had a philistine suspicion of. 'You seem very cheerful, Win!'

'You know me, sir!' I said, riskily taking his tone. He leant in, still smiling, as if to whisper something secret, raised his head, and then stepped back . . . I was slow to understand that he was trying to smell my breath.

'Music's not really allowed, of course, is it, after eight thirty. School rules.'

'Mr Hudson always plays it very quietly, sir.' It felt funny to be defending one master from another.

'And what was it tonight?'

'Oh, Janáček, sir. Yes, *On an Overgrown Path*.'

Was it impudence, or snobbery, or simple mendacity he searched my face for? The title of the magic little movement, 'Our Evenings', I kept to myself, as a private matter. He put his hand on my shoulder. 'I know Mr Willis has high hopes of you, this term, Win – well, as do we all. Don't let us down, will you now. Now go and get some sleep, there's a good lad.' And he squeezed my shoulder hard, with a hint of thwarted punish-ment in the encouraging grip.

Each new piece Mr Hudson played during our evenings was a cause to concentrate, to pick up what the form was, to sense from soon after the start if it was Russian or German or French, and above all to be involved, as I was by the mere invitation, the music beyond me sometimes, at first, but taken in gulps, on trust. We looked at the floor, or the fire, or sat back and floated abstractedly over the black Cambridge rooftops; and from time to time we looked at each other, as if what we were looking at was the music in the space between us, and then again as if asking, 'How is it for you?' Never talk while the music played, though a sharp sigh sometimes, a grunt of concession to some powerful effect. Very rarely he stretched out a hand as though to say, 'Wait for it . . . !' and fell back, jerking his head at the triumphant return of a theme. Then nothing said afterwards, for a minute, when I felt him waiting, with all his accumulated knowledge of the piece, for the reactions of the teenage boy who'd just heard it for the first time, felt it in shocks and goose-bumps and sometimes mere polite attention which I forced into excitement by an act of faith. 'Astonishing, isn't it,' he would say, and I would say, 'Mm, yes, sir, extraordinary,' smiling as I searched back anxiously over the piece and waited for the few deft phrases with which he confirmed what he thought I'd felt, so that I found, when he played it again, that I had – I flowed into it, and it was a masterpiece, of a whole new kind. My reactions then were made fiercer by the need to react, not to let him down, or squander the privilege of these hours. Sometimes, with the coffee earlier, and the drop of whisky, and all Mr Hudson's interest in me, I was too worked up to take in what I heard – I would roam back to bed with no more than a wild debauched sense of having been given an experience.

His large eyes were suggestively dark, in his pale supple full-lipped face. His wavy brown hair, short and neat, was already brushed with grey above his ears. Edmonds guessed he wouldn't mind if he asked him how old he was: though he raised his chin, stern for a moment as Hoppy or Crow, who could never be asked such a question: 'Thirty-six, boy, last March.' So he was nineteen years older than me, with National

Service and a Cambridge degree behind him, then long years of teaching in another school, in the north. Sometimes I stood close by his chair to look at a poem or an art book. He had the explorable somewhat unsociable smell, close to, of a grown-up man who's been wearing a sports coat and tie all day, and now has taken them off. My eyes slid away from the book or the record sleeve to the back of his neck, or dwelt while he talked on his strong hairless forearm and his wristwatch with its webbed leather strap. He wore grey flannels in school, snug round his seat, loose in the front, nothing clearly suggested, though the question, for me, always lurked.

On the rugger field, in black shorts and a blue jersey, running with the game for an hour and a half, he was a different person. His man's thighs, hairy on the outside, smoother on the inside where they touched and rubbed, furry at once below the knee, to the top of his thick blue college socks. 'God's Grandeur', and the radical difference of the Fifth and Sixth symphonies, went for nothing then, all the delicate questions of the world beyond the sports field were swept away in his running and rallying, the quick backward trot, the hovering and outflanking and hot-breathed authority of the referee. I was Secretary of the Record Club, I was rehearsing Lady Wishfort, I sent him winning glances as we jogged back for a line-out, but he was a stranger to me out there. Once, striding back to the touchline as he pulled off his jersey, he brought his shirt half off as well, the glimpse for five meaningless indelible seconds of his white lower back and grey waistband of his jock-strap. Then he was with us again, whistle shrill in my ear as he ran past.

Copies of *The Times* were placed in the Library after breakfast each day, and Mr Hudson left his *Guardian* beside it after tea, with the crossword filled in and two or three articles marked for us with a dilating green asterisk. One autumn night in Current

Affairs we discussed the Bill going through Parliament – six blazered Upper-Sixers around the gas fire, with responsible frowns and unruly blushes at the idea of two men who were that way inclined doing just what they liked with each other. A national opinion poll showed that 63% of respondents thought homosexual acts between adults over twenty-one should be legal; while 93% thought homosexuals needed medical or psychiatric treatment. 'So a large number of those who think it's all right for men to make love to each other also think such men need help – in order, presumably, to stop wanting to make love to each other.' He looked around. 'Yes . . . Donaldson?' And while Donaldson spoke in his stammering irrelevant way about Ancient Greece and relations between boys and older men, it was the words 'make love' that floated in the lamplit room and made the grim 'homosexual acts' into something quite normal and beautiful and a hint, so it seemed to me, as I looked at him and looked away, of Mr Hudson's own experience. He allowed Donaldson's point, he never put us down, but said, 'What about today? And indeed tomorrow?' Payne said, 'I have to admit, sir, it gives me a degree of unease,' Morton-Stuart took it impressively as a human-rights issue, and I said, with instant disloyalty of pronouns, that I thought they were doing no harm – and especially if they were in love with each other . . . 'Ah, yes,' Mr Hudson said. What he himself knew or deduced of our desires it was hard to tell: he was ironical, and contrary, as his role required. But I doubt if our 4:3 vote in favour of the Bill's proposals was an accurate index of our truest thoughts and feelings.

I mimicked most of the teachers but never him. It was part of his subtlety to speak like a sensible person, with none of the comical rhetoric of masters who'd been there for years, and had ended up mimicking themselves. I could turn for a minute at a time into Hoppy, or Charlie, or Mr Halls, and I knew the effect was heightened by my being the wrong colour, my face took the hint of my voice, seemed to soften and reshape itself into these middle-aged white Englishmen. I never did this in the mirror, it would have made me self-conscious, and I knew I could do it by instinct. I also seemed good because others were so off and approximate you wondered if they heard or noticed anything exactly. If they were school jokers, like Crowhurst or Vote, they already had credit. When Kim Wynans did Charlie, whose mouth clenched sideways when he tried to say an r, he gave him a lisp instead, and got a laugh. As for Smith's shot at Mr Hudson, it was embarrassingly bad. A breathy smile, a rapid blinking, 'Is not this poem by Percy Bysshe Shelley most moving, Smith? Does it not give you the most ginormous erection?' – Smith's own slight lisp made the words even sillier. 'He doesn't sound like that at all,' I said. 'How does he sound, then, Winny?' said Smith, trapping me more cleverly than he knew. I turned away with a withering shake of the head. 'Well, Winny's very close to Mr Hudson, of course,' said Browne. 'Well . . .' I said, secretly excited. 'What do you two talk about, I wonder?' 'Nothing you'd understand, Browne,' I said. 'I might do,' said Browne. 'Well if you must know,' I said, 'we talk about Vaughan Williams.' He turned very solemn at this. 'Gosh, I never heard it called that before,' he said, and flickered his tongue between his lips. 'Oh, fuck off, Browne,' I said, blushing and squashing a grin as I left the room. The taxonomy of love is so crude – nothing ever 'happened', as they say, between us, he never kissed me or touched my face, never uttered any formula of liking, much less of loving, me. When he wrote to me, twice in the long summer holidays before the final term, he signed off 'GRH', as if putting up a notice.

The first letter arrived in the depths of August, brought up with the post by Mavis when she came in for work. She had no interest in a letter from Norway mixed in with bills and a postcard from Auntie Susan in Clevedon, and I put it in my pocket as if absent-mindedly and took it upstairs to the bathroom. I opened it, not knowing what to expect, though my eyes ran ahead of me for something that wasn't there. He was on holiday with his mother, 'cruising the fjords', he said, with dry observations about the 'monotonous drama' of the views, the 'sad lack of culture, which Mama I suspect finds something of a relief'. He seemed almost to be counting on a shared view of his mother, and his relations with her, that hadn't in fact been established. I felt thrown by this, but excited too. It was a new kind of closeness. At the end he gave in and wrote quite poetically about the sheer cliffs and bridal-veil waterfalls, and I could tell he was having a good time.

After lunch Mum said, 'Who was your letter from with the unusual stamp, dear?' as if that were the interest.

'Oh, it was just from Mr Hudson.'

'Really?' she said. 'It's very nice of him to take the trouble to write to you.'

'Yes, I know. He's on holiday with his mother,' I said, and felt I was trying to cover up for something that in fact was quite lacking from what he had written. It was the feelings around the letter, his presence in his handwriting, that carried the charge; and though it was largely descriptions of scenery and the varieties of fish that he and his mother had eaten I felt a twinge of betrayal as I passed it to Mum to read.

'I wonder if he writes to many of the boys,' she said a minute later, handing it back, relieved but still puzzled.

'I think he just wants to keep in touch with the ones in the Upper Sixth next term,' I said cleverly, grateful now for the 'GRH'.

'Well, he's got nice handwriting,' she said, and we both gazed rather fatuously at my name and address, our address, on the flimsy grey envelope. 'And,' she said, with a look of finding a cause for worry after all, 'he tells you to keep up with your reading!'

'Yes, all right, Mum,' I said, and I went up to my room with a feeling something novel had almost been said.

The second letter came a few days before the start of term, and was brief and impersonal. The Oxbridge boys had an essay to hand in for General Studies when we got back to school, and he reminded us of this, in a friendly but businesslike way. Again, I needed to get on with it.

14

Mum and Esme kept separate addresses until I left school, and then, much as conscientious parents delay a divorce for the sake of the children, they did the opposite, and moved in together. I sensed Mum had a notion of schoolboy taunts, difficult for me, and awkward too for her, when she came to Speech Day, or to see me in a play. I never even hinted at the things I'd put up with, honour-bound to defend her against rumours I was certain were true. It would have brought the whole subject into the open, into words, which was something she avoided in all private areas of her life. It would have brought us very close to the matter I couldn't admit to her myself.

They'd had the business, by now, for two years, as a focus and a cover. They were partnered, up in Church Street, on the green and gold fascia of Wincroft, catching the eye as you came into Foxleigh from the Bampton side. Soon there was the van as well, showing the new name around town and then buzzing it out along the lanes to the villages. It suited Mum's restlessness and her creativity, and it tickled Esme to be a backer and businesswoman; friends of Gilbert came good with connections in the rag trade, as Esme called it, stiff grey boxes of beautiful work sent from Whitechapel or Manchester. The shop was a minute's walk from the flat, Mum would be there before nine, and Esme looked in whenever she felt like it. She enjoyed being there for fittings, in the section curtained off at the back of the shop – 'I don't say a word, Dave,' she said, 'I just beam approval.'

'Not entirely true . . .' Mum said.

'It's your realm, though, Av,' said Esme, 'that's really what I mean.'

Mum moved – we moved – into Crackanthorpe Lodge in May. There was so much to say that we avoided discussing it – she said, 'I think it makes sense,' as if this too was a business decision.

'Will you miss the flat?' I said.

'Probably!' she said. 'Will you?' – so I saw she was asking for my blessing.

'There's a lot more room at Crackers,' I said, which was Esme's name for it. 'And don't forget, I'll be in Oxford for half the year.'

'Esme thought you might like the nice big bedroom at the front' – which almost dared me to ask about where Mum herself would be sleeping. 'I think we'll all be all right,' she said, and her grateful smile didn't fully conceal the multiple anxieties bound up in her moment of decision. 'We had fun, didn't we, in this old place; but it's time for a change.' That weekend we started packing, and I knew that the feelings of loss that haunt even the most optimistic move were shared by both of us.

There was a week of shuttling back and forth with our possessions, marking our place in the new home for us before we got there; and then the 2 p.m. deadline, the fateful last ever descent of the stairs and loud slam of the front door, tested even so to make sure. We had shut ourselves out. There were L plates on the van now, and Mum let me drive, very slowly, down the square and up through the town – it would have been a funeral if the interest of driving, the feeling from the first time I let out the clutch and moved off that I knew how to do it, hadn't made the little journey so exciting. At the edge of the town I signalled and turned into Marlborough Close . . . the second house on the left, glimpsed through laurels, an old sycamore, at the gate a golden laburnum whose flowers swept the roof of the van as I steered us in, circled the gravel, came to a halt, got into neutral and turned off the ignition. Mum stared for a moment at the front door, the windows, as if appalled at what she'd done, then turned and smiled strangely at me. 'Handbrake?' she said.

Esme was in the hall, 'making room' for things that we'd brought and smiling sternly as she moved about. It was a tense day for her as well. I took my lamp and my clothes and my boxes of books upstairs to the big front room, which had always been a guest room until now, against a surge of homesickness and a feeling it could never be mine. I heard passing moments of Mum and Esme talking, tramping up and down stairs, friendly muttered questions and agreements, and something in their manner I'd not quite heard, or overheard, before, the tone of their unthinking closeness when no one else was there.

'Who was Crackanthorpe?' Mum said, as if now that she was living here she ought to be told. 'History doesn't reveal,' said Esme, and seemed happy to leave it at that. We were going round the garden, where I could see Mum at once had ideas, after years in an upstairs flat. At the front the square of gravel, garage off to the left, and on the right a glimpse through to the wide lawn at the back, and fir trees twelve feet high that shut off the neighbours on both sides and the field beyond. 'Gilbert planted them,' said Esme, '*dwarf* conifers, supposedly. A bit like Topsy.' Dull green, yellow, blueish, they grew and grew upwards and outwards over the lawn, one or two of them bulging and splitting under their own weight. Esme seemed to regard them as a dimly amusing fact of life that it was beyond her to remedy. To me the garden had an atmosphere, but no mystery, the lawn flanked by straight borders, a beech hedge hiding the veg patch. A sundial in a crazy-paved circle was the most romantic feature. 'You could cut out the edges of the borders,' Mum said, 'give them curves,' and she made a sinuous gesture with her hand.

'Well . . .' said Esme, shaking her head with a reasonable look as she tried to picture it. 'Why don't you have a word with Barry. See what he says.'

Bashful Barry did the garden – 'Don't be bashful,' Esme had said to him once when he knocked at the back door early, and she was still in her nightshirt. 'Not me, mam,' Barry said. But after that he had always left his offerings for her to find in the porch – runner beans and marrows his main boasts. Stuffed marrow was Esme's signature dish. 'I'm glad you like it,' she said, as we paced along beside the rows of vegetables. 'Gilbert couldn't bear it, which is probably why I got so good at it.'

'I *quite* like it,' said Mum.

'It's something I can do,' said Esme.

It was striking, and for Mum perhaps unsettling, how often she mentioned Gilbert, in those days after we moved in.

That first Saturday night in the house: the troubling new quiet. After the market square, with random sounds of cars and voices outside, disturbance so routine that it was reassuring, and in time an aid to sleep, the night in Marlborough Close extended in a lonely silence. I lay on one side, then the other, longing for the wind to get up or for men to go past after closing time shouting and singing. Later I woke at the sound of a car ticking over in the drive, got up and peered out through the curtains at the darkness, and rain pattering on the laurels.

The next morning, no one walking up the square to church, no hurrying footsteps or car-door-slammings – and still nothing outside the bedroom window to look at, just the drive and the gate and the short stretch of the close beyond, where it curved towards the next silent roadway. I sat in the armchair to read Ogg on the

Ancien Régime, and didn't know if I was grateful or annoyed when a distant indeterminate clinking and tapping sound began, as of cans being dragged along a road, but in fact with an underlying rhythm to it, like a far-off cement mixer or piece of machinery doing necessary Sunday work. Then I saw, still half-doubting, that it was the church bells, the peal of six being rung, with the same old determination and hope, back in town, half a mile away.

All of which skirts the performance of the first night, the first bedtime, the matter Mum and I had always skirted. We were in the kitchen after supper, Mum washing up as I dried. 'Top cupboard on the left, love,' she said, 'I *think* . . .' and it was obvious she knew very well where things went. These practical jobs on the very first night were a foretaste of living here, and a refuge too, something to be doing. 'I'll turn in then, Av,' said Esme. 'A long day . . .' And out of confusion and embarrassment for them, and for me, I wiped down the draining board, hung up the tea-towel and said, 'Me too.' We all moved round absent-mindedly then for a minute, backing into each other as we straightened the cushions in the sitting room and turned off the lamps. I went up and sat in my room, with the door not quite closed, until Mum called out, 'Bathroom free!' and I came out to see her retreating down the landing with a glass of water, and going into her little room at the end, which she'd already brightened up with a bedspread from the flat, the Burma box on the chest of drawers. I went after her in an unexplained spasm of worry, and kissed her goodnight. 'You've made your room quite snug already,' I said, watching her set down the glass in the glow of the lamp, and turn back the covers. She was making her old room again, in the new home, but I was pretty sure that wasn't what she'd moved here for.

*

Mum never used endearments to Esme in my presence, though sometimes in those first weeks I heard her in another room, or under her breath in a muddle perhaps about something forgotten, call her darling or love, and the words registered with me, had a weight of proof. The pretence that they were just two middle-aged friends, a widow and a divorcée, living together for company and convenience, was kept up at first so effectively that I had started to wonder if it was true, and everything Cousins and Wynans and others at school had gloatingly imagined, and forced me to imagine, was simply a schoolboys' fantasy. We established our routines, with an unexpected feeling settling around us that this was how we might go on. In the sitting room, Esme had her chair to the left of the fireplace, and Mum sat at the end of the settee nearest her, under the standard lamp, with sewing or other work spread out alongside. The facing armchair, which must once have been Gilbert's place, became my perch and my off-centre point of view. I looked up from what I was reading or glanced at their faces in the changeable gleam of the TV, and I was convinced they were acting like this because of me. When Tom Jones had his own show I sat hot-faced through 'It's Not Unusual', talked over it as if with my well-known taste for classical music I disdained the man I could hardly take my eyes off. 'Got a swing to it,' said Esme, and I think she liked the words, and was amused by the scandalous trousers I pretended not to have noticed. Then Dusty came on with 'You Don't Have to Say You Love Me'. Mum screwed up her face and said, 'Isn't she flat as hell? Well, you'd know, love,' and I said, 'She is a bit, yes, I'm afraid,' though the song went right through me because of it; Esme seemed not to hear us, she sat gazing with her lips slightly parted at the slim black-clad figure in the spotlight, with her piled-up golden hair.

*

A brief ritual developed of me making the drinks at six o'clock, gin and It for Esme, and It by itself for Mum. 'He knows how I like it,' said Esme, with a saucy look as she lifted the glass to her lips. 'He's a super little barman.' I suppose it was convenient as well as strange for her to have a young man living in her house. 'If you ever need a job . . .' she said not long after, handing back the glass for a top-up. For me she got in bottles of cider from Trinders, still my only idea of a grown-up taste in drink. I was eighteen years old. 'Sure you don't want a real drink?' Esme said; but the evening was already tingling and comical from the half-pint of cider I'd drunk. 'I'm afraid you won't be able to go up to Oxford after all, Dave,' she went on, 'it's a shame, in a way, but we need you here to run the bar.' Mum smiled at this, pleased that I pleased Esme, but I saw it start to rankle too. 'You've got bigger fish to fry, haven't you, love,' she would say. And when Esme held her glass out next time, 'I'll do it,' Mum said, getting up and bumping me out of the way with her hip.

Esme was used to service. As well as Barry she had Mrs Luke, who'd been with her for eleven years, and had stuck firm through the divorce from Gilbert, taking Esme's side and passing on as if reluctantly the awful things that were said about her in the town. All this I knew from Esme's own very approximate imitations of Mrs Luke herself. 'I don't care about the dreary little town,' Esme said, 'they can say what the hell they like.' In Mrs Luke's eyes they'd been united against a wicked man, whose main vice was too awful to be mentioned but was clearly conjured up in her silences and grim looks whenever Esme referred to him. The arrival of another lady, with her queer-coloured son, meant a lot more work, and something harder to address, the break-up of Mrs Luke's confidential bond with her employer. Esme gave her what she called a pep-talk, and a raise of a shilling a week.

*

At the end of September we gave a party. I'd just hitch-hiked round northern France for three weeks with Andrew Sparks, and in ten days' time I was going up to Oxford: Mum said it was a party for me, though I knew it was really to celebrate the move and the successful first summer of her life with Esme. We'd never given parties before, at the flat. I knew most of them now, Esme's circle of friends, and called them by their first names: Jane and Bobs and Betty Matthews, with her husband Derek, who they all laughed about, and Connie Marks and her husband Bill, who generally stayed at home. Peggy from Shrivenham, and Sally from Kingston Lisle. They were fun, but they all had their own things to talk about, their own instant rowdy impenetrable gossip, and they saw me and their faces froze, in a friendly way, as the possible problems of talking to me, finding a subject and happily discussing it, ran through their minds. Usually they remembered the last conversation we'd had, about plays I'd been in at school, and we had it again. Jane Mew had even come to Bampton to see my Lady Wishfort in *The Way of the World*, my greatest triumph yet. Jane was one of the women in the Theatre Club, which went off by coach once a month to matinees in Swindon or Cheltenham – love of theatre it seemed was not a requirement, and Esme could be cutting about 'show-offs' who banged on about Pinter all the way home – 'or Anouilh – which I believe is the French for a bore'. It was a day out with the girls, and with one or two elderly or optimistic men who everyone said were 'jolly brave'; but it gave us a link.

I busied round laying a table with a white cloth in the garden and carrying out glasses on a tray – it was a warm sunny evening. 'Is there anyone you'd like to ask?' Mum had said, and a worry of her own crossed her face: 'I don't know if the Hadlows are at Woolpeck, are they, perhaps Giles would like to come?' I said, 'We don't have to worry about the Hadlows any more, Mum, and especially not Giles. I hope I never see

Giles again' – and that seemed to deal with the larger question she'd asked. 'Anyway,' I said, to make double sure, 'they'll all be in France now with Mme Pleynet.' I thought of one or two schoolfriends who lived locally, and pictured the party and them in it, and I knew I wasn't up to it – not yet.

I made myself useful all evening, I hid in my work and I acted it out, shyness and childishness, apart from the adults, and felt the tingle of success, of delight in my performance that went beyond childish good behaviour and showing off. I was charming and admired, and I wondered if the little bit of camp, the crispness and swivel, that came into my act once I'd had a drink myself, let them wonder, in a different way, about me.

There was a new younger couple who came, George and Julie from Challow, George in a black miniskirt and Julie in blue velvet trousers. They'd been all the way to Malvern with the Theatre Club, their first time, to see Hannah Gordon in a play – 'Play pretty ropey, but Hannah . . .' said George, and narrowed her eyes as she held out her glass. 'I must say, David,' said Julie, more demurely, 'your mother's absolute heaven.' 'Oh, I'm glad you like her,' I said, and coloured on Mum's behalf as much as mine. 'We've only just met them,' George said: 'quite a find!' And it was odd because for the first time I seemed to see Mum and Esme from the outside, as a couple you might just meet, their being together taken for granted; that and thinking of Mum, perhaps fifteen years older than these women, as a star or a catch. I was happy and fairly bewildered at once, and a feeling that had lurked all summer quickened, of losing her: though there she was, in the daring red frock she had finished this morning, and smiling back when she saw we were watching her. She had put on more make-up than usual, she was giving and enjoying a performance of her own. 'And what about you?' said George, with her unnerving smile. 'Who are the most handsome actors, in your opinion?' 'Well,' I said, and looked around for inspiration – the question again seemed to take a lot for granted. 'Sean Connery?' I said, as if I didn't much care for him; 'Yul Brynner?' 'Hmm, so is it hairy you go for, or bald . . . ?' George said. 'He may not have made up his mind yet,' said Julie, with a sweet smile at me. 'Sort of . . . both?' I said, and blushed again, and raised my bottle at old Molly Carr, who'd come over the lawn to get a grip on the new arrivals. I bowed and withdrew and felt I'd been caught out and at the same time rather brusquely welcomed in.

Back at the table I opened more bottles of wine, the white with the chill off now, and took them round. 'Ah, you've got a first-rate barman, Esme,' the women said, bucked up by suddenly having another full glass.

'I'm taking him home with me, Avril,' said Connie, holding on tight to my arm. 'Just so that you know.'

'I'm very sorry, Connie, but we simply can't spare him,' Mum said, and laughed, pretty tipsy now and gripping my other arm. I saw the practical worry of the party that had eaten up the morning and afternoon was completely forgotten, and I was pleased I'd helped bring this about – we were a team, after all. And again, as I moved on to the next group, the novel thing was to hear her raised voice amid the general laughter – I felt a sudden loneliness, alongside pride, and relief.

Were there other parties going on, not far away, in summer gardens, like this, but with all men, or mainly, with one or two sympathetic women friends perhaps invited? What about Jeffrey, sexy in memory, at the cottage by the river, and Lovey, half-seen, about thirty-five, I felt, and blond, and their friend Jill they had to get away from, but who might be one of the women let in to their homosexual party. I still had his number, I could have rung him any time in the year since our meeting. 'And what about you, young man?' said Derek Matthews. 'Any particular girlfriends at the moment?'

'Oh . . . no, not really,' I said, and we both looked out, embarrassed in our different ways, at the other guests, smoking and roaring with laughter, three women arm in arm, Betty Matthews herself in a huddle on the bench with Sally and a woman in black trousers who'd arrived late. All around us the tall cheerless conifers prevented the neighbours from seeing the source of the noise, though I pictured them scowling as they sat in their own gardens on the further side.

Then things were thinning out, the trees cut off the beams of the sun to the west, and a tail-enders' mood enveloped the three or four groups still standing and chatting and sending up odd whoops of laughter. I started some discreet clearing up, and took a tray of glasses in through the back door to the kitchen, then went through to the hall for the downstairs lavatory and heard low voices from the dining room, glanced across – it was something I wasn't meant to see, but they were pretty drunk, I suppose, Betty Matthews with her arms round the waist of the woman in black trousers, whose head was on one side, undecided and smiling, before Betty kissed her on the lips, her own head moving sideways as the woman, for three or four seconds, gave in. I went into the lavatory and shut the door loudly, out of shock, and at the same time to warn them. When I came out the dining-room door was wide open and they had gone. Of course I had never seen two women kiss like that outside glimpsed pages of a dirty magazine.

'Dave will know, he knows everything,' Esme said. She was standing with Molly and Jane by the sundial, where someone had set down their half-full wine glass – it left a mauve ring on the lead when I lifted it off. 'Gilbert found it in a junk shop on our honeymoon – as you can see, it's a little bit wonky,' and she waggled the gnomon, whose now vague shadow swayed between seven and nine o'clock.

'Somewhat like the man himself,' said Molly, who had actually known Gilbert, and took a dim view of him.

'I thought it was mumbo-jumbo, but he always claimed it meant something extremely important.'

'I bet what you like he just made it up,' Molly said. Round the edge of the dial a motto had been crudely incised. I would have liked to tell them what it was, and what it meant, but they liked me just as much for sharing their ignorance.

'Well, SINE means without, doesn't it,' said Jane.

'Yes,' I said.

'And is SENSU the ablative, was it, of something?'

'Now you really have lost me,' said Molly, 'mind you, I had no education whatever.'

'So, SENSIM SINE SENSU,' Jane persisted – 'it must be to do with time, of course, mustn't it.'

'*I* know,' Esme said, 'don't you think it just means, "I make no sense"? It's a joke on all of us, for trying to work it out,' and everyone laughed.

'Well, I'm not sure about that,' I said.

'Ah, here we go,' said Molly.

I smiled apologetically. 'I think you'd have to know the context, or how it goes on, to make proper sense of it. It must be a quotation, mustn't it.'

'Frankly, if someone with a scholarship to Oxford University can't work it out,' said Molly, 'I don't think we old girls need worry about it.'

'Sense without sense . . .' said Jane, resisting the 'old girl' tag.

'Born senseless,' said Esme, and laughed and turned away, bored by the subject.

'Like the blooming motto itself,' said Molly with an air of finality.

'I will look into it for you, ladies,' I said, sounding donnish and Jeeves-like at once, and I bowed and went off with my tray to collect more glasses.

*

Then it was the end. I watched through the dining-room window as they veered towards the gate, Bobs gasping with laughter and clutching Betty's arm, all of them glowingly at odds with the silent road and the darkening sky.

'I'll get on with the washing-up,' Mum said.

'Oh, sit down for a bit, love, for god's sake,' said Esme. 'Mrs Luke can do it in the morning.'

'Mrs Luke's fed up with all the extra work as it is,' Mum said, 'since we two came on the scene.' But she threw off the apron she'd started to put round her neck and fell back with a grunt onto the sofa; I wasn't sure how much she liked being this drunk.

'I know,' I said: 'shall I make us all an Ovaltini?'

'Mm, but no tini for me,' said Mum.

'I'll have hers,' said Esme, like a good sport.

I went into the kitchen, and something cloyed in the idea, as I heated the milk, and looked out the Martini Rosso from the cupboard – it felt wilful and sentimental, and none of us needed more to drink. The clock above the cooker said 10.45. I put the three cups on a tray with some shortbread biscuits, and carried them back to the sitting room. Esme had moved from her chair to the sofa, and looked round and made a hushing gesture as I came in. 'She's nodded off, poor old girl,' she said. She had her arm round Mum's shoulders, Mum tilted sideways against her, and pursing her lips thoughtfully a couple of times.

'No, I haven't,' she said, raising her eyebrows before she opened her eyes. 'But I am rather tired.' She sat up. 'Not used to all these people.'

'I think it went well, don't you,' said Esme, 'we were rather a hit.'

'I don't know, I think we must have been,' said Mum, lifting the too hot cup to her lips.

*

I wonder now what their plan was that night, how much, in the heat of their own needs, they thought about the young man in his room at the far end of the landing. I woke up after an hour or so and opened the door like a child half-asleep, not putting the light on, a clear path ahead to the lavatory, just at the moment the door of Esme's bedroom opened, there was laughter, a spill of light across the landing, and Esme surged out. She must have slipped into her dressing gown, for form's sake, it flowed behind her untied, and in the second when she snapped on the bathroom light I saw her face, strongly flushed, a sheen of sweat on her breasts, then she pulled the robe around her as she closed the door . . . leaving a thin wedge of light still from the door of the bedroom where I knew Mum must be lying in a similar state, or perhaps was about to walk out naked herself. I pressed my door closed and after I'd heard Esme go back to bed I eased open the window, and pissed with a helpless racket on the thick-leaved hostas below.

It was when I got home at the end of my first term at Oxford that I found Mum and Esme had nerved themselves to give up the pretence and share a room. It was a Monday, and I tidied my own room as usual before Mrs Luke came in, but by three o'clock there was no sign of her.

'She's not coming any more,' said Esme that evening. 'And you know, Dave, I wonder if we need her.'

'Yes, we do!' said Mum, who had already run the hoover round the bedrooms and was about to tackle the stairs with a dustpan and brush. 'I've got a job of my own, you know.'

The next morning Esme had a long chat on the phone with Molly Carr and late in the afternoon Mrs Wilson, Molly's woman, called in for a chat. I came out of my room as Esme was giving her a quick tour of the house, and the job; she was listing all the duties and minimizing them at the same time.

'Dave's room here,' she said, and I stood aside to let her peer quickly in at my books and my posters, 'then at the back of the house, the bathroom, yes, have a good look at that, and this is where Mrs Win and I sleep' – Mrs Wilson gazing quickly through the door and shaking her head in a refusal to see anything amiss. In fact she said, 'A lovely large room,' in a satisfied tone, so that I felt some other little miracle of understanding had taken place when ten minutes later she called out goodbye and, 'See you next week!'

I'd been packing on the day before going up to Oxford when the phone rang, and as nobody answered I nipped along the landing to the big bedroom. The lacquer-red extension was on what I had worked out was Esme's side of the bed. Mum had made a new counterpane, oyster-white, which shimmered on top of the hillocky blankets and eiderdown, and I flung myself across it to reach the receiver – 'Is Avril there? Calls herself Mrs Win.'

It was the voice of a man in a rage who has said what he's going to say fifty times in his head, but whose fury, even so, might carry him off script. I wasn't unshakably sure it was Uncle Brian. 'Oh, she's at work at the moment, I'm afraid,' I said, 'can I—'

'It's Brian Slatter.'

'Oh, yes . . .' I said, with a residue of courtesy and a laugh, almost, 'yes, hello . . .'

'Tell her she's not welcome in this house. Tell her she's not coming here for Christmas, all that's over.'

'All right, I will,' I said, and found I had swung round and drawn up my knees at his aggression to Mum and his refusal to use my name, an insult I'd borne all my life.

'I'm not having that woman in my house.'

'Oh, no, all right,' I said, and it took me a second to see which woman he meant. I was sitting on her bed, and the unadmitted fear of disgrace, to Esme and Mum and all three of us, was mixed up with a sense of defiance and an underlying comfort that was close to luxury.

'Tell Avril she can be Mrs Win for all I care, she's not a Slatter any more. Her family don't know her.' I saw at once this wasn't true, I pictured Susie biting her lip, Shirley cowering, but no doubt he had waited for a moment when he was alone in the house.

'I'm sure she'll be sorry to hear that, Uncle Brian,' I said levelly, though my heart was pounding, and there was a silence, as of something about to go off, and already, in the future that gleamed beyond the end of the phone call, a first melting foretaste of relief.

'She's disgraced our name,' he said. 'She's disgraced it twice over.'

I saw this was very personal, and perhaps I was a coward to be so ironical. 'That's once too often, isn't it really,' I said. Well, it provoked him, tricked him into speaking directly to me:

'As for you, you're a stuck-up little ponce.'

'Thanks very much—' but he had slammed down the phone.

'Well, I won't be sorry,' said Mum bravely, 'not to have that drive back from Warminster,' and it went through me too, although I hated Uncle Brian, that Warminster once had meant home to her, as Foxleigh did to me. Esme said, 'We can have a special *Crackers Christmas* – so much better than the other way round,' and we laughed a lot at this, and Mum held my arm for a moment in the complex shock of release from something she had dreaded for years, yet still felt she ought to go through with. I didn't tell her, then or ever, exactly what Brian had said.

When the time came, Auntie Susie drove over by herself on Christmas Eve with her presents, and took away a box with our presents for Malcolm and Shirley. She was as always in a state of unresolved mutiny against her husband. 'I can't stay,' she said, perching in her coat on the deep-cushioned sofa, looking round wistfully at ornaments and furniture, our things mixed in now with Esme's. I felt she might have liked living with a nice rich woman herself – trying it, anyway.

Mum had a drink or two on Christmas day at twelve, not having to drive anywhere or do anything but make a huge lunch for us three. Esme teased her as usual as a too-cautious drinker, and looked forward to the moment when Mum took off her apron, raised her glass and said, 'Well . . . Merry Christmas!' much more than Mum did herself. Because I also got quickly squiffy I couldn't judge exactly how it took her. Mum was a good sport about it, she did it for Esme, she had another drink to 'keep up her spirits' while we did the washing-up, and it was hard to tell where the ritual ended and simple pleasure in the silliness and buzz of the alcohol took over – and in due course petered out.

After the Queen's Speech she went off upstairs to lie down, it was too wet for a walk, and Esme and I sat playing Strip Jack Naked by the fire. It was a game she gave her full attention to, hunched forward over the coffee table, sweeping the cards back under her pack at the end of a long run and smacking the next card down on the table with a look of demented concentration. She quickly won the first game, and got me to shuffle before dealing out the whole pack for the second, where once again she soon took the upper hand. So she simply didn't notice when the door swung open and Mum came back in, though I looked up and gasped, dazzled, almost hurt by the surprise. 'Your go, love,' said Esme tensely, before she turned and stared too, the brief blank of amazement before the flood of other feelings – 'Oh, my angel . . . ! Don't you look too extraordinary.' Mum came forward, on red-slippered feet, wrapped to

the midriff in her red tartan longyi, with a white lace blouse
and, wound high round her head, the scarlet and gold-thread
gaung-baung with its loose end jutting to the right.

'You look great, Mum,' I said, with tears in my eyes, and
a feeling that something too private for any of us really to
understand was being said for the first time in public. Esme
got to her feet, crossed the room and slipped her arms round
her as she kissed her on the cheek, and Mum raised a hand as
if to steady the tight headdress. She didn't explain, indeed now
she was here seemed unsure what to do, and even a little
astonished at what she'd already done. But she kept it up,
Esme stood back with her hands on Mum's shoulders, wide
bra-straps under the thin straps of the lace blouse, and a feeling in the room that though she was all got up she was
half-naked, bare arms glad of the fire in the cold house. She
glanced in the mirror over the mantelpiece, still saying nothing, and it wasn't at all clear what she could say. She turned
right round, with little shuffling steps, but she didn't really,
she couldn't, pretend to be a Burmese woman. It was her
sharp pretty Wiltshire face that blinked from under the lop-
eared crown. None the less, in her fancy dress she was a
stranger to me, just a little. 'You should dress like that all the
time,' said Esme, 'what a sensation! The Burmese bride . . .'
And I thought, if I hadn't been here would Mum ever have
done this, and now who was she doing it for . . . It was a
signal of some sort to me, and a present of some kind, a treat,
for Esme – who kept saying, 'Don't you think, Dave? This
is too good to keep just for Christmas.' I grinned and said
nothing, it was clear at least that Mum had never done it for
her before, and perhaps she had just been carried away by an
impulse she hadn't questioned because it was something she
so much wanted to do. It was fantasy, and self-expression, it
was the opposite of Christmas with Uncle Brian.

'You get me tight,' she said, 'and then this happens.'

'We must get you tight again,' said Esme, much tighter her-self, breathing fast and with something wild about her only just held in.

'Anyway . . .' said Mum, 'there you are,' and with a wave of the arm, haphazard, not a tragic gesture, she tottered out and back upstairs; while Esme and I sat down again to the game we seemed to have started long before. We couldn't quite look at each other, and we couldn't really focus on the cards, the play had an empty unwelcome feel, neither of us caring much when Esme saw my last card go down and gathered and squared up the whole pack in her hands. I went out, parched now and already hungover, to scrub at the roasting tin that had been left to soak.

It was Mum, not me, who kept all my certificates, in stiff manila envelopes, from Bampton and now from Oxford, the Blanchard Prize for Verse Translation, the Chancellor's Essay Prize. She came over with Esme for Encaenia, and I could see where they were sitting as I read out the showiest bit of my essay from the pulpit in the crowded Sheldonian. The event was a drama for them, and I guessed Mum was too dazed by her own nerves to take in what I was saying. There were the Latin orations, degrees conferred upon Nikolaus Pevsner, Barbara Hepworth, the President of the European Commission – the most famous people I had been in a room with, who then had to listen to an eager young man they had never heard of and never would again, declaiming on the subject of 'Inheritance'. Outside after-wards, in the post-ceremonial dazzle, bells ringing, parents posing for pictures with their sons and daughters, Mum looked at me more warily, and proudly. One or two friends shouted over her head to me, or else darted in to pat my shoulder, and glanced half-curiously at my white mother. I introduced 'Mrs Croft' without explanation, as if she was a widely known figure. I was famous myself for a moment, I mean I was singled out for those who didn't know me at all. Esme said my reading was marvellous, but rather beyond her in some respects, which gave me a peculiar feeling. I had a sense that I'd cooked something up, and had a success with it, but I was already doubting it. That's what the certificate, signed by Harold Macmillan, with my name inscribed on it in black italics, brings back – the little teetering act of taking myself seriously, of being proud of what I'd done but ready, now I'd won, to dismiss it. I'd processed through the streets in academic dress, a good twenty yards behind the preening blond pageboy who lifted the Chancellor's train. We'd been rehearsed the day before, I stood up and read, and my joke about Edward VII raised a gathering laugh from the parents and guests and even a nod of amusement from Macmillan himself, in the throne. What did I really feel, or care, what weight did I give to the applause, the handshakes, the quick shouted 'Well done's of people I half knew, whose own pleasure had something else bracing in it, a hint of a jeer in their friendly good form?

'Win, Win, Win!' said Dick Harcourt, in the year above me, slapping me on the back. 'Great essay.' We'd never really spoken before.

'Thank you,' I said. 'It's something I hope to work on further,' sounding just like Humphrey Russell, our tutor.

He grinned enthusiastically at Mum and Esme. 'It was like Oscar Wilde, read by Sybil Thorndyke' – I blushed, and Esme said to him gratefully,

'Yes, hasn't he got a lovely speaking voice.'

We drifted out through the gates and into the busy traffic of the Broad, my cap-tassel swinging, scholar's gown lifted by the breeze, among people shopping, students in jeans, tourists turning and gaping – a sense that everything should stop for us, and a sense, just as strong, that I looked ridiculous. 'Don't you look splendid!' Esme said, and Mum said I was quite bigheaded enough already.

15

'Earnest,' I said, '*earthless* . . . equal . . . attuneable . . .' Stella peered at me, tongue on lip, daring me.

' . . . vaulty . . .' she said.

' . . . vaulty, voluminous . . . *stupendous* Evening strains to be time's vast —' (now we chanted it together) '*womb*-of-all – *home*-of-all – *hearse*-of-all NIGHT!'

'I bet you can't go on.'

'I can actually.'

'There's stars, I seem to remember,' said Timbo, '*earl*-stars.'

'You two are amazing,' said Walter.

I said, 'Her earliest stars, earl-stars . . .'

'Yep, that's it . . .'

' . . . stars principal, overbend us, Fire-featuring heaven . . .'

'*Heart*,' said Stella fiercely, 'you round me right With —'

'You've missed out two lines,' I said, but we went on from there, in unison, each of us raising one arm like an orator to the sunset: 'Our evening is over us; our night whelms, whelms, and will end us.' She grinned.

'*And* will end us,' I said, 'it's the odd way Hopkins stresses it.'

'Amazing you two remember all that,' said Walter, and I let Stella share the applause.

'Well, I learned it at school,' I said. 'A poem a day for a whole summer term.'

'You never forget things like that, I suppose.'

'I just remember the earl-stars,' said Timbo.

'They sound like a great band,' said his girlfriend, Joanne, who worked in London and had just arrived. 'Walter Fowler and the Earl-stars.'

'Well of course they had a great run of hits,' said Walter, 'in the late 1960s,' and getting up from the bench he strolled towards the low wall at the end of the lawn. 'Come and look at this.'

From there it seemed one long trundle of fields running all the way down to Oxford, two miles off. The heart of the city was probed and exposed by the sunset, fine-etched rooftops and spires, chapel windows blazing. In the sky to the east, above Headington, over London soon, high elements of cloud, white Alps in the blue, took colour as we watched, burned with the fierce pink and orange and cavernous grey of a vast log fire, richer and richer. 'And the eye travels down to Oxford's towers,' I said, and shook my head gently as I spread my arms.

'Oh God, bloody Oxford,' said Joanne.

'Whereabouts was Masefield's house?' I said.

'Just down the road,' said Walter, 'I'll show you later. Robert Bridges, too, of course.'

'And Graves, didn't he live here?'

'All the poets,' said Walter.

'And I see you've got croquet,' said Joanne, turning away. 'Who wants to take me on?'

'The lawn really needs mowing first,' said Walter. It wasn't a smooth lawn, and there was long grass round the hoops, which made me think someone before had mown it without taking them up.

'Let's do it!' said Joanne. 'I don't mind doing it.'

'I wouldn't hear of it,' said Walter.

By the time he had wrestled the lawn-mower out from a lean-to shed at the back of the house, the mallets and balls had been found and a game had begun regardless. I didn't know Joanne but I saw at once she had a certain attack, on a game and on all of us swanking around in this grown-up house. 'So do you live here too, Dave?' she said, as I hung over the ball and narrowed my eyes at the tussocks ahead. I was playing with Stella, and Timbo and Joanne naturally made a team.

'No, I've never been here before,' I said, and made a sharp shot which touched the second hoop, seemed to stall there for a minute, then made up its mind and wandered through.

'Jammy,' said Joanne.

'I'm in the play with Stella, and with Tim of course.'

'You're an actor too, yes, it makes sense now.'

I raised my left eyebrow. 'What does?'

'The way you said the poem.'

'Ah, I see.'

'You've got a really great speaking voice, by the way.'

The mower roared up with an implacable effect beside us and Walt reined it in just by the third hoop, where Stella, who had struck her ball into the flower bed and fished it out, was placing it with a great show of science in an advantageous spot. 'I think,' said Walt, 'sorry . . .', with a commanding grin at me, and I went over and tugged up the hoop just before she played it; then I ran down and pulled up the fourth one, then put the third one back, and we went on like that for fifteen minutes, mowing the lawn and playing on it at the same time, with lulls for talk when Walter carried the full bin of grass to the compost and the engine idled and scented the air.

'I seem to be the hoop-upper,' I said.

'You're doing a marvellous job,' said Timbo, and put his arm round my shoulders. He was a big man, playing Sir Politic Would-be in the play and growing a beard for it. We stood gazing mildly at the house, which was tile-hung, gabled, with creeper covering the front wall and starting up the roof.

'The creeper looks very pretty,' said Stella, 'but the moment you open the bedroom window the bugs come tearing in.'

'What sort of thing?'

'Beetles, woodlice, centipedes about a yard long . . .'

'Bloody hell,' said Joanne.

'You still live in college, don't you, Dave?' Stella said.

I shrugged under Timbo's arm and said, 'Yes, no creepy-crawlies there.'

There was a haze of assumptions in the air about the house, the wry charade of Walt and Stella living in a place like this in their third year, and each of us thinking perhaps it was grander, or not, than the homes we'd grown up in, and were used to. 'It's fucking enormous,' said Timbo.

'There's Jenny and Nick too,' Stella said. 'You know it's Walt's uncle's house – he lets us have it for next to nothing.'

'Yes, we know about him,' said Joanne, and rolled her eyes.

'He's not too awful when you get to know him,' Stella said. 'Right, here we go.'

Despite Stella's artful approach to the rules, we lost the game; then Joanne challenged Walt, and Jenny, who'd been cooking, came out through the French windows calling, 'Drink?' and was coaxed into playing too. I wandered inside for a piss.

The house was out of Oxford, up on a hill, but Oxford ran through it, with a leisurely ripple of connection and assumption: framed New College photos from between the Wars, a library I looked into, like Humphrey's room, with padded fender, log basket, books, like Humphrey's, whose spines I'd stared at through unnumbered hours, though older than many of his, and deeper out of date. In the passage from the hall towards the lavatory two trophy oars were hanging, at head height, with the college arms on the blades and the names of the First Eights of 1920 and 21 painted in gold: *MR. W. FOWLER Bow*. I saw there was family history to work out, things Walter knew, and his Wykehamist friends probably all took for granted. I could ask directly but I didn't like showing my ignorance, which made too large a sense to other people who'd just met me.

I liked being alone in the shadowy house, with the tone of the voices out on the lawn suggesting I might be missed later and looked for, but for now was out of mind. In the sitting room a sofa was pulled up with two armchairs in a huddle, where last night they'd played cards in front of a fire that was now grey ashes and a scatter of fag-ends on the hearth. The watercolour landscapes had been paled and denatured by sunlight, unlike the large forceful portraits of a man and a woman, dated 1929: Walter's grandfather, it must be, perched on the window seat of this very room, books open on a gate-leg table which I saw had moved no further than the far side of the rug in the intervening forty years. The whole comfortable confident neglected mood was of the 1920s, with just a few signs of the late 1960s Walt had whimsically evoked, a small colour TV on the right of the fireplace, a turntable with the lid raised and *Disraeli Gears* on the mat.

I started climbing the stairs, which made two turns up to the first floor, with a bleary skylight above. The creak of the treads confirmed something furtive about me, as I came up level with the room across the landing, rugs on black floorboards, a suitcase flung open on arrival, a glimpse of my friends' bedroom life. Then the next door snapped open and a man came out – I saw him a second before he saw me, and I echoed his jump of surprise: a quick recoil and a grin, 'Hello!' as though he'd forgotten we were meant to meet here.

'Hello,' I said. I seemed to balance, on the stair's edge, between guest and trespasser.

'You're David,' he said, 'I saw you last year in *The Knight of the Burning Pestle.*'

'Oh, gosh . . .'

'And also . . . hang on . . . in *The Physicists*! I'm Nick,' and I went up the last three steps and we shook hands, which he seemed to find funny or unnecessary and carried on talking excitedly as if we weren't doing it. The question of why I'd been going upstairs disappeared and we went together down to the kitchen, where a tray was prepared, peanuts and Twiglets and the bottle of rosé I'd brought with me. Nick took down glasses from a cupboard and I watched him move around. He wore tight old olive-green corduroys, rubbed bare round the knees and the fly; and a plain white shirt, with the sleeves rolled up over strong forearms. The top three or four buttons were undone. He was lean and square-shouldered, with a long thick neck that excited me like a glimpse of nakedness, and gold-rimmed glasses that gave his cheerful face a lovely dimension of cleverness and reserve.

Outside, we sat on a bench at the edge of the croquet lawn. The great combustion in the sky had faded and passed and we watched the others play on in the rich even light just after sunset. Occasionally Walter or Jenny gave us a distracted smile as they strode past to line up their shots, but the violence of the game demanded most of their attention, and their calls and shouts were all for each other. I was saved from the usual inanity of the looker-on, of being both invisible and awkwardly conspicuous, by sitting with Nick, who let out obliging yelps and groans at the game now and then while still talking to me. I was adjusting to his already knowing me, though I didn't know how much he knew, as I tried to find out about him.

He was in Corpus, reading PPE, 'I'm not posh,' he said, 'or rich,' but he was a good friend of Walt's. He didn't act really, he'd once been Snug, and thus the Lion, in the college garden, twelve lines in all, and on balance enough. 'I could never be a real actor, like you,' he said, and we clinked our glasses over the compliment. 'And you're in the play too, Walt said?'

'I am.'

'I've never seen it. I'll have to read it.'

'It's an amazing play, but hard to learn, the language is very complex.'

'Do you have a big part?'

'Huge,' I said. We both smiled and looked away as we let the joke escape. 'I'm playing Mosca, Volpone's manservant.'

'Sort of Jeeves,' said Nick.

'Really not like Jeeves,' I said, with a quick doubting look at him, as if he already knew things about me no one else here did. 'Volpone calls me his parasite. I help him trick everybody else and then try to trick him myself.'

'And do you win?'

'You'll have to come and see,' I said.

'OK,' he said, and clinked glasses again and looked at me slyly, as if taking his own reading of the way things were moving forward between us.

'And you're doing Finals this term too?'

'I know . . .' I said, with a flinch at my recklessness.

'You must be very confident.'

'That's just what my mother said,' I said. And I was glad of the drink as I sensed the little squeeze to the throat, as of something planned so secret I hardly knew what it was myself. 'Well, the play's in fourth week, and my tutor seems to think I'm far enough ahead with work.'

'Oh, well that's good,' said Nick, and I couldn't tell if he was flattering me or teasing me or telling me off.

'I can do it,' I said, 'I can do it.'

We watched the game then for a minute, not without interest, but with a closer sense of feeling out the air between us and around us, and waiting, half-amused already, for the other one to speak. I asked him about living here, about getting out from Oxford into this romantic unexpected setting – I felt I was in a Chekhov play, perhaps, or some more woozy movie about Oxford's golden age. And I was feeling, without knowing it, for his own sense of the poetry of it all. He said it was great, a bit difficult at times, but Walt and Jenny both had cars; they'd been snowed in for several days in February. 'I just spend the whole time working,' he said: 'no distractions up here. I go into town once a week for classes.' It was the opposite of what I was doing, living in college, winging it at work to focus on the play. And at once it cut back the chances of seeing him again, which I knew already I wanted to do. The drink, his smile and laugh, the pleasure of amusing this man right beside me, with his right leg folded under him on the bench, and his half-unbuttoned shirt when he leant forward translucent, a three-second glimpse of smooth chest and brown nipple. 'We should meet up,' I said, floating forward into a space he seemed to have opened for us. 'Go punting – or something . . . if you'd like that.'

He smiled at me, and I couldn't tell if he was happily picturing us both in a punt or amazed at my trying to set up a date within minutes of meeting him.

Jenny seemed to rule the kitchen, she was like a mother already, but she'd had a drink and a top-up and the timings weren't right after all, the lamb was nearly done before the apple pie had even been started. She gave me the pastry to make, and the flour-scattered table in the cone of warm light was in harmony somehow with the kitchen at Crackers, or at the old flat in Foxleigh, where I'd knelt on a chair as a child to stir the cake mixture: I knew where I was. From indoors the garden outside appeared dark, though the raps of the mallets and shouts of 'Fuck you, Fowler!' came in through the open window. 'I'm sorry to beat you *so* comprehensively,' Walter said. Everyone was pretty drunk.

When it was all done, the pastry thumbed down round the rim of the dish and the surface pricked in a magic pattern, I went through to the dining room, swept off the crumbs of past meals from the table, found the heavy forks and spoons and bone-handled knives in a baize-lined drawer of the sideboard, set the wine glasses, cut glass, by each place, and re-lit the half-used candles in the white-bearded candelabrum. It was a long table, there were seven of us, and I put a place for Walt, per-haps, at the head. The room was gloomy, with flat oak panelling up to the top of the doors, and then a ledge all round, with old china jugs and plates propped out of reach. There were more dark pictures, and a red-tiled fireplace with soot-covered news-paper scrumpled up in the grate. I drew the curtains, as I might have done at home, but here with a snug sense of graduation to grown-up life, or at least to the imaginary play or film about grown-up life, in which I was happy to be cast as a servant. But when everyone had come in, and helped carry the food and more drink into the dining room, and dithered, with half-remembered etiquette, around the table, Walt said, 'You sit at the head, Dave, yeah, you're the um . . .' 'What is he?' said Stella, shaking her head, no one quite knew what he meant, and I said, 'Am I, Walt? Right, OK!' and sat down with the freeing, nearly chemical sensation of going on stage. I raised my hands welcomingly to the others, as they found their places, Nick smiled at me but didn't sit next to me, he took the middle seat on my right, with the candles in front of him drawing more subtle and fickle expressions from his features than he was aware of and at certain angles hiding his eyes behind the grubby gleam of his glasses.

There was some talk, now we were all together, about *Volpone*. 'What's it about, then?' Joanne wanted to know.

'It's about greed,' Timbo said, tucking into his lamb.

'And humiliation,' said Stella.

'Oh, yes . . . ?' said Joanne. 'Sounds fun.'

Stella said how it was Ben Jonson's most famous comedy, and 'just unbelievably hard work for everybody'.

'Everyone who's in it, you mean?' said Joanne.

'Yeah, you'll have a great time, Jo,' Tim said. 'It's a great laugh.'

'You do know, Joanne, don't you, that I play Timbo's wife . . . ?'

'I'll be keeping an eye on you, Tim Atkins,' Joanne said.

'It's only a small part,' said Stella: 'the real star' – and she made a graceful gesture up the table to me – 'is Mosca the servant.'

'I?' I said. 'Who is the real star, who is the more deplorable?' – and I morphed unresistingly into Dougie Marshall: 'Is it Volpone, or his factotum, or the grasping birds and beasts he cozens? The Jacobean City, my dear, in all its cupidity and vulgarity and polymorphous energy, translated from dry London to a treacherous Venice. What could be more fun?'

'God, that's uncanny,' said Stella.

'Who's that?' said Joanne.

'There's more real violence in this play than in many a great tragedy.'

'Stop it!' said Walt, blinking at me down the table, and I looked almost slyly at Nick, who presumably didn't know Dougie, to see the effect on him.

'Douglas Marshall, Jo,' said Stella, 'he's the famous old don who's directing. Very famous.'

'Dougie knows everyone,' said Timbo, 'you know, Beckett, and Peter Brook and people.'

'And more to the point, he knows the critics,' said Stella, 'the London critics.'

'So you'll get reviewed, do you mean, Tim, in the papers?'

'Could be quite important,' Tim said, with a candid shake of the head.

Now it was Joanne's turn to be sly. 'I bet he's queer,' she said.

'Hmm . . .' said Jenny, and stroked an imaginary beard.

'You sound it,' said Joanne, and looked at me narrowly, as if I really was Dr Marshall. I shrugged – I wasn't going to mock Dougie for that.

'His hand tends to end up down the back of boys' trousers,' said Stella. 'Actresses he leaves alone, as far as I know.'

'Has he done that to you, Tim?' Joanne said.

'Not yet, Jo, no,' Tim said. 'But we've only just started rehearsals.'

Joanne glanced round the table, perhaps thinking she was being sent up. 'Not that I care about people being queer,' she said, 'anyway, it's legal now, isn't it, they can do what they like.' She turned to Nick, who gave a little blink and shake of the head at being brought in, and said in his cheerful unanswerable way,

'No other position is possible.'

'No, well, obviously,' I murmured, I thought unobtrusively, but they all turned to see if I was going to say something else.

Walter stood and went round to fill our glasses. I felt he was a little bit fed up with Joanne.

'What about you, Dave,' Joanne said, sticking at it, 'I bet you're a bit gay?'

'Oh . . .' I said, with a smile, 'well,' and felt I could carry it off, but my pulse beat in my ear.

'It's his affair, isn't it,' said Walt, passing behind us with the bottle; and I wasn't clear how this left things, that they all therefore assumed that I was? A straight man would have had to be very principled and confident to decline to answer the question. I felt I wanted Nick to see the truth, and at the same time confusedly hoped he wouldn't find out and be put off me. 'A bit of it in all of us, isn't there, really?' Walt said, and rested his hand on Nick's shoulder and squeezed it as he leant over to fill his glass. The idea that this beautiful tolerance might embrace Walt and Nick themselves, out here all year together in this house, made everything shift again in the candlelight.

Jenny said, 'Now David has made us all a beautiful apple pie,' as if I was the best boy in the class, and I went out and came back with it held high, while a space was cleared and a mat set in front of me. But as I served it and passed the bowls round I felt a bleary threshold of the evening had been passed, and people tucked in and kept talking and drinking without commenting on the apple pie at all; I ate my own portion in a primly appreciative way. The talk had come round to Walter's uncle, Gervase Fowler, who was a Tory MP, and something quite important in the shadow cabinet. I thought now and then how we were in his house, saw him arriving unannounced, he seemed present already in the family pictures, Walter passing in front of them as he cut through the foil on a new bottle, but Jenny said, 'Oh, he never comes out here,' as if Boars Hill was impossibly remote.

'You'd vote Labour, wouldn't you, Walt?' Joanne said, I couldn't tell how satirically. 'Walt . . . ?'

'What . . . ? Yah, well, you know . . .' said Walt, and carried on looking for the corkscrew.

'There's really no excuse for voting Tory,' she said.

'Selfishness, Jo?' said Stella, 'Surely?'

'Can selfishness be an excuse?' said Nick.

'A reason, you mean,' said Jenny, 'but not an excuse.'

'Exactly. Voting Tory,' said Nick, 'is simply a failure of imagination.'

'Yes,' said Stella, 'what do you mean?'

'I mean imagining the lives of others unlike ourselves, less fortunate than we are . . . I mean look at us' – and he waved his arm at the candles and paintings and panelling.

Joanne went on, and asked us all how we'd vote if there was an election tomorrow. Nick said, 'Labour, of course,' Jenny, 'Ditto,' with a shake of the head, and it came to me.

'How would I vote, in a general election?'

'You're doing it again,' said Stella, as a low delayed laugh went round the table.

'Everyone can do Wilson,' Tim said, doing him himself.

'As a matter of fact,' I went on, an imaginary pipe in my

right hand, 'it would make no perceptible difference how I vote, it's been a rock-solid Tory seat for years.'

'Boo, abstainer,' said Jenny.

'No, no,' I said, turning back from the PM into me, 'the truth is, if we'd been able to vote in the last election I probably would have voted Liberal—'

'Oh, God . . .'

'— my Mum's always been a Liberal, and—'

'The thing is, darling,' said Stella, 'there's no point in voting for the Liberals, they're never going to get in.'

Her 'darling' had an odd effect on me, of abruptly deeper friendship, and the frankness it allowed. I felt flattered and vulnerable. My answer seemed to be waited for, a note of submission. 'But that was two years ago,' I said, 'a lot has changed since then. You know, I've been through university!' and I raised my glass in a grateful gesture at the company in front of me.

'You've met marvellous people who've changed your mind.'

'Yes, I have,' and though Nick and I hadn't yet said a word to each other about politics, or anything much, I let myself look at him – he was sitting back and smiling in a rather teasing way. 'Now,' I said, 'there's a little bit more pie, if anyone would like some,' hoping to stir some belated applause, and there was a heavy banging at the front door – I thought Walter's terrible uncle had turned up after all.

'Ah, that must be Edwin,' Walter said.

'Talking of Tories,' said Jenny.

I put down my serving spoon and stood up. 'I'll go, shall I?' I said, and there was a second loud ratatat.

'Here's a knocking indeed!' said Stella, playing our game.

'Who's there,' I cried, 'i' th' name of Beelzebub?' and I went into the hall.

The tall black man who stepped straight in looked all the more impressive for the white rowing blazer he was wearing.

'Ah, good,' he said, and strode through and looked into the sitting room. 'Where's everyone got to, do you know?'

'Well, as it happens,' I said, closing the front door, 'we're still finishing dinner.'

'Oh, really?' he said, 'then I'm on time.' He had a very deep voice, and so posh he might have been sending someone up. I couldn't tell yet if it was the sort of poshness inseparable from good manners, or the sort that absolves you of any such thing. 'By the way, I'm Edwin,' he said, and wrung my hand, pretty crushingly. 'David,' I said, and he looked down at me as if I'd said something slightly off but just about acceptable. He must have been six foot three, with the rower's air of huge-limbed power about him under the uniform. The Christ Church emblem, a red cardinal's hat, was embroidered on his white breast pocket.

I followed him into the dining room, where he was greeted and introduced, and I took my seat again and watched him find a glass and sit down facing me, at the far end of the table. I felt, as I had through my three years at Oxford, the tiny shift of atmosphere when another young person who wasn't white arrived after me at a party, a quick, often meaningless rebalancing that most of my white friends, I'm sure, had no sense of.

Soon afterwards there was a move to the sitting room and when I went back in to help clear the plates Edwin and Walter were still sitting at the far end doing something, two or three small packets on the table, and Walt fishing out his wallet, saying, 'Ten enough?' He glanced up and flickered his eyebrows at me, friendly but not engaging. I felt the little inner plunge, of shock, and raised my eyebrows too, and turned my head, as if to say I had seen nothing.

I was standing with Edwin on the hearthrug, as though the fire was lit.

'You're David Win,' he said, and waggled his finger at me.

Walter must have explained, though perhaps Edwin too had seen me in a play. 'Giles said you were a man to look out for.'

'Giles . . . oh, really!' I said, but I caught Giles's tone in him, the way of speaking to me like a middle-aged man to a disadvantaged youngster.

'Have you seen him lately?'

'Oh, not for ages,' I said.

'You won some prize he went in for.'

'Did I?' I said. 'Not the Chancellor's Essay Prize?'

'Was that it? I think it was. Something like that.'

'Oh, I didn't know he'd gone in for that,' I said, and was pleased, though I saw Edwin's praise of me for winning it was very oblique and conditional – obviously Giles should have won.

He laughed and said, 'Old Giles is a splendid character! Future PM, wouldn't you say?'

'Oh, almost certainly!' I said, and laughed myself, as if dazzled by the prospect.

'Don't you think?' said Edwin, and then gave me a second look to check, if he could, where we were on the scale between joking and hideous conviction. I nodded at him and excused myself for a moment.

When I came back into the sitting room five minutes later Jenny had put on *Das Lied von der Erde*. I couldn't resist it, and I wished it wasn't on. It was like being back at school, and feebly pretending not to mind when everyone talked over my Vaughan Williams – or indeed my *Das Lied von der Erde*. And after the second song Stella said, 'Is this *quite* the right mood, Jennifer, do you think?' in her head-of-house voice, and Timbo looked narrowly at me and said, 'Yeah . . . I mean, for fucksake . . .' Joanne was going through the records propped up in a slithering stack on the table. 'Choose something, Jo,' Timbo said. So the needle was wrenched up just as the Chinesey jingling of 'Von der Jugend' was getting under way, and after a bit of swaying and fumbling the twanging thump of 'Strange Brew' threw the switch of the night just like that. 'Turn it up! Turn it up!' said Stella. Joanne was already grooving around on the far side of the room, but she homed in on the amp and did as she was asked.

'We listened to this at least fifteen times last night,' said Walter loudly.

'Don't you love it!' said Joanne. Jenny, who didn't seem to mind her choice being overruled, got up and started dancing with her.

I was a pretty good dancer, but for now I sat back on the sofa with a mild tense smile because dancing with these drunk friends seemed to open up doors in the night ahead. Nick was sitting next to Stella on the sofa with an atlas flat on his knee while he constructed a huge joint from a bag of grass and the innards of half a dozen Benson & Hedges. He chatted as he worked, and laughed his happy laugh, but I couldn't really hear what they were saying. He fitted in some sort of filter, his pointed pink tongue licked the papers to seal them together, and at the end he held his masterpiece at eye-level and twisted its tip. 'Who's got a lighter?' he said – I watched Timbo go over and squat down with a hand on Nick's knee while the joint was fired up, and then passed round. It was Edwin who carried it across the room to me, his chin still raised as he held in the smoke and reluctantly let it go. I shook my head not knowing if I wanted it, and envious that Nick, whose smile already looked subtly different, was getting away into a high with the others. 'How do you do it?' I said.

'Aha! – a virgin,' he said, though his pomp was slightly softened, I felt. He knelt down beside me and held the flame steady as I took the thing between my lips; it was the trace of the others' mouths on the softening roach that was the induction, as much as the raw smoke. 'That's probably enough, old chap,' Edwin said, 'hold it in' – I felt its acrid tickle in my throat and fought the first-timer's comical cough till my eyes watered; I gave the joint back to him and did a large sober-sounding clearing of the throat. 'Give it a minute,' said Edwin, and stood up and strolled over to the dancing girls. I sat back with a wallflower smile, a sense of singleness and strangeness, on top of being drunk. 'Sunshine of Your Love', with arms in the air, had ended, I had the record sleeve, little posture of security from school days, though I'd heard the album over and over without learning the names of the songs: now it was 'World of Pain' – words I never quite followed, perhaps you weren't meant to, it was the voices that haunted you. Walt came in with some more of the New College hock, and yanked out a cork with the bottle between his knees. Edwin sat down in the corner, with his long legs spread out, and seemed to pass from ducal self-importance to self-communing stupor in a swift and satisfactory way. My jumbled ideas about his poshness and blackness and his bringing the dope and no one here except Walter speaking of him as a friend refused to sort themselves out, then refused to be thought about at all. Things felt somewhat discontinuous, it was odd but pleasant, and Stella was up, in her black jeans and red top, in front of me, spreading her arms and singing along – 'Is there a reason for today – Do you remember?' – then taking my hands and pulling me up just in time for what I saw, as I threw down the sleeve, was 'Dance the Night Away'. 'Fuck, I love this song!' she shouted, and soon all of us were dancing, it was a great song, with its climaxes climbing up higher and higher and then the little as-you-were bits in-between while we shook our heads happily and waited for the next ascent. When the new song came in immediately after, Jenny shouted, 'This song's *fucking* boring!' and none of us minded hearing 'Dance the Night Away' again.

I was having fun in such a new way, and now and then watching myself having fun, catching my eye and hoping to catch Nick's in the large gloomy mirror that hung between the windows. We heaved around in that further space, heads down, shoulders working, as if performing some primitive ritual. Someone had flung the French windows open and moths were coming in, the big ones batting the lampshades and the little diaphanous green ones dotting the ceiling – 'Creepy-crawlies!' said Joanne – 'I told you!' said Stella, lurching over and tugging the heavy curtains shut; though they bellied, now and then, in the night breeze.

I was sitting down again, with Nick himself now, on the sofa, when 'Tales of Brave Ulysses' came on for the second time. We were lying back, with our wine glasses held on our stomachs. 'There is something,' said Nick, 'undeniably obsessive about Joanne.' 'Yes,' I said, 'yes.' I was quite still, unable to move, and running ahead unstoppably fast on the motor of falling in love. Four or five times his hard forearm or his knee pressed against my own. After that, 'We're Going Wrong' was a harder one to dance to, and I made a coy show of resistance when Nick got to his feet and reached out a hand to me. I held the hand firmly, feeling his strength before I let him pull me up. 'God, that voice, god, that *voice*,' said Jenny, staring at us, clutching Nick's forearm as if the voice might carry her away. It filled the shadows, echoed from the vaster dark beyond the curtains. 'Yeah, the greatest,' said Tim, shifting round in a far-off style of his own, a hand now and then on my shoulder. In its remote middle section the song passed into the doldrums, Eric Clapton's guitar wound in alarmingly, and Tim and Jo weaved their hands in the air while the rest of us bided our time. Jenny gazed at Nick and me in turn as Jack Bruce came back and the voice climbed up the night . . . *I found out today, We're going wrong* . . . Nick grinned at me just as joyfully as he did at Jenny, and over the next two songs I kept up that spirit, of enjoying myself, and not dropping my head sideways in a hopeless imploring way.

When the record ended and suggestions were shouted out, 'I'm getting some air,' Nick said, quietly, explaining but not drawing attention to himself, and in the brief eddy of chance behind his words I murmured, 'Yeah, me too,' and we slid out under the heavy curtains and into the garden. He didn't wait for me, and it took me a minute to see him and catch up with him, at the far edge of the lawn.

Below us moonlight coaxed the fields and silent treetops out of blackness to the edge of colour, mixed in a misty glimmer over Oxford with the city's mild sodium glare. 'Wow . . . amazing,' I said.

'Wow, amazing to get out of it – out of Oxford, and yeah, just out of it!' said Nick. Then we sat down, sat leaning on each other, on our wooden bench. My right hand seemed to be lying on his thigh, the thumb rubbing consolingly. 'What do you think?' I said, with the certainty, in the pot, that it was part of a conversation.

'I think . . .' Nick laughed quietly, gazed into the night, 'what do I think . . . ?' My thumb lay still, my hand might not have been there. 'I think you're lovely, no, you are, you're lovely,' and again the thread of soft laughter in him, in general, and from the undescribed liberties of smoking. It was a surrender, and everything was delightful or absurd but anyway utterly unworrying. His words hovered warmly, in the hazy moonlight just above the wall – I was peering at them, dwelling on them, just as he was, like a prospect, that had materialized before us and around us as we leant together, pressed together. I turned, twisted a little, as I leaned in, my lips touched his strong white neck, the edge of his jaw, 'Ooh,' he said softly, 'goodness,' before I stretched up and kissed him, the smell and taste of his mouth, pot, saliva, his breath, the masculine truth of him, which was everything I wanted. He pushed his lips out then, closed his mouth as my tongue peeped at it from side to side.

'Goodness!' he said, and laughed again, but with a shift in the shading of the word. He was standing, and reached back with a hand which I clutched and when he'd pulled me up once more he linked his arm in mine to steer us back, my arm was squeezed against his side, he was very warm and funny but it seemed to me a pointless second-best to what we should have been doing. It was hard to see exactly where we were treading. My confusion in the shadowy time-lapse of thought and action, being truly stoned, as Nick said, muffled the dismay of rejection. It was somehow as if we'd had an affair, broken up and agreed to remain the best of friends, all in four minutes. In a few more seconds we might decide to get together again. Or had it all taken much longer than that . . . The clock in the kitchen said quarter to one. Jenny and Joanne were clearing up, after a fashion, and Jenny said, 'Where have you two been?' and Nick said, 'Ooh, just looking at the moon in the garden!' and peeped at me and giggled and put his arm through mine again.

'Well, it's legal,' said Joanne, 'we know that!' and we all laughed loudly, each in our own way, and Nick, his features strikingly downlit under the tin lampshade, looked at Jenny and blushed.

Jenny showed me to an attic room with the bed made up, surely slept in before, but I was sweaty and parched, and threw back the sheet and lay uncovered in the deep country dark. I crept downstairs to piss, and get a glass of water, crept back, over creaking landings, and I couldn't bear it, the missed chance. I didn't knock, I went in carefully. Nick's room was much bigger, and a disorienting mess. He had fallen asleep in his pants, on his front, with the bedside light on, the covers thrown back. I stood holding my tumbler of water and looking at him. I knew he was an ordinary man, normal-looking, but the sight of his long lightly muscular back and round buttocks just covered by the small white pants, the hunch of his left shoulder and plumped upper arm, scruffy back of his head on the pillow, overwhelmed me. His slow-paced breaths, little snores very nearly, persisted. And then something, some shared consciousness, paused the rhythm and over the space of four or five seconds of silent confusion he turned round and opened his eyes.

We looked at each other, and nothing I thought I'd like to say seemed possible.

'Can't you sleep?' he said, and it was that soft adult masculine note of concern and protection that pierced me.

'Not really,' I said, 'no.'

He seemed to weigh it up, what was in our best interests. He shifted himself back, pushed off the bedclothes to make space for me to get in and stretch out on the crumpled sheet that was warm from his body. I turned on my side to face him, the pillow warm too and magically damp from the sweat of his neck and his head; then he pulled up the sheet and a blanket over us. I was tensely aware of how all these sensations were new to me, the radiating heat and close breath of a grown man in bed, as novel and daunting as the bed itself, a big, broad, old-fashioned bed for a husband and wife, with a dark walnut headboard, and heavy hard mattress. We lay and looked at each other, Nick drowsy again, closing his eyes with a smile on his lips that stayed there, as if he'd forgotten it. It felt wrong to stare at him, so I closed my eyes too, and after a minute his breathing slowed and when I peeped over the rise of the pillow his smile had passed on into a sleeper's gape. And again I couldn't bear it, this hanging on the threshold of permission, self-invited but not turned away and even, uncertainly, encouraged. I put my hand on his neck as he slept, as if pulling him to me to kiss him, though for now we stayed just where we were. We didn't move, for long minutes, and the touch felt stolen as much as allowed, and a little absurd. I don't think he properly woke, but he mumbled as he rolled his head and turned over, shouldered into his pillow and shifted back against me – and then in one movement my arm was around him, my face in his smoky-smelling hair and my hand on his heart, which had a strong waking beat. No resistance, no knowing what it meant to him. He must have felt my awkwardly angled dick pressed against him as my hand wandered helplessly down to trace and lift the slumbering weight of his own. The Nick laugh, that had brightened the whole evening, was a shock now. 'Not now, Dave,' he said, 'get some sleep, put the light out,' and he twisted round and kissed me lightly on the lips before I did what he said (put the light out, that is – I lay there for agonized hours as the miracle of being in bed with him was nibbled away by the heat and the hangover and the longing).

The sun rose soon, not on our side of the house, so the room filled up with the indirect light of an early May morning, and the implacable singing of ten thousand birds, some so close under the eaves they might have been in the room itself. The large dressing table, wardrobe and armchair started to make sense, the solid world of Walter's family, preserved under the slews of Nick's clothes, cardboard boxes, books stacked and later knocked over on the floor. Something in me recoiled in judgement, and puzzlement, at being in the privacy of this room, the private space of a man I'd never heard of before last night, this night, still in force although the sun was up before five. I spent a long time, on that hard instructive mattress, gazing at the room, the damp-marked ceiling, the central light fitting with its brown parchment lampshades; and then at Nick's shoulders, and shyly, when he turned over, at his face, which seemed, without glasses, more naked than his body without clothes. My watch, nearly noiseless, showed I'd lost quarter-hours, half-hours, to sleep. By nine o'clock I ached to get up, but couldn't bear the thought of missing the moment Nick woke beside me; then wondered if I would be a horrible puzzle and shock to him. In fact when he woke, he scratched his head, yawned, groaned, lay on his back with his hands behind his head and his sandy armpit close to my face. 'How's your head?' he said. 'Absolutely terrible,' I said, 'how's yours?' '*Pretty* terrible,' he said, and that little exchange was a marvel, as if we woke up beside each other every day. There we lay, in our pants, under the tugged-about blankets, and I thought just perhaps he was as helplessly excited as I was. He got out of bed and kept his back to me as he pulled on his trousers, and when he'd gone off to the bathroom I hurried upstairs and got dressed myself.

We went down to breakfast together. Tim and Joanne had stayed over, too smashed to get back to Tim's college, and were not yet to be seen. Walt and Stella were in dressing gowns, still sleepily tangled with each other above and below the table, morning evidence of the night they'd just spent, which shocked me, in spite of myself. 'I brought you some tea,' Joanne said to me, 'but you weren't in your room.' 'Ah, no,' said Nick, 'he wasn't,' with a mysterious look. Jenny noisily refilled the kettle, and whatever thoughts she had about the night before seemed lost in the larger hindrance of her hangover. I sipped my tea, bit queasily at a corner of toast. Nick looked pained by the light, but unbothered about having spent the night with me. He allowed the assumption that something had happened between us to hover amusingly, unchallenged over breakfast in the kitchen. This felt like a great kindness to me, and our unagreed keeping of our secret had something amorous about it, even though the secret was that nothing had happened, and perhaps never would.

16

I booked the punt three days before, laid out five pounds on hock from the JCR cellar, wrapped two glasses in a tea-towel, and put them safely in my knapsack with some bits to eat bought in the market. 'It's very naughty,' said Nick on the phone, 'I should be revising.' He havered, he almost took the shine off the thing he was naughtily agreeing to: 'And you should be revising too.' 'Don't worry about me,' I said. 'And bring your books with you. You can revise all you like while I punt you along.' 'OK then, I will!' he said, with his laugh that I loved. I thumbed in another sixpence with all the cheerful neediness of the one who is calling and paying to keep the call going, and adapted to this more courtly idea of our outing, with Nick in the pampered and supine role, while I took care of everything else. I knew I could bring it off, I was a strong punter, even on the nearly unreachable mud of the Isis itself. This time I saw us going far up the Cherwell, past the Parks and into the countryside, the river winding through cornfields. There was a point when Nick put the marker in his book, rocked the boat a bit as he stood up to pull off his shirt and his jeans, and after a second's hesitation his white pants, then dived without saying a word into the cool weedy water.

I woke up, and after five seconds the painful happiness that had kept me from falling asleep until three in the morning gripped me again, the certainty of being alone with him for two or three hours, whatever happened; as I dressed I suggested to myself that nothing happening was most likely, and beautiful in itself. What had hung alive and tormenting in my thoughts through the past ten days was his night-time 'Not now, Dave.' I ran it so often in my head that I lost the pitch, the piercing lightness of Nick's own voice; then I let it surprise me and the breathtaking minute came back to me, holding him in bed and feeling his cock, a freedom he didn't resist but swiftly postponed – *Not now, Dave.* Or was that what he meant? Was this the first half of a beautiful proposition – not now but the next time, when we're not hungover or overheard? Or was it just a kind way of saying, in effect, *Not ever?*

I was early at the river, at the shed on the cobbled slipway that leads down from the road to the punts, tethered and fanned out by the gentle current under Magdalen Bridge. The boatman had a look at me, 'Mr Win – ah, yes, I remember . . .' He fetched out the cushions and I was just hopping onto the boat with them when I heard Nick's laugh from the pavement above – he must have seen someone he knew – and his voice with its happiness and cleverness made me shiver as if he had touched me. I pretended I hadn't heard him, got on with fitting in the heavy old cushions, and the knapsack with the picnic, and then trod my way back along the boat for the paddle and pole as he appeared at the top of the slipway. The picturesque tree overhanging the shed blocked my view for a second before I saw it was Walter he was talking to.

'Look who I found!'

'Sorry, Dave, Nick just told me and it sounded such a heavenly idea.' This wasn't quite how Walt normally spoke. I think I disguised my plunging sense of folly and betrayal. 'Such a heavenly day,' Walt said, and by now the air of pretence was unmissable. But Nick flung his arms round me, a pinion, with no room for amorous nonsense, though the hardness and heat of him took my breath away, and he kissed me loudly on the cheek as he stood back. So I didn't know what on earth to think.

'Do you want me to start off?' said Walt.

'Absolutely not,' I said.

'Oh . . . OK!'

'No, no, Walt' – I smiled smoothly at him – 'this is my treat.'

'Well, perhaps I can take over later on.' He handed Nick past him along the punt, and sat down facing me, with a kind of sunny presumption and I thought a clear hint of anxiety: he wasn't such a good actor as me. Nick sat with his back to me, but looked round with a grin and said, 'Great idea of yours! So glad I came.' I saw myself calling the whole thing off, in a spasm of wrecking emotion.

Then I thought, as I backed us out into the stream, and avoided the unseen hazard of the bridge that loomed behind me, that Walt believed he was doing me a kindness, saving me from the much worse wreck of an afternoon alone with Nick on the river: the two of them had agreed to that. He smiled and lifted the paddle to fend off another punt coming in beside us. I brought the boat round, and we set off up the long brown tree-shadowed stretch beside Magdalen walks.

I had a task to do, and as I whisked up the pole and thrust it down again, let it trail as a rudder before flinging it back up, I was forgivably abstracted, dodging branches, dodging tyros and tourists as they bumped round in circles, and seizing the way ahead. I was immediately fixated on not being overtaken. Nick had a carrier bag with his books in, and he took one out as if not really doing so, but soon seemed to be properly involved in it. Walt had brought nothing, he smiled at me and started to chat, then made a guilty face about disturbing Nick. 'Don't mind me!' Nick said. 'But we do!' I said.

When we came out ten minutes later from under the trees the high summer cloud quickly parted and distanced itself, and I laid the pole down across the punt for a moment to take off my shirt. 'My dear!' said Walt, looking me over, and Nick glanced round and raised his eyebrows but didn't say anything as I passed the shirt down to him to keep it dry – I shivered again as the shirt slipped from my hands into his. 'You're in pretty good shape, Dave, I'd say,' Walt said, as I took up the pole again and pushed on. 'You didn't expect that, I suppose,' I said. 'Well, I don't know about that . . .' said Walt, and waggled his head, and I knew then, if I hadn't at the start, that he was in the picture about me, he was flirting the way straight young men do with a gay one they like, not to show that they want him but the opposite, that they feel utterly unthreatened. Also perhaps he felt it would be kind, lying back with a smile and watching me work, to do some of the flirting he sensed I had hoped for from Nick. 'So, Stella says the play's shaping up well,' he said.

'Oh, she's amazing,' I said, 'so funny – well, you can imagine.'

Walt looked slightly smug at this. 'That's what she says about you. But you've got such a huge part.'

'I know, it's ridiculous,' I said.

'And you've learned yours already.'

'Oh, I'm not quite there yet, Walt.'

'Really?' He trailed his fingers in the sunlit water. 'You haven't got it with you?'

'Well, it's in my bag,' I said, 'behind you,' and he twisted round to get it.

'Shall I test you on your lines?'

I didn't answer at first, but Nick said again, 'Honestly, don't mind me,' so I said, 'Well, OK then, if you're sure.' I saw the charm of showing off to both of them. 'Just hear me through Act Three, Scene One.' He found the place, nodded at me, and with a quick gasp of self-consciousness, lost in my long breath as the pole fell through my hands, I launched into Mosca's great soliloquy on parasites. Walt was attentive, self-conscious for a moment himself as he listened, and I wished I could have seen

Nick's face. I didn't need help, I'd known the speech by heart for weeks, and I did it as a proof of my worth, a sort of offering, futile but not unhappy. And so we went on, it was oddly a public performance, a student and his parents in a passing punt turned and smiled at this Oxford eccentricity.

> ' – your fine elegant rascal, that can rise
> And stoop, almost together, like an arrow;
> Shoot through the air, as nimbly as a star,
> Turn short, as does a swallow; and be here,
> And there, and here, and yonder, all at once'

– I timed my breaths as best I could to the rhythm of punting, but there were some peculiar stresses and a cheerful feeling of doing it against the odds. A feeling too that I was in my element, like Mosca himself – in a minute Nick raised his head and gazed at the bank as I spoke, then turned and smiled up at me so that I nearly lost my place.

We all got out at the rollers, and heaved the punt up past the weir to the gleaming higher level. Then I took us through Parsons' Pleasure, and the spectacle of men, mostly older and donnish but with some tarty-looking students of our age in among them, chatting and moving around quite matter-of-factly with nothing on. They were the first completely naked men I'd seen since I'd punted last year, though I acted blasé about them. A boy dived in, I saw him welling, brightening in the brownish river till he surfaced by the punt, spouting water, grinning as he ducked back under with a flash of his arse, the happy subtext of my painful day. Walter spotted his Classics tutor, a floppy-haired old man with a white pot-belly and gigantic cock, standing and staring with his hands on his hips, and didn't know whether to wave as we thrust on past – it was a funny situation. Then we were out and alongside the Parks, with a cricket match just in earshot among the sounds of the river.

Here we had our little picnic, in the boat by the bank under a willow. I unwrapped the two glasses – 'Oh, god, I'm sorry,' said Walt, 'I've fucked up your plans, you probably wanted to be alone.' Nick said nothing, and I said, 'Well, we were hoping to have a long conversation about you' – I was still giving in, as graciously as I could. We shared the glasses, on a not quite clear basis, and ate the bits of cheese and fruit – the wine was too warm but it was good and it went to my thirsty head; the little feast had the oddest air of something secret discovered and normalized, and robbed of its point. At the end Walter hopped off to have a piss beside the tree. I busied myself with the rubbish, but Nick watched him benignly, as a figure in the pastoral scene. 'Do you want me to take over for a bit?' Walt said when he came back.

'OK,' I said.

'You must have some work to get on with too – I mean other than the play.'

It was true that one scene I'd pictured was of Nick and me tied up under low-hanging trees, each of us revising until the pretence grew absurd and we rolled into each other's arms – I'd even put Temple on the Dutch East Indies in my bag with the bottle and the Tupperware box. When I dug it out now, it was surreal as a prop in a play, like the leatherbound volume of *Punch* that I'd used in *The Tempest*. The question was whether I sat facing Nick or fitted in next to him, did I want to be touching him or catching his eye? He decided it by changing round himself, and patting the seat beside him. 'Sit here, Dave,' he said, 'and we can admire Walter's punting.'

'I'm a damn good punter,' said Walt.

'So we've heard,' said Nick. So a camp little game, of weirdly deflected interests, ensued, as Walt pulled his shirt over his head, and Nick and I whistled and grinned at him. He was still very white, with a drinker's tummy starting and a bit of reddish chest hair, but manly and nice and not remotely exciting. He crouched and angled us out under the trees with a long shallow thrust, straightened our course with a sweep of the pole through the current behind us, and took us on up the river. I slid down bit by bit beside Nick, watched him reading with something of the mystery of being in bed with him, so close as he turned the pages and marked and underlined things in pencil; I was intrigued to see his writing, neat and small and with the rapid weight of the thing I half forgot, his scholarly intellect. Soft waves of alarm went through me at the thought of all I still had to do, the term sliding past as swift and soundless as the muddy Cherwell. It was a book on Maynard Keynes and the Paris Conference he was reading. When I woke up, parched and out of place, my head was on his shoulder and his right arm along the bench behind me. Walter, red in the sun and sweating, smiled as I sat upright, and my heavy book fell down between my knees. I went through the little act of waking up in company, the foolishness and mild self-admiration. Nick said, 'Hello, there!' and took his arm back, ostensibly to write something down. I twisted round to try and see where we were. The river had wide weedy margins here, and soon a fallen tree that nearly blocked our progress. No one else was on the water this far from town. After the fallen elm we passed into a clearer stretch, high clouds in the blue above Walter's head, cattle barely aware of us as we slid past, and the far-off hum of a major road somehow sealing us into our adventure, just the flicker of the pole above the reeds to show we were there.

17

In the morning, I'd done the Civil War paper, produced a spooky simulacrum of a second-year essay on Crown and Commonwealth, and then put together in a mood of perplexity another essay on the Diggers in Northamptonshire – I seemed to watch myself tying off the ends and summing up as I might have watched a technician assemble with wires and solder some specialized but obsolete device. 'Yeah, it was OK,' I said, when we'd come out into the steeply shadowed quadrangle at the side of the Schools – symbolic quadrangle of high dark buildings on three sides but open to the street on the fourth, the airy wall through which, with the last paper done, we would pass out into the rest of our lives.

Coming in again after lunch for the Age of Empire, climbing the stone stairs and taking my place in the vast lofty room, I found my sense of estrangement extended to the hundreds of others popping their mortarboards under their chairs, sitting forward, aligning their pens and waiting for the order to turn over the paper and begin. I had just the same neighbours, I hadn't noticed them before, and I felt the current running through them all in their gowns and bow ties, heads throbbing with figures and dates and clinching quotations, about to write for dear life, all these personal reckonings happening in unison, with just a side-glance of rivalry as the race began. Staveley, the friendless scholar from Trinity, seemed by just sitting with his hand on the unopened writing-book to reach out for his First and his fellowship. He'd trained for this moment, and you knew he had no pity or feeling for the others who had failed to prepare, whose drunken whoops from outside the King's Arms had reached him as he worked each night until closing time in the top-floor reading room across the street. Next to him, beautiful Stapleford was in improvised subfusc, Jim Morrison hair tied back in a rubber band: there was something charming in his lack of expectation. I couldn't see Tim or any other friends, round the corner in the L-shaped hall. Wyatt, Wynford and Zukofsky made up the back row with me.

Now the clock in its pedimented housing showed the hour and the invigilating don said, 'You may begin!' – something courteously conditional in the phrase, to my ear, as I looked through the questions. I was almost pretending to myself I could do it, when I knew, for the first time in my life, that I couldn't. The typography, the layout, the gleaming cream paper were entirely familiar, they were every exam I had taken and triumphed in till now. Time: 3 hours. Answer one question from Section 1, and any two questions from either Section 2 or Section 3. I put my hand to my brow and peeped under it at Wyatt, a large dark-haired man writing left-handed and very fast with his arm round the page and his tongue peeping out. I looked again at the options in Section 1, with a ghostly lost sense that if they'd asked me a year ago about the East India Company I could have let them have it, but that anything I wrote now would be a mere sociable summary, as I might have explained it to someone in the pub, with none of the necessary data that Wyatt must be summoning up, as he sat back and blinked at the clock before sitting forward and scribbling some more.

I went halfway to meet the first question in Section 2, on British rule in India after the First World War – it should have been a gift, a sort of premature reward, but I had a broody feeling that Burma, which was part of the Indian Empire till 1937, was my private subject, on which I couldn't and shouldn't be examined. I understood it as much through Orwell as through any textbook. I saw it in the Atlas of the World, with its tapering tail cut off and pinned on a later page: I knew the physical essentials, the mountains, the rainfall, the three rivers. But really my feeling of possessing the place was a well-guarded ignorance, an unbreakable reluctance to learn. All this I seemed wordlessly to recognize. I got over the page, still with the morning's sense of puzzled detachment from my own actions, and with something else unpredicted rising, and rising. I saw myself playing Mosca, the sweaty chill of exertion, Marryat on Curzon in my bag in the Green Room, looked through blindly between rehearsals; I was acting revising, but the play, all that time, was my life. I took in the shock and admiration of those who assumed I was so confident I could bring off both things at once. And I had a huge success with it – the *Times* reviewer had no space for Ed Newman's Volpone, the piece, like the show itself, had been all about me. And then, since the play, a strange lethargy of avoidance, afternoons on the river, a never-faced feeling it was now too late to catch up. Now the reckoning had come, and what I'd been stubbornly preparing for was my own failure – an idea so new and repellent that the only way forward was to seize it and brandish it.

I stood up and turned, too sure to be self-conscious, I knew my unexpected action would impinge for no more than a moment on the thoughts of those sunk in concentration beside me – I was going to the toilet, forgetting the rules, not asking permission. I went swiftly and quietly, eyes ahead, eyes down, to the closed double doors at the back of the hall, and tugged open the right-hand door with a swallowed sense of the last chance and then, outside on the unpeopled landing, of no return. I went down the great stone staircase, fast but not leaping, heard footsteps above me, and a voice, stern, anxious but reined in, and now I ran, across the black and white marble expanse of the hall floor, in its passive indescribable emptiness, amid the pressure of sixteen hundred young people, in the rooms opening off it, intently and silently writing, and out, in a surge of reckless triumph and catastrophe, into the everyday High Street. Running footsteps behind me, 'Hello . . . ! I say, Mr Win . . . !' and I did glance back, to see the winged invigilator bearing down the long broad slope of the pavement, but I ran, and fast, back to college by an unobvious way, and with a feeling as I strode past the lodge and into the quiet quad of being a trespasser. I dreaded meeting Humphrey, and nipped along the kitchen corridor and into the quad from the back to avoid passing his window, where I would have been an impossible and heart-breaking sight.

In my room I dropped the catch on the door, the air unbreathable, among the books and papers I'd stared at a mere fifty minutes before, the scene of fraying preparation for the thing I'd discovered I was not going to do. I tore out of my subfusc, pulled on jeans and a T-shirt, denim jacket, snatched up my wallet, and then a notebook, from a feeling already forming that all these involuntary actions would need to be accounted for. Then I left college by the back gate and made my way with a lifetime's gathered knowledge of the place through college quads and gardens and back lanes to Magdalen Bridge and off out down St Clements till I reached South Park, where the vast open slope seemed either to swallow me up or to offer me up – I climbed in a long diagonal to the summit, and sat under a lime tree with a view of all Oxford, old Oxford, towers and spires cupped unreally between hills, flattened and condensed, like a picture from an age before perspective, an illumination. It was the view of the city from the opposite side from Boars Hill, and closer up.

What I'd done was both startling and inevitable. I couldn't tell yet if the crisis was over now or if it was just beginning. I didn't want to explain myself, I put nothing in the notebook, and I wondered if in fact there was a way back – Humphrey would argue for me, passionately, if with a painful sense that the trouble had been brewing for months. They might allow me a resit, under special conditions – everything would be focused on undoing my mistake and bringing to its proper conclusion the serious story of my first-class education.

To get to Gloucester Green I worked out a route, through Christ Church Meadow and up as best I could through the fenced-off rubble of St Ebbe's. My sense of dodging like an outlaw was the ragged upshot of having no plan, of acting irrationally, and with an instinctual feeling that I had to be kept from reason. Even so, to be sitting on the bus as it started up and headed towards Botley had something appalling about it. The familiar tree-lined road, along which Mum and Esme had ferried me for three years at the start and the end of each term, seemed to pass like a viaduct over an abyss, the bus pulling in time after time and opening its doors to let me off while I sat tight at the back. The other passengers were old people, women with shopping, students turning in their seats to chat with each other in the weightless summer of their second year. None of them had any idea about me.

I plucked the cord and got down at the Boars Hill turning, and when the bus moved off I saw myself six weeks earlier, with my bottle of rosé and no knowledge Nick existed. A van came past, a breeze stirred the roadside hedges, and in the vacant afternoon I walked on, past Robert Bridges' house, and Masefield's, where Graves had lived for a while in the cottage in the garden. That seemed a lovely idea, till I caught through an open gate the famous view of Oxford, or the view of Oxford caught me. A baler was turning at the bottom of the field, clank and rumble of haymaking, swallows diving. High up in the ash tree beside Walter's gate a thrush sang a mad scene, made it up as it went along, wild piercing runs and unconnected afterthoughts, mimicking the nearby finches and blackbirds before it came back to itself.

The cars weren't there – Walter must be in college – no, he'd have gone to meet Stella by now, out of Schools, and their shared relief that her paper was done would be cut through already by the hardly believable news. My drama now became his – theirs, my friends', who were thinking their way backwards, for signs this was coming, well, the play, of course, a huge part, and other things, probably much earlier on, thought of sometimes but never talked of, the underlying strain that someone like me must be under. No one answered the front-door bell, for a minute the breeze hissed and died in the beeches overhead, and the absurdity of finding myself here alone passed through me in a wave of despair. I thought loosely of my friends as a group but there was only one person I wanted, and trusted to help me – he was in some obvious inexplicable way both the cause and the solution. I stood back and stared up, where two upstairs windows on the front of the house were wide open, and catching the sun. I strolled round the side with the remote sense I'd had on and off of trespassing, and slouched about to show I felt at home. When I shaded my eyes with my hand to peer in through the dining-room window, I saw myself with unexpected brilliance in the oval mirror that hung over the sideboard, peering back. From the corner of the house you looked down over the lawn where we'd played croquet, and there on the grass by the bench was Nick, with Jenny. It had never occurred to me that Jenny would be with him.

She was lying on her front to read, with her bikini top undone and her breasts squashed under her against the rug. She'd tucked up the lower part into the crack of her arse, to maximize her tan. Nick was in shorts, nothing else, and sitting cross-legged with his back to me. The sizzle of the breeze in the beeches and towering poplars made a large airy cataract of sound, and I came down the steps undetected; even my 'Hello!'

had them doubting their senses for a moment, Jenny looked at me, quite blankly, then shook her head in a mime of surprise. 'What's that?' said Nick, with his nervous but tolerant laugh, before looking round.

Jenny turned away, half sat up as she fiddled behind her back to fix her top. Nick swivelled about without getting up. 'Dave! How did it go?' he said. 'Are Walt and Stella with you?' and I saw that for them the rent in the fabric was invisible, my arrival unexpected but the timings made reasonable sense. As I approached them Nick's smile had its mixture of humour, and concern, and calculation (I'd forgotten its exact but indescribable effect on me). I stood above them, like a child for a moment, bringing some unguessed calamity to the capable self-possessed adults on the lawn. I touched Nick on the shoulder as I stepped past him, and sat down cross-legged at the edge of Jenny's rug – I was in the fresh shock of his presence, raised my right hand against the sun to look at him, and also to fend off the horrible feeling that I'd broken in on some everyday, never-thought-of togetherness of theirs. Well, here they were, this was where they lived, they were old friends . . .

When I'd told them, I had my first chance to examine the impact of my news. Reflected back to me, it had a scale that in the trance of escape, the passive but ingenious mood of the past few hours, I hadn't had a chance to grasp. Jenny bit her lower lip. 'I'm sure they'll let you sit it again, Dave, won't they, you could have done it today, you said yourself you're a wizard at exams.' Nick took longer, nodding and thinking, the nervous laugh, before he reached out a hand and took mine, gripped it as he jerked it about, to show he wouldn't be shaken off. Then the telephone was ringing inside the house, and Jenny jumped up and went in. I sensed Nick for the first time was a little bit scared of me, or alarmed by my dependency on him. He was a friend, of my age, revising for his own exams next week, I was everything that wasn't meant to happen. We sat like that, cross-legged, knee to knee, my right hand clasped in his left, and the conviction that he loved me held the disaster off, beyond the lawn and the house and the trees that leant forward and drew themselves up again over and over.

Jenny came out of the house and we stood and went towards her. 'It was Walt,' she said, 'I told him you're here. He's coming back now.' Nick had his arm round my shoulders, my hand slid round his waist, smooth skin hot from the sun. In the kitchen Jenny, with the adult presence she assumed in that room, said, 'I think you should ring your tutor, straight away – Henry, is he?'

I took a while to answer. 'Humphrey . . . yes, well, I suppose,' but my idea of this talk, the shame and reproach and concern, and the tantalizing fear of being talked round to taking the paper again, loomed impenetrably before me.

'Walt says they let people resit papers, you know, if something like this happens. It happens quite often.'

'Yeah, but I couldn't do the paper,' I said.

'Well, I don't believe that for a minute.' She stared at me. 'You mean you couldn't do it just now, or you couldn't do it next week?'

'Both.'

'Well, I don't know what happened, of course. Sorry . . .' – she shook her head and looked down – 'I didn't mean to bark at you.'

Nick all this while was quiet, leaning by the sink. He had made his shorts himself, by cutting the legs off an old pair of jeans, and the square greyish bottoms of the pockets hung down an inch below the frayed hem. His legs were beautiful, the whole lean vanityless presence of him so overwhelming that I burst into tears, and it seemed to me he was the reason for breaking down, and not the afternoon's disaster. He let Jenny walk over and comfort me, which she did stiffly, herself a little frightened. Then, as I controlled myself and took deep breaths, he said, 'I think . . . well, you're a perfectionist, Dave. I bet, I'm sure, you could have done the paper, but you couldn't face not doing your best, and rather than compromise your First you thought you'd blow up the whole thing.'

I felt straight away that this was clever, and plausible, and quite beside the point. We heard a car outside, and then Walter came through, Stella tactfully behind him. She was in her sub-fusc, the black skirt and stockings, black ribbon tie undone. She brought a taste of the Examination Schools into the kitchen, and something more confounding, a glimpse of the exhausted relief of the hundreds who'd stayed at their desks and seen the thing through, and were waiting to reap the rewards.

18

The thing resolved itself, took on its own unsatisfactory form, over the coming week. I'd done something instinctual which justified itself in argument: I wanted to do things on my terms and not theirs. 'Yes, my dear David, but what?' said Humphrey when I saw him the next day.

'I just needed to act,' I said.

'Rather, you mean, than to be acted on?'

This sounded like mere cleverness, Humphrey's way of turning everything round. 'Perhaps you're right,' I said.

In college, friends who had finished Finals were extending their lunch on the grass, more beers brought out, leisure they hardly knew what to do with as the last days of all this life brightened and faded. I avoided them, I felt more than ever unknown, incomprehensible – a form of solitude that opened up a larger space within itself, since I barely understood my own actions, and had no idea, having done what I had, about what to do next. Humphrey was consumed by it, made representations to the examiners, it was upsetting how much he cared, and fought for me. The Senior Dean said I might get an aegrotat, which involved an admission I was ill. I could see a psychologist, a good man from the Warneford, the legendary madhouse that hovered on the hill above Oxford, a short walk from the spot I'd unthinkingly fled to, when I ran out of Schools. Peter Roddick, in my year, had taken his Prelims in the Warneford, between schizophrenic episodes in which he acted like a different person, attaching himself to strangers in the High Street and trying to go home with them.

Mum said she'd come to Oxford and collect me, but I couldn't face the school-like loading of the car – trunk and books and stereo and people watching. The pitiless clearing out of rooms had begun. I hardly knew which was worse, everything ending, or my not being part of it. I secured a further two weeks in my room, and hitched a lift back to Foxleigh. Standing at the bottom of Cumnor Hill with my arm out and thumb raised as car after car accelerated past me, I saw myself again through the eyes of the English driver, the boy of seventeen smiling out from the verge at the racist, the policeman and the optimistic middle-aged man who'd stopped for me and given me his number.

When I got to Crackers I let myself in quietly, as if I could avoid detection, and questions. It was half-past two, Mum was back at the shop, and it was Esme who heard me and came into the hall. 'Oh, dear, old lovey,' she said, and we stood in our usual uncertainty about how to greet each other. In the kitchen as she made me a sandwich she felt her way forward. 'As long as you're all right, that's what I said to Av,' she said.

'I'm sure I'll be fine,' I said, and she looked at me shrewdly. I sat at the table and ate my sandwich, and the eating seemed an admission of a larger hunger and need for help.

'All got a bit much for you, didn't it, Dave,' Esme said. 'Not surprising really, it makes me feel weak when I think what you had to do,' and she plonked herself down in the chair opposite. 'I'm afraid your mother's been in a bit of a state about it all.' I knew this kind of second-hand reproach, but I had the feeling Esme was suggesting solidarity with me. 'She's had a word with your tutor – it seems you could still do it.' And I saw as if in another room all Mum's grief and anxiety, and thought perhaps that was the worst thing about it, the crisis for her, who had steered me through everything, somehow, superbly, up till the end of last week.

Back in my room with its view of the drive and once in an hour, perhaps, a car passing the gate, I was something between a convict and a convalescent. I heard the car, and Mum coming home early. I felt I would get the upshot of their own anxious talks about what to do, and felt a certain embarrassment at their not being up to the task. We were stiff with each other when I went down, and she seemed not to know what tone she would take, her sternness was panicked and beyond her control. We had tea in the kitchen, trapped in our uncertainty. Was the crisis still going on, deserving hush and tenderness, or were we ready for hard talk about what to do next?

'We don't want you *slumping*,' said Mum, and her brisk almost comical tone smuggled in a pronominal subtlety: the bucking-up 'we' of the hospital nurse had merged with her first ever use, in her years as a mother, of the parent's 'we': she and Esme were in this together. It bothered me, and I said, 'I have no intention of slumping.' There was an irksome fog of cluelessness, neither of the women had been to university or knew about the theatre. I couldn't quite look at Mum, or acknowledge what she knew of the horror and hardship of going it alone.

I went out in the garden with a book, rather as I had in the past when exams were approaching – though even last vac I'd had *Volpone* with me too, sat marking it up as though revising, a reassuring sight at the end of the lawn. Now Barry had mown the grass and was doing the edges with long-handled shears. I didn't know what he'd picked up from Esme's gossip, we nodded and exchanged a few words as he came along sideways towards me. 'Hope things look up for you, then, Dave,' he said, and edged his way on past. I sensed how the idea of me that he'd picked up from the women, as a scholar at

Oxford, 'all rather over our heads, I'm afraid', was mixed up with other feelings – guesses and suspicions – unresolved for years.

Nick and Jenny and Walter and Stella were driving to Italy in Walt's Peugeot, sharing the driving. For a day or two there was meaningless talk about me joining them – 'You can drive, can't you, Dave?' Stella said. Jenny's line was practical, they were going for three weeks, they'd need to have bags on the back seat and under their feet as it was. I said, almost grateful for the snub, 'No, no, there just wouldn't be room.'

I made do with a meeting with Nick in London, an immense July day in Kensington Gardens. I was early at the Albert Memorial, walked to and fro lost between the soot-blackened Continents, India unveiling herself on an elephant, China, presumably, cross-legged at her feet. I had a fear we would be hidden from each other by the monument itself, going round and round it like a game or a dream – the gates were open, and I trotted up the wide flight of steps to look at the writers and artists in the frieze, Homer and Shakespeare and William Blake all crowded together. When I saw Nick coming, down the avenue of plane trees on the Hyde Park side, I strolled on round the corner as if I hadn't noticed him. I think I wanted to be found, not to be forever the seeker.

A minute later here he was, we were on, and time, that had crept and jumped unbearably all morning, ran forward with breathless smoothness and speed. He'd seen me and come in and climbed the steps – he gave a big smile when he strode round the corner towards me, then looked down almost shyly. He was in baggy brown trousers and a white shirt not tucked in and half unbuttoned . . . in the breeze he seemed to flow around the lean core of himself as he approached along the chequered pavement. He was what I'd remembered night after night and he was everything else that memory hadn't got to yet, and never could. We met and his tight hug and kiss on the cheek made me gasp and look round in case we'd been seen.

He said why didn't we walk up to the cafe by the Serpentine, and get a sandwich or something, and already the day was reshaped by his practicality. We sauntered down the steps and round past Europe, on to the path through the trees. 'So where are you staying?' he said.

I told him I was staying at Brian Wood's flat.

'I don't know him, do I?' Nick said.

'Yeah, he was in my college . . . It's just near here,' I said, glancing over my shoulder, 'Queen's Gate, do you know . . . ? They're all away in Spain for three weeks.'

'Well, that's handy,' said Nick. He couldn't have known how I'd tidied it up last night and put a bottle of Quentin Wood's Riesling in the ice-box just in case. 'And how have you been?'

'Oh . . . well . . . OK . . . you know . . . not marvellous—'

'And thank you for your letter, by the way. I ought to have written back.'

I shrugged this off. 'Oh, that's fine.'

'No, it was bad of me. I just wasn't sure . . .'

'I know,' I said, 'I know,' though I wasn't sure either. For the first time in my life I'd become a great burden on people, and it was part of the beauty of Nick that he never let it show.

I wanted everything about him, and at the same time shrank from his news. 'So when are you off?' I said, as levelly as I could.

'Oh, tomorrow, first thing. We're getting the ten o'clock ferry. Walt's picking me up at *five-thirty a.m.*' I'd only thought up to now of all of them in Walt's car, but it was the image of the ferry pulling out from the dock that turned me over with longing.

'You'll have a wonderful time,' I said; and we walked on under the great planes, while he told me very flatly where they were going – Pisa, Florence, Perugia (where they joined Walt's parents for three days), then on to Rome. He tried, out of niceness, to make it sound a bore and barely worth the effort, and the driving.

'It doesn't sound *too* bad,' I said, and he smiled and said, 'I'm sure it will all be fine.'

It simply didn't occur to me, in the minutes that followed, while we strolled beside the Serpentine, rowing boats and pedalos out, and the faint haunting stink of the lake in summer, that he might have had his Finals results, and the question, when I thought of it, seemed too perilous. I put my hand lightly on his shoulder, to help him through, as I said, 'I'm assuming you've not heard yet?'

'What's that?' he said, as if I had further bad news of my own.

'About Schools . . .'

'Oh,' he said, 'yes, I have, I heard on Monday,' quite matter of fact, I couldn't tell if modest in success or unbothered by defeat, but the whole five seconds had a desolating charge for me, the enactment in real life of the moment I could only know now as a spectator: 'Yeah, I scraped through.' 'Oh yes . . . ?' 'I managed it, I got a First.' He couldn't help grinning then, and I walked on a little ahead of him, my face stiff with grief. 'I'm so glad,' I said, 'well done!' I was overcome as I turned and groped for him, hugged him tight. 'Congratulations, Nick!'

'I didn't want to mention, because . . . you know.'

'Don't be ridiculous,' I said, 'it's wonderful news.' And he stood and held me and patted my back until I'd more or less stopped crying.

*

'And what are you going to be doing?' said Nick. We were perched at a table overhanging the end of the Serpentine, ducks in the weeds below making doting noises as they travelled about. I waited till the girl had cleared away the plates and paper napkins and given us our menus, and then I looked up and down at mine and turned it over as if not seeing what I wanted, though in fact I saw nothing at all. 'I hope you're going to act.'

'Thank you,' I said, and touched his hard knee under the table. 'That's what I want to do.'

'You've made a pretty impressive start.'

'Well,' I said, 'that was Oxford. It's not so easy in the big wide world.'

'I honestly don't see why, Dave, with your talent. What about that review in *The Times*? – "tireless brilliance", was that the phrase . . . ?'

I said, 'Have you noticed I don't look much like, say, Alan Bates?' and smiled, to soften my sharp tone. Sometimes Nick's absolute unconsciousness of my appearance, my difference, a sort of ethical beauty in him, seemed to verge on a blander disregard for the whole problem.

He blushed slightly and looked down at his hand as he laid it on mine. 'Don't be daft,' he said, and rubbed the back of my hand before he sat back. 'Your appearance is just a part of your talent. You are who you are.'

I think I saw what he meant. 'Well, thank you,' I said again, drily, though the wonderful rub of his hand, like any touch of Nick's, was a wild reminder of what I couldn't have.

The food came, unwanted and expensive but remotely worthwhile, a show of our coping and having lunch, at least, together. This time tomorrow he would be disembarking at Calais, perhaps out already on the road across northern France.

'What about the others?' I said. 'Has Jenny had her results?'

'Yes, she has, she got a Second – a "good Second",' with a smile at the conventional phrase.

'And what will she do?' I said. 'What will *you* do? Will you stay on – do a doctorate? – that's what everyone thought I was going to do.' It was consoling to think Oxford might keep him, within reach after all.

Nick looked down, applied himself to cutting up his toasted sandwich, with its ooze of cheese. 'I've had an offer, actually, from Harvard, I'm going to do a master's degree there.'

'Oh, amazing!' I said, in a faint friendly tone.

'Yes, I *think* it could be good,' he said, with a flinch, as if still undecided about it.

'Harvard,' I said, 'for fuck's sake!'

'Yeah, I know' – he laughed, and looked down again – 'and Jenny wants to be nearer her mother in Boston – you know, since her father died. So that all makes sense.'

'Right,' I said, 'yes, of course,' and then airily, 'I didn't know her mother lived in Boston.' It was a perilous performance, but I managed it, the selfless pleasure in its all, as he said, making sense. I saw how Nick's tact, which was a kindness to me, was also a sign of his power, of things kept from me. Of course he'd left Jenny this morning to come out and meet me, they'd talked in a firm but considerate tone about the things he would have to say. The vision of them in a hallway, her kissing him lightly as he went out, with reminders about packing, and not being too long, was also a vision of myself as a problem they shared. He was explaining now about Jenny and her plans, and I cut in quietly, 'Well, I hope it goes wonderfully for you both.' I'm not sure if this quick masochistic surrender to the idea of their happiness helped me to accept it or dug me in deeper in envy and loss. He looked at me steadily, grey eyes through the square gold-framed glasses, his large thoughtful scrupulous gaze; then blinked and looked down.

'I do worry,' he said, 'about what part I've played in . . . you know . . .'

'Oh . . .' I said, and now the water of the lake seemed to well and fill the view and block my thoughts.

He glanced round before he spoke. 'You're very special, David . . . Dave' – he laughed softly. 'I do love you, you know, but just . . . well, not like that.'

I nodded, not tearful, unchangeably corrected. The words I had longed for were spoken, and followed in the very same sentence by the others, so banal that they shocked me in themselves, as much as in what they said. I said, 'Mm, well, I love you too,' as if our being in love was his idea, to which I was responding with my own tact, a mere form of words. It was the first time I'd said it to him, out loud.

I wrote a cheque for the waitress, Nick left a small tip, and we strolled back the way we had come, at a leisurely pace, like two people talking more earnestly than we were; we barely spoke. I dreaded leaving him, though I hungered perversely for the five or ten seconds of physical contact: the sportsmanlike clinch which was his way, our way, of saying goodbye – the kiss that was his best offer, and was my inarticulate promise of all I was ready to give. This time I needed more, I pressed myself against him, so that his hidden cock glanced off mine, I couldn't see what he thought about that when I let him go slowly – stood back with my hands on his warm hips and shook him as I said, 'Have a wonderful time!'

He blushed as he laughed. 'Thank you!'

'And give my love to the others, won't you.'

'OK – yes, I will.' There was just a chance, there was every chance, of a scene – the rush of ruinous emotion that I always kept back.

'And . . . you know,' my last shake a little melting stroke before I stood back empty-handed, 'keep in touch!'

'Will do,' said Nick, 'will do,' and I turned then and

walked off fast down the path, and veered away under the cover of the trees.

I went at a relaxed-looking pace down the tree-shaded length of Queen's Gate, windows open on the lounge bars of discreet hotels, cream-stuccoed consulates where Filipina maids swept the areas and put out the rubbish, all the beautiful business of London going on, and let myself in at the black front door of the house. The second post had come, and I took up a postcard for Brian's mother in the lift with me to the fifth floor: a beach on Tresco, 'Dear Connie, The boys are having a whale of a time!' I got into the flat, the little learnt procedure of the three locks, and snapped the bolt behind me with a strange sense of imposture. The flat was at the edge of its tolerance, in fact it was offended that I was still there. The sun shone down steeply into the empty sitting room, the cool kitchen at the back, with its pans and scales and electric clock, seemed to frown as it watched me open the cupboards and stare without knowing what I wanted at the spices and jams. In the ice-box the Riesling was frozen solid, the cork forced half out of the neck of the bottle. I stood it in the sink, not wanting it or knowing what to do with it.

In the hallway of the flat there was an entryphone, a white handset fixed to the wall, silent throughout my stay, and now it buzzed, and buzzed fiercely again, a new sound, as unlike the telephone as a fire alarm. I felt incoherently that Nick had found the place, rung the bell, and after a heart-stopping second of adjustment I lifted the receiver and said hello. Only the weirdly magnified sound of a van that I could hear at the same time through the open window as it went down the street below. Then two voices, the words indistinct, out on the front steps perhaps, some helpful exchange. I said hello again, as a matter of form, a car door slammed, a car moved off, and in the

London silence that followed, steady murmur of the city, with a faint low-pitched buzz from the entryphone itself, I stood waiting and listening, and then hung up.

Esme was at Swindon to meet me. I threw my overnight bag on the back seat and climbed in beside her with a heavy live feeling of distress and exhaustion it was hard to conceal. 'Meet up with your friend OK?' she said.

'I did, thanks, yes.'

'Everything all right?'

'Oh – fine, yes,' I said, as though I'd already forgotten about it.

'You know,' she said, checking in the mirror as she pulled out onto the main road, 'you can always ask him, Nick, he's called, isn't he, to come and stay with us.'

'Yes, I know,' I said, 'thank you. Actually, he's just going off to Italy for three weeks, but it's a nice thought.'

'Well then, after that.'

I couldn't tell if Esme was tactfully waiting for me to own up to something that was obvious to her, or if she just thought I needed more company of my own age.

'The college forwarded some post for you,' Mum said. 'I put it in your room.' I could tell from her casual tone that she was curious about this post, and I said, 'Oh, I'll have a look at it tonight.' A few minutes later she said, 'Do have a look at your letters, love – you know, just in case there's something important.' I went up to my room and closed the door, and opened the post in order, two from the Faculty that I couldn't take in, and an unexpected postcard from Tim's Joanne, to say how sorry she was and how something was sure to turn up. The picture was Olivier as Othello, cork-black to the navel, with the six wavy lines of the postmark impressed on his face. On the top left-hand corner of the last envelope the three forward-leaning sans-serif capitals were so familiar and so momentous that I couldn't face opening it for a minute or two. I went to the bathroom with an illogical feeling that the contents could be good or bad, like the exam results my friends were getting every day now.

'Any developers?' said Esme, when I went down. Both she and Mum were languid with anticipation. When I told them, she mixed extra-large gin and tonics for all of us to celebrate. 'It's not, you know, playing Hamlet,' I said, 'it may not even happen,' but we were all shuffled up for an hour or so into a dubious kind of cheerfulness. Esme asked to look at the letter again and by dinner time she had it more or less by heart.

'So you have to go and *read for a part*,' she said. 'I wonder what that entails, exactly.' I tried to be offhand about it, and teased her for being excited. I said, 'The casting director saw me in a Jacobean play set in Venice and thought I'd be just right for a hotel receptionist in Torquay.'

'Well you've got to start somewhere, Dave,' Esme said. 'And I've always loved Torquay.'

Mum shifted the sizzling onions in the pan but her cook's concentration was divided. 'I suppose you can play a character like that,' she said, 'I mean you've been taken for Malayan before now.'

'God knows,' I said.

'It's acting, isn't it,' said Esme sensibly. 'I mean, look at Olivier, all blacked up like an old . . .' – she stared into the distance, but I knew then she'd been through my post. 'And this is on the Beeb! We'll get the girls round to watch.'

'I'll probably only be on for three seconds.'

'I don't think I've ever seen anyone I actually knew on telly,' said Esme. 'Have you, Av?'

'No,' said Mum, 'I'm not sure I have.' I saw her old belief

in me, her trust that everything would pay off, at odds with her new wariness and sense of danger.

We had our supper in the garden, not yet a tradition, but suggested as a treat for me, celebration winning out for the evening over worry and unfocused blame. I opened the French windows and set up the card table on the path, small stones from the flower bed wedged under the feet to keep it steady. A white cloth over the baize and two candles in jam jars. A tray then with glasses, cutlery, Mum's best red napkins, the Crown Derby cruet that Esme had had as a wedding present. I brought out three heavy chairs from the dining room, stagey and out of place. I took all my usual care with presentation, folded up the napkins like fortune-tellers, brought out the silver bowls of ginger and sugar for the melon starter, and it felt like a pathetic consolation, I wished I wasn't doing it, or was doing it for someone else. All the time as I went in and out I was dawdling and wincing through thoughts of Nick and me together, and ideas, blurred and slipping, of the evening he was spending in London without me. I looked at the perfect table. I had everything except my meal.

We sat down as the last sun went off the garden. The candles in their jam jars burned steady while the breeze got up and pushed Mum's hair across her face and flipped the corner of the tablecloth into the sugar. A touch of English stoicism stiffened our smiles. Esme had opened a bottle of Moselle, but Mum covered her glass with her hand. 'Cheers,' I said, keeping up the positive mood, the audition in London next week to look forward to. The card table brought us close together, Esme and Mum facing each other, partners, and me in the middle, turning from one to the other, or at times simply gazing at the empty place facing me.

'So London, love, yes, how did it go?' said Mum, as if I'd just arrived. 'It was all right at your friend's flat.'

I hated this kind of stilted talk, and then felt it was better than the serious talk it was a fragile defence against. 'Yeah, it was fine, Mum,' I said – and heard my adolescent mumble. 'It's where I stayed last summer, if you remember, for the Proms. It's five minutes' walk from the Albert Hall.'

'I don't think I knew who you stayed with, you see. What's his name?'

'Brian – Brian Wood. He read English in my year. He's very nice – big Delius man. He's going out with Fiona Harris – you know, who used to be Giles's girlfriend.' It was craven, my need to reassure her about Brian, I seemed to dream up her suspicion that I might be going out with him myself.

'How funny . . .' she said.

'And you saw your friend Nick . . .' said Esme, coaxing things along.

'Yeah, I wanted to catch him before he goes off to Italy.' I said this very calmly and in the silence that followed it seemed transparently inadequate.

'So, Dave, what about this Nick?' said Mum, in a funny house-master tone I hadn't heard before. The thump of my pulse in my ear was so loud because the looming frankness wasn't just about me. It seemed to me all three of us were about to declare ourselves.

I set down my knife and fork, sat forward, laid my hands flat on the table, in candour and steadiness. 'Mum, I love Nick,' I said, 'I'm in love with him.' Esme shifted in her chair but said nothing. I didn't know which of them to announce it to, so I said it to the garden in front of me: 'I'm a homosexual.' Then it was Mum I looked at first, and I couldn't tell if her gaze as she took it in was one of shock or pity. The words had a physical presence – it was like being high in the garden with Nick himself, words printed on the night, imminent, and so obvious in prospect that you thought you might have said them already. The candlelight on Mum's features made her strange. There was a throat-clearing from Esme.

'Well, we rather gathered that, I think, didn't we, Av?'

'Well,' I said, and shrugged as I turned to her, 'there you are then.'

'I'm just worried, love, about you generally, you know, at the moment,' Mum said. It wasn't clear if this included a worry about me being homosexual or if that barely figured in the larger concern.

'I know, Mum,' I said.

'I'm glad you've told us what you just have, but you must know it makes no difference to us.' And she reached out and took my hand, a quick warm clasp giving confidence and seeking it too, and which we both knew in the moment she did it was very unusual.

'I mean, for god's sake,' said Esme, and reached out and gripped my other arm. 'I've glad you've come out with it at last.'

Then an awful perspective opened up, as they sat there holding on to me on either side, of having to go into the thing, with tearful confusion, and shy reminiscences, and the still unsubsided shock, for me, of having spoken. 'I'll get the main course,' said Mum, and I think we all saw that the subject I'd come out with over the melon could not be kept up through the chicken casserole and the trifle. It left me at least with a breathless feeling of being launched and treading air, waiting to touch down. The relief of our each having said what we'd said was so great it was almost an anticlimax, as we nattered about Wincroft, and what Jane and Molly Carr had been up to – though Molly and Jane themselves appeared now in a subtly liberated light. I felt in an unexpected way that I'd joined the girls.

*

Over coffee, with Mum in a shawl now to keep warm, our faces, in the soft but unwavering light of the candles, were mask-like, so shadowed and private as to seem unknown, but then again frank, and even mischievous.

Esme sat back, a small brandy glass in her hand. 'I have to say, Dave, about you, you know, if you won't mind me saying, that it's been pretty obvious to me since the first day I met you. I have a nose for these things, I just know,' and she wrinkled her nose like someone amusing a small child.

'Oh, really!' I said, 'was it . . .'

'Certainly when we had that holiday in Devon – the way you stared at men all the time – look, I don't want to embarrass you.'

'No, no,' I said – almost curious now about how I'd been seen, and read.

'That young waiter you couldn't take your eyes off – do you remember?' I looked down, amused and ashamed. 'And then when your mum and me came to see you in that play, where you were so brilliant as the old woman. If I didn't know before, I knew then.'

'Well . . .' I said, 'that was years later,' and I wondered if she had kept these suspicions to herself – it brought back those glimpses, on the sands at Friscombe, and in the hotel dining room, of the talk that she and Mum must have without me, and at night, in their shared room: the first seeping awareness that they knew each other better than they pretended to me they did.

'I've known a lot of gay men, as we say now, in my time – Christ, I was married to one for four and a half years!'

'Yes,' I said, 'I know you were,' and felt almost envious of her and gorgeous Gilbert, as she sometimes called him.

'Gilbert had a number of good friends in the theatre world, so if you're going to be an actor, my impression is you'll be absolutely fine. In fact it will be an advantage, won't it, Av?'

'I don't know,' said Mum: 'I mean, so I've heard.' I wasn't sure at first if she liked this candour; but I think it was the fact of speaking candidly that took some getting used to, more than the things that were being said. 'I think I will have a brandy,' she said. 'A tiny one, love,' and it wasn't clear for a second if it was me or Esme she was looking at. I got up and went into the house for a glass. It seemed a moment for them to talk, to come to some murmured agreement, but I heard nothing, and when I stepped back outside they both smiled calmly up at me, as if to say that harmony was now restored. 'Ah, you're having one too,' Mum said, and I poured out half an inch for each of us. It wasn't expressly a toast, but we touched our glasses, all three, in a delicate chiming collision, before we drank.

Esme said, 'I think we just want you to be happy, love, like your mother and me.'

'Mm, quite,' said Mum, in a considering way.

'And, you know, we couldn't be more delighted that you've got Nick.'

I looked down, breathed deeply, very grateful for her kindness, then lifted my glass and peered ahead, at the lavender and the low wall, the garden losing colour to the night, the tips of Gilbert's conifers like cypresses against the deep blue sky.

II

19

Mark and Cara drove down to Greenwich to see me in *R&J*, and came round afterwards, with a disorienting scent of money and privilege about them as they chatted with my friends in the small hot dressing room I shared with the Romeo, Johnny Dingali. Capulet flung open the door with a whoop, half-naked men with faces still purple and ginger in make-up squeezed past them like satyrs, there was only a third of a glass of Veuve du Vernay each. Mark and Cara were patrons of the arts, Cara herself was an artist, and they couldn't have been nicer. But none of the cast had met them before, and their name, when they learned it, caused a certain awkwardness, and inhibition. Only Johnny, determined not to grovel, went straight into first names, 'So, Mark, do you see much theatre?' – aiming for an argument Mark was far too clever to get caught in. 'Lord Hadlow,' said Johnny, 'in our humble dressing room . . .' and Mark did say, quietly but firmly, 'I'm not a lord, actually,' while the others looked unsure about baiting a man so friendly and so rich. Cara tapped her card into my shirt pocket and told me to get in touch, and as soon as the door had closed behind them Johnny almost shouted, 'Right! Where's that other bottle?' and a laugh of guilty relief filled the dressing room.

Later that night, over curries round the corner, Raymond showed a certain sarky fascination with the Hadlows, once he learned that they'd been in. 'I'm sorry you didn't meet them,' I said.

'I don't mix much with plutocrats,' Ray said, and raised a hand to stay my objection. 'No doubt you will argue that plutocrats don't as a rule seek out radical work such as ours.'

'They're not your usual plutocrats,' I said. 'They're quite left-wing.' Ray chuckled at this idea, and I felt that the question of my own status, as the one member of the company who'd been to public school, was looming yet again – it didn't need to be mentioned, it was a presence, conjured up noiselessly in Ray's thin smile. 'Anyway,' I said, 'Mark isn't a plutocrat. Plutocrat means someone who rules through wealth.'

'Your innocence never ceases to amuse me,' Ray said. 'Though it strikes me this very rare and special kind of left-wing plutocrat you've identified might be worth your prompting.'

'Prompting?'

'Into an act of generosity, negligible to him, life-saving to us. You might care to have a word?'

This made obvious and exciting sense and at the same time, as I wiped my plate with the last cold corner of naan, I shrank from the prospect of having to ask Mark for money.

I rang Cara the next day, and began with an apology which she talked straight over. 'We were excited by the play,' she said, 'by the whole approach.'

'That's wonderful to hear,' I said.

'Delighted, of course' – with her remembered effect, that was almost a stammer, of drawing on a cigarette in mid-sentence – 'mm . . . to see you doing so well.'

'Thank you very much, Cara. It meant a lot to me that you came,' consciously moving to first-name terms myself.

'And you looked marvellous, by the way. A star, we both thought so.'

'Ah . . . ! I wish you'd been reviewing us for the *Nottingham Post*.'

'I've not seen that,' she said drily. 'But you've read this morning's *Guardian*?'

'Oh, no . . .' I said. In fact I'd only just got out of bed. 'Is it all right?'

'Hold on.' She put down the phone, and from my fixed position I seemed to follow – with the opening of a door, the whining of a dog, Cara calling, 'I'm on the phone . . . I'm talking to Dave . . . Dave Win,' and another voice like a far echo – her movement through the rich perspective of the Holland Park house which I had never visited. I caught a sense of its atmosphere, in the busy but unsocial morning, as I heard her come back, nearly with me again, then, 'Right, here we are . . . It's their new man Billington, who we think's rather great. Shall I just read it to you?'

'If it's good,' I said; 'and, obviously, if you don't mind.'

'It is good' – she laughed lightly and I pictured the quick overridden distraction of stubbing out her cigarette before she began. I wanted to know what this man had said about my own performance, but I hummed appreciatively as Cara went rather slowly through the first paragraph – about the political acuteness of Ray's vision, and the physical excitement of the action, the unusual violence of Tybalt's death. 'Now here we are, "The boyish Mercutio, David Win, has great presence, and an instinct for verse-speaking undeniably at odds with the roughed-up delivery prevailing elsewhere; his technically dazzling Queen Mab speech stands out. He is of mixed Burmese heritage, and an interesting foil to the half-Indian Romeo, Jonathan Dingali, hinting that the dynastic purity obsessing the Capulets is threatened also by larger historical processes of empire and race. Ray Fairfield's Terra is one of several new companies making politically disruptive readings of the classics, with performances evolved through collective decision-making in long

rehearsals. More than other such innovative directors he presents an unusual range of races on stage. With young actors of
the calibre of Dingali, Samson and Win they are among the best
hopes for a new British theatre of the left.'''

'You're right, it's not bad,' I said – with a levitating feeling
of pleasure, relief and vindication. It needed to be dwelt on, but
I couldn't ask her to read it again; I almost wanted to get her
off the phone so that I could dash out and buy a copy myself.

'Mark was saying something similar last night – it would be
good to see you tackle something more explicitly political next,
he thought perhaps *Julius Caesar*. Well, I don't know what you
are doing, of course. *J.C.*, I suppose you'd call it – though that
could be confusing!'

'Well, we've got some ideas,' I said, 'and more political, yes.
Really we'd like to do a brand-new play.' The point, both obvious and extremely delicate, was the money. I wanted to tell her,
without sounding pathetic or reproachful, that we were a touring company, paid a mere subsistence, sleeping on floors and
sofas or in cheap bed-and-breakfasts. Our old Bedford van,
with its hand-painted lettering, broke down quite often, costumes and props and the minimal abstract sets marooned in a
lay-by hours from the hall we were due to open in that very
evening. Our 'present-day' aesthetic at least let us act in our
jeans, if the van didn't make it. We were desperate for cash, and
I sensed, as I smiled at my image of Cara in her house, that the
future of Terra might lie, much more promptly than I had
expected, in my hands. Too promptly for me to be able to start
begging. I said, hesitantly, 'Well, I'd love to talk to Mark about
it, you know, and hear his ideas.'

Her pause made me wonder if even this was too pushy. I
had an embarrassed sense of them bothered by people for
money all year round. But I also thought if they showed an
interest it meant they expected it and might in fact be tacitly
opening the way for a request. Patrons needed something to

patronize, after all . . . Then, 'Tuesday next week?' she said. 'Or will you have left town?'

'Tuesday . . . I'll be here, I may have rehearsals, but I'll certainly be free by five or so.'

'Have dinner with us. I mean, if you *wanted*' – and again I pictured her way of squaring up to things – 'you could come to a drinks party with us first, it would mean you could see Giles, if you'd like that, it's given by his new boss.'

'Well, thank you, Cara, um . . .' Her tone left me guessing at her feelings about this party, and indeed about Giles's new boss, but I could hardly say I didn't want to see Giles.

'He's working for Norman Upshaw . . . do you know?'

'I know the name,' I said. I saw myself painfully out of place at Upshaw's party, and also curiously, mischievously, enjoying it – such was my mood these days. 'It will be an experience,' I said.

'I'm afraid it will,' said Cara. 'But a much nicer one for us if you're there too.'

I remembered Mark as a risk-taking driver, ten years earlier, on the blind brows and dips of the road under the Downs, but when they picked me up outside Notting Hill Gate station they were seated together in the back of a grey Mercedes. I ducked my head to smile in at them and nipped round to sit in the front; a young Indian man was driving, and reached across to shake my hand before looking in the mirror and moving off. 'Ashok . . . Dave,' said Cara, 'good friend' – which seemed to apply to both of us. I was turning round sideways to chat to Mark and Cara, and observed Ashok's half-smiling way of attending to the conversation without taking part in it. He was soft-faced, darker than me, in a blue suit and tie with a red pullover under the jacket. I thought he had that watchful desire to please that I'd had myself in the Woolpeck days.

'It's wonderful to see you again,' I said.

'And you, Dave,' said Mark. I felt the friendship was resumed, without fuss or reproach, after a gap which had quite naturally happened – my guilt slithered for a minute, seeking for a purchase, a chance to apologize for being out of touch for so long, but by the time the car was circling Marble Arch I knew it wasn't necessary.

The Upshaws lived in Old Queen Street, in a huge Georgian house overlooking St James's Park as if it were its own garden. In the car I toyed with a joke about the address, not sure if Mark and Cara would think it funny, or if I thought it was funny myself. It was doubtless a very old joke, and Mark had the look of someone so used to the name of the street that a joke about it would be almost bewildering. Still, as we got out of the car, I said quietly, 'Who was the old queen, I wonder?' 'Mmm?' said Mark. 'Old Queen Street,' I said, with a smirk. Mark looked about as if for inspiration. 'Is it Queen Anne, I suppose?' he said. We went in to the party.

The hour we spent there, escaping now and then into a further room, urged upstairs to an almost empty drawing room where we peered obediently at the pictures for three minutes before creeping back down again, only made me fonder of the Hadlows. They had been my benefactors, not only mine, but I felt their goodness tonight almost intimately; I stuck with them, and with Cara when Mark was taken aside, and saw how their decency glowed in this setting steeped in values we could never share. I'd put on a suit and tie, the only suit I owned, which was the one I'd taken and walked out of my Finals in, but I felt my dissidence showed. The quick look away when I caught someone staring was familiar to me since Bampton days – the suspicion that I shouldn't be here, and the subtler suspicion that since I was here I might be someone important: a question they probably wouldn't have time to sort out. By now I was quite at home being out of my element, I even enjoyed it, in small doses, and the element here was bracingly alien and unconstrained. Did I escort Cara or did she protect me? At her elbow I leaned in as she spoke to another guest but my eyes slid aside to take in the exact weight and angle of a *Telegraph* columnist's head or the furious frown with which his wife refused the canapés offered by a beautiful black waitress. It was a useful education, for the actor, in the language of disdain. Quite soon, a heavyish drizzle set in, so no one could go out onto the terrace overlooking the Park, and the downstairs rooms grew roaringly noisy.

There was no sign of Giles at first, though I was keeping an eye out for him over Cara's shoulder, and Cara herself glanced round now and then as she talked. I hadn't seen him in the three years since Oxford, I hardly thought of him from year to year, although I dreamt of him sometimes, which showed he was still in my system. In dreams he was certainly Giles, though he didn't look much like the teenager I'd known or the man he must now have turned into; we were roughly intimate, sometimes in bed together, with hugging and even kissing which in the dream seemed like a revelation about him, but on waking of course could only be a small and unwelcome revelation about me. Now a grand old woman in diamonds had got stuck to Cara, in an impasse of good manners, discussing sponsorship for young artists – Cara torn between impatience at wasting her own time and a principled need to talk up the Hadlows' work. The old woman's good manners stopped short of acknowledging me, so I was free to analyse her desiccated accent, her flawless hair and clothes, the little nods and recoils with which she mimed thought – she had a mistrust of Cara and more so of Mark that she couldn't quite conceal, and a confused sense, even so, of kinship, money recognizing money, however gained or spent. 'Yes, well, we give out twenty scholarships a year, to children from deprived backgrounds,' Cara said.

'And have you had any luck with them, I wonder?'

'Sometimes, yes,' said Cara, 'we have. But it's not all about backing winners – it's about giving them chances they wouldn't have had otherwise. It's really up to them what they do with it.'

I felt I could testify to this, but the old woman gaped at the madness and waste of philanthropy. A white-aproned waiter refilled our glasses, and as he did so I saw a small door in the panelling open and Giles slipped in – a glimpse of an office beyond him as he pulled the door to. He buttoned his suit jacket and looked round, I saw him nod and smile at someone – not as a prelude to joining them but as a sign he wasn't going to; he peered blankly into the room, his gaze settled on us for three seconds, on his mother's back and then on my face: so that I caught the instant of shock, immediately disguised, before he looked down and pushed through the crowd towards us.

'Hallo, Winny! This is a surprise' – a balance in his cheerful tone between comradely pleasure and a clear hint that I was a gate-crasher. 'Mother, hallo.'

'Mother is it now?' said Cara, as he kissed her on the cheek. 'And do you know Lady Harwell—' but Lady Harwell had seized her moment and swivelled, and was being kissed herself by a red-faced old brute in a kilt.

'Isn't Dad with you?' said Giles.

'Of course he is – we were wondering where you were.'

'Oh, yes, I had various things to finish up for Norman.'

'Ah, I see . . . of course,' said Cara, rather drolly. Giles was junior in this world, which meant mimicking the senior attitude. 'Anyway, we thought you might like to see Dave again.'

Giles put his head on one side as he thought what to say, and I had no idea myself what the terms were – new maturity and sympathy, the erasure of silly old squabbles, or reinforced suspicion, with fresh chances for mockery. 'Well, how are things with you, Winny?' he said, but with a faintly anxious look, as if now remembering my famous meltdown.

'Really terrific, thanks,' I said.

'Dave's been having a great success in a play at Greenwich,' said Cara. 'Your father and I went to see it last week.'

'*Greenwich* . . . ah,' said Giles. 'Yes, I think I heard you were doing a bit of acting.'

'And you're working . . . here?' I said, sounding almost as supercilious.

'I'm here some of the time,' said Giles. 'The main office, obviously, is in Mayfair.' And he turned, his face clarified, he almost forgot us as Jasmine Upshaw herself came near, greeting Lady Harwell and the kilted brute. 'Just a moment,' Giles said.

The Upshaws were undeniably impressive. They'd come in a few minutes after the start, and I'd watched the way they carved up the crowd, as efficiently as royalty. They were very much a couple, but with no glimpse of Mark and Cara's obvious fondness for each other – they seemed to suggest that at their speed and pitch little time was left over for shows of affection. Norman Upshaw was tall, pale and sleek, in a chalk-striped dark suit and large black-framed glasses that seemed meant to signal both money and genius. He sniffed smugly if something he said raised a laugh, but grew restless if the answer prevented his going on. Jasmine's manner made no claims to his intellectual standing, but her brisk smile and firm little nods, as she came through the room, suggested a greater fund of common sense. She questioned, she advised, and she moved on, in a way that left people unsure what she really felt. I thought they took from her what they wanted, like consulters of an oracle. When our own moment came, Cara introduced me, 'David Win, the actor' – Jasmine narrowed her eyes, as if not to be taken in, and then tapped my wrist: 'I know,' she said, '*The Yellow Flower* – Norman thought you were awfully good,' and turned away before I could say, for the umpteenth time, 'That wasn't me, it was Ken Danby, the Chinese actor who is much shorter than me and five years older.'

*

A man at the edge of a group that was breaking up in a mutual hunger for new faces caught my eye for the second time, and suddenly alone turned doubtingly but pleasantly towards me. He was aquiline, handsome, perhaps twenty years older than me. 'I think we met at Brighton?' he said.

'Oh, did we . . . . ?' I said, shaking hands slowly, as if doing so might help me remember. Brighton had been over a month ago, with good houses and a surge in confidence among the cast. 'David Win.'

'Yes . . .' he said, narrowing his eyes: 'Martin Causley.' The Sunday after the final performance we were down on the shingle beach beyond the pier in a late-summer heatwave, a blur of drinking and nakedness all afternoon. I thought I might remember Martin better if he'd had nothing on. 'It was a pretty good show, wasn't it,' he said.

I grinned. 'Yes, I thought it went well. Everyone was on great form. And of course a great audience!'

He laughed modestly. 'Put like that,' he said. 'The mood of the whole party was very good, I thought.'

'I certainly had a wild time, I don't know about you.'

'Well . . .' he said. 'We may have been at different meetings.'

'Oh . . .' I said.

'I know some of the Scottish groups got quite rowdy.'

'*Oh* . . . !' I said more emphatically.

'And Norman himself of course gave a very good speech to the business committee.'

I said, 'You're talking about the Conservative Party Conference, aren't you?'

'Aren't you?' And I couldn't help laughing as I explained.

'How funny!' he said, not wholly pleased, looking away and then back at me – we chuckled guardedly, unsure if we were enemies, revealed in our true colours, or if in fact we were enjoying the unexpected intimacy of two strangers caught up in a mutual muddle. I saw how he regretted blushing, and yet

perhaps the blush was a shortcut, a skipping over pages of pre-
amble to other rosy possibilities. Now his handsomeness was
sexy, it was as if he'd been switched on.

I started to say, 'But I wonder who you thought I was' – the
usual dull thing of being taken for some other brown person (a
keen Asian Tory, well, there were plenty of them) seemed for
once to have fun in it.

'Ah!' he said, 'excuse me, I see my wife's signalling,' and he
slipped past me with a hand raised to part the crowd. I didn't
bother turning round to see him go.

At just the right moment Cara announced we were leaving
in ten minutes. The promise of imminent freedom broke the
spell and I saw us already as winners, escaping a house where a
hundred others were condemned to sink deeper in drink and
claptrap long into the night. 'Can you see Giles?' she said. I
craned round for her and spotted him near the window, in
fawning conversation with a tall white-haired man who stared
over his head as he spoke to him. 'Oh god,' said Cara, 'he's
sucking up to Inglewood.' She sagged and sighed. 'Do you
think we've bred a monster, Dave? And if so, how did it
happen? Feel free to tell me!'

I laughed and looked over at Giles as she made her way
towards him, his face half in shadow but gleaming and revealed
in the rainy light from the window, thick chestnut hair longer
and swept back, a surly new heaviness to the student jaw. I felt
he was caught, like someone starting a beard, in the awkward
middle of a transformation into a new impressive self that he
had imagined but we hadn't thought of at all – not that growing
a beard was itself something Giles would ever do. I could tell
from his smile he was pleased by his own thoughts and plans,
and barely listening – he must have been forty years younger
than George Inglewood, but he thrust himself forward even as
he nodded his head in apparent submission to the scrawny old
monster. But if Giles was a monster too . . . What happened

when monster met monster? Did they fight it out like stags, one insisting on dominance, or might they come, sooner or later, to some wary accommodation? A man pressing on me as if trying to get past spoke in my ear: 'I hope we're going to see you on telly again soon.'

'Oh, thank you . . .' I said, and leant back a little to take in his face, but he was confidential, chin almost on my shoulder as he went on,

'I thought you were the best thing in *Hibiscus Hotel*.'

'Oh, it wasn't a bad show,' I said.

'Very naughty, I didn't say it was, far from it.'

I laughed, 'Well, thank you.'

Now I looked at him. 'Chris Canvey,' he said, offering a firm hand, which held on to mine for five seconds or more till I said,

'Canvey. Like the Island . . .'

'Flat, polluted, prone to flooding . . .' I laughed and pulled back, took in curly grey hair cut short, grey eyes behind large brown-framed glasses, a tight double-breasted suit in which he seemed to wriggle with unspoken intent. Then for a moment we both looked half-seriously into our drinks.

'And what brings you here?' I said, with a little wince at the whole thing.

He gave me a quizzical look, and I thought perhaps he was another insider, Upshaw's personal assistant, say, one of those ambitious younger men who adapt themselves to the ethos of a useful employer. 'I work for Westminster Council,' he said. 'God knows why they asked me.'

'You must have an idea,' I said. The buzz of connection in a setting like this felt all the more wicked. He looked in my eyes and when he looked away I was already awkwardly hard. I saw Cara signal with a tilt of her head towards the door. She and Mark would have been staggered if I'd told them I wanted to stay at the party after all, or at least to leave it with Chris

Canvey instead of them. But they were taking me on to supper, and whatever was suddenly happening would have to hang fire till another time.

'Your friends?' said Chris.

'Yes,' I said, not sure if he knew who they were. I leant against him. 'Well, I hope we'll meet again.'

'Me too,' he said, with a quick smile at Cara.

'I'm in London till Monday. A drink on Saturday, perhaps?'

'Could do,' he said, 'yes, could do. Or how about later tonight?'

Ashok was there at once when Cara and I came out of the house into the still aftergleam of the drizzle. Mark had been snagged by someone in the hall, and we stood by the Mercedes waiting. Cara lit a cigarette. 'You don't, I think,' she said, slipping the packet and lighter into her bag.

'No, thanks,' I said, as if it was hopeless of me, looking back at the bright doorway, smiling in courteous submission to their plan for the evening, but distracted by the thought of Chris, and the fear of a missed chance. Mark came out, we all got into the car, and I felt the reassurance of being in their hands. In the dressing room at Greenwich, bouncing with adrenaline, I'd hardly taken them in, though I'd noted that Cara seemed leaner and more lined, and Mark a bit stockier, with new glasses and a shy shot at sideburns. Tonight I was struck by the complementary way they functioned as a couple, as efficient as the Upshaws but very much nicer. Mark always approached you smiling, Cara never did; but this meant little. In Cara's quick frown and stare a good deal of mere introductory pleasantness could be taken as read; whereas Mark remained with you for ever in the gleam of a preliminary charm, a busy man's way of making things easy and agreeable. In his smile there was perhaps a promise of getting to know him better, and finding further things in common, if ever time allowed.

Ashok drove us westwards, and it was all an impression of parks, with lamps tracing paths here and there under the vast dark height of the trees. I'd pictured dinner in a restaurant, but it seemed we were going to their house. 'Now, I hope you like quail,' said Cara, and I said I'd like to try it. I had a feeling the Upshaws' party was still being absorbed, analysis postponed until we were alone. I said, 'They've got some impressive paintings, haven't they?' 'No, they have,' said Cara, and Mark said, 'Expensive ones, anyway,' and I laughed at the clarification.

I'd lost my bearings, after the parks, in the sequence of wide streets, white-stucco crescents, white-pillared porches in misty succession, a tree-lined avenue with high walls and houses that stood back – now we waited at a gate that opened slowly by itself on to a shallow paved driveway with a bright glass lantern shining in the porch between its own two white pillars. Ashok sprang out and I was just as quick, so that we opened the rear doors in unison – Cara climbed out with a glancing smile that registered the courtesy and perhaps too my little bit of play-acting. Ashok said something to Mark about the next morning before getting back into the car and driving it away round the side of the house. I had a shadowy sense of hierarchies and at the same time, as I followed Cara up the steps and into the marble-floored hall, a quickly evolving idea of the Hadlows' wealth. It was at once, almost embarrassingly, clear to me how I had seen them out of their own true element at Woolpeck, which was where I'd always pictured them till now. And time had been at work, over the decade since we'd first met; surely they were very much richer. I laid my old mac on a chair in the hall, and wasn't sure whether to loosen my tie and relax, or to tighten the knot and shoot my cuffs. I hadn't thought it through – of course left-wing plutocrats were rolling in money just like the right-wing kind. I was having a sarky little argument with Ray in my head, and torn between my affection for Mark and Cara and taking mild offence at the style they lived in. I really didn't want to be disillusioned by them, though a small part of me now had a taste for such disruptions.

We went through into a lamp-lit drawing room with large windows, shuttered at the front and at the back looking out on to the blackness of a garden with the lights of other houses glowing some way off through the trees. I felt clumsily disoriented, already half-drunk and half sobered up again, as well as on my best behaviour. We stood looking at the painting over the fireplace, the teasing watchful silence when a host lets a guest take something in, and when I said, 'This is, er . . .' Cara said,

'Yes . . . do you like it? It's by someone Mark discovered.'

'Well,' Mark demurred, 'we discovered him together.'

'It's exciting,' I said, and it was, a tall furious mess of red and black, like a burning town.

'A young Trinidadian artist, called John Constable, funnily enough.'

'Probably not *much* scope for confusion,' I said, and the joke was fresh for me, at least. I turned and looked at the room, almost as if congratulating them. There were obvious differences, weren't there, between the Upshaws and the Hadlows, clashes of belief, about how you spent money, and also about how you made it – though this was always vague to me, in Mark's case. 'How long have you been here?'

Cara looked vague, and Mark said, 'A couple of years, I suppose, now?' – so that moving house seemed one among many transactions. I smiled at this, and he went on, 'Yes, the Hampstead house felt a bit too small for us once the children had moved out,' with a sly smile of his own. I think that was what I gathered, from these first few minutes in the place. This wasn't a house Giles and Lydia had any part in, or a house in any way adapted for children – it was a new stage in the parents' own story and a statement of their independent taste and ambition.

I said, 'My mum sends her best wishes, by the way.'

'Ah, how is she?' said Mark. 'Is she still, um . . .' – gazing at me as he searched for the proper formulation, and perhaps for a name as well.

'She's still with her friend?' said Cara.

'Oh, with Esme, yes . . .' – it was a low, vaguely worrying fence we'd hopped over quite matter-of-factly.

'And that's all all right?' said Mark, with a cheerful shake of the head.

'No, it's great,' I said. 'Their business is doing very well.'

'You must tell me more about that,' said Cara. 'Shall we go through?'

We went across the hall and into a small dining room, where a dark-haired young woman in a jersey and skirt was lighting the candles. She was introduced as Angela, with the same implication of her being a friend as much as a servant. My own role as we sat down felt subtly ambiguous too. It was related to the role I had played before, as if in far-off episodes of a long-running series to which I had now returned, to find it all imaginatively updated: I felt I was allowed to be myself, but should at least bear in mind the original conception of the part. Their own roles had been expanded, and I saw again how at Woolpeck they had been on holiday from the grandeur of their normal lives.

Angela served a green soup, a white wine was poured. There were somewhat difficult things we seemed likely to talk about, and I sat forward and unfolded my napkin and felt what it might be like to account for myself to parents, to a couple always talking to each other about their own child, rather than edging and skimming things past my single mother and her friend. It was an odder sensation so soon after seeing Giles.

'I so liked seeing you acting again,' Mark said.

'Oh, thank you!'

'And of course a very striking production.'

'I don't think you met Ray Fairfield, did you?'

'He's the artistic director?'

'Yes,' I said, and smiled at the thought of Ray having that title. I said something about the principles of the company: improvisation as democracy in action, 'openness and maturity from everyone' and so forth. Mark was intrigued by the idea of the democratic rehearsal process, and I tried to hint without open disloyalty that the democracy in question was like that of a fascist state. 'In the end,' I said, 'we all do what Ray says, just like any ordinary production.'

'And what's he like?' Mark said.

I could hear myself saying, as Johnny had once, when asked this very question by an awestruck punter in Bristol, 'He's an absolute cunt!' But I was, yet again, an ambassador; I said,

'He's rather a genius, I think. As I say, he's demanding, but he gets results' – and I let my smile and eyebrows do the work.

'How long's he been going?' Mark said, and I felt an appraisal of Ray as a business prospect was now under way.

'Terra started last year,' I said.

'I see, so you were in at the beginning.'

'Not quite,' I said, 'but early on.' I hesitated. 'I was in a thing on telly for a year, before I joined.'

'I wish we'd seen that, we're rather hopeless with the telly.'

'Oh, I saw a couple of episodes,' said Cara, 'you were awfully good, but you didn't have enough to do.'

'Oh, thank you, Cara,' I said, 'I didn't know you'd seen it.' I felt my mixed-up pride and embarrassment about *Hibiscus Hotel* all the more in this grand house.

'And it was telly,' she said, 'you were famous when you joined this new company. He must have been thrilled to get you.'

'Well, yes . . . I had experience, but I didn't have training.'

'No . . .' said Mark, and the question of my going off the rails seemed to loom for a moment. I felt tipsy again and candid on a further glass of wine, but tense too at the thought of another coming-out. I'd been learning over the past three years that it wasn't like putting a notice in *The Times*, it was something you had to keep doing, and awkwardly on occasion, over and over again. 'Anyway,' Mark said, 'acting's something you can do or you can't. And the point is, you can. We're both so glad to see you doing well. And, you know,' and he held my eye, as he had done that first time we met, 'triumphing against the odds.'

'Well, thank you,' I said once again. I was behind with my soup, and hurried to finish it off.

'I'd imagined them bigger,' I said, when the quails were brought in. 'Sort of pheasant-size.'

'No, no,' said Cara. A small complete bird, browned, legs gaping helplessly, lay on its back on each white plate. 'There's another one for everyone, but I always think two birds on a plate looks a little offputting.' They were good hosts, they let me get on with it but kept half an eye on me.

'Easiest probably to tackle the legs with your fingers,' said Mark, when I was stooped like a surgeon winkling the last strands of brown flesh from the bones with my knife, and Cara stood up from the table just as the door opened. 'Ah – I think finger-bowls, Angela,' she said, as if they hadn't been sure how much mess I was going to make.

'Mm, delicious,' I said, when I'd finished and cleaned myself up a bit. 'No, I won't have another, thank you' – I held up a hand and sat back with a sense, that perhaps was my own paranoia, of the quails as not only a treat but a test and almost a warning. I shook myself out of it and had another glass of wine.

And then, with a spurt of the heart that coloured my face like some other embarrassment, I thought of Chris Canvey and the call that I'd promised to make in an hour or so's time, that Mark and Cara had no idea of at all.

Nothing so far had been said about Giles, the review of the Upshaws' party hadn't happened, and I didn't know quite what to say, as a guest – they both clearly knew not to think of me and Giles as friends, except in some meaningless nominal way. It was Mark who then said, 'So, what did you make of Giles? You hadn't seen him for a bit, I think.'

'Not since Oxford,' I said. 'And actually not much there. We moved in rather different worlds.'

'They've gone off at odd angles, our children,' said Cara, demonstrating with her arms, 'Giles one way and Lydia the other.'

'Giles to the right, evidently?'

'Just so.'

'And how is Lydia?' I said.

'Oh, I think she's well,' said Cara.

'She's in New York,' said Mark, genially, but narrowing his eyes.

'Oh, yes . . . I remember her talking about going to New York years ago. Is she still with . . . Rory? . . . . *Roly*?'

'Oh, lord no, that's long over,' said Cara. 'No, these days she's very caught up with the whole Andy Warhol scene.' She brought out the name firmly, though I sensed a tremor of unease.

'Well, that's exciting,' I said.

'Yes, it is.'

As it happened, I'd seen *Heat* the previous week, but thought it best not to recommend it. 'I remember seeing *Chelsea Girls* years ago,' I said, 'at the ICA.'

'Ah, we rather wanted to see that one,' said Cara.

I wondered how to put it to them. 'Three hours,' I said, 'on two screens simultaneously. I'm sure I was the only person still conscious at the end.'

Mark laughed and said, 'I gather things are much more on a business footing there these days – you know, at the famous Factory. It's really some sort of office job that Lydia has, I gather.'

This sounded like what Lydia probably thought her parents wanted to hear. I'd been kept awake in *Chelsea Girls* by hoping something sexual might happen, in front of a camera oddly detached from all human agency and interest – it was bizarre now to think of Lydia at the Factory, in that labyrinth of dirty couches and silver-foiled walls.

'But she comes back to London now and then?' I said.

'A bit,' said Mark.

'We don't see a lot of her,' said Cara.

'Right . . .' I said, and looked from one to the other of them, though they were looking ponderingly at each other. The door opened in the white wall and Angela came back in to clear the plates. I sat back with a smile, and gazed up past the paintings murky in the candlelight to the fancy white cornice with white flowers like a daisy-chain all the way round, and slow-wittedly saw how far both their children had got away from Mark and Cara; the magnificent house was the brave face they'd put on the fact.

'Where do you stay while you're in town?' Cara said, when the time came to leave.

'We're all staying at a place in Acton.'

'A hotel?'

'In a sense. It's very cheap, anyway.' I thought she might be going to suggest I stayed with them, but she was wiser than that.

In the hall, Mark shook my hand, and said, 'You might ask Raymond . . . *Ray* to come and see me.'

'I will,' I said, 'thank you very much,' and feared already for the meeting, just from Mark's tone. Ray, though desperate for money, was too proud to think of coming with a begging bowl. Still, I'd done what he told me to. I put on my coat, and gazed round at the marble-floored hall, and I half felt the Hadlows should be kept from funding us, the gulf between the paupers and the patron seemed so vast.

20

Mark retreated from the hall with a wave and Cara came out on to the drive to see me off. I kissed her respectfully on both cheeks, a new un-English practice we both seemed to like, and opened the gate in the wall onto the damp nearly noiseless vista of the avenue. 'We'll be in touch,' she said. When the gate clicked shut behind me I walked a few steps in a swift soft confusion of feelings, released but alone. The moist air glistened under the streetlamps and on the roofs of parked cars. I was drunk but unexpectedly nervous, now the moment had come, about seeing Chris Canvey. At the far end of the road was a busier, very different street, with a lit phone box and a minicab office – everything I needed was there, and still I might have fluffed it, but I didn't.

It was a deep-voiced woman who answered, like an echo of the woman I'd just left. 'Hullo,' I said, 'it's, um . . . I wondered if Chris was there, by any chance?'

'Whom shall I say is speaking?'

'My name's David.'

'Ah, yes, indeed,' she said warmly, and I heard her put the phone down, and after ten seconds brisk footsteps and then a voice, 'Hello?' as if he hadn't been told who it was.

When I got to the house about thirty minutes later it was Chris who let me in, but I was wary somehow of the woman, and I could hear the whine of a tap running somewhere and the bump of it being turned off. It was a biggish, rather dingy-looking house. Chris took my coat politely, but he was smirking as he hung it up. He was in shirtsleeves now, large round bum in suit trousers as he led me down the hall. It was strange to see a second time, and so soon, a person I had had no chance to memorize the first time. It was him all right, it all made sense, but he wasn't quite the man I'd been picturing on and off throughout dinner. I saw straight away the plumpness, the smudged glasses, things I didn't think sexy, which seemed only to confirm and heighten my first feeling, that he was irresistible. We went into a sitting room – closed red velvet curtains, the last of a log fire and cigarette smoke, loose covers of the sofa threadbare on the arms. 'Will you join me in a whisky?' he said, and out of nerves and my own politeness I said, 'Yes, OK.'

'Cheers!' he said, with a grin, and we clinked glasses and sipped as we stood in front of the fire. We were close to what we wanted, but self-conscious without a crowd around us. 'So how was your dinner with the Hadlows?'

'It was all right,' I said, 'we had quail.' He narrowed his eyes, a joke seemed to lurk here, but neither of us could find it. 'How long did you stay at the Upshaws'?'

'Oh, I left soon after you.'

'Don't we sound grand, with our plutocrat friends . . .'

'Mm, not really my scene,' Chris said. 'Anyway, it felt very dull once you'd gone.'

'You must have known other people there?' – trying not to smile.

'One or two, I suppose, but, you know . . . zero homosexual interest.'

'I had a funny encounter with one man,' I said, 'Martin Causley.'

'Oh, Martin, yes, did he try and pick you up?'

'I think he wanted to. Then I made him blush, which I don't think he liked at all, and he said he had to speak to his wife.'

'That poor woman.'

'He's quite good-looking.'

'No, he is. Huge cock.'

'Oh, really?'

'Well . . . apparently.'

Perhaps it was the thought that Chris might have got off with Martin Causley instead of me that made me say softly, 'For god's sake,' holding my drink out in my left hand as I kissed him. Then we looked at each other in a scheming kind of way for five or six seconds, and sat down close together on the sofa, his arm round my waist. The sofa half swallowed us up. I heard the squeak of a floorboard, a sigh as the draught-excluding curtain rose on its rail and a woman in a dressing gown looked round the door – 'Hello, Claudia,' Chris said as if he was quite used to being found here with his arm round a stranger. Claudia herself seemed unsurprised. And in a way I still hadn't adjusted to, I wasn't a stranger. 'You recognize David, don't you.'

'Well, I just had to say,' said Claudia, 'before I turned in, how much we enjoyed you in *Hibiscus Hotel*.'

'I've told him that,' said Chris, but quite pleasantly.

'Thank you very much,' I said.

'We were so excited that Christopher met you tonight,' and as she looked at me, from the edge of the lamplight, I wondered if I'd been lured into something odd.

'This is Claudia's house,' Chris said. 'I'm just her lodger.'

'Oh, rather more than that, I think, Christopher, by now,' Claudia said.

She came forward and reached out a hand – I could only half stand up to shake it. 'Well, pleased to meet you,' I said, taking my lead from Chris's cool tone with her. She looked down at us with a confident smile.

'I'll see you in the morning, I expect,' she said.

'Well . . .' I said, thrown by the mood of permission, almost put off by it, so that I saw myself making some silly excuse and going back to the lodgings in Acton.

'There are a number of things I'd like to ask you,' she said, ' – about the theatre. The actor's life.'

'Well, goodnight, then, Claudia,' Chris said.

The curtain rose again, a minute after she'd gone, as we were starting to chew at each other – 'I forgot my book,' she said, and tiptoed out again with a guilty grimace.

Upstairs he closed the bedroom door and stood there, so eager he was almost hesitant, eyes reading my look for instructions, ready for whatever I wanted most. I hardly knew, beyond the basics, but I took on the role, I sat on the edge of the bed, and had him kneel in front of me, where I could also admire him from behind in the wardrobe mirror. At first I avoided colluding with my own expression, but it took on undeniable interest as things got more serious – until I stood up, and we both got properly undressed and moved on to the astonishing next stage.

It was a mixture, Claudia's house, of comfort and squalor. Next morning, on the alarm, hungover, happily amazed, I had to pick up Chris's rhythm, he was out of the room, then back: 'Just a quick one, please,' he said, the bath already running – he needed to be out of the house by 8.15. I worried about Claudia, but apparently she was a late riser. I got into the water after Chris, to save time, and again, as I dried with a towel that I felt had been used before, the figure whose eye I held in the mirror seemed amused if a little bewildered to find himself here, and to be doing this. Chris went to make breakfast, and I followed him downstairs into the red-tiled hall with a wary fascination at seeing it in daylight. I went into the sitting room, the light switch not working, so I stepped through the shadows, past sofa and bureau and fringed standard lamp, to tug open the dark velvet curtains, which slid back smoothly enough with a click of wooden rings on the oak rail. Outside there was a lawn overwhelmed by a bay tree thirty feet high – I thought of Gilbert's dwarf conifers at Crackers, and the mood of helplessness that grew with them, year by year. In the room, in the curtains themselves, there was the smell of cigarettes and of the ashes of the fire. The large friendly sofa, which had nearly rolled Chris and me up in itself last night, sprawled like a drunk out cold in the early light. The room had an atmosphere, old family furniture, I guessed, handed down and knocked about in the process, china dogs on the mantelpiece, and above it a portrait of a bishop, perhaps, in his robes, in a fancy gilt frame that had lost a corner. The little side tables, the photographs on one, the figures and ormolu clock on the other, were grey with dust, but a confidence in background, Claudia's accent, posh but louche, could be heard. I opened the door, the curtain rose on its rod, and as I went into the hall I wondered about seeing Chris again, before Terra left London to scandalize Ipswich and Colchester. I didn't know, but one small scheming part of me ran on into the months ahead, and being with him, and this house being the setting. It had the glamour of London in it, just a bit, of people doing what they liked in the great blended hum of the city, which hung in this empty hallway even now, the faint far-off roar like a noise in my own head. In the hall I caught another mood, dreamy for a second then sharper-edged – the big family house on Boars Hill where Walt lived with Stella and Jenny and Nick a long-lost three years ago: a different sort of house, but with a lasting aroma of dust and old carpets and yesterday's fire.

When I got to the theatre in Ipswich there was a letter at the stage-door for me, in writing I didn't know, but which then had the lovely and almost alarming interest of being Chris's. Pale mauve flame of the envelope opened in near-darkness backstage, and two folded pages with the ghost of the Rothmans he'd smoked as he wrote them – round-handed, blue biro, fast and efficient and also childlike, pressed hard into the paper. I'd never had a love letter before. I went into the Gents to read it properly, glowing at its rudeness and its confidence, his allusions to what we had done and were going to do. By the next day I knew it as well as my own part – I could hear him clearly, sensed his live presence in the stale cigarette smoke, but the words he chose and the way he formed his letters made me see him in a new light.

In Ipswich we did *R&J*, fairly settled in by now, and boosted by a further good review in the *New Statesman*. There was also an annoyingly positive notice in the *Telegraph*, which Esme had clipped out and sent to me; Ray reduced this to the one word 'Startling' for the poster. Like many resolute outsiders he had a tortured idea of success. Praise in the *Guardian* for a Terra production was welcome, and in the *Workers' Weekly* valuable and true, but almost identical phrases in the *Times* or *Telegraph* showed he'd failed in his mission to outrage. His greatest dread was of acceptance by the mainstream – eunuchry he called it. The grant he received from the Arts Council was an insult he could neither mention nor forget. He never admitted to me how much Mark Hadlow gave him.

I loved arriving in a new town and seeing the posters up. There was the glamour of appearing for a few nights only, and the much sharper sense than in London of being judged, against last week's visitors, and the ones who came back every year and were so popular. In London we merged with the life of the surrounding streets, but on tour we stepped off the train as a troupe, a multicoloured rabble of men and women with a cheerful and possibly threatening appearance. We straggled along with our bags to whatever cheap boarding-house had been found for us. Sometimes when we got to the theatre the van was already there, and quite often it wasn't there yet; on such occasions Ray installed himself in the pub, or if it was the afternoon in a cafe, and made himself available for interview by the local press. When the van rolled up with Betsy at the wheel there was all the rush and excitement of the get-in, and the pressing inescapable sense for the whole team of time moving rapidly on. I liked the different moods of places we played in, and in larger towns the sense I had even while acting of the pride that the regulars took in having a theatre and going to it. The stage lighting gave glimpses of all these shadowy spaces, warehouses, drill-halls, now and then the gilt mouldings and two boxes of a proper old playhouse, or the concrete and blue plush of a brand-new building. The Arts in Ipswich was more like a chapel or church hall, narrow gallery all round, and a stage at knee-level of the front row of the stalls. The first night we pretty well filled it, almost three hundred people, though it thinned out a certain amount at the interval.

Johnny got our landlady there to take our photo outside her establishment – a risk, as the slightly blurred and sideways-sloping print confirmed when he got it back from the chemist's. But there we are, a team, an amazingly motley fifteen: Ken Mallow in the middle, Capulet and about to tackle Lear, 'Instinctive actor,' Ray said, 'does amazing things, but has no idea why', our senior member but too grouchy and scowling to be a father-figure to the rest of us. Pale little Wendy and skinny Jack Marks, big dark Derek Dos Passos, with Olu Samson from Lagos beside him, burly blond Gary Molesey next to Betsy the Jamaican SM in her desert boots and dungarees. Johnny, whose father was an immigrant from Goa, stands next to brilliant red-haired Ruth, whose Bristol accent Ray treasured and mocked undecidedly, and then there's me, Dave Win, looking very happy and also, as often in photographs, residually anxious, in a way I think the others never noticed.

Ray stands with pointed modesty at the end, small but with a large despotic presence; his style is professionally nonde-script, tight faded jeans like everyone else, belted tan-leather jacket, thick greying hair swept back under the wide-topped workman's cap that he kept on even indoors. He looks as if he might be on his way to the pub or the bookies', an off-duty salesman of some sort, with a battered briefcase in one hand; but in fact he was a well-connected artist, he'd worked with Charles Marowitz and David Hare, and he was a 'good friend' of Peter Brook, who'd come to his *Titus Andronicus* in Margate and 'very much seen the point of it,' Ray said. With his other hand he holds a cigarette just under his chin, impatient to get on with smoking it once the picture's been taken.

'We're on tour,' Ray would say, 'not on holiday.' And oddly, with no homes to go to, we felt a bit trapped – my first taste of the new isolation of touring, a bleakness beneath the adventure and the focused energy of work. In the days in Ipswich and then in Colchester we fitted in rehearsals for *Lear*, Ray's most ambitious show yet, due to open in Leicester six weeks later. I was Edgar, and grappling already with the problems of having three plays in my head at the same time. We were all in at ten the first morning, more or less, basic warm-ups, and then Ray said, 'I was thinking the Death Circle.' This was an exercise he'd borrowed from Marowitz but typically customized and made more alarming: the whole cast had to tramp round in a circle, singing whatever they liked at the top of their voices, and at unexpected moments Ray would clap or whistle and who-ever was beside him had to drop down dead, while the others carried on until only one person was left marching and singing their song, often with a quaver of genuine terror. But today Ken said, 'Can we not do that, Ray?' – no one else could have done so and been listened to, but Ray listened to Ken, and with only a hint of reluctance said, 'All right, then, Ken, as you like, let's get started.' That remission made us all more cheerful.

I rehearsed in the soft blue tracksuit I'd had at school,

rescued from Crackers and given a new life: it showed I had barely changed size in the past six years. We were working in a first sketchy way on Act Two, where Edgar learns that he must flee the court, and decides to disguise himself as a beggar. Scene Three is simply his twenty-line speech, in complex language of the kind I liked learning, and I was off the book already – it came easily to me but it made Ray disgruntled, 'If you learn it too soon you run false, by the time we open you've forgotten what the fucking words mean.' I jogged into the middle of the space among the chairs and tables, and expounded Edgar's situation. 'My face I'll grime with filth, / Blanket my loins, elf all my hairs in knots, / And with presented nakedness outface / The winds and persecutions of the sky.' As I spoke I pulled at my clothes and devised other gestures I knew Ray was bound to condemn and replace with his own ideas straight afterwards. He paced round me, smoking and nodding slowly in a way that in him rarely signalled approval; and left a long silence at the end, so that I looked at him and said, 'Or do you think, perhaps—'

'I hope,' he said, 'of course, very much, that Gielgud can be persuaded to play the part of Edgar the next time round. But for now can we please have Dave Win, young man with a grievance and a healthy suspicion of fine words. Thanks so much.'

I took it, as you had to with Ray, and half listened as he said what he thought I should do, and I wondered, did I have a grievance? I felt most of the company, without looking far, could find something that had harmed them, and oppressed them, and unfairly held them back. I tried not to dwell on it, thought it healthier not to, though I knew that I'd lived my short life so far in a chaos of privilege and prejudice. 'So we'll run it again, and as I say, find the panic, the spirit of improvisation.' 'OK . . .' 'His life's in danger, he's not singing an aria.' 'Well,' I said, 'some arias are very—' 'And this time for god's sake strip off, get used to all that.' 'Oh . . . OK,' and I glanced at the others, at big camp Gary studying his part with raised eyebrows and a hint of a smile – it was almost, but not quite, a joke for the actors, the nudity in Terra shows. Gary got his kit off whenever he could, Jack and Olu I'd seen naked in the Arden play, but this was my initiation. I couldn't say I hadn't seen it coming. So I did it, and as I said, 'whiles I may scape I will preserve myself' I pulled my top over my head and threw it aside and felt the cool, close to chill, of the room. It was a fair bit of business to add to the speech, prising off one shoe and then the other in the following lines, and then for good measure my socks. Ray sat now, staring through smoke, and when I got to 'presented nakedness' I tore off the bottoms and my underpants, and threw them away too. I poked and scratched at myself in the lines about Bedlam beggars mortifying their bare arms. I felt it was going down well, it was a relief and in fact rather more than that to the secret exhibitionist in me. 'Poor Turlygod!' I shouted, 'poor Tom! / That's something yet. Edgar I nothing am' – and here Lear and the Fool and Kent, waiting to come on, did look a bit uncertain, as I strolled back to pick up my clothes, and I knew that the mood of the rehearsal had been stretched and changed by my nakedness, though everyone studied their scripts as if a little private appraisal had not been smuggled in as a question of art.

It was a different sort of challenge the next week doing Stan Creeley's *Bodies* at Essex University – not in a theatre but in a large low room in the students' union. The whole campus was less than ten years old, and already weathered by student use and a recent three-week sit-in. The cafe on the 'plaza' had windows papered over with posters and stickers; and in the hallway too there was a whole wall of curling and dropping posters, the old pins pilfered to put up the new ones. Each time the tall glass doors from the wind-tunnel plaza were flung open by someone arriving or leaving, the notices chattered and whispered across the length of the board. The massive self-involvement of student life felt far off, but not dead to me, I saw red and yellow fliers for their own Dram Soc's *Merchant of Venice*, and I felt anxiously excited for them, and the ideas of future careers as actors that some of them were bound to be gripped by.

For *Bodies* the audience were seated on three sides of the room, and the cast, for ten minutes before the show started, were seated in a row on the fourth, hunched or bored and vaguely restless, as if waiting their turn at the barber's, not talking to each other and showing no interest at all in the public coming in. This neglect quickly gave the audience an unexpected interest – they stared it down blokishly or talked among themselves, but a certain discomfort at being a spectator had crept in, the latent embarrassment of theatre that Ray liked to work on. One or two nodded and smiled at us, as if to a professor about to start a seminar; we let our eyes run over them unseeing. The show came after their supper in hall, when they could have been doing something else, or nothing at all. We of course were doing our job, but at such times our job seemed to ride very free of the usual concept of acting, which as Ray said was bourgeois crap. Even so, I was running through my part with the quick steady heartbeat of anticipation and noting the whole rows of empty chairs. Then the customary chatter crammed in before the lights go down faltered, and we sat in spontaneous silence for a minute or more, till the blackout.

Bodies was already famous for its long first scene played in total darkness. Voices are heard, very quietly, '. . . or between the thighs . . .', '. . . you see she likes it better from the other side – yes, round the backside . . .', '. . . he has such stamina, doesn't he . . .' Two or three conversations, or strings of exchanges, which the audience try to make sense of, as coming from characters, while gradually the green exit lights illuminate the space, eyes adapt, and just about make out six figures, four men and two women, seated on the ground, and talking with insouciant frankness about sex. Sex with persons not present, and then, pretty clearly, and imminently, with each other. The near-darkness is an obstacle, and a blessing. Then as stage-lights edge up out of nothing the weirdly free talk becomes inhibited, the players react with dismay to the sight of the audience, they stand up, peering at them, Creeley says, 'as if at a long-feared threat made manifest', and the minute or more of dumb show that follows seems to the audience agonizingly longer, as the actors do what they declined to do before, they face them down, hold their eye, refuse to be intimidated, before turning and stalking off into another blackout. We all had evening dress under our scrubs, and now there was one of Ray's famous quick-changes, before we re-entered for a second scene, a party, all rococo chit-chat, some of it quite funny, with the catalogue of sexual positions and perversions still fresh in the viewer's mind. 'Puerile' the *Evening Standard* had called it, 'undeniably clever' *Time Out*, and again, just by seconds, as the lights slowly strengthened on the students' faces, I thought what on earth would I have made of all this at their age, virginal and knowing sex mainly through images and hearsay. I saw them taking it, some grinning nervously, some loving it, some upset to be listening, and then seen listening.

The day I got back to London Chris said he needed to see me at lunchtime, couldn't wait till the evening. He worked in a tall gleaming building in Victoria Street, high up on the twentieth floor: some time, he said, he would show me his office, the view of the Cathedral and Westminster Abbey, but not today. I chose the bridge over the lake in St James's Park, and got there unintentionally early. The Blue Bridge it's called, its arc so slight it barely rises in its stride across the water. The lake was broken and glittering in the breeze, and I didn't think, till I stood at the centre, of my meeting with Nick three years earlier, in another park a mile or so away, our miserable lunch, and the ducks on the Serpentine below. Here much more exotic-looking water-birds were pushing about, and I had a sense of life now at a brisker tempo, in a brighter key.

I was the one with the news, and we ate a sandwich sitting on a bench while I told him about *R&J*, and *Bodies* at the university, but for some reason I kept the *Lear* rehearsal to myself. I think I wanted it to surprise him, when he came up for the weekend to Leicester to see it. But I said how the sex-talk in *Bodies* had been tricky for the actors, in rehearsal, and how I saw it all differently since I'd met him and done quite a few of the things Stan Creeley's characters described. Chris loved this, he was easy to flatter and amuse, and anything to do with me seemed to have an exaggerated magic for him; but after a minute, as I talked and made it all as entertaining as I could, it was clear he was smiling in helpless excitement at my being there touchably and kissably in front of him, his head shaking, dumbly biting his lip and not taking in a word I was saying. 'I don't think you're really very interested in how the play went, are you?' I said.

'I am, honey . . . the audience were laughing and Wendy hurt her foot.'

'Mm, OK,' I said, but a sort of satire had come into his attention. All he really wanted was me.

He had to get back to the office, and I went with him that way, onto Birdcage Walk. There was no one within a hundred yards of us, on the tree-shaded pavement, and we kissed goodbye, had a hug that turned into a bit of a snog, reckless somehow but not to be resisted. It should have been Chris, but it was me who said, 'God, I can't wait for tonight!' We stood back, laughing and thinking, hand in hand, rather sweetly, though I heard

voices and I glanced aside, through the railings and low shrub-
bery, into the garden of the tall grand house beside us. French
windows were open, and at a table on the terrace an older man
in a dark suit was talking to a younger one, who had his back
to us and seemed to be writing things down. It took me several
staring seconds then to focus, and to levitate, and hanging high
up swivel the scene round. The older man's voice was unmis-
takable, the quick surges in volume when he made a point, and
of course the daft architect glasses; the bulkiness of Giles I still
hadn't grown used to, the hair thick on the collar, and Chris I
think had never met him or taken him in: he meant nothing to
him. I made a funny face, pulled his hand and drew him away;
I don't think he knew we'd come back to the beginning, though
now, thank god, on the other side of the fence.

21

Each day when I went off on tour again, to Liverpool and Chester and Leeds, Chris wrote to me, sometimes on Westminster City Council paper and franked 'First Class Urgent' at the office. They were the filthiest letters I've ever read. 'You must be behind with your rates,' said Ken when he saw another envelope arrive. I hadn't told the team much about Chris yet, for unexamined reasons, but I let myself be teased about having a boyfriend. They called them love letters but the love part was slapdash, charming and conventional, compared to the sex part. Sometimes I found a spare half-hour to reply, in whatever lodgings or travellers' hotel we were sharing in, twin-bedded rooms for non-sexual couples, washed-out underwear drying on the radiator. Sometimes I just sent a postcard, which saved me from trying to match his inventiveness; I saw Claudia stooping in the dusty hall to pick up the afternoon post, then taking it into a better light to read my tiny writing.

Then it was back to the house, where various small annoyances had become routine for me now, and almost endearing – the way you had to open the front door again, when you left, and slam it harder, the problematic geyser, the pink silk lampshades scorched brown by the bulbs and threatening to burn the place down. I went up to Chris's room and unpacked, and lay on the bed, which he'd changed and made hotel-smart for my return. I was randy as hell, but I loved lying there for the first time without him. Sometimes he asked me if I'd picked anyone up, 'had any adventures' when I was out of town – once

I gave him a merciless account of an older man who'd come to the stage-door in Chester and taken me back to his hotel, watching Chris as excitement and uncomfortable jealousy coloured and stiffened his face, before I gave in and said, 'No, of course I didn't!' Still, the idea was there, actors on tour, it turned out, were known to be up for it, and Gary seemed to get off with someone everywhere we stayed – though he was big and forthright and a natural comic, where I was, as he candidly put it, 'a more specialized taste'.

When Claudia raised her glass that evening and said, 'So good you've settled in,' I saw myself for a moment in the long light of her phrase – matrons' letters, school reports, the note of relief, and surprise, that I seemed to have found my place in one difficult environment after another. The effect at Claudia's was less of settling than of sinking, into squashy beds and sofas and a haze of booze and cigarette smoke. She rolled her own, in her ladylike way, and her commonest gesture when she stood up to refresh her drink was to brush off the crumbs of tobacco from her front.

I was sitting by Chris, thigh to thigh on the amorous sofa, and with the funny little feeling I'd had on my first visit weeks before that I was somehow a project for both of them. I said, 'I wish I could settle properly, Claudia, but we spend so much time on the road.'

'Nice, though, I hope, for you to have a London anchorage. That hostel place sounded too awful!'

'Oh, much nicer here,' I said, as Chris put his hand on my knee and after a second or two I wove my fingers through his. Excitement in my tight jeans was hard to hide, but I made a bit of absent-minded play with a loose cushion and pulled it into my lap and teased out the tangled fringe with my other hand.

'It's so marvellous for us to hear about your work,' said Claudia, still smiling at me warmly. In someone else, this might have been mere bland twaddle, a note of encouragement close to condescension, but she'd seen me on TV in *Hibiscus Hotel* and Chris, I was sure, had talked up the glamour of the man he was bringing into their strange cosy life together. 'And I feel it's only fair to you, honestly, if I don't charge you rent for the weeks when you're not here.'

I think she read my little gasp as one of gratitude. 'That's very good of you, Claudia,' I said, blinking and staring away as if shocked by her kindness rather than what felt at that moment like her greed. 'And of course if you want to see one of our shows when we're in London, you must say.'

'Well ... thank you, David, very much,' she said, and looked down modestly; I could tell she was rather nervous at the idea. She seemed never to go out, she went to the hairdresser's, and she went to the nearby Sainsbury's, with the wicker shopping-basket on wheels of a much older woman; but she was there in the kitchen or in state in the drawing room whenever I came back, and our evenings at the house were largely, as she said with a smile, 'à trois'. She slept at the far end of the landing, but I wondered more than once if she'd heard Chris and me going at it. I saw her being always there.

At the end of the week I handed her ten pounds, which she tucked in her purse in her bag on a hook in the hall cupboard, and it was that little formalization and folding away, and the closing of the hall-cupboard door, that told me I was caught. I was moody and kept to myself that night in bed. 'Tired?' Chris said. 'I am a bit,' I said; and lay awake as he settled down and his breathing slowed. His last move, a mumbling, nearly unconscious upheaval, was to back up against me and pull my arm round him; and I lay there for ten minutes, with the smooth weight of his belly warm under my hand, until, a bit later, I rolled back into myself.

*

Soon enough, the question of meeting my family started working its way into Chris's talk at the table, or in bed. 'I don't have a family,' I said, though I'd told him about Mum, I'd explained myself, as I so often did. 'She sounds really adventurous,' he said. 'And she's . . . she lives with another woman.' I could see him getting on better with Esme than with Mum, but it was Mum he was intrigued by and prone to little speculative remarks about. 'I suppose your mother must . . . Does she look like you?' 'Well, so people say. She's a different colour, obviously.' He seemed to look for her fondly in my features. 'So daring, what she did.' 'You mean getting pregnant?' 'Does she ever talk about it?' 'She says there's nothing to say – it happened twenty-five years ago, and on the other side of the world. It was a terrible mistake.' 'She doesn't say that?' 'No, she doesn't, but I made things very difficult for her.' I couldn't convey to an outsider the force-field Mum had set up round the subject of my father, a strong mutation of maternal power.

Extraordinary the multiple anxieties, the unimagined perspectives, of a weekend at Crackers with Chris. He rented a bright yellow Cortina, and I drove us down in it. I'd been home so little in the three momentous years since the Oxford disaster that the visit was a sort of rapprochement in disguise, with Chris as the ostensible subject. 'It'll be nice to have someone in the spare bedroom again,' Mum said on the phone, and I didn't know what she envisaged, or was licensing; I'd never brought a boyfriend home before. Esme at least had known Gilbert and his many close friends but Mum had never been friends with a gay man, much less a gay couple, before. 'You won't mind if I'm not all over you while we're at Mum's,' I said in the car.

'Absolutely,' he said, 'of course. Are we nearly there?'

The road was just gathering and focusing in the primitive way it had, a mile or two from Foxleigh, before the long descent into the town. I said, 'In a moment you'll see the pillbox where I used to play as a child.'

'Fascinating,' he said, 'could you pull over at this lay-by?'

'Are you feeling OK?' I drew up at the far end, under trees, beside an overflowing bin that I gazed at unseeing, and with glances in the mirror, while he went down on me. He finished off, wiped his lips and his chin with his handkerchief, and gave me a kiss: 'May not get a chance later!' I felt lightly scandalized to find that I'd had sex so close to home – when we pulled out again onto the main road we soon came up behind a grey Rover 90, trundling forward at 26 mph. From the rear it seemed not to have a driver, though I knew very well how old Dr Grahame, bent low with arthritis, looked out through the steering wheel rather than over it. 'The man driving that car,' I said, 'is our family doctor, he's known me since I was four years old.'

'So you do have a family,' said Chris.

Chris had never heard of Foxleigh before he met me, so I saw it a little through his eyes as well as through the odd prosaic trance of knowing every shop-sign and doorstep. It was Saturday afternoon and Wincroft was closed, but I turned down Coach Lane and into Church Street so as to drive past it. 'That's Mum and Esme's shop,' I said. In the window Betty and Tricia, the two tireless mannequins, raised their right hands and gazed out, as if they'd just seen something wonderful on the far side of the road; they were in smart new autumn suits, Tricia's with a belted jacket and slightly flared trousers. Chris said it looked very chic, and I thought myself it had a gleam and presence out of key with its street and its town, it was a triumph but also a risk.

As we drove up Marlborough Street I seemed to see the house already, see through it, Esme staring at the *Telegraph* crossword and Mum in the kitchen peeling potatoes to fill up the anxious time between lunch and our arrival at 'round about three'. We swept into the drive, and the house had a blank look, plain and capable but not quite sure what was coming. Oddly enough, I hadn't brought my keys, and rather than ringing the bell I led Chris round the side of the house so that we saw them first through the sitting-room window, Mum in fact knitting and Esme watching the horse-racing on TV: I gave them a start by tapping on the glass. Heads turning, the second's fluster and confusion erased at once by the act of delight and surprise. Mum unlocked the French windows, and welcomed us in – the old hug, forgiving, instinctual, as Chris looked on smiling: then, 'Mum, this is Chris Canvey,' and they shook hands and Chris said, almost laughing, 'So fabulous to meet you!' and meant it, I knew, though to her I think it sounded affected. 'Hul*lo*!' said Esme, crossing the room, and looking in those first clear unconditioned moments magnificently active and glowing. I'd forgotten her glamour, which clearly struck Chris too, and they laughed as they went straight in over a handshake for a kiss on the cheek. 'Let me turn this off,' said Esme, 'now do sit down,' and Chris sat by Mum on the sofa while I found myself going back to my old chair by the fireplace. 'I hope you weren't held up too long by the roadworks on Chalk Street,' Esme said as she dropped down opposite me, 'they've been causing some terrible hold-ups.'

'We were stuck there for about ten minutes yesterday,' Mum said, and glanced at Chris for signs of sympathy or indignation.

'It's the Water Board,' Esme explained, 'not known round here for their efficiency, I'm afraid!'

I said, 'No, it was fine, wasn't it, Chris?'

'What can I get you?' said Mum, jumping up.

'Oh . . . !' I said, 'let me . . .' sitting forward, and caught in an undefined role between host and visitor and prodigal son.

Chris asked to have a bath before dinner, and this left me alone for the first time with Mum and Esme. 'Well, your beau seems to like it here,' said Esme.

'You should see the place where he lives,' I said with a funny face to cover my confusion at her being so open about things.

'What's it like?' said Mum.

'I mean, it's comfy,' I said, 'but it is a bit squalid.'

'Oh dear!'

I gazed round at the order and smartness here, the yards upon yards of Ladies in Waiting that Mum had made up half-satirically and now found herself living with.

I wasn't sure if they found Chris's greater age reassuring or disconcerting. 'He's probably pretty well paid, I should think, isn't he,' said Esme. She'd rather basked in the boredom of Chris's stories about Council business, the shenanigans over budgets. 'Fascinating, isn't it Av, to have this insider view?'

Mum hadn't been paying much attention, but she shook her head and said, 'Absolutely.' I wondered if her idea of a gay man wasn't something a bit odder than this, if she wasn't rather worried, now she'd met Chris, that I would soon be as bored by him as she was.

We all got fairly drunk at dinner, and afterwards over the *Nine O'Clock News* Esme would sigh and start to say something you assumed was to do with the report we were watching but turned out to be about some other programme she wondered if Chris ever looked at. He answered quietly, respecting the self-conscious attention Mum and I were paying to the *coup d'état* in Chile. Another drink was offered, but Chris did some plausible yawning and stretching and we all suddenly agreed it had been a long day. I hadn't been to bed so early since I was at school. Chris pulled me into the bathroom when he was cleaning his teeth for a horrible peppermint snog, and I half expected him to creep along the landing later, but when I crept out myself about eleven to the lav I could hear his soft snoring through the spare-bedroom door, and talk too quiet to make out from Mum and Esme's room beyond.

*

The next day while lunch was being made Chris said could I take him for a walk round the town, show him where I'd grown up? I wanted to do it, to be given the treat of a lover's attention to the shaming and touching little details of my past, but then I was worried that he wouldn't see the point, and wary after all about the self-exposure. Also I imagined he was hoping for a blow-job, at the very least, and as I put on my jacket and called out, 'Back soon!' my mind ran ahead for a copse or a corner where it might possibly be had. As soon as we got out into the Close, still in earshot, he said, 'David, they're fantastic!' and flung his arms round my shoulder as we walked so that I nearly fell over. He'd been saving it up, to tell me. 'I love them.'

'Oh good, I'm so glad . . .' I said, relieved and laughing and in some unexpected way upset, as if he'd at once seen the point of them, adult to adult, while I was still tangled in teenage resentments.

'Esme's complete heaven, she ought to be on TV, I adore her.'

'Well, I think she likes you a lot too,' I said.

'I think we have rather hit it off.'

'What do you see her doing – on TV?'

'Ooh, a chat show, I think, don't you? – one with plenty for the guests to drink, my god she knocks it back.' He peered at me. 'Sorry, love, I'm not being awful about her, you know that.'

I shrugged and grinned to show I didn't mind. Praising Esme first left the question of Mum for the moment in the air, and I wondered if she hadn't lived up to the idea he'd formed of her. 'Mum's much quieter, of course,' I said.

'Well,' said Chris, and shook his head, 'she's completely amazing.' I thought there was something very loving to me in his saying this. 'And beautiful, too.'

It wasn't for me to deny this, and it was probably leading round to a compliment to me – that I was 'so like her' and so on. I said, 'People don't often say that, actually.'

'You really need to be a lesbian like me to appreciate her properly.'

'Maybe that's it,' I said.

'You can bet all those girls that Esme keeps mentioning are mad about her.'

'Well,' I said cautiously, confronted again by this idea of my mother, so well known to me that I hardly saw her, emerging in her new life as something of a stunner. I was pleased, and still smilingly doubtful, and again a little worried, that we'd lost each other, just as she found herself – the old problem.

'It was lovely to hear her speaking about you – she's so proud of you – well, they both are, of course.'

'Really?' I said, and now I thought he was inventing diplomatically – he always liked people to get on.

'She said they'd both really like to come to your shows, but they feel you don't want them there.'

'Well, I've asked them to come,' I said.

'Anyway, I thought I should tell you that, because you always seem a bit embarrassed about her.'

'Do I?' I said, and knew that he was wrong, that he misunderstood my tone, as the accusation sank in and took hold. 'I'm very proud of her myself, actually.'

'Yes, that's what I told her,' Chris said, and kissed me on the side of the head to stop me sulking before I had started.

As we came down Chalk Street there was something unlikely if not quite impossible in seeing his reflection moving beyond mine in the shop windows. I had brought a man home, a small, barely perceptible victory. One or two people glanced at me, half smiled as they passed, and either they remembered me, vaguely, from my childhood, or they thought I looked a bit like the young man who'd been in *Hibiscus Hotel*. To others who noticed, I suppose I was an unexpected foreigner, being shown round the town by his English host. Was my secret visible at all – that I performed homosexual acts with this man twice a day, and three times, sometimes, at weekends? We walked up the Square and I pointed out our old flat, strolled on past so as not to attract the attention of whoever might be up there, invisibly looking down. The windows were nearly opaque in the sun, the cream-coloured linings of the curtains just showing in my old bedroom. It was a test for Chris, the completely uninteresting thing that was charged with meaning for me. 'I'm picturing you there very clearly as a teenager,' he said, with the guileless expression that masked his dirtiest thoughts, but as we went on he put his arm through mine and seemed unexpectedly more touched by the sight of those blank windows than I was. It was me who had failed to see the point.

We came home through the top of the town, past the Regal and Bishop Alfred's, and crossed the main road, and though the first field had recently been harrowed I took him over the stile for the loop back through Ansell's Farm. The line of the footpath had already been trampled down, but we went single file for a while, me following with the ongoing unexpected finding of the weekend, that he was the leader. I had my eye, on and off, on the hem of his short outdoor jacket as it edged up and down with each step and then as he thrust both hands in its pockets was pulled tight across the small of his back – my thoughts were of the common kind but my heart wasn't quite in the scene I was picturing, if we turned right at the stile instead of left, and crossed to the large dusty barn where the drier was, an adult dare laid over a childish one. I realized, not as a flash, but in a slow welling-up of unresolved feelings, formless and confusing but rising into clarity, how cruel – how neglectful, and unkind – I had been to my mother for the past three years, my shame at myself taken out on her.

It was Chris who had helped me to see this, in his generous straightforward way, and I loved him for it, even as spasms of resentment, and dismay that he'd had to do it, went through me. Over the stile into the next field, and the stretch of path marked for ever by the old trout who'd sneered at me and Mum years ago, and we turned left for home. I came alongside, my shoes in the knobbly half-soft crust of the ploughed edge, and took Chris's hand as we swung along. I don't know if he understood what was going on any better than I did.

22

'I can't drive,' said Derry Blundell on the phone, 'I mean I can *drive*, I drove a fucking *tank* in the War, but I don't have a licence, not at the moment, so I'm afraid I can't meet you at the station. Or are you driving down yourself?'

'I do have a licence,' I said, 'but I don't have a car.'

'You'll need to get a train from Waterloo to Gillingham, with a hard G. For Christ's sake don't go to the soft-G one. Then take a taxi from the station. The house is *somewhat* hard to find, tell the driver to head towards Shaftesbury, and take the third turning on the left after the Melton Arms. He probably won't want to, but tell him he's got to. There's a ford at the bottom, it's not too deep, and it's the first gateway up the hill on the right after that. There's a statue of Boadicea outside.'

'That should be easy to spot,' I said. I wasn't sure if he was trying to be funny, or if I was.

I looked up where I was going in the road atlas, which I'd bought as though I did have a car. Great Gores, the notably secluded old house which Derry and Bill Severne had bought before the War, was right on the Wiltshire / Dorset border, and disowned, according to Derry, by both counties. 'We pay our rates to Dorset, but they say we're in Wiltshire when it comes to collecting the rubbish; and then there's the whole sewerage question, of course.' It seemed a sad matter for a once adventurous man to be bothered with. On the map the lane where he lived was a thin thread taking the longest route possible between two B roads, themselves of a rambling and dilatory nature. But I knew nothing yet of the hills they were making their way through.

Ten days later I was on the train, clattering out through south-west London and into the safely mindless prospect of two hours' travel – Woking first, and then on across Hampshire and Wiltshire, and into the surprising topmost little corner of Dorset. I felt a mild relief at getting out of town by myself, a grateful expansion into the air and space of the country; I'd been a bit ratty with Chris since we'd got back from tour, my irritation channelled confusingly into non-stop sex – he was grateful and resentful in rapid succession, and as reluctant as I was to talk about what might be wrong.

I don't know what I expected from the visit to Derry, or why I'd said I would go. A small handsome grey-haired man had come round after the *Troilus* in Southampton, excited and critical, and keen, above all, to have a word with me. I was still getting dressed when he knocked and walked in. He had the bearing of a soldier and made no bones about watching me button my shirt and pull on my jeans. He'd seen me in nothing but a leather thong earlier in the evening, but this was more intimate. Something touched my vanity, the much older man with an element, a residue of sexual challenge – my response to an imagined observer, someone else in the cast, was 'Of course not!' with a smile that protected my right at least to flirt. I had the feeling, I had it all the time in the mixed world of artists and actors we moved in, of almost knowing his name; so I was cautious and polite, and he was flattering and candid, as if used to success, and expecting one with me. The next day, in the Southampton Art Gallery, I saw a photo of him and Bill Severne by Beaton, in rehearsal at Sadler's Wells – forty years ago nearly, jackets and ties, cigarettes, stage brilliance in a circle of shadow. Bill, ten years older, was tall, fair and feminine-looking; and I remembered then that he'd come to Bampton, to give the Art Club a talk on theatre design, a bit beyond our needs or understanding; he had died of Parkinson's disease last year. In the photo Derry had oiled-down dark hair but otherwise looked much like he did now.

At Gillingham, the taxi driver let out a heavy sigh when I told him the address, then muttered to me to get in. It was a former London cab, now with ads for an Indian restaurant in Shaftesbury nodding surreally on the back of the fold-down seats. Once we were out of the town, the driver found a way to get at the subject. 'Staying the night, are you?' he said.

'I hope not,' I said. I'd only brought my briefcase, with the *Guardian* and Derry's book *Staging an Opera* for him to sign. In the driver's glance in the mirror, suspicion and possible collusion seemed to mingle, as if I might need putting in the picture about the man I was going to see. I focused on the landscape. It was beautiful country, of the kind that filled me with the old mixed longings, to be there always and to go straight back to town.

'Been in England long?' said the driver.

'Twenty-six years,' I said. He seemed caught up then in some sour calculations.

Before long I saw the Melton Arms looming, and soon after that we slowed and turned into a steep narrow lane between high hedges. At the bottom it levelled out and the driver changed down to first gear to enter the ford. 'Got your lifebelt on?' he said. It was the deepest ford I'd ever been through, and the driver himself started looking very anxious as the unrelenting water pushed round us and seemed to want to sweep us away downstream. I wondered breathlessly if that had ever happened but just then we started to shake free of it and we shot up the ramp on the far side in a frothing roar.

I'd formed my own idea of the statue of Boadicea and it was only as we were turning off the lane that I saw it, a mossy helmet and sword sticking up above the bushes. The taxi made its way down the track, rocking from side to side, coming almost to a stop in the waterlogged potholes, the driver's caution mixed with a certain satisfaction that I was getting what I asked for. I sat absorbing the jolts and smiling remotely, while thinking we might actually be on the wrong track altogether. Then chimneys and a gable appeared among the trees below, and I felt the gentle clench of arrival, and the encounter about to happen. The trees opened out into a gravel circle in front of the house, where Derry himself was standing with his hands in his jacket pockets as if wondering where we'd got to. We seemed to go straight for him – there was a moment's war of nerves with the taxi, which pulled up almost on his toes. I crouched inside, passing money to the driver through the sliding screen, and with no more than an impression of the house as I glanced out – urns, a pediment and a pillared porch, stuck onto what looked like an older and humbler building.

There was challenge as well as greeting in Derry's tone. 'You look different,' he said.

'Hello!' I said, grinning, unsure what to call him, but letting him peer at me. He shook my offered hand as if it really wasn't necessary.

'It's the glasses' – with a hint of reproach.

'Oh . . . oh, yes . . . well, I generally don't wear them on stage.'

'No, of course,' he said, forgivingly, with a hand on my shoulder to guide me to the front door. 'Cyril Matthews was blind as a bat too, you know. I once saw him deliver the whole of Polonius's speech to Laertes to the extra who was playing his servant – brought the house down, and he felt he'd had a great success, without having a clue what he'd done to deserve it. It didn't stop him from being one of the greatest actors of his age.'

'No, I'm sure,' I said. 'Did he ever trip over things?'

'Well, I wonder. I never heard that he did.'

I followed Derry into the house. In the dark panelled hall, with an oak staircase rising beyond, he seemed unsure if he was merely a host or a guide as well. 'Gosh . . .' I said, propping my briefcase on a chair as I gazed around. He said, 'What's that . . . ? Ah, yes,' pleased and perhaps a little bored that he would have to explain it all to me. 'I'll give you a good look at everything later.' In the light of the one small window behind them it was hard to make out exactly the three or four busts on plinths, bare-shouldered young men with strong features and licks of hair in white plaster and reddish clay. The light threw its own glaze over the framed and mounted drawings, clearly costume designs, perhaps for some ballet with an Oriental subject.

'Amazing!' I said.

He drew a sequence of short breaths, as if each time about to start explaining, but then said merely, 'I'm glad you like them.'

We went down a stone-flagged passage and before he had lifted the latch on the sitting-room door he said, 'What will you have to drink?'

I glanced at my watch, 'Perhaps just a glass of water?'

He crossed the room and moved around for a minute, rather grim-faced, saying nothing. 'You won't have a sherry or something?'

'I won't, thanks.'

He went out, to find some water for me. When he came back he had a vaguely contrite look, as if feeling it might be my race, or religion, that kept me from alcohol. He smiled indulgently as he passed the glass to me. 'Bill had occasional spells on the wagon,' he said.

It was a long low room, oppressively full of furniture, objects and pictures, all no doubt interesting in themselves. As my eye ran over photos, small portraits, small table-top bronzes of soldiers and naked wrestlers, I wasn't sure what was fine art and what was mere memorabilia – the framed set-designs perhaps were both. There was bric-à-brac that looked fairly ordinary to me, and there was a bronze of a Burmese boy, bare-legged in a tucked-up longyi, that was very like things I'd found on my drifts through the unpeopled Far Eastern Cultures wings of large museums. I tensed with the nearly subliminal sense I had now and then, in the house of someone new, of entering a trap, however gilded and apparently comfortable. I was still adjusting and pretending not to notice the Eastern theme as I homed in on the portrait that must have been Bill hanging opposite the main window. 'Well I know who this is,' I said warmly, as I tried to decipher the artist's red signature. It showed him very young, golden, lips parted, perhaps a bit too much pink in the cheeks.

'Yes . . . I'd like to say it was how I remember him, but the fact is the chap who painted it was madly in love with him, and I'm afraid it shows.' I thought of the photo by Beaton and the old man at school with his vague pansy look and drinker's high colour.

'You have some marvellous things . . .' I said. Of course I was very aware of being in a homosexual house, objects and pictures more or less eloquent of the fact, a rich anomaly, buried deep in the country – I wondered if Derry had someone like Esme's Mrs Wilson, calmly dusting the bronze boys and smiling at the photographs on the piano as if they were her own old friends.

'Well, I'll take you round in a bit,' he said. 'Let's have a drink first,' and he fell backwards into a large squashy chair that seemed accustomed to the shock. 'Sit there, where I can see you.' I looked round and picked a little French armchair a few feet away from him. As with the unnecessary handshake I felt a bit unsure about what was good form. 'Well, as I say, I enjoyed your show,' he said.

'Thank you – yes. We were all very glad you came.'

'Not everything about it. It was much too noisy for my taste.'

'A lot of people thought the same as you,' I said.

'You don't need all that noise to make a point. Whatever the point was supposed to be.'

'I suppose we were aiming to convey the relentless effect of war.'

'Mm, but it's a play, isn't it, not an actual war. A few bangs and screams would have got that across.'

'I must say I sometimes had the same thought, you know, being in it night after night!'

He shot me a winner's glance. 'Of course,' he went on more admiringly, 'we could never have had all that bare flesh on stage in my day,' and gave me an odd little smile. 'You know, actual cocks.'

'It keeps us in the news,' I said.

'You've never done it yourself?' he said airily.

'What's that . . . ?'

'Gone nude on stage?'

'Yes, I have,' I said, 'once or twice.'

He didn't quite know what to say then. I peered at the brown grand piano beside me, with the half-dozen framed photos clustered on the lid. Did Derry play? I had a feeling the Cole Porter songbook had been open on the stand for a long time. And I had an awkward sense that I ought to recognize the faces – I was trying to decipher signatures scrawled at steep angles, possibly when drunk. I made out Tony Britton and Cocteau, was it? and a very young Rudolf Nureyev. One of them showed a handsome Asian man, perhaps older than he looked in theatrical make-up, and bare-chested, 'To Derry, love Tony' written slantingly at shoulder level. 'Who's that on the left?' I asked.

'Ah, yes,' said Derry, again with a stare and a heavy breath as he took up the task of explaining a subject from scratch – he could do it, he'd done it before, and in a way of course he wanted to do it, but the gap between his knowledge and my youthful ignorance had to be imagined and spanned. 'There's a better picture of him, in fact, over there,' and as I turned round: 'Tony Sein – you may well have heard of him.' We got to our feet again and crossed the room. The other picture was a small painted portrait, dark and hard to see, but Derry switched on a lamp underneath it, and it leapt into colour – it was like a little shrine in the corner of the room. It showed the young man full length, in jewelled costume and gaung-baung, right arm raised behind him, the left stretched forward, hand flexed. I'm not sure I'd have known it showed the same person. 'It's a lovely image of Tony by old Gerald Kelly,' Derry said, 'who died the other day, I don't know if you saw, ninety-five.'

'Oh . . . Sir Gerald Kelly PRA,' I said, '"A Tragic Gesture"!'

'Ah, yes, quite so,' said Derry, tilting the lamp so that I was lit up by it too. 'Though this gesture's different, obviously. I imagine you must know about Burmese dance?'

'Mm, not *really*,' I said. I felt him looking from Tony to me and then back.

'You've got something of his look.'

'Oh, do you think so? It's a bit hard to tell.'

'Something about the eyes' – embarrassed, perhaps, but pushing on. 'You told me you're half English, but you're pretty dark, I'd say.'

'My father was very dark.'

'Was he, yes,' said Derry, in a reasonable tone. 'Anyway, that's Tony – he was a great love of mine.'

'Aha.'

'He came to London with a Burmese dance troupe not long after the War. Most beautiful man you ever saw. Everyone said so.'

I sat down again on the hard fauteuil with a deepening certainty of being not only an interesting young man but a particular type of young man that was especially interesting to Derry. 'Where is he now?' I said. Derry fell back into his armchair and smiled tenderly across at Tony's portrait as if about to answer, but perhaps he hadn't heard. I couldn't sort out my feelings about being a type, when the type was one he felt such tenderness for.

When we went through to have lunch it turned out there was a woman in the house, who brought in warm plates as we sat down and helped us to some sort of cutlet, with vegetables. Derry muttered at her as if she was being a nuisance, though I could tell straight away she did everything for him. She wasn't friendly exactly, and I felt I might be suffering for some row she was having with him; she'd made an effort, not a huge one, for a visitor from London, and I was too charming to her, and felt she didn't trust me. I was glad when she went out of the room. Soon a radio could be heard very faintly, singing and laughter, and a louder noise of clanging pans, which Derry seemed used to ignoring.

We sat on either side of a round oak table, Derry framed for me by a high carved mantelpiece of dark leaves and flowers, his grey hair swept back and gleaming: the picture of a country gentleman in tweed jacket, red tie and breast-pocket handkerchief. Behind him in my mind's eye was the elegant, impatient young man in the black-and-white Beaton photo. His high colour now I guessed was due as much to drink as to country air. He'd had a good War, as he passingly told me, MC in North Africa, and when he got up to fetch a bottle from the sideboard the stiffness of age was defied and disguised by the military squareness of his bearing. I accepted a small glass of a red he said he thought I'd enjoy. But as lunch went on something more troubled came into his stare at me over the polished oak.

It was obvious he fancied me, but he had to keep forgiving

me too for not having heard of people he talked about, and this in some subtle way seemed to put pressure on me not to disappoint him further. He moved in an atmosphere of connections, largely in the past, with possibly brilliant people, dancers and designers, certain émigré painters, librettists of pre-war operas that were 'very well-received' at the time, and very rarely heard thereafter. He was excited by Marowitz and Peter Brook, I could tell he'd enjoyed the way Terra shattered the decorum, the habit of disguise he'd mastered in his own career (his shock wasn't that of an ordinary elderly play-goer but of a gay man who hadn't been allowed to go nearly so far). There was an air of pride in what he had done, and weariness too, a mixed sense that his past had been notably interesting and that the past was all he had left. I said he should come back and direct something new, and he said no one would want him, 'and besides' – as he refilled his wine glass for the third time – 'I'm not sure I'm up to it now.'

'And what about books?' I said blandly. 'Are you writing something new?' He looked pleased and then also rather pained.

'The books were very much a sideline,' he said.

'Still . . .' I said . . . but didn't press on, not even having read the book of his I'd brought with me and not wanting to suggest that at his age a sideline might be something to be grateful for.

'Since Bill died,' he said, staring at me and blinking, features maudlin for a moment, and I looked down shyly.

I started to say, 'How long were—' and he said heavily, 'Forty-three years,' and then at once, changing his tone, 'on and off, you know, with some bloody awful upsets all the way through.' He laughed as he took another swig from his glass. 'Once he buggered off – and I use the word advisedly – for a year and a half.'

'And did you ever bugger off yourself?' I said, feeling this was allowed. He seemed not to have heard, but then shrugged and said,

'Oh God yes . . . more than once. But we always came back, you know? Always came back.' He seemed to notice his half-eaten meal, and went at it again irritably. 'And what about you, David?' he said.

'Oh . . .' I said, 'I've been with someone for a couple of years now.'

'Another actor,' said Derry, sawing at his cutlet.

'No, not at all,' I said. 'He works for Westminster Council.'

'Oh, really, I see . . .' – undecided, it seemed, if this was original or deadly dull.

'He's quite a lot older than me.'

'Of course that was the thing with Bill and me, he was ten years older than I was.'

'Just the same with me and Chris,' I said.

'There were some very striking young men in your cast,' Derry said, as if I might consider living with one of them instead. 'The young Negro actor, for instance, who was playing Aeneas.'

'Hector,' I said.

Derry looked at me strictly. 'Hector was a burly blond fellow.'

'No, Hector Bishop is the name of the actor.' It was a joke, pretty threadbare by the end, throughout the rehearsals, and Derry seemed more cross about it than amused.

'A great stage presence.'

'Yes, he's just joined us, a few months ago.'

'Hard to take your eyes off him.'

'I'm glad you liked him,' I said, and gave a little laugh that disowned the mildly romantic feelings I had about Hector myself.

The awful upsets in Derry's love life impressed me as much as the unimaginably long time the two men had shared. I thought more fondly, after my glass of red, about Chris, it was how I lived now, and imagined continuing to live, slowly changing, but with something that had never changed from the start, my feeling that it was temporary, and fun and sexy though it was I surely wasn't going to spend the whole of my life like this. Not a feeling I could share or discuss with Chris himself, of course.

After lunch we went back into the sitting room, and Derry's conversation became rather more unbuttoned, he talked about getting the clap in the army, and the relative dimensions of famous actors' cocks. I didn't mind this, but I wasn't used to his particular mixture of sex talk with sharp, rather technical remarks about Mozart and Sheridan. He said he wanted to show me the garden, but he seemed to have settled into a monologue and I was starting to wonder about ordering a taxi and before that securing some promise of help from him for our next Terra production. I had settled down myself, in an appreciative pose, smirking and tutting as he rambled on, while also now thinking unstoppably about what I was going to do to Chris when I got home later tonight, and I missed a transition in what Derry was saying, though his last phrases hung in the air, available still to my unattentive mind in the silence that followed – 'I don't know what you think . . . but I always say, why not, actually? . . . you know, mutual interest . . .' He gazed at me with a kind of unfocused confidence from some way off, in the land of drink. I smiled back, politely ignoring what he'd said, though to him I may have appeared to be flirting. What he seemed to be suggesting was only thinkable in one way, and might perhaps, if I really let it happen, tap into the excitement I was already feeling about someone quite different. I looked away, then smiled at him again, with what seemed to me a mixture of the practical and the unexpectedly amorous. Perhaps that was what I felt.

Derry stood up, went over to push the door closed, came

back and stood by my chair with his faraway look, thinking how best to proceed. Then he was down on his knees, with a creak and a grunt, his hands on my thighs, as I made a small move to unzip – 'Let me do it,' he said mildly, a tone of seasoned competence and a glimpse of his taste for the drama of the moment. I was so hard he had a struggle to get it out through the fly. 'Goodness . . .' he said then, reassessing the task. He was like an old man praying in stoical discomfort, and also, as he flexed his jaws and brought saliva to his mouth, a workman who could deal with most emergencies.

'The garden's not quite as large as it wants you to think,' said Derry. He conducted me round it on a route which made the most of its secret corners and sudden views. There were hedges, and steps and lead cupids, a certain air, as the fallen leaves dotted the lawn, of a deserted opera set, say Act Four of *Figaro*, or perhaps just the garden scene in *Twelfth Night*. It had been beautifully designed, but there was something lonely about it – no Feste and Maria were hiding here. The garden stepped downhill, with a view beyond of fields already being ploughed. At the bottom, sheltered by a beech hedge, and getting the best of the sun, was an oblong pool, paved round like a fishpond, and murkily ambiguous, dead leaves making islands on the surface, a faint blistered blue showing through from below. 'You're welcome to have a dip,' said Derry, and when I pulled a panicked face he gave a grunt of a laugh, as if to say it had been worth a try. 'You must come again in the summer. Bill and I used to have marvellous parties down here, with all the young dancers and so on – no one bothered with bathing-drawers, you know, we just jumped straight in.'

'It sounds fun,' I said.

We turned back towards the house, his arm now through mine, as if more infirm than he was. From here you saw clearly the low range of the old building, with the grander embellishments tacked on at the front, the pillared porch and the urns on the parapet disguising the farmhouse it had been before. 'Bill and I added that higher front bit, just after the War, for guests mainly, and parties,' and he squeezed my arm against him to emphasize the word. As we went back up the steps I seemed to gather, faint on the breeze, a sense of the liberties the house had been host to, the excitement, principled, and muddled too, about other races, black singers, Burmese dancers, the smart English queens turned on by the dark skins, the difference. Or was this merely my fantasy of what had gone on here, since I knew almost nothing about it? I couldn't think yet about what had happened just now in the light of what had happened long before. In the moment I came I had thrown back my head and caught the cool gaze of Tony Sein.

When the driver had given a second sour blast on his horn, I went into the hall and collected my briefcase. 'I'd love it if you'd sign this,' I said, and passed him my copy of *Staging an Opera*. It was a nice question of etiquette, what he might write. In fact he just struck out his name on the title page and put 'To David Win best wishes Derry Blundell', and handed it back.

'Well, goodbye,' I said, unsure which of us should thank the other.

'Bye-bye, David,' said Derry, 'and, you know, do come again!'

'I'll be in touch about our new show,' I said – and with unexpected forwardness, 'and of course if you felt able to support us in any way, we'd be extremely grateful.'

'Well . . .' said Derry, and opened the front door.

In the cab the driver gave me a narrow look, as if trying to measure his suspicions against my mood. 'Good lunch?' he said. 'Oh . . . yes, thank you,' I said. 'Will we make the five fifteen train?' I think he read my keenness to get home as mere relief at getting away – which was perhaps a small part of it, along with something else, not guilt exactly, but a feeling I had quickly to make up to Chris for what I'd done, or allowed to happen. If I told him, he would think it was another of the fantasies I cooked up to excite him, when I'd been away. I didn't know how he would take it when he found, for the first time, that it was true. 'We've been advised not to go through the ford, after last night's rain,' the driver said, advice I suspected had been issued by himself. So we turned right when we came out of the gate, and into those twisting lanes I could still vaguely picture from the map. He drove fast but it was slow, overall, with dull misgivings about heading for so long in the wrong direction. I saw myself missing the train and having to crawl back and spend the night with Derry after all. Dusk was filling the valley, and now the lights of an oncoming vehicle could be seen, then were lost again in the winding of the road, and then much nearer with a looming question of which of us would give way. I couldn't see my driver yielding at all readily, but then I couldn't read his mood, or tell if he saw me now as a victim to be rescued or a fare to be soberly thwarted and screwed.

23

Late that afternoon we rehearsed the long scene between Marcus and Hildebrand, and acted it so overwhelmingly it felt definitive, too soon, perhaps not easy to repeat. Ray let it run, and surely sensed that something new was happening. Hector was electrifying – in a way that can turn the other actor into a mere stooge, but can also charge him up. My big speech in reply came out as one great gathering climax, and when I turned forgivingly at the end (I was kneeling, he standing up behind me) I saw tears in his eyes which I knew weren't simply a tribute to my skills or the playwright's. We looked at each other as we might have done after a great argument in real life, and also with a kind of wonder, amorous and half-doubting, at what we had just done together. Ray let a long silence follow, blinking, hesitant, before he said, 'So we've been playing our old Sarah Bernhardt records again, have we.'

This was brutal, but the fact that our great transport of art had been 'worryingly self-indulgent' was no doubt worth learning – Ray's adverb, as so often, undermining. And then at once I knew it was for Hec and me to take, or not, the path our 'public wank' had privately revealed to us. We packed up, Ray chatted smoothly with Ken about something else, and I sensed I was being avoided by the others as I left the room. In the entrance-way in the dusk we were self-conscious, from the corner of my eye I saw Hec fold his flares under his cycle-clips, button his donkey jacket – then he stood thinking, looked up and said, 'Night, pal,' and kissed me gently but squarely on the

lips. No one saw, and as I went out to the bus stop I felt a longing to run after his disappearing tail-light, and then the lovely
reassurance that I didn't have to. At ten the next morning we
would do it all again.

Lots of actors are in love with each other, there are husband
and wife teams as famous as couples offstage as they are on it,
dear old Hettie Barnes and Lionel Wilshire have been at it since
their twenties, their whole personal and professional lives a
shared enterprise. But falling in love in the course of rehearsing
a play made its own drama, there was a new energy that I saw
at once could be focused or disruptive. I knew we would both
want to keep it secret, though in a group like ours, both tight-
knit and unbuttoned, this might be hard. I feared it would be
obvious to the others.

I went home on the Tube wrapped up among the five
o'clock crowds in my own sensations, of a new chord that had
sounded, and sounded again just as surely each time I found my
way back to it. I felt entirely open to it, as a thing in itself,
thrilling and unquestionable. I started thinking for the first time
about making love to Hector. He had never appeared naked in
one of Ray's shows, but I'd warmed up with him often enough
– I found I had a phantom memory in my hands of his heaviness and heat. I was puzzled and amused at how cheerful I felt
as I came down Chris's street, opened the gate for the thou-
sandth time and let myself in to the dark musty hall. Claudia
was moving round the kitchen in her usual stately way, oblivi-
ous of the sink full of dishes and the smell of the fridge. 'What
are you boys up to tonight?' she said, and even this little logis-
tical check to my fantasies failed to trouble me.

I sat in the kitchen drinking tea with her and eating one of
the horrible sponge cakes she made as a treat for me. I don't
know where she went wrong, something basic in the quantities,
then too brief a time in the oven. 'Not as good as your mum's,
I bet,' she said, pressing damp crumbs into a pellet on her plate.

'Well . . .' I said, weighing it up.

'Another slice?'

'I couldn't, darling,' I said, and raised a regretful hand.

'Save it for tomorrow,' she said.

When Chris came in and kissed Claudia on the cheek and then me on the lips I held his face to mine until he pulled back with a wary chuckle. 'You seem pleased to see me . . .'

And I was – in my stunned excitement I almost wanted to share the good news about falling in love with Hector, if that is what had happened: about the psychic jolt that was a physical experience, I was certain, for both of us. I sat in a bizarre glazed excitement, insulated from the circumstances of my actual, perfectly enjoyable and sexually gratifying life. I smiled up at Chris himself with straightforward affection, and Claudia said, 'Aah . . . ! It's lovely to see you two.'

'How was your day?' Chris said, feeling the pot – then refilling the kettle, a barely conscious routine.

'Well . . .' I said – and here a vague sense of diplomacy did begin to impinge. 'Ray was an absolute . . .' – I paused and blinked, since we watched our language in front of Claudia; she was at worst a 'darn' and 'bother' sort of woman, and I felt I was pushing it a bit when I said, 'Ray was an absolute *bastard*.'

'Nothing new there, then,' Chris said.

I smiled as I conjured it up. 'I was doing a scene with Hector – you remember him in *Troilus*, the new black guy?'

'Oh, yes, he's amazing,' said Chris.

'Mm, I remember you liked him, Christopher,' said Claudia, in a rather pert manner.

'Yah – no, he's a lovely guy,' I said. 'Anyway, we did a thrilling run-through of the end of Act One, a long scene, just the two of us – I wish you could have heard us, actually: the sort of thing you just know is genius.'

'And Ray tore it to shreds.'

'I won't tell you in front of Claudia what Ray said.'

'Oh . . .' said Claudia, with a little shrug.

'Well, you've said before,' Chris said, 'the painful path to self-knowledge, and all that' – as the kettle on the far side of the room started singing like a bore and rose in three seconds to a scream.

The next day I got in early, not with any plan beyond wanting to be there and see him. I paced about muttering a speech in my head, then put myself in charge of the coffee, the big drum of Maxwell House, mess of sugar on the table, people having their particular mugs. I was in the Gents refilling the kettle at the basin, the door opened, and there in the mirror was Hector himself, his astonishing neat presence, in his coat still, knapsack on his shoulder, and a shiver went through me, a smile of triumph and good luck, as I said, 'Morning!' and he said, 'Oh . . . ! Morning . . . yes . . . yes . . .', and after a glance at the vacant urinal went into a cubicle and bolted the door. There was a lot of rustling and banging then in the tiny space as the water ran over the brim of the kettle and I twiddled furiously at the tap. I was back at the table, saying, 'Ken, yours is the Superman mug, right, and Jack, you're Klimt' – acting, really, over my fear that I'd made an agonizing mistake. Perhaps his kiss in the hall last night, so sudden and promising and true to our new mood, was no more than a kiss of condolence for the bollocking we'd had, and to him was as chaste and devoid of intention as the kiss of an aunt.

In the warm-up I did stretches and pat-a-cakes with Gary, forceful and businesslike as ever, and in the general activity, while Ray smoked and circled and took us all in, I looked across at Hector, on his back, with Wendy almost riding, like a child, on his foot as she stretched his raised leg. Then he was doing the same for her, and I was shaken, astonished by how his presence in the room had a charge for me today – though of course I knew the sensation, a shadowy line-up of men I'd adored unavailingly in the past seemed to roam and jostle out of reach beyond him. After this, we did the Death Circle, the usual madhouse of clashing tunes as we strode round the room singing. Jack went down first, and I was nearest to Ray when he made the next signal – dropped where I stood, cardiac arrest. I lay on my front with my eyes shut as the feet tramped round, bodies thumped to the floor and the singing grew quieter and clearer, with an uncanny feeling each time when Hec's forceful bass-baritone came closer and he skirted my corpse and strode on, as he had to do, until he was the last one alive and we all lay still for a minute or more listening to him marching and singing and waiting for Ray's coup de grâce.

The Death Circle was always unnerving, a taster of tragedy, nothing giggly or Pyramus-and-Thisbe-ish allowed. It was designed to shock us into the other reality of acting. And it put me in a strange mood for the big last scene in Act One, which Ray started us off with – 'now you've both had a chance to think about it'. I laughed submissively and Hector nodded and pursed his lips to show he wasn't so forgiving.

Ruth did the end of her short speech and went 'off' and then it was Hector and me, in the imaginary prison, observed by the others, blank-faced as they perched or sprawled at the side of the room in the practised double act of being our audience and working discreetly on their own lines. Hector circled me again, spoke his opening accusation, with a bitter kind of lightness, action and intention scarily distinct, unlike yesterday's blind rush at feeling. It made me tremble on the spot about how I would answer him – it was, what? ninety seconds to the climax of the scene, I had the words and spoke them, as if I'd just thought of them, as if they were only accidentally in verse. I came up to him, put my hand on his shoulder, looked in his eyes, the words ran on, and I was nearly thrown by the multiple intimacies of acting – the lurking business of my real-life feelings and the terrible closeness of the characters we were playing, at a pitch of emotional conflict I'd never experienced offstage. When he spoke next he was loud, his breath strong in my face, and his large dark eyes seemed from moment to moment to be glittering surface and unreadable depth. I fell to my knees, he moved away behind me, I was aware of Ray watching, and I felt he was right, the broken, unmusical style that he liked had made the scene modern and gripping to the others. At the end, they weighed in at once, with nods and murmurs, collective affirmation before Ray could open his mouth and spoil it all. In fact he smiled, shrugged, spread his hands – 'Very good.' He was pleased, above all, to have imposed himself and got his way, but he was pleased with us too. 'Act Two, Scene One . . . ?' Hector sat down, and I looked for a place, sat where Ken had been sitting, some way off. A little later he turned and found me looking at him, raised his eyebrows in mild enquiry, then nodded slowly, to say we'd done it, and perhaps – who knew? – would do more yet.

Jack gave a party at his flat – 'any time after seven', Chris very much invited. They'd met a few times after shows, and Jack fancied him, I could tell, and Chris in his ever-ready way no doubt fancied Jack, and more than that loved to be included by the Terra gang, who were friendly but never took much interest in him. So I felt vindicated and also just a little on guard. Chris, eager and liking a drink, chafed at my saying there was no point in arriving before eight. Big Ben could be heard striking eight fifteen across the river when we rang the bell, against a thin pulse of music from an open window up on the fourth floor. I put on a smile at the top of the stairs and went in at the door that was left half-open, into a narrow hall and beyond it a bright room with the chairs round the walls, and the emptiness of a party getting ready, Beach Boys playing, crisps in bowls, two or three voices from the kitchen beyond, and an ugly roaring noise – when we looked in we saw Jack was making hummus in a liquidizer, amid a mess of garlic skins and squeezed half-lemons. Johnny was there with a dark young man, Mick – the first time we'd been allowed to see him. 'And this is Chris!' I said, and Chris beamed 'Hi!' and handed over our bottle of Chianti. In the small kitchen there were also two friends of Jack's, a Dutch artist called Hans and his girlfriend, who was helping Jack make the hummus and had her own ideas about it; she was Malaysian, and I felt the flicker of affinity and of resistance to it as we introduced ourselves – 'No, Burma!' I said. 'Oh, Burma!' she echoed. 'But I've never been there,' I said, to get that out of the way.

It was clear Jack wouldn't be ready for another hour, and Chris and I felt so superfluous, or I did, that we sat down and chatted to each other as if we'd just met, and drank most of a bottle of Rioja before the rest of the party arrived. All the time I was wondering if Hector was coming, and the drinking was an answer to the tension, close to worry, that he would or he wouldn't – I didn't know which was worse. He wasn't in the big batch of guests who came in just after nine, but things livened up then at once, and soon Chris was deep in discussion with Jack about Westminster Council politics – housing budgets and road schemes. Jack had a look of mesmerized fascination, at this unexpected access to the inside story, or anyway to Chris, and stroked his arm appreciatively now and then as he listened.

The party didn't reach capacity till after ten, but by then I was so exhausted by drink and drunken chit-chat and waiting for Hector while keeping an eye on Chris flirting with Jack that I was ready to call it a night. I was sketching out a miserable story for leaving, when a vision arrived, too large as it squeezed through the narrow hallway, then uncooped into the room in an explosion of stiff skirts and writhing feather boas. It took me a good ten seconds to understand it was Gary – with Derek behind, in severe grey separates, a sort of lady's companion. I was dazzled, slightly frightened as well as amused, and Chris stared happily. Gary had all the licence of drag, glittering, challenging, a display of power to which we all had to adjust. 'It's Zeta!' someone said. 'Zeta, what can I get you?' I said. Zeta looked at me quizzically: 'Have you,' she said in a deep voice, 'a very small dry sherry?' – so I had to laugh. 'Ooh, they're so posh 'ere, they've got a fuckin' butler!' At which Chris laughed rather sharply too. 'Buttle me, darling, will you?' Zeta said, back from Cockney to Coward, 'buttle me sideways.' And then, 'I'll 'ave whatever she's 'aving,' nodding the stiff height of his blonde wig at Chris. 'Hello, darling, I'm Zeta, who are you?' 'Hi!' said Chris, with a grin, and holding out his hand gamely, as if they hadn't met a dozen times before: 'I'm Christopher, David's other half.' 'Awfully good to meet you, Christopher,' said Zeta, and wrung his hand like the second-row forward he'd once been.

I came back a minute later with a glass of red for Zeta, but it was hard to get his attention, rushed along as he was by his own performance and throwing the rest of us off. His feet were forced into gigantic high heels, and he controlled, surprised by it himself, the odd dangerous wobble. 'Have you met Ethel?' he said. 'Is she your sister, then?' said Chris, entering the game. 'Sister, how dare you!' Gary said. 'She's my great-aunt!' I must say Derek was marvellous in his role, and did clever things with it that weren't quite in Gary's range: the unflagging but subtly mutinous support of his mistress, self-effacement turned into a steely kind of display. I don't know how long Hector had been there, but when I saw the back of his head a few feet away, nodding as he talked to somebody I couldn't see, the whole room with its real and its would-be dramas was remote for ten seconds as if I was about to faint.

*

Then Hector and I and Malaysian Sue were all waiting outside the bathroom, which by now had a pillaged look, damp towels on the floor, the loo seat coming off, and the lock broken, so that the front person queuing was also the guard. We gallantly let Sue go in ahead of us, and then had to talk nonsense to a woman who'd just arrived while I tried to guess how we would be talking if she hadn't been there. Sue came out of the bathroom with a flinching look at what I was about to experience, and as I went in I gave a sideways glance at Hector – only half closed the door, and he looked from one side to the other and then nipped in too. My hands were round his waist, and he said, 'I'm not sure we ought to be doing this,' and leant back against the door, but he let me kiss him, a mad pouring out of all my unagreed feelings; I felt he was rather marking his part as I pressed myself against him, but then half giving in, and his hard-on was the real thing. He doubled up with a gasp when I gripped the black denim. 'You're very bad,' he said, straight-faced, and didn't smile when I giggled at this and put my head on one side. 'Things to think about,' he said quietly, 'things to think about.' Nothing more was said, and after a minute I slipped out first, and went with a racing heart back to the living room, where now only the strung-up party lights were winking and Chris was slow-dancing to 'Walk On By' with Wendy and Johnny's Mick, not quite in the same style as them, but he was a nice mover, he'd waltzed me round Claudia's kitchen once or twice, and been patient teaching me the steps. Now he took me in very smoothly and happily, and I grooved about for five minutes not daring to look round until I said I really must go home.

'You'd look great in drag!' said Chris as we went down the stairs.

I said, 'Ah, you should have met me twenty years ago . . .'

It was agony to leave but impossible to stay. I saw Hector loosening up now we'd gone, getting drunk and hitting on someone else in the hot crush of the dancing – it was a poky little council-flat living room but it expanded, took on depth and mystery . . . from the street the music was much louder now, reddish flickers at the open window, screams and laughter and in the unexpected chill of the night the certainty the party had forgotten us already.

'That was fun, actually,' Chris said. 'Jack's a great host.'

'Oh, yes . . .' I said – Jack had got so drunk that hosting wasn't quite the word.

'They're all so lovely, your gang – not like my lot.' And I thought of course they had been nice to big smiling Chris, they'd liked him and fancied him and it was only me who shamefully hadn't wanted him to be there. 'Very nice to have a chat with Hector.'

'Oh, I didn't know you'd spoken to him.'

'Well, just for a minute,' said Chris, with a glance at me. 'I told him how wonderful we both thought he was.'

'Oh, yes,' I said, and my unsteady grasp of the evening slipped again.

'So, so handsome.'

'You old tart!' I said, and slapped him quite hard on the arm.

'Ow!' he said, 'anyway, don't you think he's handsome?'

'No, he is, of course,' I said. 'He's got great presence.'

'He certainly has,' said Chris. I walked on, head held high. 'Oh, baby, don't be silly!' – he gripped my upper arm and nuzzled up, 'Nothing like such a big presence as you.'

So there was a fraction of an atmosphere upstairs on the bus, half-disguised, half-excused by tiredness, and more complex than he knew. The air was foul with beer and cigarette smoke, an empty bottle rolling down the aisle and after a while rolling all the way back. 'I'm going to sleep well tonight,' I said, with a convincing yawn, and though I didn't look at Chris I sensed his lips shaping the phrase he then decided not to say. But as the bus crawled on, with its long stops for ranting drunks and shrieking kids to get on and then in a great lurching line clatter downstairs to get off, later for cooks and waiters from half a dozen restaurants to clamber on amid their own tired smells of turmeric and saffron, we slumped together, his thigh pressed against mine on the narrow seat while I pulled a cuff over my hand to wipe the window and see if we weren't, as we ached to be, at our own stop.

On Monday in the lunch break Hector said, 'Fancy a stroll?' and we slipped off with our sandwiches to a small nearby garden that was part of an old churchyard; the headstones had been lined up like a fence beside the path, and giant plane trees blocked the blue above. It was clear that things had moved on since the party, though I'd acted blank with him all morning, to get through, and Hector spoke with careful clarity. We sat on a bench and there was a strange active atmosphere, for all the quiet, sparrows waiting for crumbs, a squirrel in the branches overhead. Hector ate his sandwich before he spoke.

'You all right?' he said.

'Well,' I said, 'I don't know . . .'

'I don't like breaking something up,' he said, so responsibly that I felt he had made the decision to do so. 'You know . . . ?'

'Sometimes these things happen,' I said, as if speaking from experience. It was fairly astonishing, now it had been said.

'I mean Chris seems a nice guy. How long have you been together?'

'Oh . . . two and a half years?' I said.

Hec was cautious. 'Right. Right. I wouldn't have thought, necessarily, that you'd be a couple.'

'Well, there you are,' I said – now it came to it I wasn't

going to talk down the man I lived with, though Hec was inter-estingly opening the way for me to admit certain frustrations, incompatibilities . . . He was five years younger than me but I felt for a moment like his pupil, and this itself was so unlike being with Chris that it gave what he said seriousness and something like inevitability.

We had our first night together in the hotel on the edge of Leeds: low glare of car park outside and beyond it the whine and rumble of a major arterial road building up before dawn. Not that we cared, we were exhausted from travel and doing two shows in a day, and the romantic certainty we were going to go through with it struggled with the timetable of sleep. He locked the door and took me in a tight strong grip, and it was beautiful to be kissed by him at last, the shyness of waiting still felt in the first sweet seconds of letting go. When he pulled back and touched my face and kissed me again I had an almost solemn sense of reassurance, a taste of what was to come. He sat on the edge of the bed to undo his laces, and in between pulling off one boot and the other he gave an enormous yawn – he turned it into a grin as he looked up at me, and said, 'Let me do that,' stood up and unbuttoned my shirt and ran his cool hands over me under my vest while I undid his belt and prised open the stiff top button of his jeans.

24

He lived in a tall council block near Latimer Road, in a ninth-floor flat that he shared with a mild-mannered white boy called Perry. The rooms were small, and they both kept their bikes on the balcony outside the living-room window. There was an old pub umbrella out there too, London Pride, loosely furled and propped up, and two picnic chairs like Esme's along with other things scavenged locally and lugged home. The balcony gave you a weirdly dissociated view across West London, other council blocks, church spires, long streets of red-brick housing far below – all cut off beyond a deep dual carriageway, whose night-time sigh became a darker sound as dawn broke and the city came back to life. If you took the stairs you looked out the other way, at the wreckage, like the path of a hurricane, of streets being cleared to build a new estate.

There were two bedrooms, with the beds head to head on either side of a thin wall. Hector had made his room his own with pot-plants that he tended scientifically, and a large red and brown batik hanging with a radial pattern, which covered the wall above the low wood-framed bed. There was a stale smell of joss-sticks, revived each day, no bulb in the fitting overhead, and at night-time thick red candles the main source of light. It was all very different from the stuffy comfort at Claudia's, with the dinners and the whiskies she gave out gratis, from old bourgeois habit and a need for company. I hardly felt the loss because of the intensity of Hector, the austere and principled way he ran his life, the rationing of sex. Sometimes, after two or three tantalizing days without, my thoughts flitted down from the tower through the night-time streets to the big squashy bed half a mile away, where perhaps even now Chris was being seen to by someone else – he was wounded, shaken by the break-up and on his dignity, but he was skittish and insatiable too. I put him over my knee and it all started up again, the hot-faced possession of our nights together; I turned away carefully to keep my excitement from Hector as he lay beside me, apparently asleep. He could fall asleep in seconds, as if acting. I was the one then to blow out the candle – the red tip of the wick on the dark and for five or six seconds as it cooled the fading pink glow of the molten cup of wax. Already as I slid down and shrugged the bedcover round me the thin curtains glimmered like the dawn, and the mild glare of the West London night took over the room.

Hector and Perry had nothing in common, and got on well enough, each being self-contained, but friendly and funny if the mood was right. Often Perry was in bed when we got in from work, and we took off our shoes in the cupboard-sized hallway and did what we had to do in whispers. On a hot night, Hector would roll a spliff and take it out onto the balcony, where he seemed to commune for ten minutes with the lights of the city, the traffic far below and the dimly visible stars. Then he came in, sleepy and smiling, cleaned his teeth and got ready and slipped into bed. He was at his most amorous after a smoke, and backed up against me with possessive grunts and purrs. He never said he wanted it, or acknowledged on any later occasion that it had happened. In bed he shushed me, whispered 'Go on' or 'It's time' or 'What's the problem?' – this with a kiss and a sly grin. We were quiet as could be not to wake up Perry, and that was a trick in itself, sometimes bungled in performance, when the bed-frame rode against the wall. Perry himself the next morning made his breakfast and went off to work in White City with no hint or protest or smothered smirk that he'd been woken in his bed beneath his Blondie poster by our outrageous coupling, feet away.

He was a context, and also an excuse, for Hector, for the private life, unseen, undiscussed; no one else was ever asked back.

We were both broke, but I saw at once he was serious about money in a way that I realized at the same time I had never been. It was a part of his larger air of caution, and forethought. He had the very small Terra wage each Friday, and his dad gave him twenty pounds a month, to see him through, he said, until he was settled – we looked round the room at the batik hanging and the spider-plant, uncertain how we'd know when that was. 'It's all right for you,' he said, and when I said I'd got nothing he said, 'Yeah, well,' and of course he was right in a way. On Sundays if we weren't on tour he went to see his parents, who lived in Beckenham, forty minutes by train from Victoria. He was touchy and deflecting about them, and I was cautious but curious, as I generally was about my friends' families. I knew at least that Hector had been born in Liberia, and I suspected his family had once had money; now it seemed they ran a hardware store – but I didn't press Hector about them, perhaps out of some fellow-feeling about fathers.

It was one Sunday evening, about nine o'clock, when Hector came back to the flat. Perry was watching TV in the living room and I was in bed with my clothes on, for warmth, learning a long verse speech from *Andromaque* – Ray had decided it was time a French classic was given the once-over. 'Hi, honey,' I said, 'how was it, how were they?' with a carefree tone, and perhaps just a hint of the hurt I was starting to feel at these moments when he got back from the family I was never asked to meet.

'They're well,' he said, 'they're well,' and came over and kissed me, and bustled round in a preoccupied way.

'I'll tidy that up later,' I said.

'Actually, I just thought I'd show you this,' he said, and came back and sat down on the bed beside me, and teased a small photograph out of his wallet. I took it with a half-smile, a feeling of guesswork, ready to be surprised. It was a group photo – a white couple, whom I felt I half recognized, on the back lawn of a whitewashed semi-detached house, and in front of them four children, two black boys and two white girls, sitting cross-legged on the grass like a team. The seconds went past as I worked out the larger boy was Hector, perhaps fifteen years old. 'And aren't these your old friends,' I said, 'who came to the show in Greenwich? They were a bit shocked by it. Patrick, was it?'

'Yeah, Patrick and Amanda,' he said.

'And these girls are their children, by the look of it.'

'Yeah, well . . .'

'You look so sweet, and very serious. When was this taken? Sort of eight or nine years ago—'

'David, they're my mum and dad.'

'Ah . . .' I said, and focused on them, not knowing what to say, my own foolishness, the further little hurt of being kept in the dark, was as nothing to my rush of love for Hector. I put my hand on his thigh and gripped his hand, too overcome to say the thing I at once almost selfishly wanted to say, that I'd felt from the start we had something deeper in common.

'Yeah, well,' said Hector again. 'There it is.'

Something cautioned me not to ask questions. 'Well, thank you,' I said, and flung my arms round him, still holding the photo so that I saw it, over his shoulder, the man I was holding as he had been eight or nine years ago, in the safety of his family.

I decided early on I wanted Hector to meet Nick and Jenny, who said it should be soon, for their own reasons – Jenny was eight months pregnant with their second child. They were back, Nick was teaching Politics at Sussex now, and the meeting in my head was a proof of my doing well too, of being over him, though my need to stage the scene at all perhaps implied otherwise. I wasn't sure what to tell Hector, though he'd spoken of a crush of his own, on a schoolmaster, and on other boys, never admitted or acted on. So I half explained, out of tenderness to all concerned and a feeling it could never really be made sense of. We were drying after a bath when I suggested the meeting. 'Yeah . . .' Hector said, with a shrug and a shake of the head. He was shy about being shown off, and awkward, I felt, about being embraced by my old friends as half of a new happy couple. 'Yeah, I can't go next Monday, though.'

'Oh, OK,' I said, 'why not?'

'I've got my art night.'

'Can I come?' I said. 'I love art.'

'I don't think that would work,' he said, with a rough little laugh.

'What is it, then?' I said.

'It's just at Molleson's, I've been doing it for the last couple of years – on and off, you know.'

'I know Molleson's. I had a friend who went there. It's a great school.'

'Yeah, well,' said Hector. He was full of quietly nursed ambitions, he took nothing for granted and often almost secretly was seriously at work on something.

He unscrewed the brown jar and rubbed a pinch of cocoa butter between his palms, started massaging it into his warm dry skin. 'What course are you doing?' I said.

'I'm not studying there, David,' he said, and impatience with me seemed to mix with embarrassment in his face.

'Oh,' I said, 'I see, you're modelling?'

'I am.'

'What sort of thing?' I said. I was thrown, just a little, by the news, and again by not having known.

'Just standard art-school stuff . . . you know.'

'I've never been in an art class,' I said. 'Do you mean you pose naked?'

'Drawing from the live model, is how it's described.'

'So you stand there just like you are now.'

'I do.'

'Except without a hard-on, I imagine.'

Hector suppressed a smile. 'The chances of getting a hard-on in those conditions are next to zero, my friend. It's more like a medical.'

I took hold of his hard-on to stop him from getting away. 'So you never fancy someone in the class?'

He sighed. 'You don't even look at the class when they're working. You have to look at the floor, or the corner of the room or something. You certainly don't think about sex, or your jealous little boyfriend hanging on to your dick, or anything like that.'

'What do you think about, then?'

'As a matter of fact, my love, I think about Hotspur . . . Thersites . . . the Jook of Clerrunts' – he took on his thespian tone.

'How do you mean, think about them?'

'Just old parts, parts I'm playing now, parts I'd like to play, once I've moved on from Ray's.'

'You learn parts you haven't even been cast in?'

'It fills the time,' he said. 'Now, if you wouldn't mind . . .' I pecked him on the cheek and let him go, but I was dazed by this vision of unnecessary readiness, a refusal to be sidelined, I supposed, by all those lazy chancers who strolled into the best jobs. It was ambitious, and exemplary, but pitiful too, since no one in the big world that he dreamed of was going to offer him more than the *mauvais rôles*.

Hector asked me to the Molleson's end-of-term party in such a mumbled, offhand way I couldn't tell if he hoped for a refusal or was shyly longing for me to come – I thought it best to accept. We made love quickly and fiercely before leaving the flat, and set off to the Tube in a flush of private confidence just touched, as we bought our tickets and climbed up the stairs to the platform, by a lonelier feeling.

I knew the famous street-front of the art school, with its terracotta roundels of Dürer and Reynolds and Landseer perched between the first-floor windows, but I'd never been inside before, into the battered and echoing atmosphere of student life, the mood, mixed up like the chalk dust and turps smells in the air, of pride in the place and fury against it. I drifted into the sculpture room on the ground floor, the welded frames and looming plaster maquettes like scenery for later acts crowded in the wings, but Hector quickly pulled me away and I followed him upstairs, among students running up and down, and smiled through my self-consciousness at being an outsider in a school. The big life-drawing studio was on the top floor, with a sloping skylight half-covered by blinds, and it was here that the party was now beginning.

A grey-haired man in a brown suit and paisley cravat turned round from a group near the drinks table. 'Ah, Henry!' he called, 'so glad you could come,' and I glanced over my shoulder for someone behind us and then made a grimace at Hector at this stupid little slight, which seemed, in the context, to be part of some larger indignity, though he smiled through it. The man waved his arm to bring us into a group of young students who seemed rather bashful at first in their model's presence. They shook hands, one girl and then a second stepped up to kiss him on the cheek – I saw there was a fascinating shock for them of intimacy, almost of exposure, in meeting him not as a model but as a fully-clothed person. A girl with dyed red hair, trying her luck with him, plucked at his sweater and said, 'Hello, Henry, aren't you boiling in all those clothes!' and amid the immediate laugh about the situation I made my own quick adjustment, and found some fun in it too – I took it up as a kind of improv. 'This is my friend David,' Hector said, and I said very smoothly and earnestly how glad I was Henry had invited me.

The man in the cravat was Mr Trivet, who ran the life class, and who, as we stood drinking and chatting, seemed to feel he had a special claim on Hector – he turned his back on me to talk to him, laid an encouraging hand on his shoulder and left it there. I realized he'd stared at Hec's naked body for hours at a time, much longer than I ever had, in the supposedly clinical conditions of this very room, the little platform wheeled into the corner now and the chairs and easels stacked away. It had the subtly excluding presence of someone else's workplace, the trace and echo of unknown routines. It was a room that Hector was accustomed and inured to, and I wasn't – the skirting boards, the skylight, the suspended heaters were imbued for him with the hours he'd spent here, the runs and ripostes of Hotspur or Vladimir or whoever it was, all the unguessed mental activity through which he escaped from the place but also, to my now vaguely uneasy mind, assumed it as his own.

I felt Mr Trivet must know Hec's body best of all, because (as I pictured it) he paced round the circle, examined the chest and the thighs and the cock and balls from each student's angle, leaning in to shape an ankle, or enhance a student's shading of dark brown skin. And sometimes, I assumed, he got stuck in and drew him too. I soon understood they knew nothing about Hector, so I had a little audience suddenly keen to learn more. I toyed with telling them things, for the cheap amusement of their surprise, and simply from the feeling he didn't need this veil of protective secrecy. But I said merely that he was a wonderful actor, and that they should all come and see us in a play some time.

'Do you want to see my best drawing of Henry?' said the red-haired girl, who clearly had a thing for him.

'No, no . . .' I said.

'I don't mind,' she said, and went off to the lockers at the far end of the room. She came back with her large sketch-pad, the worked pages curling at the edges, and looked through it rapidly, 'Not that one . . . not that one . . .' but I glimpsed other goes at my boyfriend, from the side, seated and standing, the beauty and evident difficulty of him as a subject. 'There!' she said, and displayed it to me, and from where we were standing we could look up at Hector, in a similar stance, across the room, but in his best jeans and black roll-neck sweater.

'Yes, very good,' I said, though it was intensely romantic, the figure standing out heroically from the thickly hatched space behind him. 'Thank you for showing me.' I didn't want to hurt the girl's feelings, though I found she had somehow hurt mine.

'Would you ever consider modelling?' said a sweet-look-ing boy with a wispy blond beard. 'You'd be an interesting subject – if you don't mind me saying.'

'Oh . . . no,' I said, 'I don't think so.'

'Too shy?' he said.

'Mm, not that exactly,' I said, and seemed to be flirting back.

'Henry's a great poser,' he said, as the girl went off, 'but his body's unusual. He's got really wide shoulders, great physique, by the way, but unusual proportions, if you like. I spent ages the other night working on his bum,' and I saw this boy was quite a character, after two glasses of wine I couldn't help it:

'Mmm, me too!' I said, and he looked at me narrowly and then laughed.

'So you're . . .' – and he nodded his head between the two of us. 'Yeah, some of us were wondering . . .' – and I realized that a further part of Hec's self-preservation in this room, exposed for whole evenings on the shabby old dais with its stack of boxes and torn Turkey carpet, would be to make an absolute mystery of his own desires, a serious matter, but as private to him as religion. 'Henry keeps things to himself,' the blond boy said, and I looked vaguely at Mr Trivet for a second, forgetting who Henry was.

25

For a long time in the 1970s I barely thought of Giles at all. Sometimes, at Edinburgh perhaps, in the dodging and jostling of the Festival, at a bar or street corner, I snagged on some mutual acquaintance from Oxford, from Bampton even, and as the smiling conversation quickly ran dry they would cast around and say, 'Do you ever see Giles, I wonder?' 'Giles . . . ?' I would say, 'Oh, *Giles* – no . . . not for years,' with a dismissive laugh at something so remote from my concerns. 'Oh, really . . .' they'd say. Often they'd seen him just last week, he was doing awfully well. I was told that he'd moved on from Norman Upshaw – he wanted to make money before he went into politics, and now there was a property business, and some magazine he'd bought and completely turned round . . . I heard he had fallen out badly with his father, which made me, at least, feel tenderly for Mark. They showed they were excited to know Giles, they allowed a moment of shared irony ('You know what he's like!'), but I knew they saw me as a foolish heretic, excluded from the story of his rise, though excused in part and made less threatening by costumes and greasepaint; to know an actor had a marginal glamour for such people, it was tradeable among stockbrokers and barristers, often flashy little actors themselves. And besides, I was darkish-skinned and half-foreign, even if I spoke, as Raymond said, like Anna Neagle.

But there we were, people who had known each other, more or less, on the cusp between stopping in the street and walking on by – sometimes with a little catch, as we passed, an 'Oh, *hi!*'

and a grin, half turning but sharing the instinct to keep moving. In Edinburgh that year, I ran into Alec Adams, my fellow-editor of *The Hive*, our school magazine, in town to give a reading. 'David!' he called across the busy Grassmarket. 'David Win!' and I puzzled for a moment, over and between the passing traffic: glint of glasses, red beard, denim jacket – then the two-second tussle of instinct and good manners: 'Aha!' Strange dynamics as to which of us would cross; but he stood his ground, legs apart there, with his satchel round his neck, and I waited then darted among the cars and vans with an involuntary appearance of eagerness. He was a test-case for my good and bad feelings about the success of contemporaries – two collections from Faber, on the shortlist with men twice his age for the new Whitbread Poetry Award. 'I thought it had to be you!' he said, as we shook hands. 'Did it?' I said.

I saw him as ripe for satire, and wasn't quite sure if he deserved it. I felt he twinkled encouragingly at my own obscure efforts – whatever they might be. When he opened his satchel to take out a pouch of St Bruno and a long-stemmed pipe, he brought out in the rummage for matches his copy of *Magritte at Sunset*, bristling with paper slips marked up for his reading, the book itself dog-eared and stained, but no less fresh to him for that. I wanted to say, 'Don't you get sick of reading the same fifteen poems over and over again?' but it was hardly a question an actor could ask. Alec's self-belief was perfect, the drudgery of trotting out those same gimmicky similes and shameless last lines was the least he could do for himself, and the chuckles and satisfied sighs of the audience were proof that his magic still worked. In personal style he was rough, a pub man and a shagger, but as a poet he was precious as a Meissen figurine. He teased the tobacco into his pipe, tamped it down with a brown finger, all the while talking, a polished bit of business. 'But Dave,' he said, with a stammer of quick puffs between words as the match-flame dipped and he drew in and tested the smoke, 'how about you, now?'

'Well, I'm in a play here, all this week.'

'Ah, you're still acting, good.'

'Come and see us, Terra Productions – the Scottish Play as you've never seen it before!' – I was charming, for the hell of it, and I also thought it wouldn't be a bad thing if this oddly influential young poet spread the word about us. But I knew as he sucked at his pipe once again and half hid himself for a second in a bloom of smoke that he was one of those perfectionist literary types who keep their distance from the theatre and its risky collaborations.

It was Mark and Cara who kept in touch. They had always sent a Christmas card, a completely unseasonal picture from their own collection, but with hand-written season's greetings. Once you were on their list, you stayed there – I did, anyway, with an almost physical sense of being warmly thought of, and undroppable, among hundreds of others I knew nothing about. What they did at Christmas now I wasn't sure. Giles's rift with Mark seemed to me an anomaly in nature, the wilful rejection of a generous father – and I hardly saw Lydia flying back from Manhattan to be with her parents.

A new habit had started of meeting up two or three evenings a year with Mark and Cara, when they gave me dinner at the Ivy. 'Have what you like,' said Mark over cocktails and I gazed at the menu with a feeling there would hardly be time to read it all before the restaurant closed. I was so money-conscious I almost wished I wasn't there, or that they'd given me the cost of my meal in cash instead. I'd been brought up always to choose the cheapest things, for years I'd had the chicken when I longed to try lobster, but now I felt this would disappoint and even offend my hosts, who took pleasure in giving me a treat; so I ordered the caviar and filet mignon and a special pudding that took twenty minutes to bake, and Mark and Cara, who chose something much plainer and didn't want starters, seemed delighted. We all got a bit drunk, they were happy occasions, and at the end I spoke confidently to Cara about my plans while Mark made out and tore off a three-figure cheque for the waiter.

When we made our way through the restaurant together and into the lobby, I felt the world outside, beyond the peculiar multi-coloured diamond-paned windows, begin to loom very differently for them and for me. I saw the inner warmth of the evening's treat dispersing pretty quickly on the grimy trundle back on the Underground. The girl reading by the heater in her coat-lined cupboard looked up, saw Mark's two pound-coins on the saucer already, smiled as if charmed as she fetched our things. I didn't hear him speak to the black-coated doorman, but as we came onto the street a cab drew up beside us, the door was tugged open and just before Mark clambered in after Cara I caught the smooth passage of a five-pound note to the hand of the commissionaire. I was leaning in saying goodbye when Cara said, 'But can't we drop you off?' – so I got in too, and for the first two minutes sat facing them and smiling uncertainly on the fold-down seat.

'I get sick, I'm afraid,' I said, 'if I travel backwards.'

Cara looked at me. 'And you've just had that chocolate thing.' They pulled their coats round them and I fitted myself in between them and stared ahead as we thought about a new un-expected half-hour of conversation. We were cool for a minute or two, for all our cosiness. I had never been so physically snug with them but there was an echo, in my self-conscious image of the three of us sitting there, of the long-ago evening at Woolpeck, when we'd walked up together for the first time through the garden to the tennis court. The meter kept mounting in stubborn increments as we sat in the dense West End traffic, the theatres coming out, the audience's faces in the marquee lights somehow crazy with relief; then it ran up in a more high-spirited way as we rattled along Piccadilly and round Hyde Park Corner. In my new life, in the new economy I shared with Hector, two pounds bought the means for a nice home stew that would last us two nights; five pounds was the cost, plus a penny, of a big new novel I might read for a fortnight and keep for the rest of my life. I thought, rather childishly, about these things as we drove down the length of the darkened Park, until Cara asked me to explain where it was – 'Not too far from us, I'm sure' – that I lived.

Hector's problems, his unhappiness and his doubts. I don't mean he was indecisive. In a way he was too decisive. But he changed his mind, sometimes radically, about decisions he had made – he would stick with Terra, he would look for work elsewhere, he would give up acting altogether. Who wanted a brilliant black actor when they could have a just about adequate white one? 'Yes, but . . .' I said. And, 'Well, I do know what you mean,' and he looked at me, giving me, this time at least, the benefit of the doubt. Then, a week or two later, the gloom came to seem quite unnecessary, the self-doubt ridiculous, and with a new keen-eyed excitement he would detail a plan even bolder than the one he had renounced earlier on.

Then a plan came off, an audition, a second audition to make absolutely sure, and he was offered a season at Stratford; which turned out to have its own complications. At least with Terra if you hated it in one provincial town you knew you'd be off in a few days to another, whereas at Stratford . . . He wrote me letters, for the first time, in his elegant hand with looping ascenders, loving and funny but charged with feelings his humour couldn't wholly contain. He doubled Harcourt and Bullcalf in *Henry IV, Part 2*, and was Barnardo in *Hamlet* (with Roger Jessop, and Marcia Delano as a glamorous Gertrude). 'In the first play,' he wrote, 'I have thirteen lines in all, but in the second thirty-nine, which is three times as many.' I pictured him naked and abstracted in front of the Molleson's students, running through Hotspur and the Duke of Clarence in his head. I thought of the hefty parts Ray had given him. But it was, when all was said and done, Stratford, 'with the audience fifty yards away instead of five feet, and a full house every time'. To me there was something furtive about casting a black actor in such tiny roles: the surprise was swallowed up, and no reviewer even mentioned him.

We were in Coventry for two weeks that autumn, and some of us went over to see him in *Henry IV*, and he on a day off got the bus to see us in our new play by Snoo Wilson. There was a sad strain of suspended judgement, of mutual regret, about these reciprocal visits. Terra had always been friable, we crumbled off to take small parts in film and TV, which paid a lot more money, and Raymond wasn't always too happy to see someone return from a shoot in Spain or six months in a West End hit to the rigours of our little outfit: the two worlds were at odds with each other. In Coventry Hector joined us for a curry after the show, and seemed almost miserable to be with the gang again (Ray notably absent). We spent the night together in a room above a pub, with singing from a lock-in in the public bar rising up until late from two floors down. 'I haven't come for ten days,' he said – he shivered as I touched him, there was nothing more moving than his nakedness, my sense of it even before I undressed him, his stare and his gasp as I brushed my thumb across one nipple, then the other, under his shirt. I felt I played him, and his need, and his need was the astonishing secret, never so nakedly admitted. 'I do love you,' he said, and his stare and his trace of a smile were a beautiful dismissal of every compromise and disappointment.

The next morning I walked him to the bus stop and we sat clumsily in our coats with our arms round each other's shoulders. We both dreaded seeing the bus swing in, and the speechless half-minute between the doors opening and closing again with Hector aboard; I watched him pass back through the bus as it moved off, searching for a seat by himself, which meant having an empty seat beside him. I waved, longing for a signal, but he was closed at once into the prospect before him, the subtle humiliation of the work he was going back to, and the loneliness (though he didn't admit it) of being away from us all.

When he rang me from Stratford, I had the dislocating feeling I was speaking to him in character, not as Bullcalf or Barnardo, but as somebody's secretary, with a pleasant impersonal tone. Was this the voice, and the manner, he projected to the world when I wasn't there, and he was making his own way? I thought perhaps he was constrained, in the hallway of the lodging-house, by the presence of other members of the cast. When he rang me from a phone box we were in a hurry from the start, talking over each other, but with something hesitant about it all too, as if we couldn't quite get going on the special things we wanted to say, and if we did there were the pips cutting in, the repeated impending distraction of the money running out till, with only one 10p piece left, the knowledge that the call would shortly be over seemed to rob us of words, there was no point in starting a new topic, or going for a minute into something more heartfelt, when in our minds we were already hanging up; which then, with a little more time in fact left than we'd reckoned on, we did: leaving both of us, surely, in a mildly disconsolate state. I felt Hector could have saved up more 10p pieces, and yet I understood that he didn't really want to talk, and that perhaps things had changed between us. I wondered if I sounded equally altered to him, over-bright and implausible – if we were simply two actors taking different views of the same role, the absent lover.

The RSC came to do their season at the Aldwych, and we were in London too for ten weeks and things seemed better than I'd feared between us and not as good as I'd hoped. He got me in to the first night of *Hamlet*, with the cast party afterwards, at a nearby hotel: 'Do you want to come, Olivier's going to be there' – just a moment of throwaway pomp in his invitation, disowned as soon as heard. I went round to the stage-door, he came out in three minutes flat, and as we walked up the street away from the theatre I took his arm, and felt his glamour embraced me too – even passers-by who hadn't seen the show must have known he was a star. 'I'm so proud of you,' I said, and felt him, in his five-second silence, test my phrase for a note of condescension, but tonight he took it. 'Thank you, my love,' he said, and then, smiling politely at a woman who scowled at us clinging together, 'I've now had a chance to work out the number of words in my part.' 'Oh yes,' I said. 'It's two hundred and twenty-seven words,' he said, 'I counted them twice, just to make absolutely sure.' Still, as we arrived, among the first guests, I knew he was happy, the thrill of something done, and the lift of the party, the celebration, beginning. We went through to the cloakroom to leave our coats and scarves, and when I turned round there he was, glowing and beautiful in new black slacks and a white silk shirt, elegant as I'd never seen him before, and slyly (or had he done it unawares?) like Hamlet himself. I was abashed, in my shabby dark suit and my reheeled black Oxfords – I fell in love with him all over again, and kissed him quickly on the cheek to cover the rush of emotion.

We came back through the lobby as other guests were dodging in through the revolving door, Olivier we respectfully pretended not to notice, two other actors of different generations who'd also played Hamlet, being snapped with their arms round each other for 'Londoner's Diary'. Then Hector nudged me and murmured, 'It's Julie,' as Julie Halberton came in, she had her clever look of being both a star and a bit lost, needing attention but not to be approached, hand at the throat of her long red coat as she gazed round – I hadn't seen her since I was the barman in two scenes in *Ramsay and Rose* (she was Rose), and her eyes swept over me and then, as tends to happen, swung back. 'Oh my god!' – she was still peering round the lobby as we kissed both cheeks, then grinning and shaking her head at me as she shrugged herself out of her coat, with that actors' sense of sharing memories too numerous and disordered to know where, or even whether, to start. I liked being seen on such friendly terms with her, and having the chance to introduce Hector, who had said more than once how much he admired her. 'Wasn't Marcia amazing tonight!'

'She certainly was,' I said, amused by her performance of bewildered admiration for a fellow star, 'such an ungrateful role, though, isn't it.'

'Well, I know,' she said, almost under her breath, as if now she might say what she really thought.

'But she transformed it, I thought!'

'Well, she did. You're right!'

'And Julie,' I said, half turning to Hector who was smiling expectantly at her – she glanced at him –

'Oh, thanks so much . . . let me give you this,' she said, and passed him her coat, heaved it up again as it threatened to slip from his arms. He held it stiffly, for three or four seconds, as if he'd never seen a coat before, and then, 'Whoops,' she said, 'sorry . . . hang on,' and tucked her scarf into the pocket.

'Oh, Julie!' I said, with a despairing gasp at her mistake, 'this is —' – but Hector had turned without a word, holding the coat up and out in front of him like something disgusting in itself, and walked through the thickening crowd to an open space in the middle of the room where without looking round he dropped it on the floor and strode on into the bar. 'That's Hector Bishop,' I said, 'he was Barnardo . . .'

'Oh, my god,' she said, hand over mouth, 'I thought . . .' – though as she mugged dismay at me her self-reproach stiffened into a frown, 'Did he have to be so horrid?' I didn't argue it out with Julie; I knew how in those few seconds Hector's admiration for her would have warred with his hurt and his fury at being taken, yet again, for a servant. Young actors can be as star-struck as anyone else, and with the edge of intimacy in sharing a trade with their heroes. 'I'm sorry!' she shouted, in an airy way, after him, and then had to cross the room herself and curtsey, in her tight frock and high heels, to retrieve the coat, as I was damned if I was going to do it. 'Do you know him well?' she said.

'Well, yes,' I said, 'we're together.'

'Oh Christ, Dave . . . can you take me to him.' So I did, uneasily, being frightened of his anger, and dreading to appear, in his eyes, to be on her side.

In the bar he had started talking immediately to a small group of people, he had a glass of wine in his hand, and he was telling them in rapid impersonal terms about some aspect of the production. He paid keen attention to a question, as we came up behind him, Julie clutching her coat and stretching out a hand but not quite touching him. The man Hector was talking to smiled at her as he listened, and seemed keen to bring her in, while she hovered, fearing to offend him further by interrupting. 'Look, I'm so terribly sorry,' she said, 'I was . . . I was utterly thoughtless.' Hector half turned.

'Forget it,' he said, not the forget-it of forgiveness but of there being no chance of it. She looked at him, pained and panting, bit her lip; and said,

'Well . . . all right then,' and then almost crossly, 'but I *am* sorry – you see, I had to miss the first half, I've been filming all day, I hadn't seen you or of course I would have known.'

But this small extenuation meant nothing to Hector; she went off by herself to find the cloakroom and after that the little group broke up rather nervously and he and I were left alone.

'God, how much longer have we got to put up with this shit?' I said, and meant it, though even to myself I sounded out of character. 'You know, that still happens to me, with people I don't know, sometimes, or who don't know me.'

He said nothing, a powerful silence, a hidden chain of thoughts, as we stood looking into the crowd like two guests who were yet to be introduced. I flinched in my mind through his possible replies, and phrased my inadequate rejoinders. I kept nearly speaking, but his presence was forbidding, it would have chilled a packed house. Then Roger himself was coming towards us with Joan Collins, who said she wanted to meet Hector especially, and the surreal glamour, gleam of flashbulbs on the retina, sliding and dissolving, seemed to stun him at first, like another assault. He shook her hand stiffly and it was as if she had charged herself with undoing the hurt, and against the odds coaxing him into a smile. She asked him about his career so far, she'd never seen a Terra show but she'd heard of us, and said she meant to see the next one – 'at least if you're going to be in it': she flirted and she was also a little like royalty, to those who are susceptible, bestowing the magic of her attention. Then Claudius and Laertes, who were watching and smiling just behind her, jumped in, the photographer called and the group turned away from us while Hector said, tersely and quietly, as if it shouldn't need pointing out, 'David, you're not even black.'

Whenever I could, and Hector had a comp, I came in to see him open *Hamlet* with his sonorous 'Who's there?' and feel the surprise in the house as he stepped out from the shadows and dry ice. Francisco answered with his own challenge, but really the audience were waiting to hear Hector again, and work out what they thought . . . I thought if I had never seen *Hamlet* before I might have expected this powerful figure in the first scene to play a commanding part throughout – not vanish after Scene Two, never to appear again. It seemed to me Hec played it as a statement of intent for some much larger performance than this one – one where he wouldn't have to wait backstage for three and a half hours to join the blood-soaked principals at the curtain call.

The second time I was in I went round in the interval, and climbed up the stairs past the comfy Edwardian suites that were the stars' dressing rooms ('Mr Jessop', 'Miss Delano' on the doors) to the one Hector shared on the top floor with Fortinbras, Marcellus and Guildenstern. It was hierarchy, and it caught my breath for a moment as I went up. I knocked and went straight in with the feeling that as an actor myself I was allowed to find them in their underpants. Marcellus had popped out to get something to eat in Drury Lane, and Fortinbras, who didn't appear until the end of Act Four, was sitting in his vest and doing his make-up. Guildenstern was on. Hector was sitting in an armchair under the window with its small but disorienting view of the evening outside the theatre; in his posture, his nod at me, he seemed to communicate his right to be here and a sense even so of its strangeness. He introduced me and Fortinbras nodded in the mirror and said he'd seen me in *Volpone* at Oxford, and how great I'd been. 'I saw you the other night,' I said; 'you were great too.' I went over to kiss Hector, but he started talking to head me off. Fortinbras stood up and put on his doublet, and over it a stylized piece of leather armour. 'Could you?' he said, so I helped him tie it up at the back; Oxford terms seemed at once to prevail. 'I'm not on for long, but I will need to breathe,' he said, so I laughed and let him out a bit; he was posh, handsome, plumpish round the hips – he took me straight back to the mood of college plays, all the boyish self-regard that Ray so deplored. 'Don't worry about the bows, I've got this fucking great enormous cloak.' 'You look splendid in it,' I said, and dusted off his shoulders and looked at him. 'You're not his blooming dresser,' Hector said. 'I must say,' said Fortinbras, 'it's bloody good of you – David, isn't it – to come and see this reprobate now he's deserted your outfit for the RSC.' 'Yeah, well,' said Hector before I could explain further, 'no doubt I'll be back with his outfit at the end of the run.'

Then Fortinbras's call came over the tannoy. 'Right you are, then,' he said, pulling himself up: 'Go, captain, from me greet the Danish king.' 'You've got it,' I said, amused by the sudden grip of nerves, the change in his breathing. He swept out and we heard his boot heels dwindle down the concrete stair. Far below, the play was going on non-stop, he would be hearing it now as he entered the backstage, among the watchful technicians, then looking on for a minute from the wings till Hamlet, shouting, 'Come, for England!', exited towards him, sweating, no eye contact, and Claudius, ten yards away, in a cone of light, spoke secretly to Rosencrantz and Guildenstern. He would hear for the first time, beneath the towering twilight of the flies, the presence of the audience, unseen in its dark plush shell beyond. He would only have a moment to gauge that sound, its quality of attention, before the stage was emptying, the lights went quickly down and slowly up again, and he was on, his Captain stage right, perfectly on cue – 'It's like life, isn't it,' I said to Hector, 'the little people's fleeting contact with the great ones.'

'You said it, my love,' he said, and moodily allowed me to kiss him on the cheek. 'Welcome to the West End.' I stroked his hair, which he hated, though I did it in a stew of admiration and embarrassment and the longing to make love to him, a remote chance in this place and moment. It didn't escape me that it was he who welcomed me to the West End, not me him.

Across the street a couple in their flat were having dinner: to them the bleak undomestic back wall of the theatre must be an almost picturesque aspect of living there, and the crowds in the street below when a show came out, honking of taxis. They were used to thesps; their new guests were intrigued by the things that they glimpsed in the dressing rooms across the way, but they themselves were blasé about them.

I watched the man get up and go into the kitchen. Then he came back to the window and without quite looking at me closed the curtains.

After the show the quick backstage demob, scatter of a tired cast for distant homes and hotels. A youngster's 'Goodnight!' for old Ron in his glass cabin, veteran of one hundred and seventeen plays, so he claimed, in this theatre, and their fleeting stars. The autograph hunters at the stage-door looked past us to whoever was coming out next – it was Roger they wanted, or Marcia, and their moment with her, as she took the book or programme and asked their name, would be filled with their tongue-tied praise for her past work in *Upstairs, Downstairs* as much as her Gertrude tonight. 'Will there be another series?' they wanted to know. This was something Gertrude was never going to have. 'Oh, excuse me!' said a man with an animated look and Hec turned like a star himself with a minute to spare for a fan. 'Leicester Square station, mate – is it this way?'

Then we were alone together in the street, Hector abstruse with his own tiredness, the empty fatigue of having worked and not worked, and me tongue-tied too in the face of his mood. The Central Line was suspended, so we took the Piccadilly, to change at Hammersmith – we pressed into a carriage that was full already, friends who entered by two different doors shouting over our heads to each other, drunk, and then singing started up. Other passengers frowned, or smiled timidly, seated or standing, some holding programmes for *A Chorus Line* or *Tosca*, enduring the disenchantment of the journey home. A sour smell from the smoking carriage next door crept in through the end windows, lowered for air. At Knightsbridge the singers got off, twenty more people joined, and Hector dropped into the last seat by the door, ahead of a woman in a beret with a bag on her shoulder and a large shopping basket and her own look of exhaustion. She winced and sighed and I saw her wanting and then fearing to say something to him. I swayed from the strap a few feet away, squeezed in from behind against a crop-haired, muscular man who stood with his back to me, unnervingly face to face with the exhausted woman. The doors closed at the second attempt, and the train moved off, with a jolt after two seconds that threw those of us standing off balance, though we couldn't fall over. The crop-haired man looked sharply over his shoulder. 'Watch it, mate,' he said. I scowled and said, 'Not my fault,' but his look added menace to the powerful presence of his shoulders and his broad arse, and I pushed back myself so as not to be thrust against him. It was the old business of carefully avoiding a contact I could justly be accused of wanting, though he worried me more than he turned me on. Once or twice I caught Hector's eye, and he answered my stoical smile with a nod; then he rested his head against the narrow glass screen, and closed his eyes. He had slipped out of reach. And so we went on through the long twisting tunnels at what seemed a terribly sluggish and jolting pace, as if the train laboured to carry so many of us: all I could see, with my arm raised to the strap above, was the shoulders of the man I was trying not to press against, and beyond him the white woman peering down now and then at the black man who she thought should have offered her his seat. I couldn't tell if Hector was actually asleep. The white man nodded scornfully at him, the woman gave a nervous smile, half-grateful, half-bothered by his taking her part: he was very close to her. And in my own trance of exhaustion and discomfort I saw oddly clearly the potential of the scene, the tired, short-tempered hatreds and fears that were ready, at another fierce jolt of the train, to kick off.

After the Aldwych season the RSC let Hector go – the parts they had given him were too small for them to judge his fitness for larger ones, and as several people said to him quite frankly, as if sure he'd understand, it looked pretty daft having one black person in Elsinore. Ray took him back, in a new John Arden play, and gave him the very small role of a cook to teach him a lesson. Life back on the road was unsettling, with an undertow of tiredness, and there were times when Hector and I seemed no more than two people travelling to Chester or Durham who had found themselves sitting together. In London we were either in the room I borrowed at the top of Robin Boyd's house in Islington, big, newly done up in a crumbling terrace, four floors, double drawing room and a certain expectation of tiptoes and order; or we were in Latimer Road, with the broken lift and Hector's plants and candles. Small resentments built up of the guest-like self-consciousness at Robin's and the pokiness at Perry's. 'This place is getting too small for us,' said Hector. I smiled, nervous, charming: 'It is a bit on the titchy side . . . But it's home.' 'I need more space,' Hector said, and I knew it was one of his simple statements in which weeks of silent thinking were prepared and packed. He didn't smile back.

We tried going away – after *Timon* in Exeter we cut off from the cast and took a bus across the Moor to Friscombe, a room in a B&B just in from the front. I rang before and booked it, felt the warm Devon tone of the landlady, and beyond it the pleasure of showing Hec where I'd stayed long before with Mum and Esme – I saw all the lovely ways to entertain him, the funny stories about Maureen and Marco, loutish Ollie with his trunks falling off; it was late September but still warm and with a chance of swimming.

The bus set us down at a stop by the north beach, the tide out and the sea tumbling grey on a far-off dazzle of wet sand. Behind us the long row of guest houses, with their stark salt-lashed sunrooms and indomitable hydrangeas. Memory crawled and shifted to fit itself to the facts, the steps and railings unim-agined until now. The Cliff Hotel had lost its place, slipped further round towards the harbour, a white block of flats this side of it. We set off towards it, I didn't press Hec to react, but I watched the hotel looming, in its blank diminished way, and as we came along in front of it I said, 'Well, this is where we stayed, Mum and Esme had that room there with the balcony,' and he glanced up. It was spindly and rusty, the balcony, and by now surely as dangerous as Esme had claimed at the time. The door was open into the late-morning vacancy of the hall, through the dining-room window the first lunchers could be seen with an impatient old waiter, grey hair oiled back, left hand hooked round the order-pad. 'Good god,' I said, and when Hec raised his eyebrows – 'I'll explain later, it's the same waiter from fifteen years ago.' 'Well, that's life,' said Hec. Marco I was certain was married, ran a cafe in Bari, had ten-year-old children, never thought of the Cliff Hotel or the old bully Terence from one year to the next; while the thread of old Terence's life was laid desolately clear. We walked round the corner, I sprung the surprise of the harbour on Hector, high black walls, boats resting on the mud, gulls on the narrow creek of water that remained. 'That's nice,' said Hec, and I wasn't sure about his tone, I grinned at him and we went on. A black guy, in his forties, perhaps, the first person of colour this side of Exeter, murmured, 'Hey, man . . . hey, man,' as he came towards us, Hec gave him his tutting lift of the chin, and I said, 'Hi!' 'Place is crawling with immigrants,' Hector said as we went on, we both laughed, and I knew with a lift of the heart we were going to have fun.

Hector nipped into Boots for essentials while I went down the side street and rang the bell at Tralee, the name one holiday inside another – I watched the woman through the glass front door, as she came towards me smiling, before she saw that I wasn't a guest: with my shabby suitcase perhaps a rep of some kind. 'Can I help you?' So I was Gielgud first, then toned it down because it sounded to my ear like satire. 'Oh! *you're* Mr Win, I see . . . well, you'd better come in . . .' – I saw her still adjusting, and reassuring herself that I wasn't something worse: 'Are you down here on business?' she said, regaining her footing – it would be a local restaurant, very probably. She seemed to talk herself into liking me then, and I saw how she quietly admired herself for doing so. 'Just two nights, is it?' It would be something she could talk about, I didn't like to think how. 'Yes, please,' I said, and added fatuously, 'then, I'm sorry to say, we'll have to be off.' She looked in a thick desk diary, the pages curled up with the summer's bookings, though there was no sign on the present page of anyone else staying, and the small lounge behind me had the look of a waiting-room, seldom used. 'A twin, you said?' she said, turning to the board in the miniature 'Reception' (there were only four rooms) where the keys were hanging. 'Yes, my friend's just coming,' I said, and saw her flinch but surmount the idea of an unmarried couple; there was a bump of the front door and Hector came in – I see him with the wallpaper behind him, and the wrought-iron wall-lights, and the bright-featured holiday map of the sunny south-west as the woman looked back and blinked very fast while the rest of her face adjusted itself, as if to an insult, as if seeing her own goodness abused. 'Let me just ask my husband,' she said quietly, and as she went through the door marked Private she glanced back, unsure now about leaving us there unwatched. Hector stood expressionless, staring over my head. In a minute the husband came through, cardiganed, comb-over, round-faced, with the twinkle of a good host, the wife behind him, nodding, knowing she'd done the right thing. Where she was brittle, he was smooth, and implacable. 'I'm very sorry, lads,' he said, 'there's been an awful cock-up, double booking.' He looked from one to the other of us, he had his own ingenuity, he took the blame, 'All my fault, I should have told my wife, the whole place is booked up for the next week.' I said quickly, 'We'll try somewhere else,' and picked up my suitcase. Hec's kitbag was halfway off his shoulder. 'Oh, you shouldn't have any trouble, at this time of year,' the man said. 'I agree,' I said, 'we shouldn't,' and went out past Hec, who stood staring in a great deep ordering of thoughts in front of the man, with his wife now beside him, triumphant and a little frightened. The narrow hallway, with its fuse-box, its notices, its makeshift conversion of a house into a guest house, was so mean and ugly I was ashamed of my forgiving holiday readiness, two minutes earlier, to make the place my temporary home. The dead air tingled with things none of us, probably, was going to say, though I felt Hector's readiness to speak, the unscripted eloquence of his response to any assault on himself.

'So, where shall we go?' I said when we were out, and a few yards down the street. I wasn't sure from his silence if he'd banished the subject instantly for ever, or was still building up to a furious accusal. Absurd, but my own position felt compromised by the woman's readiness to let me have the room. Hector shrugged his bag round on his shoulders, spread his hands.

'This is your idea, David,' he said. Of course the holiday was over, there was no true recovery from a start like that.

'We don't have that much money,' I said, 'or we could try one of the hotels.'

'The Race Relations Act makes it illegal to refuse anyone accommodation on grounds of race or the colour of their skin.'

'Yes, I know that. The problem, as we both know, is proving that those were the grounds for refusal.'

'I'm not stupid.'

'The woman was going to give me a room.'

'So she hates homosexuals, is what you're saying.'

'No law against that, honey,' I said. And I wondered if anywhere here would let us share a room. Hotels were more impassive, but in B&Bs you were the helpless prey of the host family.

We turned left along the curve of the harbour. I had a glimpse, in the gleam of the water, the breeze, and the racket of gulls, of the holiday we might have been having, as inaccessible now as the one I'd had here as a boy. 'I need something to eat,' Hector said, 'and a drink. Christ!' It was very rare for him to swear.

We went over the cobbles to the Ship in Dock, 'Friscombe's oldest inn', saloon bar low and timbered, beer-pulls and optics shining in the gloom. It had the sour hoovered smell of a pub in the morning, before the next day's smoke and beer and food-smells warm it up. 'Yes, gentlemen!' said the girl behind the bar. As she drew our two pints of the local IPA, Hec said, in a rather measured way, 'I see you have accommodation here.'

'We certainly do!' she said. 'Though I think . . .' – craning round, as she pulled down the handle, to look at a list – 'no, I'm wrong, we've got a couple of rooms free. Was it for tonight?'

The 'couple of rooms' had the making of a fresh misunder-standing; and I thought about the noise, being over a pub, but it was Hector's call. 'We just want one room for the two of us,' he said.

She lifted his pint forward, and smiled at him narrowly. 'I know I've seen you before,' she said. 'You're an actor, aren't you. I could swear I've seen you in a play.' Hector was blank in the face of this charge, then started speaking to conceal his smile. It was one of his perilous, magical changes of mood.

'I am, madam . . .' – basso, melancholy – 'but a walking shadow – a poor player . . .' – he raised his right arm . . .

' . . . that frets and struts . . . is it? *struts and frets* his hour upon the stage' – they smiled and shook their heads at each other.

'And then is heard no more,' I said. 'Don't forget.'

'My friend too is a player,' Hector explained.

She hadn't really looked at me, it was Hec, in any offstage situation, who had star power and held the eye. 'Hi!' I said.

'Mr David Win: you might recognize him from sundry epi-sodes of *Hibiscus Hotel*.'

'I expect you're too young,' I said, 'to have even heard of *Hibiscus Hotel*.'

It turned out she was doing English at Bristol, this was her holiday job, and she'd seen Hector (and me too, come to that) in *Catchpole's Army* in the students' union theatre last year. 'Yes, it was a . . .' – she looked over our heads as she cast her mind back – 'it wasn't a . . .'

'It wasn't really, was it,' I said.

She had a word with the landlord, who came through to check the book; he had the red-faced look of one of his own regulars, the same potential for malice as the host at Tralee, but seemed in fact utterly indifferent to what we looked like and what we might want to do in bed. 'Have a look at the rooms and take your pick, gents,' handing over two keys each attached to a bit of driftwood with the number burnt on. We went down a passage beside the bar and up a dangerous little staircase, with a feeling of being allowed a treat, a surprise. One room, at the back, was almost filled by the bed, the one at the front was twice as big, but above the bar, which could be mumblingly heard through the floor. From the two low windows there was a view over the harbour, the brown sea, the silver horizon. Hector let his bag slide down from his shoulder onto the bed, and the decision was made.

After a pie and a second pint we strolled out with a not very clear sense of purpose. I felt parched and bleary from the beer. The sun went in and came out, the sea was coming back, and I smiled at the disappearing rocks and the commonplace shops and cafes like an anxious host – when I called up my crushes on Ollie and our dramas with the hotel staff I saw Hector struggling to see the point and the point itself shrivelling in the light of explanation. He'd had holidays with Patrick and Amanda in Paignton and Cromer, he'd played on a beach with white adults keeping an eye on him year after year, in the equivocal freedom of the seaside. I knew nothing was simple, and the outrage at the couple at Tralee still burned in him, and blocked the view. I bought a few postcards, each exactly the same, on the spinning and jamming rack, as fifteen years earlier – colours filtered and simplified, sea turquoise, sails white or red. I got the one in which the Cliff Hotel could be seen on the right across the beach – it was the card I'd sent the Hadlows when I was fourteen. Other people in the shop fell silent, as we came out an old couple sketched a brisk courtesy as they swerved aside and glanced back and murmured to each other once they'd crossed the road. On tour the theatres and the company explained us and licensed us, people paid good money to see us. Here they scowled at us – or anyway three or four of them did, turned and stared and nudged each other: I filtered them out while Hector, I knew, stored them up.

I went into the Gents where I'd once read the graffiti with a pounding heart, where a stranger's eye had gorged on me through the wall – the first half-terrified imagining of another town, another world, of men together, indifferent to cold and filth, burning their own heat. It appeared, as I stood on the step, to have been thoroughly cleaned up. In a minute Hec came in too, right beside me, and I stood with my arm round his waist as we watched each other finish. 'Very nice,' he said, and I knew with a melting of the heart that he meant it. 'Let's get back to the room.'

In Room One at the Ship in Dock I sat up in bed, Hector face down, unreachable in sleep, the actor's held-back exhaustion. I wrote gently, not to shake him: 'Dear Mum and Esme – As you see, back in this old haunt, just for two nights – staying in a quaint old pub on the harbour. Went past the Cliff Hotel – looks like Terence still there but no sign of Maureen! May go in later for a drink.' I was conscious, in my hesitations, looking out at the boats as they rose bit by bit into view on the tide, of avoiding my first-person pronouns, no hint of the man in his vest and pants lying flat out beside me. Was I writing the card while he slept to keep his own absence a secret from him? I went on, 'I'm with one of the other actors,' which was the truth, and not enough of it to make them care much, one way or the other. Oddly difficult to say then that this other actor and I had been having an affair for the past nine months. I was baffled and depressed by my own reticence, a slight to them as much as to Hector and to myself. But then to tell them at this stage that we were a couple seemed dangerously ill-advised. I saw Mum's smile, as she got her mind round the new idea, adjusting soon after to the wince of letting it go. I tucked the unfinished card into my Iris Murdoch, and edged down beside Hector, to share his sleeping breath and then, I hoped, to sleep myself. I had a sense of precarious refuge.

In April, after three auditions, Hector got a part in a Hollywood movie, set in New York. I thought of putting him in touch with Lydia, but it turned out the film was being shot in Toronto, a much cheaper stand-in. Something seemed to stretch then, to breaking point, the never-spoken assumption that I would travel with him. I knew I couldn't, I was after a TV part in Manchester myself, and I knew he wouldn't ask me, or express disappointment at going there alone. 'Let's keep in touch!' I said, brightly but barely in control of myself, and he agreed to that amiably enough.

I didn't know when he was back, and then I saw him announced in a new play by Mustapha Matura at the Royal Court Upstairs. In a hopeless performance that took me back to school holidays and ringing up other people's parents, I found Patrick and Amanda's number and called them. Patrick answered, he was pleasant, remembered seeing me act, though admitted that the play hadn't really been their kind of thing. I felt they had probably been prepared by Hector with some knowledge of the situation. I asked them to give him a message.

Now I was staying full-time at Robin's place, my old Oxford friend who'd gone into the City, and was often out later than me. He didn't mind having me, was lonely himself in these large white rooms, but I heard a new crispness in his greetings when he came in and found me there, a hint that I ought to start looking for somewhere else. 'You never seemed all that happy together – if I can say that,' said Robin, and I frowned and said, 'Oh . . .' and searched back for the moments when we had been. 'He's had a lot to contend with,' I said. 'No, of course,' said Robin.

In the pointless quiet mornings alone in the house I went through Robin's LPs, some we'd listened to together in Oxford, already eight or nine years ago, we had a craze for French songs. Here was the record, with that past still awake in the sheen of the sleeve, the typeface like a wedding invitation, *Mélodies françaises*, and the singer in open-necked shirt – Gérard Souzay, the grainy authentic old baritone, with Dalton Baldwin, his half-secret long-term lover, as accompanist. I put it on, the side with Duparc's 'Soupir', the words known by heart, 'Ne jamais la voir ni l'entendre . . . toujours l'aimer'. At the door of the long double drawing room I saw Hector coming in, just three months ago, his red socks on the dove-grey carpet, face blank with the presence of something not yet being said. Perhaps we could never have been truly happy, but I missed him, I missed our life together, and I missed, incalculably, the future we were now not going to share.

26

'Yes,' I said, 'it's my first time back.' A group of girls, folders clutched to their bosoms, hurried past outside the Headmaster's window.

'You'll see a fair bit of change,' he said. One of the changes, of course, was him – younger than me and with an active and fairly compelling sense of having his own agenda. Full co-education in the sixth form was a part of it, which no one but a sexist or a sexual nostalgist could object to. To be back at school twenty-six years after leaving was to plunge into more nostalgia than most well-adjusted adults would admit to, while seeing the scene of my past with a disbelief close to mockery. It was wonderfully disorienting. 'It's good of you to say you'll give a talk.'

'Oh, not at all,' I said.

'I've put it down simply as *Acting as a Career*. There's been a fair bit of interest.' I wasn't sure the Headmaster had ever seen me act. Or that I'd made a career of it. *Struggling to Make a Career Out of Acting* might have been nearer the mark. 'The talks are all between four and six, then the BOBs meet for drinks and then supper in Hall after the students have had theirs.'

'I suppose you have BOGs now, too,' I said.

'Indeed we do,' he said, 'though not of course at this reunion.'

'We're the Sixties leavers.'

'Not a very high response rate, I'm afraid, among your contemporaries, but I think you'll see some old friends.'

'That's the Sixties for you,' I said.

As I left his study – new secretary, new decor, fire doors breaking up the once dreaded hallway – I saw Kim Wynans coming towards me, and though he was almost bald and had grown a moustache we were both for a moment offenders on the HM's list: he seemed to look at me for signs of what to expect, and this was part of the comedy of our meeting, as well as the great change in his appearance. 'Well, *you* haven't changed a bit,' he said, 'and I don't suppose you ever will.' We agreed we would catch up over drinks – and even drinks had an atmosphere of illegality. I wasn't sure I could tell him I thought he'd changed for the better – there was something weedy about Wynans as a boy, blond and slight, bullied for being queer, and joining in timidly when I was bullied for other reasons. I left the building, and suddenly shy again, avoided the other BOBs and walked off over the lawns to the Balustrade.

I was caught off-guard by the park – the gang-mower moving briskly over the outfield in a low haze of cut grass, while its smaller cousin puttered intently down the length of the pitch, turned, and came back again. Widely spaced posts marked the ring of the boundary; beyond them rose the dark arboretum-like wall of the Bampton woods. The whole scene was casually graceful, the mowers plying capably up and down in the sunshine just as they had thirty years ago. Anticipation seemed to tighten and shimmer in the rising and receding thrum of their motors – close by, you would have had to raise your voice, but from the Balustrade two hundred yards away you heard a kind of music, the beautiful integrated drone of English competence, and habit.

'Winny, is that you?'

I glanced sideways, half-prepared to forgive – it was Fascist Harris, with his mocking look just a little abashed by our transformation into middle-aged men. He was fat, fashionless, red-faced, with a gratifying air of having gone wrong, perhaps without knowing it himself, but something bothered him. He smiled narrowly as he came up, didn't shake my hand but touched my shoulder, and nodded as he gazed at me. The old hatred was there, it was our element, but I saw him enjoying his thin pretence that he'd moved on. 'We saw you on the telly,' he said, 'you were really rather good, Winny.'

'What did you see me in?' I said.

'A crime thing, wasn't it? You played some inscrutable Oriental, as usual' – and seeing my reaction, 'actually you were the best thing in it. I said to Claire, "I know that chappie! We were at school together." Of course, she didn't believe me at first.'

'And what are you doing these days, Fash?'

'Ha!' He flinched, then shrugged. 'Oh, the law, old chap, yup.'

'And what does Claire do?'

'She's a JP, as a matter of fact. I'm a barrister, she's a JP, you don't want to mess with us.'

'Any children?'

'Three girls, yes. And are you . . . ?' – he shook his head in pretended innocence. I had every reason to be frank with him, but I felt I heard already the things he would say to Claire about me and the straight-faced innuendo he would traffic in tonight, and I said simply but conclusively,

'No children, no.'

I went along the Top Corridor with a silly feeling of not wanting to be caught, waited for a moment by the warm frosted glass of Mr Hudson's door, other voices busy inside, and somewhere ahead of me a louder voice, Giles, yes, speaking in a halting but businesslike tone, I supposed to a group of pupils – his talk was on 'Making Our Own Way: Britain and the EU'. 'Start again,' he said, and then more decisively, 'I advise you to approach the Prime Minister's office directly, and make clear

the urgency of the September, is it? The *October* deadline—'
Now I was outside the half-open door of Dorm 3, which he
must have commandeered for his pep-talk, with his exciting
knack for improvisation . . . sunlight on brown lino, white
pillow of a tightly made bed under a red rug and for a long
dissolving second lovely Barker naked in it until Giles said,
'Kathy, look up last Monday's minutes would you and check
the date, um . . .' The floorboard squeaked in memory as I put
my head round the door, and there was Giles, perched on a bed,
papers spread out beside him, and a small black device held
close to his chin like an electric razor. 'Hullo, Dave,' he said,
'exploring?'

'I thought you were giving your talk, for a moment,' I said.
'I didn't want to miss it.'

'Ha! No, I'm giving my talk in the Library at half-past five.'

'Damn,' I said, 'that's when I'm giving mine, in the Chapel.'

He stared at me – it was the first time I'd seen him in
glasses, and he seemed conscious of them too. 'I just needed a
quiet spot to catch up with departmental business,' and he gave
me the firm little smile which told me I should let him get on
with it.

'That was Andrew Sparks's bed,' I said.

He was blank. 'What?'

'You slept over by the window. Sparks had the bed you're
sitting on.'

He tutted, turned back to his papers. 'Your memory,
Dave . . .', and I wondered if his touch of colour implied that
he remembered making Sparks strip naked and wank off in
front of him, and was worried that I might, in my needling
needless way, bring it up. Do married men, fathers, Secretaries
of State, remember such things, or are they buried for ever,
unreachably? – I've never known.

'And I had that bed in the corner,' I said, 'next to Gary
Stapleford.'

In the centre of the dormitory was the Slab, two tall chests of drawers back to back, just as they always were. I had a blurred image of scenes enacted on top of the Slab, but again I kept them to myself. Besides, the mood was so changed, the new curtains and lockable bedside cupboards introduced a clean hospital note to the night-time menagerie of thirty years earlier.

I ran into Kim again about five minutes later – we seemed cosy at once, quite unlike our relations when we were boys: it was forgiveness, immediate and mutual, and it bonded us against others we weren't so ready to forgive. I said, 'I've just found Hadlow in Dorm 3 dictating letters to his secretary on a tape-machine.' We looked at each other and giggled.

'Isn't everyone doing what they wish they'd done all those years ago?'

'He must have wanted people to hear him,' I said.

'Very good of him to be here at all when he's so busy,' Kim said. It was charming how little we needed to explain – in our different ways we'd known Giles as a teenager, and now shared unshakable doubts about him as a forty-three-year-old. 'You were the Hadlow Exhibitioner, weren't you, I remember. I don't think Hadlow himself was very pleased about that.'

'I suppose he was annoyed he didn't get it himself.'

'Giving it to a bloody – well, I won't tell you what he said.'

'Oh god . . . Anyway,' I said, 'what's your thing that you're doing?'

I thought he coloured too, very slightly. 'I haven't done it yet, perhaps I never will. I don't know . . .' with a smile, a flicker of the eyebrows, then he seemed to close again.

When we gathered for drinks before dinner, all of us in black tie now, a number of masters, as well as two mistresses, joined us. 'Yes, we'll be rather a shock to you!' said one of the women, the new Head of Maths.

'A very happy, and very timely, shock, if I may say so,' I declared, unexpectedly Jeeves – I nearly added, 'madam'. I saw that to her we were historic, remote, a maze of stories she was barely going to grasp before we all went home again; it made the one or two prominent careers, like Giles's, stand out reassuringly. Giles, heavier now, clearly felt he was the most important BOB present, though naturally the other BOBs had a range of feelings on the question. The Tories among us were excited, others humorously intrigued by his presence; in some the spirit of reunion ran up against a loathing that had only intensified since schooldays. The Headmaster was above the fray, but I liked his line: 'I've been looking you up,' he said: 'you were never Head Boy.' 'No, no,' said Giles, with a shake of the head, as if he'd already had much more important positions in mind. We milled around there, in the Library, guessing and concealing our shock at who some of the others were. There was an instinct to use nicknames, slight struggle in fact for forenames, and a tone of pretended friendliness in using them that half the time turned out to be quite genuine. We felt open and connected, as people sometimes do at funerals.

'And whom have we lost?' said Peter Leatherby. I looked round as if for late arrivals, or counting the squad back after Field Day long ago. 'There was Tim Franklin, of course, from your year, very sad business.' 'Cancer,' someone said. 'Only thirty-five, I liked Tim . . .' 'Indeed . . .' said Leatherby, 'how could one not.' 'And Pringle, wasn't there . . .' 'Not Derek?' 'No, Piers, his younger brother, you remember.' 'I didn't know him.' 'Climbing accident, in Nepal I think it was.' 'Oh, really . . . god . . . how awful . . .'

There was a darker tide that had risen through the years since we'd last been together, too dark, it seemed, to be easily mentioned. But someone said, 'Andrew Cousins, of course,' with a little wince and indrawn breath.

'Kissing Cousins,' said Giles, 'what on earth happened to him?'

'Well,' said Leatherby, but looking at me, 'it was, I'm afraid it was AIDS, wasn't it, yes.'

'He always was—' said Giles, then thought better of it.

'What did he do?' said Charlie Boxwell.

'He was a male model, wasn't he?' Kim said.

'For a while, I think,' I said. 'Then he trained as a dental surgeon.'

'Oh, did he, yes . . gosh . . .' and a brief silence fell. Did anyone else here dare to remember how Charlie had fancied Andrew, been really madly in love with him, in the autumn of '65? Perhaps, under other conditions, someone might have teased him about it.

'I remember you giving him the slipper, David,' said Kim, and I had the split-second shock of remembering this was Harris's name too.

'Oh, Christ, did I really?' said Harris, with a flinching look, at his own beastliness, and also, remotely and horribly, as if he might have caught something.

'You were quite keen on discipline, weren't you,' said Kim.

'We all remember your great speech,' I said, '*I have the power – you don't.*' I felt he could be teased in public, and he smiled very decently.

'In what way, Winny,' he said, 'was I wrong?'

Soon the conversation turned to wives and children, a dull part of the reason I'd never come back before: an odd craven worry, a gay thing really. I said, 'I've been single for a while now, actually,' as if it was a bracing but rewarding choice. 'Well, for an actor,' Charlie said, 'it must be so much easier, you know, touring a lot, and so on,' and making excuses for me. Of course I was expecting all the time that someone would say what they'd seen me in, and how good I was, but so far it was only Fascist Harris who had done so. As Charlie was talking my eye found my name on the Honours Board, in slanting gilt capitals, with a quarter of a century of subsequent scholarships to Oxford and Cambridge pushing it further and further back into the past.

At dinner I was seated next to a young black man I'd noticed at the drinks: we shook hands, Brian Mitchell, he taught English – small and serious, with wire-framed glasses and a light Yorkshire accent. I tried to picture having a master like him here in my day, a destabilizing intervention, not quite imaginable now in 1960s terms.

'I hear you were a Hadlow Exhibitioner,' he said, peering narrowly at the seafood starter, prawns and bits of something else, a bizarrely fancy presence in a school dining hall.

'Yes, I was,' I said, 'in 1961. They're still going, I suppose?'

'Oh, very much so. It's the fiftieth anniversary next year – we're hoping as many old Exhibitioners as possible will come back for a reunion.'

'Well, if I'm free,' I said, feeling one reunion was probably enough for me.

'Of course, for an actor it must be hard to say.'

'Our evenings are rarely our own,' I said, in a tragic voice, with a sly little smile at him.

'No, quite,' he said. No wedding ring, but no covert collusion either, in his voice or glance. 'Can I ask if you're about to be in anything?'

I answered a slightly different question. 'Actually, I've just finished shooting a film about the Burma campaign, called *Wingate's War*.'

'Oh, yes?' he said, a little hesitant – I guessed he was twenty-five, the War in Burma the sort of historical blur it had been to me in my years at Bampton. 'I've never been to Burma.'

'Well, who has?' I said. 'We filmed it in the Philippines.'

'Oh, really! You mean you've never been yourself?'

'Oh, I expect I will one day,' I said.

To many white English people this was a barely explicable omission, a great symptomatic avoidance, but Brian Mitchell seemed to understand. 'Well, I've never been to Jamaica,' he said, with a quick shake of the head. 'Do you often get a chance to play a Burmese character, though, I wonder?'

'It was the very first time – it was quite refreshing.'

'Interesting. So your . . . *father* is Burmese, I assume?'

'Was, yes.' I looked round the hall, all the black-tied forty-somethings at the three long tables they had sat at as boys. One or two of them might still recall elements of stories I had told about my father, and I wondered if just for consistency I should come out with one of them now, the fighter pilot, or perhaps the assassination. 'Actually,' I said, 'for all I know he may still be alive. I've never met him.'

Brian glanced at me. 'Oh, I see . . .'

'It's all very obscure,' and I explained a little more about it, since he seemed interested, and in this setting it took on a subtly different interest for me too.

'I don't know if you'd ever be willing to come and talk to the Race Relations seminar I run with the Middle Sixth.'

'Race Relations seminar,' I said, blinking at the thought. 'I don't know, all these things are very personal.'

'Well, see how you feel. I hear your talk this afternoon went extremely well.'

'Oh! That's nice to hear. It wasn't really a talk, I got them to do an audition.'

'Enobarbus.'

'Yes, and "Give me my robe, put on my crown" for the girls.'

'The kids were very excited – they watched your *Midsummer Night's Dream* in General Studies last week.'

'Oh, they didn't say.'

'A bit star-struck, I expect.'

It wasn't false modesty that made me look down and murmur, 'Well . . . I don't know.'

'Anyone stand out, would you say?'

'In the end I gave them all the part . . .'

'I wonder what you made of Georgia, tall, nice-looking girl, blonde hair . . .'

'Oh, yes . . .' I said.

'She's a very bright kid.' I heard then in a second his way of being on the kids' level – sharing their ambitions, not hearing a bad word about them, while being also of course a clever young professional, and no doubt a good teacher.

'No, she *was* good,' I said. And I felt there were other things to say, very personal too, about the multiple sensations stirred up in me by working with these boys and girls in the very chapel where at their age I'd knelt with a beating heart to take Holy Communion, a phase of devotion I had almost completely forgotten; but I wasn't going to say them to Brian. The truth was I was frightened of children, just a little, and I felt they didn't take to me. I hadn't quite reckoned how my standing, as an old boy of the school, made me a fine example to them of what could be achieved. They hadn't known me as a child themselves.

On the other side I had Keith Bagshaw, who had come in late, hair thick and wild, improvised black tie, with brown shoes. 'David Win! Hello!' he said, when I turned to him. He had the inattentive warmth of a nice but almost entirely self-absorbed person. 'You haven't changed a bit!'

'Oh . . . !' – I looked at him. 'What are you up to now, Keith?' I said.

'I was just telling Charlie Boxwell here . . . I've got this organic farm in Wales. Part dairy, mainly arable. We burn the cow-dung to heat the house.'

'Enterprising.'

'We aim to be completely self-sufficient by the start of '94. A lot of people are coming round to it, of course. It's the way forward!' And he smiled pleasantly, waiting for another question.

'But you're not writing any more?' I said. In the years after university he'd done a series of unrelated things, all promptly reported in the BOBs' newsletter: published a sci-fi novel, gone to live in Indonesia for two years, taken a law degree in Edinburgh, then opened a vegan restaurant in Lewes. It seemed the need to do something overrode any long-term idea of what.

'I'd like to write another book, I'm not sure, probably something quite different . . . you know' – even here the desire to be busy seemed the main thing. He smiled at me, head on one side, with a hint of pity. 'And what have you been up to, David,' he said, 'this past quarter-century?' I had to laugh, in humility, of course, but also at him.

It was muggy when we came out onto the lawn and drifted towards the Prefects' Path and the Balustrade. Night had fallen, and the wingtips of a plane coming in to Brize Norton were pulsing and then hidden in the pinky-grey gloom. Beyond the Balustrade the reach of light from the large sash windows gave a ghostly presence, like a calm sea at night, to the near expanse of the cricket field beyond. Taller trees in the park showed as dim silhouettes against the sky, the wellingtonia high above the rest. The fireworks were going to be set off by the Temple, and there was a random dance of torch-beams against steps and pillars as a young master and two of the prefects made final checks. The boys and girls had massed on the lawn, in a murmuring army. Kim Wynans was leaning beside me on the stone coping. 'We never had all this in our day,' he said. 'No, we didn't,' I said, as the first earth-bound fireworks, two Roman candles and a Catherine wheel that stuck before it started to fizz round, announced the start of the display.

Then a pair of rockets, a fraction out of synch, shot upwards into the murk. Nothing happened for a bit, till high above two gold chrysanthemums of light bloomed dazzlingly and seemed for the space of an indrawn breath to die, then flared and scattered in a dozen frazzled comets traced on darkness, leaving a spilling column of pink smoke as a deep boom, with a certain grandeur of delay, reached us and re-echoed from the house beyond. All this in three seconds, perhaps, but a gap in time opened at the wonder of the thing. Rattled birds flew up out of the trees. Kim's arm was round my shoulders, and I found myself in a mixed-up mood of readiness and near-indifference. 'So good to see you again, David,' he said, pulling me closer for a second, and I felt his moustache as much as his lips pressed lightly on my cheek. I smiled pleasantly, at the fireworks and at him, and other figures, the Headmaster, passing in front of us, staggering as he gazed upwards and then blinking round to share the enjoyment with us.

'I have to ask you,' Kim murmured.

'Oh, yes . . . ?' I said.

'If . . .' – another rocket went up, a strangely whirly one. 'Well, I can still see you,' he said, 'in the showers – one day after cricket . . .' I thought back lazily but I couldn't remember Kim naked at all. It's true I'd been famous in the changing room, for obvious reasons, which sat oddly, half praise, half slanted blame, with all the other things that were thought and said about me. Kim's words seemed more a confession than a question – though the question I suppose concerned what was happening next. 'Then I saw you as Edgar,' he said, 'you know . . . It sort of brought it all back,' and he giggled; I think he was drunker than I was.

'That was fifteen years ago,' I said, 'no, it was more than that. I didn't know you'd been in.'

'It was in Exeter, with my aunt. I'm not sure she'd seen a naked man before.'

'And how did she find the experience?'

'Wow . . . !' – the great hushed unison of the children as one very spectacular rocket towered and tumbled high above two lesser ones.

'All she said was, "Why did he have to be Siamese?"'

It wasn't at all unpleasant having Kim hit on me, but I felt the whole thing unravelling. And where would we have gone, after all, for the long-deferred fulfilment of his fantasy? I smiled at Keith Bagshaw who was drifting past, 'Marvellous!' he said. 'I know!' I said, and started slowly after him, eyes upward, but Kim stuck with me a bit longer.

'Where are you staying tonight?' he said.

'Oh, I'm going back to my mother's,' I said.

'Ah, of course – you're local.' Two big simple mortars went off, very loud, not exactly enjoyable. 'Yes, lucky you. I'm staying at the Crown.'

'Oh, good, yes.'

'Looks pretty ropey, but there's nowhere else much round here.'

'You'll be fine,' I said, and patted him on the shoulder, thinking it cleverer not to say goodbye. I felt I'd got all I was going to get out of this party, and now I must revisit that trapped column of humid and unhappy air, the pupils' phone booth, and call a taxi to take me home.

'How was it?' said Mum, when the cab had left me back in the forgotten adolescent silence of the Close and I'd let myself in, checked myself, incongruous in bow tie, in the hall mirror, as if with something to conceal . . .

'I'm not sure why I bothered,' I said – a lifelong habit of disparagement, a way of not telling her things.

'Was the famous MP there?'

'He was, and in his own eyes very famous indeed. Prime Minister in waiting.'

'He didn't say that.'

'No, he said someone else had said it.'

'Well . . .' Mum said. She saw what was awful about Giles, but loyalty and obligation were strong in her too. We went into the kitchen and she made some cocoa, while I pinched one of Esme's Alka Seltzers. It dropped swaying and fizzing and twisting in the glass, and I knocked it back with a shudder.

'How is she?' I said.

'OK,' Mum said quietly, 'she's gone down,' as if she were a difficult baby.

'I thought she seemed a lot better this afternoon.'

'Oh, yes, well, she is getting over it,' Mum said. 'And she's been so looking forward to seeing you.'

I was a bit drunk, and I put my arms round her and said, 'She'll be all right, Mum,' with a stare over her head at the future in which I was wrong, and she wasn't.

We sat in the sitting room, in our eternal places, and the large emptiness of Esme's chair made the case for that other scenario, when a much bigger stroke, perhaps, would finish her off. Something perilous had entered the house, and their lives together.

I said, 'I had a long chat with a man called Tony Bales.'

'Yes, I remember his name.'

'You're amazing. He was the year below me. Followed me as editor of *The Hive*. He makes arts documentaries now. He said he'd like to make a film about me – well, about East Asian actors, but with a section about me in it. You know, beyond *M. Butterfly* . . .'

'Oh, good,' she said, in her practical way, and looked down as she sipped her cocoa. 'I just think of you as an actor, of course.'

'I know you do, Mum,' I said, and took it as a compliment, an intimacy, and of course an evasion.

'How did your talk to the boys go?'

'Well, the boys were mainly girls, in fact.'

'Oh, yes, of course!'

'There were three boys, and six girls. Most of the kids had signed up to hear Giles laying into the Common Market.'

'Is he still going on about that?'

'I have the feeling he's hardly got started – "a diet of Brussels" and so on. You know Giles's sense of humour.'

'I don't really.'

'He hasn't got one. If he did he'd be groaning at the terrible joke of himself.' Mum snuffled at this. 'No, I got my lot to do an audition – Enobarbus or the death of Cleopatra – five minutes to prepare.'

'Sounds pretty difficult.'

'It was, wasn't it. One of them, a Chinese girl funnily enough, was rather brilliant.'

'Oh, good . . .'

'Anyway, it was better than depressing them with stories about agents and not getting work.'

'I should think the school are jolly proud of you,' she said, almost indignantly.

I smiled at her, her face gaunt under the sewing light. 'Who knows?' I said. 'But I don't think I'll be going back.'

'Am I slurring, a tiny bit? I think I am,' Esme said the next morning, back in her chair, Zimmer frame parked beside her

'Say something else,' I said, as though I hadn't noticed. 'A tiny bit,' I said, 'sometimes. Nothing to worry about.'

'What will people think!' she said, and laughed in a way I'd never heard before, a sort of heartless chuckle. This was something Mum had told me about, and was hoping would die away before it stuck. Esme appeared to be just the same, aside from the fading bruise to her left cheek, where she'd collided with the dining table when she fell. She was large, robust, good-looking, looked fifty-five rather than seventy – she was the old inexhaustible Esme, and yet she was puffed and puzzled by the effort of crossing the room, and she laughed like someone we didn't know at all.

I brought her a glass of water. 'The doctor says you have to drink a lot more of this, Esme.'

She gave it an unrecognizing glance. 'Fancy me having a stroke, love, eh! Just a small one, though,' she insisted, as if I were pressing a real drink on her. 'Could have been much, much worse, you know.' She picked up the glass and drank it placidly. 'Poor old Av, I scared her half to death' – words I felt more aptly described where she'd just come back from herself.

'I'm sorry I have to go straight off to London,' I said. 'I've got rehearsals this afternoon.'

'Don't worry about me, Dave. Your mother's being an angel, and Jilly Wilson comes in every day now, for an hour or two.' She reached out to take my hand, and gazed up at me quite tenderly. 'It's just a god-awful fuck-up, love, let's face it,' she said, and gave her deep mechanical chuckle.

27

All my spoken part was in the can, and there was a short silent scene the director was happy to do as an insert later. 'She was a second mother to me,' I said, and he said, 'Yes, of course I understand, I'm so sorry, David,' but as I went out of the room my satisfaction at saying the decent thing was spoilt by unease that I hadn't quite told the truth. I came back to St Pancras by train, and then drove out to Foxleigh, and it was only as I came over the Downs and into the Vale that I realized the new life had now begun, though what its terms were Mum and I had yet to discover. She was widowed, and I was what she had left, I was needed more than ever. I dropped down through the town in a tender kind of dread, not knowing how I would find her. Sometimes it is the evidence, the spectacle of another person's grief that harrows you, more than the loss itself.

I got out to open the gate, and the red unremarkable house seemed charged and set apart by the crisis. I looked at the windows for light or movement, a glint of the life that was still going on after the other life had come to an end. 'Oh, hello, love,' said Mum when I let myself in. We hugged and she turned almost at once and said, 'I've got this frock to do for Mrs Bardsley, she's being rather difficult about it.'

'Oh, dear!' I said. 'Can't it wait?' but I saw she was caught in the mercifully practical phase between the fact of a death and the gathering breaker of loss.

'Her son's getting married on Saturday, and she needs it for his wedding.'

I said gently, 'Mum, you don't really do this sort of thing now,' but she had taken it on as a favour, and also as something to occupy her mind and her hands while Esme was in hospital. Mrs Bardsley had been short with her on the phone. 'Imagine it was your son getting married, Mrs Win!' she had said: we had to laugh at that. We went through to the sitting room, and Esme's vacant fireside armchair nearly did for me, after all. In the ten years since her first stroke it had been more than ever her throne and her habitat, till the new stroke, a week back, had carried her out of her chair and her house for ever. Mum took up her sewing, I sat in my usual place and gazed at the grey, mildly convex screen of the TV, which reflected the room so dimly we seemed not to be in it ourselves.

I'm pretty sure Esme hadn't set foot in a church since my Confirmation in 1964, but she'd wanted a Christian funeral, and Mum asked the Vicar for a drink at Crackers to talk us through it. 'It's a lady vicar,' she said, 'Annette.'

'Do you prefer that?' I said.

She shrugged. 'It doesn't make much odds, does it?' I felt how forced they are, these transient occasions, not exactly deceitful, when an unbeliever sits down face to face with an unknown priest to discuss her needs.

It was one of those high cloudless August evenings there, which had me longing disloyally for London. The bell chimed at six thirty, and I went to let her in. Annette was a well-built woman in her forties, with a cheerful look and that hint of defiance, a sort of coming out, in topping off her sandals and blue slacks with a clerical shirt and dog-collar. I saw it must save her from countless explanations. 'I'm Annette Roberts . . .'

'I'm David, Avril Win's son.' She stepped in with a respectful smile and something provisional behind it, a sense of matters to be sorted out. 'How long have you been in Foxleigh?' I said, as if casting my mind back fondly to earlier vicars.

'Oh, six years now.'

'Really! Gosh . . . Come through . . .' – and I led her into the sitting room. The French windows were open, and I saw Mum had gone outside, she was dead-heading the roses rather than sitting and waiting. I called her and she came back in, holding the secateurs, and with an odd mix of gratitude and resentment in her face as she put them down and shook Annette's hand.

'Mrs Win – I'm so sorry,' head on one side, as if seeing her pain and hoping with time to ease her out of it.

'Mm, thank you,' said Mum.

'Do sit down,' I said, with a gesture at the room which to Mum and me was so full of Esme I wondered if Annette felt her presence there too. She seemed to sense, with a glance round, which had been Esme's chair, and settled herself instead on the end of the sofa. There is always a question of what people already know, and I wasn't sure what a vicar would have heard, even after six years, about two of her parishioners who never went to church. I offered her a sherry, feeling faintly satirical, and she said yes, and so we all had one, as if it was what we wanted. A sherry's such a small drink that it's hard to pace it, socially. Annette set hers aside and sat smiling tentatively at us both. I thought she was about to ask us to pray, but she came at things in a more sociable tone, with questions about how long Mum had lived here, mere chit-chat that helped her feel her way forward. I said, 'My mother and . . . Mrs Croft were together for nearly forty years.'

'Gosh . . . yes,' said Annette, with an intake of breath.

'You possibly know they had a business together.'

'Ah, yes,' she said, more decisively, and I saw that of course she would be gathering facts and anecdotes for one of those warm-hearted makeshift addresses in which priests attempt to conjure up a person they haven't known for the benefit of those who have.

At the end she noticed her sherry, and drank it in a minute or so, showing an interest in the framed photos on the bookcase, which gave her a sense of what Esme had looked like. 'I'll show you out,' I said. I stepped down with her onto the gravel, with a sudden sense of allegiance with her, as protectors of my mother. 'It'll take time,' said Annette, and laid her hand for a moment on my forearm, so that I saw she was also helping me. We walked slowly towards the gate, the stupor of the Close in the evening, a lawn-mower throbbing and fading a few houses away, our particular crisis silent on the air.

'Thank you,' I said. She had really been very helpful. I lifted the iron hasp, and tugged the gate open.

She looked at me then, with her thoughtful clarity. 'I think you were at school with my brother.'

'Oh . . . !' – holding on to the gate as the past quiet hour rearranged itself in a new perspective. 'You don't mean . . . *Dominic* Roberts?'

'Dom, yes. You do remember him?'

I had the three or four irreducible images. 'I remember cleaning his shoes . . .'

'Oh, dear!'

'Well, he was a fair bit older than me.' I peered at her, wondering. Perhaps the sherry had gone to my head, I said, 'He was incredibly handsome, everyone was in love with him.'

'Oh . . .' – Annette looked sadly aside for a second. 'He was, wasn't he.'

'Ah . . .'

'I'm afraid Dom's no longer with us.'

'I'm so sorry . . .'

'Yes, things didn't go well for him.'

'Was he . . .' – but I saw a screen of tact had descended the moment after the disclosure.

'Just three weeks ago. It would be nice to talk to you about him – later on, I mean. You have your own troubles now.'

And so, I saw, as she went off with a nod and a further handshake, did she. I saw death all round, coming from far and near, and maybe it was just the shock, the news heard no more than a minute ago, but as I closed the door and went back to join Mum, I had a tumbling feeling that the death of this beautiful boy – what, nearly sixty, but to me an unchanging eighteen – had moved me more sharply than the death of the woman whose house I'd called 'home' for thirty-five years.

The funeral took place at a new crematorium on the edge of Swindon, a grand old gateway, old parkland, freshly parcelled out for graves, then the chapel like a steep white tent came into view, with the chimney half-hidden behind. We were both very quiet, I crept over the gravel in low gear, and turned into the car park. 'A lot of people . . .' I said, then saw of course, once we'd parked, that most of them were here for the service before Esme's, just getting started. We were early, but not the first – Connie Marks, and her husband, in black, locked their car and made their way, with a stricken look, as if arguing with each other, towards the garden of remembrance, stooping to examine the floral tributes from earlier funerals laid out beside the path. When we followed a few minutes later, past the wreaths and the crosses, I felt both their plea for fellow-feeling and their elaborate intrusion on our own grief, 'DAD' and a Saint George's cross in red and white carnations. 'Oh god,' I said sniffily, but Mum was beyond noticing. She was wearing a black hat she'd bought for an earlier funeral, with the wide brim sloping downward at the front over the eyes, a little claim on privacy. She took my arm as we walked along the path, the sad known routine of a score of other funerals about to take hold of her and carry her blindly through, the focus of the drama. She was exposed, by the starkness of the facts and the occasion – the widow of a woman, glad of her many friends' support but best able to get through it with minimum acknowledgement that she was there.

Before long there was a crowd of us, some grim-faced but friendly, gathered in small groups in front of the high glass triangular front of the chapel, which reflected the trees and the cloudy sky behind us – though we could half see into the building, the timbers of the steeply pitched roof, and the entrance hall, where our mirrored selves already hovered. It was in its way a remarkable gathering, perhaps thirty-five of the elderly lesbians in Esme's life – a world with its own little salutary challenge, its fine independence of spirit. Some had brought their husbands, of course, and there were others, friends or tradespeople, Bashful Barry with his pretty wife in a wheelchair, and Jilly Wilson the cleaner, flowered hanky in and out of her sleeve as she dabbed her eyes. Auntie Susie was there but without Uncle Brian, not seen by Mum or me since the late 1960s, and with her a very stout grey-haired figure I had no idea was my cousin Malcolm until he pressed my hand and said, 'Sorry for your loss, David,' in a quiet and reasonable tone. 'Hello, Malcolm!' I said, in a daze of recognition that felt like fondness. No one else was with them, I think he hadn't married again after his wife left him, the volley-balling *Health & Efficiency* family had never been his. Then Annette appeared, in her white surplice and purple stole, black walking shoes peeping out beneath.

We'd made up an elegant order of service, with photos of Esme as a girl, and in the ATS; and on the front a picture of her at her seventy-fifth birthday party, champagne glass in hand. Esme wasn't a reader but there were three or four poems she quoted from repeatedly, and Mum and I found ourselves agreeing that I would read 'A Subaltern's Love Song' at the funeral, Esme's favourite bit of Betjeman. Really a woman should have read it, and made it a solidly same-sex poem. I rehearsed it, wondering methodically what a subaltern sounded like in 1945; the words were comical enough without making him sound too socially inferior to Miss Joan Hunter Dunn; I was a reader at a funeral, not a stand-up. So I gave him the voice of a standardized Englishman and found, like the Englishman I was, that I already knew the poem almost by heart.

In her address, Annette wove the platitudes of solace in with something unconventional, the narrative of Esme's life, the word lesbian never used, but the subject not shirked either. She spoke of Esme's bravery, which drew nods and sighs from the crowds in their forgiving funeral mood. I felt this was something I must have neglected or grown used to – to me she was a funny, domineering, self-indulgent and immovable presence, I was stirred by the mutinous frankness of opinion that sometimes follows a death. 'She found great happiness in her life with Avril, and the business they ran together so successfully for over twenty years. And in Avril's son David she gained, as it were, a new family member, in whose work she always took great pride.' This was humbling even if, I felt, not entirely true. Or was it again a truth I'd been stubbornly, unkindly blind to?

There was a further lobby that we passed through on our way out, where we shook Annette's hand and said a few platitudes of our own. She held my hand in both of hers for five seconds, soft experienced hands of a female priest, she looked somehow yearningly at me, in sympathy, of course, and reassurance, and also I felt, as I gazed back, with some private confirmation, that Esme's bravery was something she admired and understood. She seemed to look over the fence of her religion, at a freedom she had knowingly denied herself.

*

I drove Mum back to the house, where the gathering was to be held – wake, party, reception: we couldn't settle on the word. I laid my hand over hers as I drove, and she said at once, 'Don't worry about me. Concentrate on the driving.'

'I can do both,' I said, but I took my hand away.

There were already cars in the drive when we arrived, a sound of voices from the open front door, and Mum went in (it was dreamlike) as if to someone else's party. 'Ah, here she is, poor love.' I took charge while she went upstairs, and when she came down a few minutes later she went straight into the kitchen, fretful about arrangements, but really I think over-whelmed by the sense that from now on everything depended on her. The new reality was gripping her, so tightly that she hardly knew what was going on; but she kept herself together, just about. When she came back into the hall, Jane lurched up to her, and gave her a hug.

'Don't be nice to me!' Mum said sharply, stepping back.

'I wouldn't dream of it, love,' said Jane. 'Now what can I get you?'

Mum had no idea. 'I don't feel like a drink.'

'Maybe not, but you're having one' – and Jane went to the table and got Mrs Parry, with a quick glance at Mum, to pour her a stiffish whisky and ginger ale.

Soon the sitting room was full of the friends, the French windows open and one or two stepping carefully over the sill with their sticks and their drink and their sandwiches and sitting down on the bench in the sunshine with the air of both guests and survivors. Mrs Parry's girl from the Bull went out and back again with the bottle, and the old ladies teased and flirted with her and forgot their everyday caution. They started to forget about the funeral too, and chatted as they had done here when Esme was alive, about what they'd seen on telly and items they'd liked in the sales that were not in their size. When they remembered again, they were as candid as I'd felt in the crematorium – they couldn't hurt Esme now by joking about how bossy or greedy she was capable of being; though not all were like this, some repeated treasured sayings, spoke of very generous gifts, and more virtues I'd never associated with her were extolled: it was posthumous flattery, which Esme herself might have seen through.

Back in the sitting room one or two had pulled a bent order of service from a pocket or handbag and were looking again at the photos, Esme as a schoolgirl in Ware, something stubborn already in her smile, though otherwise it wasn't her – not the palpable Esme of six years later in brown shirt and tie, brass buttons glinting on the thick serge tunic, cap perched at an angle on dark curls. 'You did a good job, Dave,' said Jane, loyal humourless friend of more than forty years, who appeared in a later photo herself, a Theatre Club visit to Cheltenham. Others blinked in amazement and regret at the well-built young woman of 1948 or '56 who wasn't yet their friend. On the back, above the sentences inviting the mourners to come on to Crackers, was the picture taken by the oily photographer at Friscombe in 1962: 'That was the beginning of your little family, Dave,' said Jane, encouraging but somehow stoic too.

'You're right,' I said, and I warmed to the idea a little more now, looking at Mum's face. 'I would never have guessed, but it was.' The photo had stood in a cheap silver frame in her bedroom in the old flat, and for decades at Crackers, reconciling the two sets of brushes and make-up, the two different styles of the shared dressing table. 'I know it so well,' I said, though I saw it in a new light now, it was like that long-ago holiday itself, full of strange hints about all our futures. I saw the lurking photographer, getting in our path, camera raised, but waiting a clever second to have our assent and not waste an exposure. He must have lived for the season and the trippers, their guard down and their consciousness of leisure hemmed in by a consciousness of time: this was something they would want to remember. He was instantly friendly, and his act depended on everyone knowing and not minding that he was a chancer. Did he sense Esme's normal disdain for flirtatious men? I'm sure Mum kept walking, with the brief firm smile that prevents engagement, but Esme's smile was more artful, as if to say she'd seen through him too but knew she could get something out of him.

There had been some shuffling about, me in the middle, or on the outside, beyond Mum? We look as if we might move places again. There's Mum on the left, slight, dark-haired, 'so interesting', as Esme said to me one evening in the lounge, as we watched her coming in: middle-aged in those days, at thirty-nine, though she looks to me now like one of my students, in a full-skirted cotton frock with a white belt; next, me, fourteen, in an Aertex shirt and sandals, head slightly back, with an adolescent look of worrying at matters the women have no idea of; and then Esme herself, whose age at the time was a diva-like mystery, but who I now know was forty-one. If Mum is interesting, Esme is glamorous, French, you might think, in her white shorts and plimsolls and loose blouse knotted at the waist. She's a big woman, large bust, broad hips, and she smiles at something the cameraman doesn't understand, the beautiful new turn in her life.

Jane said, 'I can still hear Esme telling me she'd met someone special.' I smiled at her. 'She'd done that all right!' And a look of yearning that I'd never seen before opened up her old face, and threatened a collapse, for a moment or two, before she shook her head and sniffed and looked almost crossly around the room.

I went back to town for the read-through of *The Country Wife* and drove down to Foxleigh again on the Saturday. I heard the noise, like snoring in another bedroom, as I turned into the

Close. Barry's van was in the drive at Crackers, and an unaccustomed light made the house stand out, as if singled out for change. On the back lawn, beyond the sundial, Barry, in his eighties now, and Jason his son, with his own landscape-gardening business, cutting down the conifers, the long orange cable of an electric saw snaking over the grass. The noise was snarling and almost vengeful as I came closer. I knew people had sudden ruthless clearouts after deaths – a way of not being passive in the face of the inevitable, of taking control, in a stark form of consolation which called for destroying the traces of the dead and longed-for person. But I was shaken by the release Mum seemed to find in felling the trees, and by the nearly demented urgency with which it was done. 'Yes, get them all out!' she said, something gleeful about her as she stood hands on hips, in a brief respite from the tearing and snagging noise, on the lawn between Barry and Jason, surveying their progress, too far in to turn back or admit any kind of dismay, though I knew the result wasn't quite what she'd imagined.

Things I'd never seen in my life had come starkly into view, the flat roof of the Carpenters' extension, where (so Esme claimed) they'd sunbathed in the nude for decades in complete security. A large greenhouse showed, two gardens on, and the Fletchers' bedroom windows seemed to blink as they woke up to this unagreed exposure. I felt it would take a lot longer to adjust to the change in our own garden, robbed of the old claustrophobic suggestion of the trees. Near at hand, there was the narrow sunless strip of ground between the new stumps and the Carpenters' tall fence. It was the sort of space I might have explored on all fours if we'd moved here ten years earlier – I thought for a second of Woolpeck, and the dry child-tunnels under the yew hedge. Now it was a deep rotted mat of brown needles and grey toothless pine cones.

I sensed it was something Barry himself had long wanted to do but was feeling a certain reluctance about now he was actually at work on it. It made a huge pile on the lawn, one pile after another, springy and difficult, rough foliage grey and green and blue at the tips, and within the trees and in their ruinous splitting crowns, brown, brittle and dead, so that some fierce principle of upward growth and inward decay was laid out like a diagram, horizontal on the beautifully mown lawn. Jason tripped backwards, dragging out the fallen branches, the sawn-up sections of the scaly and bifurcating trunks. Barry again, who'd been devoted to Esme and no doubt half in love with her, seemed often on the point of saying what he knew he couldn't say, that she wouldn't have liked this at all.

In the evening, all down, Mum and I walked out over the lawn that was covered still with small fronds and sprigs and in the air the sweet sickly scent of the cut fir-wood. The effect was enlightened but bleak, we breathed deep but fought off a note of panic too. It changed everything, and the house itself, when I turned and looked back, was stripped bare of its last little margin of mystery. Mum stood and gazed astonished at what had happened – for the first time in my life, she broke down with me, she turned to me, mouth creased and tears tumbling from her eyes, and allowed me to take charge of her, stoop round her seventy-eight-year-old frame and hold her tight while she shook and gasped with sobbing. Then she was calm, with her old look as if she'd been silly, and said simply, almost flatly, less to me than to the great blank influx of evening light, 'I miss her so much.'

28

It was one of those smaller book festivals which flourish on the snob appeal of spending a weekend in the home of a duke. It's true Brasing is open to the public – not all year round, like a station, but on alternate weekdays between April and October. 'Curated' tours of the state rooms can be had by appointment at other times, according to the website, where a photo of the present duke, in red cords and hacking jacket, 'welcomes' you to the house where his family has lived for four hundred years. Like all very rich people, I guess, he has large outgoings, and he makes what he can from his palace with a calculated mixture of accessibility and lofty remoteness. Mum and Esme once went over the house, and reported having spotted his Grace, as Esme called him – a great lanky red-faced bloke and very rude, according to Mum. Esme had asked him a question, and got a brief snuffling answer. 'You couldn't say he had the common touch,' Mum said. 'Well, no . . .' said Esme, as if that was the last thing she was looking for.

I was invited to talk about *The Stage Is All the World*, and when the festival brochure came in the post, with a view of the house overlaid with thumbnail photos of TV gardeners and right-wing historians, I had a cold familiar feeling. I leafed through in search of myself, and it wasn't till the middle spread that I saw the boxed photo of Giles Hadlow MP, kept off the cover, but given a full page inside. He would be talking about his forthcoming book *Our Laws, Our Borders*, 'Place: Great Hall. Time: Sunday, 12 noon. Tickets: £10' – exactly the same time, it turned out, that I was on in the 'Playroom', which I immediately saw as an old top-floor nursery, holding at most ten people: 'Tickets: £4 (Concessions)'. I read the inane but flattering description of myself, beside a small prune-like photograph I had never seen before. I was to be in conversation with 'the writer Richard Roughsedge', which meant nothing to me, and I flipped back reluctantly to read about Giles. He was, as I more or less knew, Shadow Business Secretary, one of our leading Eurosceptics, and a prominent thinker on the right of the party. It was only a blurb, but even so 'thinker' was funny, and disturbing too. At the end it said that to mark his sixtieth birthday this year a *Festschrift* had been published, with contributions from many leading figures, and a foreword by Baroness Margaret Thatcher OM, a fact so absurd that I laughed out loud. In the photograph he wasn't smiling – he never did that publicly – but still had a misleadingly patient and approachable air.

It meant an early train from Paddington, changing at Reading, and a car with a nameboard waiting at Theale to drive me to the house. I felt more and more, being sixty myself, the bleakness of making such journeys alone. The festival was run, with active but somehow impersonal friendliness, by a woman called Francesca. She'd sent my tickets, with a letter telling me what to expect, and I studied it with interest, since this was my first book, and I'd never been to a literary festival. I shared her hope that copies would be available for me to sign 'in the Morning Room' after my event. She said that on arrival I would be shown to the Green Room, 'which this year is in the Red Room!' The helpful naming of the rooms gave the whole thing in advance the air of a weekend-long game of Cluedo.

I travelled in the car from Theale with a woman whose name I knew, a historical novelist, bestseller, about my age, smiling but businesslike – 'Have you done Brasing before?' she said.

'No,' I said, 'it's my first time.'

'Oh, you'll love it, it's really one of the nicest – not too big, and of course a fabulous setting.'

'I've not read your latest book,' I said rather cunningly.

She gave a great sigh. 'I'm nearly worn out with it,' she said. 'I've just done Cork and Carlisle and Ilchester and Hay.'

I'd heard of Hay, and assumed the others were literary festivals too. 'But you must enjoy it,' I said.

'Oh, I do, of course,' she said; and I saw it might be addictive, the packed-out events, the flattering questions, the sales. 'Now, here we are,' as we slowed and turned off the road through a triumphal arch set back between two low lodges. I couldn't resist the emotions of arrival, the curiosity and excitement and the faint Gothic fear. We went in a deferentially low gear down a good half-mile of curving drive through open parkland – oaks and chestnuts, ancient branches buckling groundwards or jagged against the sky, dense newer copses fenced against the deer, the long grass faded to gold after weeks of hot weather. 'Just wait for the first view of the house – voilà . . . !' – there it suddenly was, still far off, gloom and glitter, incomprehensibly big. It seemed, as we got nearer, to be all periods – Tudor turrets, steep roof of a great hall, first touches of Palladio chaste and grey beside the vast baroque front staring at the park. I was leaning across the historical novelist to see, and she enjoyed my amazement. 'Incredible to think it's lived in just by Edmund and Annabel and their three children.' We parked in a roped-off area on the grass, and I got out and stared at Brasing, staggered, almost laughing, for a moment, at its beauty, the English antiquity and persistence of it all. As Bertie Wooster says of his Aunt Dahlia's country seat, the place was simply ill with atmosphere.

*

I felt the tension of coming in to a new kind of event, where you don't know if a certain briskness and indignity are just part of the form, like the first day at a new school, or if you are alone in being neglected. Others around me seemed to know the ropes, to be busy in discussion of their imminent events, or talking in a way that suggested they met each other regularly on the great circuit of festivals, and also perhaps in houses like this when festivals weren't going on in them. I felt it was important not to sulk. In the Green Room a long table was spread with sandwiches and coffee and piles of today's *Telegraph*, and I withdrew to a big bay window and went through the extracts I was planning to read. Jeremy Paxman, far more famous than anyone else here, came past with a touchingly uncertain look. 'Have you seen Francesca?' he said. 'I haven't yet,' I said, and he shook his head mildly and walked on. I felt it was a kind of solidarity, involving for me the remote chance that he knew who I was. More present to me were the loose lines and knots of the punters on the drive outside the window, the audience gathering, even if most of them were here to see Giles, or indeed Jeremy. They were mainly in their sixties or older, like a matinee crowd, and as I watched them through the old rippled glass they focused my mind.

'David . . . ?' A man in a brown tweed suit was standing beside me, pleasant-looking, dark hair grey at the temples like mine, though he must have been ten years younger. 'Oh, I'm Richard . . .' We shook hands, and he dragged up a chair beside mine. He was one of those men who keep the soft-faced look they had as students, pinched and pulled about a bit since, and with a smile still boyishly effective. 'I'm so pleased to be your interlocutor,' the smile hesitant, perhaps a hint of innuendo. A ring on his right forefinger, no wedding ring.

'It's very nice of you to do it,' I said, as if I knew who he was and what he did otherwise.

'Have you been to a lot of festivals with the book?'

'No, no. This is the only one.'

'Really! Well, that makes it all the more special. I saw you five years ago now in *Up Country*,' he said.

'Oh, yes . . . ?'

'I've wanted to meet you ever since.'

'I'm very flattered,' I said, and watched the smile, both of us still shy. I suspected he was one of those heavily gay-friendly men who after a while, as intimacy deepens, have awkwardly to come out as straight.

When he went off to get coffee I watched him from behind: the air of youthfulness wonderfully kept up – it inhabited his fifty-year-old self like a barely concealed secret. He came back and sat down and smiled again – I saw then it was the still incredulous face of a fan in the presence of a star, something boyish in itself, a way in but also perhaps an obstacle.

We sat and ran through his outline for our event. I'm never nervous in public, but I was glad of his help with this new kind of performance. For an actor, used to houses full of people night after night, the publishing of a book feels weirdly disconnected from any sustaining reaction. So far I'd received eight reviews, and I had a feeling that the 2,214 people who had bought the book in its first six months were sitting on their hands to keep themselves from applauding. 'Ah, have you met Francesca?' Richard said, as the door at the far end of the room opened and a pretty blonde woman came in with a tall red-faced man I knew from the website was the Duke, who hung back for a second to usher in Giles Hadlow himself. It was Giles, as he entered, who had presence, and made people sitting and talking look up before he'd said a word. 'Yes, the Green Room's in the Red Room!' Francesca exclaimed and waved her arm as if still finding this funny. Giles's gaze settled on me for two seconds, as he called 'Hello' to someone else. 'I'll introduce you,' Richard said, and we got up and went over to them. 'You must be David!' said Francesca, and shook my hand: 'Welcome to Brasing . . . and have you met the Duke?' We shook hands too and the Duke blinked down at me with his mouth slightly open though only a perplexed sort of murmur came out. 'And David, I don't know if you've ever met – Giles Hadlow!'

I smiled narrowly at him. 'I have indeed met Giles Hadlow,' I said, 'we were at school together.' It was a rare occasion when I wanted to make the claim. Giles's head went back a fraction, as though no one could be expected to believe such an imposture. Then he gave in. 'How are you, Dave?' he said.

'I'm very well.'

'So you two know each other of old,' said the Duke, perhaps seeing some interest in me after all.

'We rather drifted apart,' I said.

'It has been absolutely ages,' Giles admitted, almost smiling as he took charge of the situation. 'We must find a moment to catch up.'

I was so sure this wouldn't happen that I said, 'We absolutely must.' He had the social impregnability of the politician, the pretended inclusiveness and readiness for anything, but of course what intrigued me, and amused me as much as it wounded me, was the way I embarrassed him. There was a little silence, no one knowing if something had just started or just ended, until Francesca glanced at her mobile,

'Forgive me, I must get on – oh Giles, by the way, I've had those papers sent up to your room – if you could look at them before dinner.'

'Thanks so much, um . . .' said Giles, and I held my thin smile at this glimpse of the unchanging order: Giles, of course, would be staying in the house, while we day-labourers were shuttled back to Theale station, with our tote bag and the hand-stencilled china mug, a copy of one in the house itself, which seemed to be our fee, or 'thank-you', for appearing. I'd been put in my place, but my resentment was nothing to my relief.

'We're all looking forward to your session,' the Duke said, I thought to me for a second, before he swivelled to Giles, so that I felt co-opted in his excitement.

'Should be a good one, I think,' said Giles. 'And with the stirring news from Ireland.' Somehow this sounded, in this cut-off country house, historic – Cromwell's massacre at Drogheda, perhaps. It took me a moment to work out what he meant, the alarming vote by the Irish to reject the Treaty of Lisbon. 'You'll see, Edmund, the tide's turning.'

'You'll have a lot of support here, Giles,' the Duke said. 'A full house, I'm told, for your event.'

'Oh . . .' said Giles, 'yes . . .', and shook his head as if indifferent to numbers but still expecting nothing less.

'I'm sorry I can't come and heckle,' I said: 'my session's at exactly the same time.'

'Ha . . .' – the Duke peered at me to see if I was joking, and I went back to my seat feeling both frivolous and right.

'I didn't know you were at school together,' Richard said when we'd sat down again. I made a face of impotent regret. 'What was he like?'

I glanced towards the door, but the two men had left the room. I felt already Richard could be trusted with the truth, but still I was diplomatic. 'He was an absolute shit,' I said.

'OK . . .' he said, and giggled.

'He was a cheat and a bully, and I must say very good at being both. He cracked the whole thing early on.' We grinned at each other. I didn't want to interest him too much in the subject.

'Do you mean he bullied you?'

I said, 'He used to go for me a certain amount, yes.'

'Mm, how do you mean?'

I held Richard's eye – it seemed we'd started on a bit of mischief together. 'Oh – ambush me, give me a half-nelson.'

'It sounds very childish.'

'Once or twice he chloroformed me and locked me in a cupboard.'

'Ah . . .'

'We were only kids, I suppose. Though it went on for over a year. He used to call me a brown-faced bastard.'

'I see.'

'Which I am, strictly speaking. He always did have a way of casting the truth as an insult.'

Richard nodded at the window – Giles was setting off with the Duke for a stroll by the lake, in a mime of relaxed authority, heads down in confidential talk as they passed by the punters gathering on the drive. I had always to remember that for others, millions of them, Giles had the heft of a senior politician, a man who could be looked to to change things, with all the glamour and gravity of government about him, his mastery of arts unknown to his followers, who trusted him to get things done. And maybe it was a limitation in me to see him only, or in essence, as an adolescent sadist, a spoilt hand-biting brat, who could never, surely, be taken seriously by anyone.

As expected, the Playroom was less fun than it sounded. It was a large square chamber on the second floor where, Francesca said, battledore and shuttlecock was played on rainy days. I said, 'Is that the same as badminton?' and Richard said it was a much older game, played without a net – you just scampered round whacking the shuttlecock till it fell to the floor. There was a box of equipment, like a school trunk, pushed into a corner, and a few half-occupied rows of chairs had been set out.

It helped that I'd spent much of my life in front of audiences, and could master in two seconds the performer's disappointment when he finds that the empty seats heavily outnumber the others. My smile embraced all those who had shown up, as if it was only them that I'd wanted to see, and to counter any faint anxiety they might have started to feel that the audience was as tiny as it was for a good reason. While we waited patiently for any latecomers, lost or out of breath on the second flight of stairs, Richard sat looking through his notes, and I leant by the window as if offstage. The view from the Playroom was really the best thing about it – formal gardens below, with a ha-ha, and beyond it a sweep of parkland rising to dotted woods, and nothing whatever to tell you it wasn't two hundred years ago. 'Well, I think we'll get started,' Richard said, and as I took my place in the other low armchair he turned his enormous smile on the audience who all as if hypnotized smiled back. Then he smiled at me.

He'd said he'd been interviewing writers for years, but I was uncertain, in my new role as author, what to take for granted. I felt the room was a mixture of sceptics – staring their challenge to me to impress them – with the decently encouraging and a few to whom it meant a great deal to be there; a young woman at the back wrote down everything I said. Richard had asked me to prepare two readings, and I did the section on auditions and not getting parts because of my appearance which made the audience reassuringly uneasy. A bit later I read my account of the notorious *Troilus* in 1978, which got at least half of them laughing. I wasn't used to seeing so clearly who did and who didn't.

In the interview afterwards Richard was very upfront about gay things: I had an unexpected feeling I was more self-conscious about this than they were. 'You mention Hector Bishop playing Aeneas in *Troilus and Cressida*, and later on Timon of Athens – I think you and he were very close in your twenties.'

'Yes . . .' I said ponderingly – 'well, we lived together for some time.' This was feebly ambiguous, as if tamed for the country-house audience, but I knew that in Hollywood Hector still felt the need for discretion and it probably wasn't for me to out him, even to an audience of twelve in a remote Hampshire attic. Then this seemed absurdly cautious. 'No,' I said, 'that's slightly misleading: we were lovers for about a year,' which struck a different kind of personal note from the talk about being bullied or slighted for not looking English.

'And he's a great Hollywood star now.'

'Yes, he is – well, he's more than that, he's a magnificent actor. I wish he'd come back to the theatre, play Shakespeare again.'

'Are you still in touch?' Richard said, finding out how far he could go.

'No, no,' I said quietly and shook my head and he moved to his next, quite closely related, question.

'Are actors easy to live with, would you say?'

'They're – we're – very demanding,' I said. 'We can't be relied on, because we're often out of work, and when we are in work we're not there when we're needed.'

'I suppose perhaps if actors marry other actors . . .'

'In that case, I'm afraid, they tend to have affairs.'

The audience laughed, and Richard, smiling prosecutor, said, 'So a fairly self-sufficient person, but with a keen love of theatre, might be the ideal partner for an actor?'

I laughed, as if to say he'd got me. 'Ideal indeed,' I said.

After a while Richard said we had time for questions from the audience, and I smiled sweetly for ten seconds at their torpor and shiftiness until a small tweedy man in the second row, one of the non-laughers, put up a hand, and then stood up. 'You won't remember me,' he said. I winced apologetically. 'But I have some very clear memories of you.' I signalled a different kind of dismay. 'I don't know how many people here today realize that two of our speakers were at school together.'

'As half of them went to Eton,' I said, 'it's not really surprising,' which drew another good laugh. He let it subside, and said,

'I was thinking of something less obvious. You and the Right Honourable Giles Hadlow, MP' – said with undecidable pomp and irony – 'both went to a school called Bampton in the 1960s.'

'I can't deny it,' I said, with a grimace that drew another laugh.

'As, I should say,' he went on, 'did I.'

'Oh, yes,' I said, 'what's your name?' and truly had no idea.

'I remember you both very well, and I wondered if you'd like to tell us something about those times.'

Richard said, 'I'm not sure it's really relevant to the discussion,' looking round for agreement from the others. But in fact they'd rather perked up at the question.

'I merely wondered if you recognize in our leading Eurosceptic the school prefect of forty years ago – and more?' said the man.

'It seems reasonable for me to ask if you do,' I said smoothly, and wondering who the hell he was.

He let out a short breath as if seeing and of course disallowing the point I had made. 'It's you we've come to hear,' he said.

Richard said ingeniously, 'Well – I wonder if the Shadow Business Secretary showed any interest in drama as a schoolboy?'

I cast my mind back obligingly. 'I remember his Sea Captain in *Twelfth Night*, because I was the Fabian. That was in the Junior School play. Later on he was Stanhope in *Journey's End*, I remember, where he has to act drunk a lot of the time.' I sat blinking and letting the audience picture it.

'And whom did you play in *Journey's End*?' Richard said.

'I was Raleigh.'

The tweedy man was very pleased with this. He half stood up again to say, 'Raleigh, of course, who hero-worships Stanhope.'

'It was a play!' I said, lifting my hands in the air, and wondering, for a mazy second or two, what other gossip and secrets from forty-five years ago this man might be about to produce.

'Please tell us your name?' said Richard, as the man sat down again, and it took a nudge from the person next to him to get him to say rather crossly, 'Ian Barker.' I shook my head as if to say I had no recollection of the boy of that name, the show-off of Dorm 3 and a bit of a tart.

'Any other questions?' said Richard. 'Yes!' to the woman at the back, who I'd thought from the start looked more serious than the others. I gazed at her encouragingly.

'I was just wondering,' she said, 'about Giles Hadlow, if . . .'

Coming down from the Playroom I found myself mixing with the crowd emerging from Giles's event, which had been allowed to overrun. I glanced past them through the door into the Great Hall, lit as if for TV cameras, a scattering of leaflets in the disarranged rows, the amplified atmosphere of a big room that empties after a meeting where challenging things have been said and excitement has run high, and which carries on in the chatter of the audience outside. Giles himself was engaging with a small group of questioners at the far end by the dais, Francesca hovering to bring him through to the book-signing table. When I reached the Morning Room, the crowd blocked the door, and I was eyed like a queue-jumper as I wriggled through. The signing table was covered with blue baize, with three chairs aligned with three pens and three bottles of water. 'Splendid,' said Giles, when a way had been cleared for him, and he came towards me, pushing back his grey-streaked forelock in a gesture both businesslike and inveterately vain. 'Now, where do you want me?'

'I thought Giles on the right – of course!' said Francesca, 'and Amanda on the left . . . and David, perhaps you'd just like to pop in the middle.' Amanda was a surprise to me, but when she came in I knew I'd seen the end of a programme of hers once or twice just before the News. It turned out she too had had a rival event, in the Orangery, on the sanitary habits of the Tudors. 'Yes, sold out!' she said to me as we shook hands and turned to face the crowd, who had gathered, deferential but impatient, in unregulated lines stretching out into the Marble Passage. We all sat down, like some motley new panel about to get started. I took up my pen, and sat forward with a welcoming look.

As it happened, the first person in the queue was a woman with *All the World* open at the title page and a secretive manner. 'I wondered if you'd just like to write something for me – just a thought, you know, something inspiring . . . yes, wherever you like.'

'They'll all be here for Dave,' said Giles to Amanda behind my back, 'we might as well leave now.'

'Not quite so fast, Giles!' said Francesca, stewarding the first members of his fan-club towards the table. I had to have a think about my inspiring remark, and by the time I'd written it, and signed it, and then taken the book back and dated it, the other two were already on their third or fourth customer. I had a hunch that a kindly attentive approach to each person, finding out what they did, where they lived and what plays they'd seen recently, would fill up the time and disguise the dreadful shortfall in my own fans. Amanda and Giles worked with bright and practised speed. On my left Amanda was writing, 'For Jenny and Clive, with very best wishes' in a quick businesslike hand, but Giles didn't bother with any of that. I felt his signature, when I glanced across, could have been scrawled there by anyone; it was a gesture one had to take on trust, with perhaps one decipherable letter in it. It felt dismissive of the person who thought it worth paying and queuing for.

Of course I thought of those huddles at stage-doors for the

stars in plays I'd been in, the madness of fandom, and the fan's hope, now and then, of going further, of being greeted as a friend. I was quickly unoccupied, and sat as if admiring Giles's performance. A man of about our age came forward who had met him socially somewhere, and gave his name and exacted a quick handshake. 'Good to see you,' said Giles grumpily.

'And how's Laura?' said the man.

'Laura's very well,' said Giles, in an emphatic tone, as he took the book and opened it at the title page.

'She's not here today?'

'She's not, no. In fact she's at another literary festival elsewhere.'

'Oh, *is* she. I saw she had a new book out.'

'Oh, they're making a great fuss of her,' said Giles, and made his one-second scrawl.

'We'll get her here next year, I hope, for the paperback,' said Francesca.

'She'll have a new one out by then,' said Giles, with ominous brightness, handing back his own book.

'Well, do give her our love. We look forward to reading it.'

'Yes, it's quite, er . . .' and Giles looked past him with a nod to the next person in the queue, who seemed as impatient as he was. I knew almost nothing about Giles's marriage, and cared even less – beyond a generalized pity for Laura, and a pleasing feeling her novels were a problem for Giles: beach reads, a bit racy, with a clear invitation to see real people in their adulterous MPs and power-mad media types; thus, presumably, a kind of revenge on Giles for the life he made her lead, and a marginal annoyance for a man who was so violently self-important. He had to be a good sport about them, not his natural mode.

After I'd signed three books, and an odd scrap of paper for a woman who claimed she'd bought the book but had left it at home, I pushed back my chair, and since no one protested I left the bestsellers to their buyers, and drifted round the books tables, still within reach should one last devotee of radical theatre come panting in.

At the back of the room, I found a tall stack of Giles's *Festschrift*, which at £48 was moving less quickly than *Our Laws, Our Borders*, marked down to £12 for festival attenders. In fact the stack was so tall that I was able to stand unnoticed behind it while I flicked through a copy. The lack of a jacket gave its dark blue covers an academic look; it was published by an outfit called Excalibur, with a PO box address in Boston, Lincs. Thatcher's 'foreword' was only a few sentences, in facsimile, for the fetish of her signature and the House of Lords notepaper. She dwelt on Giles's early successes in her government, but you could see there was tension between her ideas about Europe and his, which she had somehow been persuaded not to go into. The contributors included some big-name monsters, some perhaps offering pieces in the right general area that had already appeared elsewhere. Others I had never heard of, and it was then, as I dredged through the lower list of the well-wishers, that the necessity of getting to the Green Room before all the sandwiches had gone became unignorably clear to me.

I saw Giles once more before I left – we passed in the cold corridor that led to the lavatory reserved for the speakers. He had his look of habitual success, but he was almost confidential. 'I never asked you how it went?'

'Oh, not bad,' I said.

'Well, you'd be very good at these things,' he said, with a sort of inverted vanity, as if he dreaded public speaking. The briefly hushed and weary tone, I realized, was there to shut out our differences with a specious intimacy, almost a suggestion that whatever our public divergences might be, in private I really agreed with him. 'Are you sticking around?'

'No, I have to get back.'

He smiled resignedly. 'Well, good to see you, Dave.'

Before I reached the door I said, 'Perhaps we'll meet at Cara's private view next month.'

He turned, and said slowly, 'Oh, yes,' blinking as if at some quite unexpected idea, 'mm, I'm not sure about, um . . .' and with a little nod went on into the lavatory.

In a minute Richard Roughsedge came back, and I was happy about that. He told me my driver was waiting, and he walked out with me onto the gravel. 'I have to chair another event in twenty minutes,' he said. I didn't know him well enough to ask how he tolerated working for these people, I felt I had to be ready for the dreary disclosure that under the beautiful smiles and the sexy rapport he was one of them himself.

'Well, I hope you get a considerably bigger audience,' I said.

'Oh, I doubt it,' he said, though his blush as he looked away suggested he would. I thought he was a little embarrassed on our hosts' behalf. 'It was certainly bad luck to be on at the same time as Hadlow.'

'If luck enters into it,' I said. To me it felt too pointed a coincidence to be quite covered under luck. 'And with the Tudor Toilets woman too, who seems almost as popular.'

'Oh, god, I'm sorry . . .'

'I'm glad to have seen the house, though.'

'Staggering, isn't it.'

'And of course to have met you,' and we shook hands, smiling at our own formality. 'Thanks for everything, and, you know, do let's stay in touch.' The terms of courtship felt almost too old to recover, but still worth it, surely.

'I'd like that very much.'

'You have my e-mail,' I said, tugging at the sliding door of the van with a feeling I'd have liked to stay the night after all. So I came out with it: 'I'd love to see you again.' He raised his hand as we moved off, and gave me the full reckless smile.

In the van my thoughts about him were mixed like a secret success with my sourer sense of the indignity of the day. As we waited at the lodge for the gates to swing inwards and release us, it was Richard I was asking if it was better to be included, to be on hand to remind this unconcerned crowd of the existence of a world elsewhere? Or did coming here and speaking to twelve people about alternative theatre serve only to confirm in the eyes of the Duke and the others our abject marginality? Of course, I'd been in plays that were just as unsuccessful – but even for those I'd been paid. I opened my tote bag and looked at the horrible mug.

'Had a good time?' said the driver.

'Fine,' I said, old trouper, uncomplaining – 'not really my scene.'

'They get some good people there, mind you.'

'Oh, do they?' I said.

'I hear Giles Hadlow was there today.'

I hated asking. 'And what do you make of him?'

'I think he's got a lot of the right ideas,' said the driver, 'you know, on immigration and all that,' and then looked for me in the mirror.

It was consolingly subversive to picture, against the dark running trees beside the road, the soft sexy face of my *interlocutor*, to sense the first warmth of friendship and further ruttish feelings and imagined actions too, touched in with sudden clarity. I was imagining then, and over the following days, our second meeting, where the undeclared feelings of the first would sweep us together – I saw us go at it, at my flat, with a light-headed confidence I'd forgotten and which I laughed at even as it gripped me. It was true I knew nothing about him – he could have been happily settled with somebody else for years. And I still wasn't sure what he did for a living – interlocution alone surely wouldn't keep the lights on.

In fact it was a while till we met again, a tense little interlude explained by doubt or confidence – which of us could tell? I was at Richmond for two weeks in Charlie Reid's *Fever Ward*, not a Richmond sort of play, and thin houses, the upper circle closed and the audience coaxed down towards the front. You carry on as if the house is full, but those faces in the nearer rows of the stalls mean more to you than they would if six hundred others were breathing and stirring in the darkness beyond them. He hadn't said he'd be in, and I was halfway through Dr Tan's humorous monologue in Scene Two before I saw he was there, near the end of the third row, and almost lost my place. I smiled as if Dr Tan himself was savouring some wicked memory, then looked away and projected the rest of my speech to the empty gods.

At the end of the show, jogging back to the front without leaving the stage, just in case the applause expired altogether, I grinned at him directly, and he smiled back, clapping with his hands up high. There was still a small uncertainty. Was he alone, or with the older man next to him? Would he know to come round? I got changed very quickly and wiped and washed my face and glanced critically at the beige-coloured dressing room with its frosted window and noisy little fridge. My good-luck cards were tucked in round the mirror, the *Standard* with a notice of the previous night's show lay untouched on the table. To Richard, I hoped, it might look beautifully authentic. There was a loud knock, I warbled, 'Come i-in!' and Hettie Barnes stuck her head round the door at a commiserating angle. 'Well done, old love,' she said. 'They don't know what they're missing.'

'You mean the seven and three-quarter million inhabitants of London who didn't come?'

'Them and all the rest.'

'Well, I'm glad you came, Hettie,' I said, looking past her into the passageway outside. 'I didn't know you were in.'

'Lionel's coming. He's just a bit slow on the stairs.' And in a moment I heard shuffling, Lionel's histrionic wheeze and a voice that I hadn't exactly been able to remember, Richard speaking up and holding his elbow as they came round the corner. Our eyes met, and I made a face, but then Lionel asked him something and he looked down.

'Hettie Barnes and Lionel Wilshire,' I said: 'my friend Richard Roughsedge,' my hand on his shoulder to present him and simply to touch him.

It was typical of Hettie and Lionel to carry on as if Richard was someone they'd long been hoping to meet, and were even slightly in awe of. 'Hello, hello!' said Hettie, her old actor's modesty mixed with her simple confidence of being a treasure. 'Wasn't Dave good?' She was tiny now but magnetic, her real-life and stage personas practically fused. Lionel was larger than ever, in a handsome plaid cape and fedora, as if for convenience staying in costume from one West End cameo to the next. I soon saw that it was Richard who was in awe of them.

'I saw you both in *An Ideal Husband* in Malvern,' he said, 'when I was a schoolboy.' I think he sensed that with Hettie and Lionel their longevity was now their main point – they'd gone beyond the vanity of concealing their age. 'I've never forgotten how funny you were. I got your autographs afterwards.'

'Did you really?' said Hettie, as though she ought to remember.

'And how do you know David?' Richard said.

'We were all in a bit of seasonal hokum on telly,' I said, 'four or five years ago. *The Spectre of Tappington*.'

'Great fun,' said Lionel, as he did about pretty well everything.

I said, 'Champagne?', with a feeling the play they'd just been watching deserved a bit more attention. I kept a half-bottle of sparkling wine in the fridge, enough for a quick symbolic drink if people came round. 'Do sit down, won't you.' And again, when I gave Richard his glass, I gripped his shoulder for a moment. We were in a theatre, it was theatre that brought us here, and now it was the habits of theatre, the coming round, the cheerful loyalty and nostalgia, that I felt stifling me.

'Are you doing anything else soon?' Richard asked them.

'Sweet of you to ask. We are, we're doing *Trelawny*, aren't we, Lionel.'

'I believe we are, my love.'

'We're the ancient Trafalgars, do you know the play? – the grandfather and the great-aunt, isn't it.'

'Yes, I do,' said Richard.

'We're tremendously dull,' Lionel said, with a genial chuckle. 'All great fun.'

A brief silence fell, in which the question of *Fever Ward*, and what to say about it, seemed at last to confront them all. Richard raised his glass: 'Well, congratulations on tonight, anyway.'

'Yes, bravo,' said Hettie.

'Thank you,' I said.

'An odd sort of play . . .' said Lionel cautiously, as if he might well have missed something. 'But a cracking part for you, Dave, I thought.'

The truth was we'd all been in enough flops to know how to cope, but the dying adrenaline was mixed with the tension of seeing Richard, and I felt impatient.

*

'Do you have to go far?' Richard asked them, when we were outside the stage-door.

'We live just round the corner. We've been there since 1956!'

'Handy if you're in something here.'

'Oh . . . yes, I see what you mean,' said Hettie. 'We still really love being on tour.' And as they went off past the bins and barred windows of the back street I couldn't help thinking how happy they were, a childless old couple who lived for acting and each other, and even in their eighties didn't mind that their evenings were rarely their own.

'Well . . .' I said, and smiled at Richard, shaken at being alone with him again, and at last. He gave me his smile, half-smile, wonderful but hesitant, and I saw that the two old actors had been a cover for his shyness, and guessed that like me he'd been living our affair in his head through the weeks since we'd met, so that now was a kind of reckoning. 'Are you hungry?'

'I am rather.'

'I wonder . . .' It was 10.05 on a weekday, just a pizza joint open as we turned down the street, and further on a shadowy Tandoori with a last couple paying. 'Or we could,' I said, taking a leap, 'just go back to mine.' It was a longish leap, a good forty-five minutes on the newly dubbed 'Overground'. I wondered fleetingly what we would talk about on the way.

'Oh . . . all right,' he said. 'I mean if you don't mind.'

'Mind?' I said, with a saucy look. We set off towards the station, two minutes' walk, and something breathless about Richard, as if faced with a misunderstanding he needed to sort out tactfully and quite fast. I thought I'd been an idiot, of course this beautiful cultivated man ten years younger than me didn't want to flog back to north-west London for . . . 'I don't know where *you* live,' I said, to make it easier for him.

He glanced gratefully at me. 'Well, that's what I was thinking,' he said. 'I'm just in Turnham Green.'

'Oh, you could be home in no time,' I said.

He gave an awkward laugh. 'What I mean is – would *you* like to come back to *mine*?'

'Well, thank you!' I said, and as we strode up the sloping forecourt of the station I slipped my arm through his.

It was only three stops on the Tube, and so much was unsaid between us that it was hard to say anything. The lit back windows of houses, little settlements and commons of south-west London, ran past outside. Richard took a serious look at the flimsy theatre programme. 'I thought Nina Adeleke was very good,' he said.

'Oh . . .' I said, 'yes – well, she's going to be a real star, don't you think?' – I saw we could natter about actors, something I do easily, if rather drily as a rule.

'Your scene together was the high point of the play, I thought.'

'Well, thank you, very much.' To me our relationship on and off stage was a touching and instructive one – the brilliant young actress looking to me for reassurance and advice, but burning with a gift that was far beyond anything I've ever had.

At the station, at the barrier, I tapped out with my senior's Oyster card. 'Ooh, lucky you,' said Richard.

'Well, it is rather great,' I said, and added, as I put it away, 'I've only had it since April, of course.' The privileges were also the badges of age. I waited for him. There was a first scent of autumn in the air, and the puzzle of the small green spaces just outside. 'So this is Turnham Green,' I said.

'It isn't actually,' Richard said. 'It's Acton Common. Turnham Green's half a mile . . . thataways.'

'You mean the bit I can see the edge of over there?'

'No, no, that's Chiswick Common.' I could see he was used to sorting this out for people. When I needed greenery I went to Hampstead Heath, an hour's walk wide. These little salvaged triangles, low railings, street lamps glimpsed through trees, seemed meagre and genteel to me. I wondered if anyone met here after dark. If you dragged a man into the bushes you'd be in full view of the street behind.

'Terra incognita,' I said, 'down here, to me.'

'Oh, I've been here for fifteen years.'

'It's jolly nice,' I said, and took his arm again – I thought in a romantic rather than geriatric way.

His road was very quiet, leaves on the pavement, a few lopped old limes surviving still among daintier replacements, cherry trees and silver birch. The houses, behind their gardens, were red-brick, Dutch-gabled, arts and crafts on a budget and up to a point. I hadn't gone home with a man for years and years, as long perhaps as Richard had lived here, and I'd forgotten the topographical element, the way curiosity about a new place plays its part in the excitement. There was a TV on in the wide-windowed room beside Richard's front door, and the *Newsnight* theme as he led me through the hall and up the stairs to a further locked door. 'I've got the first-floor flat,' he said. In the room he showed me into, the TV could still faintly be heard from down below. 'Give me your coat,' he said. 'And let me get you a drink.'

'Thank you,' I said, the whole shape of the imminent minutes and hours unknown.

'Shall we stick with champagne?' – which was very gracious of him. He went out and I stood bringing the room into focus. It was absurd, but I still didn't know exactly what Richard did; I felt it was almost too late to ask such a basic question, and that a long detailed answer would undermine the mood. There were floor-to-ceiling bookshelves on each side of the fireplace and a desk with an up-to-date iMac and two stacks of typescript, pens and pencils in a British Library mug, everything neat. I heard the stifled pop of the cork and called out, 'It's awful, I don't know what you do when you're not doing what you did to me.'

He came back with two tall flutes of champagne, and a secretive smile that seemed to put off an answer for now. 'Well, cheers!' he said. We clinked glasses, sipped, and looked at each other. 'I can't believe it, I've got David Win in my flat!'

'Incredible, isn't it,' I played along. It was charming but slightly absurd from a fifty-year-old man. It needed to be something more than fandom that had brought us together. 'You know I'm very happy to *be* in your flat,' I said.

He bit his lip, 'Are you really?' – pleasantry and longing all in one. I inspected him, rather teasingly, close up – round chin, the hesitant smile, grey curls at the temples, brown eyes. I knew I had no idea what he'd done with himself, and with others, for the thirty-five years of his adult life, and I wondered for a moment or two how he imagined my past and my love life. The faint metallic taste of his mouth, his tongue along mine, the yielding and pushing of his lips were both reminders and promises – and the hard-ons, new friends jumping at each other, straight off. For now, there was little more to say.

29

In a mini-reshuffle in the spring of 2012, Giles was made Minister for the Arts. He was so laughably unsuited to the role that his appointment was itself a grim warning. I remembered his father's sad comical stare, across the bonnet of his red Citroën DS, 'It pains me to say it, but my son has no sense of beauty.' In fact Mark was deployed, in a cynical way, to justify the decision. In *The Times* it said, 'Giles Hadlow, as the son of the famous collector and cultural benefactor Mark Hadlow, grew up in an environment where a feeling for art and music was paramount – all of which will stand him in good stead as Minister for the Arts.'

And then, for a while, we kept seeing Giles, on his busy, rather threatening appearances in a world he had hitherto ignored, if not scorned. He had the rueful but undeflectable manner of all hard-line exponents of 'austerity'. He was there, in effect, to give the Arts a good kicking, while parading in another kind of virtue, that of protecting his sector from a worse kicking yet, 'seeing what he could do', 'putting in very urgent pleas' to the Chancellor of the Exchequer, with whom in fact he fervently agreed. We were in the crowd at the British Museum one evening, when a major exhibition of European goldsmiths' work was being opened; Richard had co-edited the catalogue, and we smiled and sidled our way through a nice jostling mix of groomed lenders, officials and aficionados – discussions in German, Catalan greetings, a gathering roar of polyglot talk in the echoing concourse. A tentative drawl, very loud, through a microphone brought us all, over five or six seconds, to attention: the speeches ... accepted, even welcomed, for a minute or two, as a time-honoured ritual, that confirmed the significance of being present. First, briefly and brilliantly, the Director, and then the head of the German museum where the show would be seen next, whose own team were out in force and applauded him warmly. That was it, the talk started up again, and the Director, with a hint of apology as he raised his voice to ask for our attention, called the Right Honourable Giles Hadlow to the microphone. The Brits knew who Giles was well enough, but to the European guests he was a never-heard-of sixty-something in a double-breasted suit, the sort of speaker you barely pretend to put up with as you try to catch the eye of the wine-waiter working through the briefly quietened crowd. I couldn't tell if he was aware of his own insignificance to these guests – I thought I glimpsed it, the little indurated reflex of defiance in the face of our disdain, which always brought out the sadist in Giles, the more or less subtle reminders that he had the power and we didn't.

Of course he was happy to take credit for the exhibition, and he put over resolutely, as his own thoughts, what were clearly the main points of a well-researched briefing. The years-long efforts of the curators, the frustrated diplomacy and excited last-minute additions to the catalogue, which I'd learned about from Richard, were quite reasonably unknown to Giles. The show was the thing, with its spotlit vitrines of gold masks, cups and amulets, and the government was ready to bask in its accumulated glow. 'We're tightening our belts in the Arts sector,' said Giles, 'as every one of us is in all areas of life. But we're committed to delivering a leaner, better future for our theatres and orchestras and arts organizations.' I think it was the first time I'd heard the cant use of 'deliver' – which over the following years came insidiously to mean its opposite, to mean 'take away'. The Director stood near him and a little behind, eyes raised as if both listening and looking beyond Giles to better and saner times. Giles's speech wasn't long, but the grip of boredom was nearly instantaneous, and murmurs of talk resuming at the back of the crowd in Italian and German were spread by the echo of the space into a larger mutiny, freeing others to start talking too. He had the microphone and we didn't, he sensed the collective resistance and rode over it, but there was something wounded, and dangerous, in his smile as he was winding up. I blanked out what he said, tipped my head back and gazed at the great glass dome. Beyond it, in the slow transition of dusk, silver planes could be seen escaping, bright in the last sun above the darkening city.

A week or two later in a *Newsnight* feature on Tory Eurosceptics Giles was interviewed at home: what sort of home, I wondered, would he and Laura have made for themselves and their elusive children? A discreet exterior shot of the house, the Range Rover's number-plate fogged out, then a long shot of Giles and Laura walking and talking on a wide lawn. In the unmiked distance they might have been locked in a bitter disagreement. It was a big West London house, perhaps not far from his parents' place and not unlike a smaller version of it – at least until you stepped inside. A shot in a kitchen where everything was panelled in carved oak, like a Bavarian inn, then a minute in a posh sort of Georgian drawing room with paintings out of focus, before we got down to business in Giles's study, leather armchairs, signed photo of Thatcher, framed prints, and a heavy male atmosphere of a standard kind. Over the fireplace was a portrait of Giles himself, of the sort that dutiful colleagues commission on someone's retirement – clearly Giles had decided to get in first. I thought how his father, in that same spot in his study, had hung a large Prunella Clough that was like an electric circuit, where the mind travelled happily between the blue flashes of ideas. With a ponderous show of tact, Giles voiced the dissatisfaction on the right of the party with Cameron's dawdling approach to a referendum on leaving Europe. It was tedious and pointless, it would never happen, and I got up to find the remote, although Richard said he wanted to watch more – we stood there distractedly just in front of the set, so caught up in our grumpiness about whether to watch it or not that again we blanked out what Giles was saying. Was there a slight – a very slight, and perverse and ingrown – jealousy on Richard's part of my 'knowing' the man now filling the screen in disturbing close-up, just eyes and nose and speechifying lips and teeth? A sense that I was once as close to him as that myself? 'He has been described,' the voiceover said, above archive footage of Giles speaking at Conference, 'as one of the party's leading intellectuals' – that idea again, a self-perpetuating tag. I started on my madman's laugh, then squeezed the off button when I saw it was probably true.

At the end of June I was in Aldeburgh, asked at short notice to take over as the Speaker in a strange late piece by Vaughan Williams, *An Oxford Elegy*, written when he was eighty – it's rarely performed, and the only time I'd heard it before was in Oxford itself, over forty years earlier. There's a chorus, but mainly wordless, while a speaker recites chunks out of Arnold's 'Scholar Gypsy' and 'Thyrsis', some of the same chunks then sung by the chorus, who I remembered feeling had a clear advantage. It threw me into a muddle, of critical squeamishness, unshakable love for old VW, ironies aplenty about Oxford itself, and unironized emotion triggered by the words. I doubt I'd read the poems for fifty years, though lines glimmered forward for me, unforgotten.

On Spotify and YouTube I played five recordings, different actors in each, and a sober feeling growing in me as one followed the other that I would soon be in their shoes, though not, I hoped, sounding like any of them. It was a brief history of declamation, as a form between free acting and notated speech. 'Heeah till sun-dyne, shepherd, will I lie' – I saw the glow of the childhood wireless and the imagined announcer in evening dress. Well, I'd had all that beaten out of me, decades ago. And the later performers on record moved with the times, though cornered somehow by the oddness of the piece, and now and then forgivably doing the thing they were famous for on stage or TV. I felt I wanted to make it as intimate and natural as I could, but the orchestra shimmering and surging around me would force me to project. With each listening the piece felt less odd, and the elegiac emotion more gripping. I read that the Speaker at the first performance had wept as he declaimed the words, 'and he was a Cambridge man'.

We drove out to Suffolk two days before and stayed at a hotel overlooking the front, a five-mile drive from Snape, where the concerts take place. Richard swam from the shingle and had lunch in the town while I went off in the car to rehearsal. There was something very happy and confident in these arrangements, work and holiday plaited together with the third strand of the place, the long coast and the marshes where the festival had happened every summer since the year I was born. Our piece began the second half of the concert, before Britten's *Young Person's Guide to the Orchestra*, which they ran through in the morning first: I sat halfway back in the empty hall and was fourteen again for a minute or two at a time, airborne as section after section did its thing, then dropped back to earth by each ragged pause for correction.

I'd never rehearsed with a conductor before, but it turned out to be mainly a matter of cues, and all very clear: he perhaps thought it beyond him to advise on how I actually spoke the words. A quietly climactic line early on was 'And the eye travels down to Oxford's towers' – one old thesp I'd heard made a virtual aria out of 'Oxford', another reverently breathed it, a new recording by a Bafta-winning star barely noticed the word but pulled all the stops out for 'towers'. A lot seemed suddenly to ride on this, and I felt when we finished our run-through that when we did it for real I would land on a reading that magically combined what Arnold, Vaughan Williams and David Win all felt about that loaded subject.

When I got to the band-room that evening the normal careless buzz about who was in had a more wary and jaundiced character. The Minister for the Arts had arrived half an hour ago, by helicopter. I went out to verify this. The pilot had landed on the lawn beyond the hall, where normally only a large Hepworth bronze intrudes on the wide view of reedbeds shifting in the wind. An Alouette, I was told, its drooping rotors menacing in their stillness. The audience strolling with pre-concert drinks were curious but kept their distance. 'Has to be in Brussels later tonight' was the straight-faced explanation when I went back in – 'No other way of doing it.' I thought it ominous that Giles, 'tone-deaf' and proud of it, should go to such expensive lengths to catch a concert – flattering, for a second, his not wanting to miss us, but sinister, above all. The chopper underlined his importance and the limited time that we had to impress him. I knew how he would have relished flying in across the sunburnt countryside, the dazzle of the sea beyond as they turned and saw the concert hall and car parks laid out beneath them, the small square of turf waiting – then the hellish roar of the touchdown, the wind-whipped greeters standing by, the military urgency as he leapt out and strode to shake their hands. Backstage among the members of the orchestra milling and fiddling, the whole unfamiliar white-tie world of music, there was a frail sense of safety in numbers; but I couldn't help finding it sinister, again, that Giles had elected to come to a concert that I was performing in.

I joined Richard in the audience for the first half – they'd put us in the very back row, with a tumbling view down beneath the high timber roof to the far-off stage, where the players were quickly assembling. It was strange to be watching a stage I was due to appear on myself in an hour or so's time, and I wished they'd put our piece in the first half instead of the world première, *Storm Warning*, for choir and orchestra, by Fricka Garrett. The woman next to me said, 'Hello, we're looking forward to hearing you!' and introduced her husband, so I introduced mine, it was all very friendly; and we watched Giles come in, with a man on the festival board, an old Aldeburgh hand, whose face was a study in awkward diplomacy. They were sitting on the wide cross-landing, just below us, with expansive legroom and easy access to the exit. Giles was still texting as the lights went down, and slipped his phone into his pocket with a hint of reluctance.

Storm Warning turned out to be quite a racket, and I glanced now and then at Giles, wondering how he was taking it. Perhaps if you're really tone-deaf it makes no odds if it's Boulez or Boccherini. His demeanour seemed, from the back of his head and a bit to one side, to be stoical, the quasi-royal stillness of someone trained for boredom. There were aleatory sections, with the choir and then half the orchestra whistling and clapping, and shattering effects of tam-tams and bells, but they made no discernible impression on the Minister. Maybe he thought all concerts were like this. When it ended he got out of doing much clapping by questioning his host, and staring blankly at the bowing performers, the composer as well, bounding onto the stage in red dungarees, as he listened intently to the answers.

A concert hall isn't as dark as a theatre, but the lights were lowered and the audience appeared from my spotlit place at the side of the stage as a slow climbing wave of glimmering white hair and glasses, fading into deep shadow. Though I couldn't see him, or allow his presence to distract me, I sensed there was a fine, an invisible, filament of connection between me and a suited figure on the wide cross-landing, a tiny tension of mutual awareness, as I waited to open my mouth and say, 'Go!' It seemed to me too, as I held up the open score like a choirboy, that it was in my power to swing this, a degree or two, for the festival and its funding, to give Giles, what he might not have felt he'd been getting so far, a good time.

There's a lovely orchestral introduction, the chorus, still wordless, blows like a warm breeze over a cornfield, and then, about two minutes into the piece, the small nod from the conductor, and I begin. 'Go, for they call you, shepherd, from the hill . . .' – as if it was a play, I'd learned the words, I held the listeners with my eyes, and felt the curiosity about what I was saying override the immediate embarrassing quality of anything spoken to music, as I went on to evoke the scene and sounds of summer, the 'bleating of the folded flocks', the 'distant cries of reapers in the corn' and – one of the lines I remembered from school – 'All the live murmur of a summer's day'. A very beautiful line, which seemed to open up the view of wheat fields from the Bampton woods, and to speak just as freshly of the day we were all still sharing, amid the reedbeds and the ripening crops. The chorus started to repeat my words, in atmospheric harmonies, the 'live murmur' blurred and echoed among the parts, and mingled strangely, to my ear, with a far high note, not quite a string tone, out of tune with all the rest, jarring now with the texture of instruments and voices, and after a minute, as it kept steadily on, very clearly not coming from the stage. The air-conditioning, or feedback, possibly, from the mics that were recording the concert. I shared a glance with the conductor, who like a pro pressed on, focusing the orchestra with his own stoop and stare, but the passage that followed was terribly quiet, and full of floral filigree for me, pale pink convolvulus and air-swept lindens, which I'd meant to read *piano*, and without quite being rattled I eased up the volume, and pressed on too, doing my best to hold their attention with the colours of my voice, though I soon felt I had to acknowledge that something was wrong. I saw I was the face of the piece for the audience, and I spoke with a faint and I hoped reassuring smile as I closed in on the crucial line – I was sorry as I did so that the performance Giles had chosen to drop in on was being spoiled for us all by this freakish technical occurrence, it would harden him further against the place . . . The hush deepened on the stage and it was just as I uttered the key words 'the eye travels down to' that the noise beyond rose abruptly in volume and pitch, a noise, now, like a braking train, the long penetrating screech from the rails, and I understood, perhaps everyone did, I threw 'Oxford's towers' like a javelin to the back of the hall, as the scream rose up into the air with a throbbing roar that shook the roof of the building, hammered and faded and came back even louder as it passed overhead, and the conductor set down his baton and bowed in defeat to his players. A mild hubbub broke out in the hall, and it was pure improv that made me say, 'Ladies and gentlemen, the lark ascending!' The Minister for the Arts had left for Brussels.

We drove back next day a winding route, stopping off at village churches lost down Suffolk lanes. Richard's drawn to churchyards, he loves both the atmosphere and the detail. Quite often we've had our coffee and sandwich on a mildewed bench with a view of leaning headstones, a fenced-off table-tomb, mown grass sweet and sour on the air. The hidden angle where a boiler room or vestry sticks out at the back of the church makes a good place to pee afterwards. This time we found a very good church near the Essex border and spent an hour, strolling and stopping among the graves, Richard taking pictures on his phone of amusing inscriptions and good lettering: he likes the early Victorian ones with every line in a different typeface, like printers' samples, and any account of an odd life or comically unusual death – mauled by a tiger, killed by a falling rock. There was no one else around, an English mood, sedative as sunshine, the church above a gentle valley, hay ready for harvest in the field below, and last night's Vaughan Williams still in my system.

On the far side of the churchyard, where half-hearted battle was done with the grass and brambles from the field beyond, there was a fresh grave, wooden interim cross, flowers pretty well dead in their cellophane. A week or so old, but the presence of the mourners still felt in the trampled grass and the message pinned to the flowers. I said, 'I wonder which of us will go to the other's funeral?'

'Oh . . . please,' said Richard, moving away.

'Well, it's going to happen.'

He stopped and looked at me earnestly. 'Not necessarily. We might both be wiped out at the same time, by a neutron bomb for instance.'

'Ah,' I said, 'I hadn't thought of that. Or we might have a suicide pact, I suppose.'

'Then we could both be at each other's funeral!'

'Perfect. Though I hope,' I said, 'for obvious reasons, that you will be at my funeral.'

'Oh, darling, of course I will . . . you know, if I'm free,' he said.

That evening back home I said, 'It's awful, isn't it, I spent several minutes in the churchyard today imagining I was giving the address at Giles's funeral.'

'They'd be bound to ask you,' Richard said.

I let this sarcasm settle. 'I was terribly good, because although I pay as little attention to his actions and ludicrous pronouncements as possible, I have known him for fifty years, and I know how he ticks. I'm almost ready to write the thing now.'

'Does it ever occur to you that it might be him speaking at your funeral?'

I thought for a moment. 'The trouble with that plan is that Giles never understood me at all, and most of his ideas about my life, and actually about my whole make-up, would be laughably wrong.'

'That's a worrying thought, isn't it,' Richard said.

30

Then I left her in the ward, between her curtains, to the half-curious glances of children and couples visiting their own tubed-up mothers and grans across the way, whose cases seemed pitifully worse than Mum's – and went out, into the early night-time of the car park. I'd put the car round the corner, past the stale roar of the kitchen fans, fuggy warmth of frying in the frosty dark – it was her dinner getting ready, I saw the tray, small hot dish, clingfilm on the trifle, and a piercing image of her alone there, trying to eat it. Then, with a sense of weighty and uncertain freedom, I started the engine, drove to the barrier, and out into the evening traffic.

From the moment I unlocked the door and reached in for the light switch, the stillness in the house was posthumous. It was there, unannounced, and admitted no doubt: the unimagined truth of absence, known in an instant for what it was. I dropped the car keys in the bowl, walked round functionally to turn on lamps, draw curtains, saw her chair, with the paper beside it, notes of people to ring. I stood in the gleaming stillness of the kitchen, the silence broken for the millionth time by the whirr of the fridge and then the brief but heavy-going rumble of the boiler firing up and clicking off, and I reasoned with it, as best I could: she should be home in a couple of days. But there are premonitions, it seems, too heavy to argue with.

*

But then, on the actual night, eight months later, I was blind to all these things, I saw nothing as I went from room to room. I had been warned, and I was wholly unprepared. I remembered my clench of hesitation before the visits to the hospital in the spring – eagerness to see her miserably weakened by the fear of what I might find.

I poured a large whisky and put on the dishwasher, and sat till the lapsing green numbers of its timer were the brightest light in the kitchen, the mechanism whooshing and shuddering behind it as usual. The instant drunkenness was woeful, whisky the wrong thing, and not reversible: I had to live through those first hours of confounding aloneness with a nagging headache and no chance of sleep. The intricate network of seasoned professions would stir into life at nine in the morning; I knew from Esme's death what to do, whom to see, the visits to registrars, solicitors, funeral directors – the same receptionists, perhaps, in strip-lit offices, the same undertaker, fourteen years older. For now, though, it couldn't be put into words, or it could, but the words didn't want to be spoken. Then Richard rang. I stared at his name and his holiday photo, the ringtone harp sweetly insistent. And in fact I had no idea how I would put it, once I touched the screen, and said hello. 'I just wondered . . .' he said.

'Oh,' I said.

'So . . .'

'Yes . . . yes.'

I'd just opened in a new play, *Practice*, at Hampstead – four nights of tense previews, and Press on Friday. It was a powerful two-acter by a young African American writer. The dialogue was quickfire, comically banal and brilliantly heard, and the English cast more or less kept a grip on plausible accents for a story set in Alabama. I was playing an old Mexican, a first for me, and an interesting relief after a life-time of touring East

Asia. The main tensions in rehearsal were technical: there was a staggering coup de théâtre at the end of Act One – the programmes on sale had the middle pages sealed so as not to give away the surprise. A certain omertà makes me shy to reveal it here. The play has since travelled all over the world, but for every person there's a first encounter with even the most famous surprises in art.

Mum had sent me a good-luck card, which she sometimes wanted or remembered to do: 'Sorry I can't be with you!' That Friday, her evening and mine took very different courses, and when I looked at my phone in the dressing room afterwards, there was a text from Eileen her carer: *Sorry Dave Av's had another small episode. In Best Western. Not to panic but pls ring when you can.* Best Western was Mum's name for the Great Western Hospital, 'Oh, I often stay there, yes, very good service and delightful staff!' It was one of her brave, much-applauded jokes. 'Some of the guests *are* getting on a bit . . .'

I made phone calls and spoke for two minutes to Mum herself, on her ward; she sounded determined but confused, and weak of voice. There were the Saturday matinee and evening performances to get through, and it was just after midnight on the empty M4, doing ninety in the moonlight over the Downs, when I saw another text flash up, slowed and glanced at it: *Come as soon as you can X*, which I knew meant that I was too late.

Her car still sat in the left-hand garage, but it hadn't been used for six months and the battery was dead. Up till then, Mum went out, to Tesco or to lunch, in the red Suzuki like a postman's van, bent forward at the wheel and putting her foot down – I drove past her once, on the long straight outside Buckley, going the other way: chin up, white hair, gleam of square-framed glasses, urging the car on – she saw nothing, except the road immediately ahead, I started to wave but thought better of it and drove on in the excitement and alarm of it having been her.

'Should she really be driving,' Richard had said later, 'at ninety-one?'

'She's been driving for seventy-three years,' I said, 'and she's not had an accident yet.'

'Well, that's something,' said Richard, seeing through my argument.

'I mean, it's a lifeline for her, isn't it.'

'Not so much of a lifeline if she kills herself – or somebody else.'

'Mm, that won't ever happen,' I said, and I knew, with a sort of weak certainty, that I was right.

I opened the bureau, thinking I'd like to reply to the letters from George and Julie and Jane Mew with the Osmiroid Mum herself had used when she wrote to me at school, in her square blue hand – marbled shell, broadish nib, gold band and clip, a lady's fountain-pen. The bottle of Royal Blue Quink was in its pigeonhole, with a stick of scarlet sealing-wax only used once, and a folded sheet of blotch so old it might have held in its blurred and crossing depths the mirrored traces of those fifty-year-old letters. The pen's nib was a good clean durable gold, but the bladder was perished – it was useless, and indeed Mum herself, as I knew, had written for the past twenty years with thick fibre-tip markers which gave her rare letters the look of notices or recipes. Older still, in her office upstairs, was the typewriter I'd smacked at the keys of at just the time I had learned to write and read. Mum had bought it when I was a baby, to earn her living, and through the Wincroft years Esme had taken charge of it, and bashed out all their business letters, orders, invoices. Now it stayed on a low shelf, under a fitted blue shroud. When I heaved it onto the desk and tugged the cover off, it seemed caught for an instant between reawoken readiness and stark obsolescence. The letters, when I tried to type 'Dear', reared up in twos and threes and stuck there, an inch from the paper.

In her last eighteen months the present-day world offered up in the *Times* and the evening news had become more opaque to her – ever more bristling with nonsensical terms, jokey-sounding phrases that were slung about by millions but which were meaningless to her – crazes, institutions, phenomena . . . What was Buzzfeed? – a pop group? a TV show? something you ate? What, really, was Bitcoin? She would sit down after breakfast with the paper, folded neatly back, right hand flattening the page and marking her place, head slightly bowed, now and then at an angle, as if in shock or doubt about what she'd just read. Perhaps it was eye-trouble, that sideways look she gave at an article; her shake of the head as she turned the page seemed to hide inside a general despair at the things she had read a sadder admission that she couldn't quite take them in. 'You'll understand it,' she had said to me for decades, and it was part of my role, to be active in the world and full of opinions about it. From me it drew out an odd mixture of impatience and showing off – 'I'll explain it to you, Mum.' From her it required, for a long time, a passive belittling of herself, a tough unconventional woman, quick as a needle, who had somehow accepted a general suggestion that she couldn't keep up.

The TV Mum chose to watch was not just pap for the nursery of second childhood, it was a place where she recognized humour, smiled at kindness, saw conventions observed. The programmes themselves were conventions. 'Oh, look at the time!' she would say, and get up to tug the front curtains shut against the 3 p.m. sun. The image welled up in the screen, the urgent inescapable music made the little china boxes rattle on top of the set. *Countdown* was a lovely half-hour, the start of a channel-hopping sequence of quiz shows, through tea-time and ending up warmed and benignly attentive with a six o'clock whisky and *Eggheads* with Jeremy Vine. She called out answers, scornfully at times, and dismissive of right answers when she'd got them wrong. Towards the end I felt she had a nearly abstract reliance on the ritual, a satisfaction in its being performed, the combat of questions asked and answered; it became harder and harder to be sure what she actually knew, and perhaps in the last few months, when she was quiet and withdrawn, the familiar stages of the game show, the dismissals, the forced climaxes, the ad-breaks, were above all a pattern and marking out of time for her. There was something to look forward to, then something to be doing, then something that was over and done.

I went to see Bob Buscott, the funeral director, in the villa on the Radstow road that is his office and works. Grim things that no one can bear thinking of go on behind the white door at the end of the hall, but in the sunny south side of the house a stilted domestic comfort prevails. We talked, as before, in the front room: gas fire, everlasting flowers, tissue drawn up from the box; tea and coffee offered and religion available too, of course, should the signal be given. Bob is more badger-like now, broad and stocky, his thick head of dark hair streaked with grey. He let slip all over again that he'd been born and raised in the town – 'and no doubt I'll die here, too!' I chose a wicker coffin, bassinet shape, a D-ended escape from the eternal hexagon. 'More coffee?' he said, as if he had all day, and I drank up, smiling at the fire. Gas fires always send me back, for a moment or more, to Bampton, to Roland Hudson and our evenings, an invisible breath reignited. I stood and shook Bob's hand, glad of my dry-eyed self-control; it was in part my horror of the peeping tissue, the anticipated need. He sent me home with a list of questions, about the texts and music, and unexpectedly about what Mum was to wear. I saw I must send her off in her finest, in one of her creations I most wanted to keep.

Many things to be done in Foxleigh, accounts settled, people visited and told. Each encounter unpredictable, for me and for the person on whom I watched the news breaking and then sinking in. I saw Frank Fletcher, Mum's butcher for forty years, very deaf, glancing round in the street, thinking someone had spoken: I said, 'I think you knew my mother' – he looked at me as if this was very unlikely: 'Avril Win?' 'Oh . . . oh, yes?' – and the quick flux of reactions in his face and tone, respect for the dead, and for my feelings too, rueful fondness for another old-stager who'd gone, and with it (I don't think I'm wrong) a never-shifted unease about her life with Esme. In some people there was spontaneous affection; in others, none of that. I found Mum's address book and rang Judy Dawes, her old neighbour, who sent a card each Christmas, and as far as I knew was still living in a Devonshire village not far from Friscombe. On the phone she sounded just the same, bright and unfoolable. 'Well, she was even older than me,' Judy said. 'I've had two new hips, but I'm still managing.' 'Oh, have you, I'm glad,' I said, and pressed on, 'I don't expect you'll be able to come to the funeral, but I wanted you to know when it is.' 'It's probably too far,' she agreed, 'I am ninety-one.' 'Anyway,' I said, 'I felt I should let you know at once, since you were *such* old friends.' '*Well*, it's inevitable, isn't it,' she said. I asked about her, but she was very dry, and she asked me nothing about myself. When I hung up I wondered if the dryness was partly resistance to me, a man so unlike anyone else she knew, perhaps the only man of colour she'd sat down to lunch with in her long nine decades. Or did it convey, now she'd gone, some never-voiced reservation about Mum herself?

In some of these encounters, calling round kindly in the car at an old person's bungalow, the few last survivors of the long-dispersed girls, I felt I was a youngster, the one just setting off from this small country town to a dubious future elsewhere; I felt they saw the boy in me still, and not the lined sixty-eight-year-old who caught my eye in the mirror as I left. It was clear to me too that these were my last visits, and that within a few months I would be leaving Foxleigh for good.

That was the light, more and more, in which I walked round the town with Richard. He knew his way well enough by now, but of course he couldn't see, through the Oxfam shop window, the glass counter and tobacco-jars of Timmy Hogan's, or after that for decades the three black chairs of Smiths, Barbers, the nylon-sheeted farmers, solicitors, other people's fathers, talking into the mirror as I waited for my turn, the sweat smells and tang of the lotions in waves as scissors dawdled around ears and clippers pinked up the back of the neck. It was there Kissing Cousins's photo appeared in the window, blond head tipped forward, one of the newer styles seen on TV and in Swindon, and now offered here, more or less, just in case. All my past in the town was present on these walks, as if glowing and fainting on gauze beyond gauze. Sometimes it was no more than a mild awareness of a lost impression, the barely registered pulse of recollection, a face at a corner, a school morning in the rain. 'Are you lost?' said a helpful old man, seeing a tourist staring at nothing.

The memories opened and spread with a magic, a pictur-esque interest of their own that distracted me for minutes on end from the recurrent black pain. As we ambled around something stirred of the childish dreads and lures and skipped-over boring bits on a walk, summer afternoons with awnings down, aura of doorways, doors open all day on dim hallways, the polio lady, Captain Lingard, Cooper's sweetshop and tobacconist on London Street, unequal doorsteps of big houses on steep streets, four up one side, two down the other and not to get caught. And the edge-of-town places, the goods yard, the scrap yard, and then stiles into fields. 'This was all fields,' I said. 'And up there is where Miss Rowse lived, who babysat sometimes, she was stone deaf but she could still hear children.' We glanced at the row of small pink-brick houses where her ancient collapsing cottage had been. 'You'll just have to imagine it, it was like something out of Hardy, or Tolstoy perhaps – outdoor bog, oil-lamps and candles.' I could see Richard thought I was overdoing it. And was it worth trying to explain? To tell him about Mr Andrews, cobbler and leather goods, left leg in a calliper, who wrote down his real name for me, with his thick shop pencil on a paper bag, wrote it slowly and clearly and in letters not like ours: Andrzejewski, which he said, with a sort of pained twinkle, no one ever got right. He was a Polish airman who'd been wounded and stayed on, and was spoken of still with wartime sentiment. I learned the spelling of his name by heart that day, but never, it seemed, the exact pronunciation.

And can I possibly capture that further thing, elusive even at the time, but subtly pervasive: the way I was seen as a child by these teachers and tradespeople in a small market town in the far-off middle of the previous century? The old woman in Cooper's whose reactions to me were unreadable – doting, mocking, a part of the complicated thing of being myself seen and remembered by everyone as different. It struck me now, and for the first time, that to Mr Andrews too I was a foreigner, and more obviously and pitiably so than him.

I'd shown Richard on earlier visits where Mum and Esme's shop was, 'Wincroft, Dressmakers' (Esme'd wanted 'Modes', but Mum prevailed). They'd closed up thirty years ago, bereft but relieved, and leased the shop to Victoria Wine, who in due course had closed down themselves. Now it was a brightly lit charity shop for Children in Need, appeals for the orphans of earthquakes and civil wars taped up in the window once commanded by Betty and Tricia, imperturbable mannequins. I tried

440

to describe them for him, their role in our lives. Mum had got them ex-display from Elliston and Cavells, and they were different colours, Betty pink, Tricia milk-coffee brown, but with no other suggestion of racial difference. Both had sharp forward-looking faces, small busts, long thin legs and pointed fingers; Tricia's bust was in fact a bit larger, though both used padding, and they wore interchangeable wigs. Locked in week-long colloquies at elegant angles they seemed caught for far longer in a well-mannered standoff: neither could let down her guard, or leave the other alone. They were slightly sad, endlessly patient figures, as well as a joke, a proxy couple, with Esme taking Tricia's part. 'Tricia's sulking this week, because Betty's ignoring her,' she might say, and it was left to me to guess if the game meant something more. Behind the two mannequins on their narrow forestage ran a waist-high curtain on a brass rail, which half-concealed the front room of the shop beyond. Once or twice, as a schoolboy, when it was time for them to change, I'd slipped off my shoes and stepped into the window, tickled and excited at being on display myself. I seemed to flirt suavely with the women as I helped undress them, Mum showing me the handling of the wigs, the way to pack the bosoms with crumpled-up tissue-paper. When I came to play Lady Wishfort, I knew just what I was doing. Now there were two or three coats in the window on hangers, and when we went in for a minute, with temporizing smiles at the volunteer, we were brushing past shoulder-high racks of jackets and shirts which gave off, not the impersonal promise of the new, but the worthy collective must of the second-hand.

Even in the time I'd been coming here with Richard the town had decayed. The famous old Bull was boarded up, though a light shone year round in an upstairs window, as if one unevictable guest stayed on, while wind-sown saplings sprouted from the gutters and chimneys. At the Crown across the square garish boards announced pizza and pasta with encouraging photos, and loud dance music played at mid-morning in the near-empty bar. Mason's remained, and had answered the challenge of a Tesco with late opening and a deli counter. Otherwise not a single shop was what it had been when I was a boy; and even those that looked prosperous five years ago had gone under. A cute cafe with vegan options seemed to look to a newer kind of customer than the elderly couple seated in the window grappling with a focaccia sandwich. Elderly couple ... they were probably a few years younger than me.

31

Back in London we've found room for 'A Tragic Gesture' and the Burma box, and we have the framed photo of the man Richard calls 'your Dad' or sometimes just 'Dad', as if he's taken him on too. Mum had said it was lost in the move to Crackers, and I hadn't seen it since I was a schoolboy. The frame has a prop that folds out from behind, but the ribbon that keeps it from doing the splits has perished, and after five seconds at eighty degrees Dad is flat on his back, sending other things flying. The photo itself is a puzzle to me: it could hardly be more personal or more remote. It is also very different from how I remembered it. The two or three friends we've shown it to say they think they can see me in him. What I see is a lean young man in a wide-shouldered Western suit and a tie, shiny black hair cropped short at the sides and parted in the centre, complexion dark as pewter; he has a full-lipped mouth, no question of smiling, and the sheen on his wire-framed glasses half conceals his eyes. The setting has the studio props of an age already over when it was taken, a chair, a carved teak table with books stacked on it, and a painted backdrop of a balustrade, airy trees, and in the distance a pagoda in silhouette. There are shallow undulations in the backdrop, shown up by the studio lights; Dad pays no heed to any of this as he stares at the camera, but you feel it's what he wanted, what any customer of Cashel & Nephew, Rangoon, was counting on getting.

It's dated on the back in pencil, 1945, with the name, Aung Kyaw Win. Perhaps by the time he met Mum, two years later, he had grown more supple and seductive. He doesn't appear in any of the other small photos I've found since she died, and I have no image, physical or mental, of these two as young people together. His colour intrigues and absorbs me, in part because it eludes me: I know how different exposures, different stock, variable processes blench or burnish skin tones in black-and-white. It's part of the endlessly slippery game, or ordeal, of distinctions, discriminations. Mum said to me once or twice how in her day the old-school Brits in Rangoon still divided the Burmese into two types: Orientals (more or less OK) and Blacks (uniformly inferior). I think Mum thought she herself had met an Oriental, but I can't be sure if she thought that, or if she had.

Richard knows of course that I've been writing another book – though not exactly what it is. I seem to need some secrecy, even from him; and no doubt I'm wary of his editorial eye. If I'm home in the day I climb up here under the Velux and close the door, but I'm aware on and off, when he crosses the room or takes a call from one of his authors, of Richard at work in the room below. He's just started editing a book on the Burmese junta – a curious choice, it seems to me, and clearly very slow work for him. He has tried to involve me by asking if I'll check the proper names, but I feel the author, who has actually spent twelve years in the country, is much more likely than me to know the right forms. Richard has taken on a broody look, himself knowing far more by now about modern-day Burma than I do. He shares terrifying details and statistics over lunch. His view is that the author of the book is deeply informed but can't write. Anyone Richard says 'can't write' is of course someone who does so; and there's a lot of them. No doubt this makes me more nervous about sharing my chapters, though I'm sure he is curious, and pained, just a little, at being kept out.

He said to Ken and Edie over dinner the other night, 'You know David's at work on his magnum opus.' 'Ooh – what is it,' said Edie, 'a play?' 'It's his *memoirs*, I *think*,' he said, holding my eye. Both Edie and Ken murmured that they couldn't wait, and seemed lost for a minute in picturing what might be in it.

I looked at them – Richard's friends, originally, now part of the month-by-month pattern of my life, though I don't think I would otherwise have sought them out, or followed them up, as friends of my own. Edie is still lovely, face delicately lined, streaky blonde hair pinned up and escaping; Ken is tall, bald, denim-jacketed, barely knowable from the photos Richard has of them all together, at Bristol, circa 1979, where they look like a folk band, tight jeans and shoulder-bags, Ken with dead-straight black hair down to his chest. I've never asked but I'm pretty sure Richard was in love with him then, and still, once they've gone and we're clearing up the kitchen, putting left-overs in clingfilm for the fridge, Richard at the sink half-drunkenly scrubbing a pot will say, 'So nice, old Ken, don't you think?' and I'll say, 'You go back a long way, don't you.' The truth is I don't believe Richard and Ken would be friends either, if they first met now; and yet their being so is more than habit, a long loyal tribute perhaps to how they once were.

Now Ken said, 'Rich says you were at school with *Hadlow* – at public school.' They're not Trots any more, but they're old-style left-wing, and anyone like Giles is stripped down to one name, like a sentenced criminal, or a schoolboy indeed.

I said what I always say, 'It's not something I boast about.' I could see he was already forming an idea of what I'm writing, as anyone does of a book they've only heard of but not read: in Ken's case, vague but dependable images of things I sense he doesn't really like about me: private education, affectations of actors, worse things than that, tripping through his mind like slides through a carrousel. I said, 'I've no intention of writing a book about Hadlow, there are more than enough of those already.' I pictured the ludicrous privately published *Festschrift* for his sixtieth birthday, that I'd leafed through eight years ago, on the very day I met Richard – which showed, once again, the ability of Giles to butt his way into my life at even quite intimate moments.

'You saw him on TV last night?' said Edie.

'We missed it,' I said.

'Yeah, *Question Time,*' Ken said. 'All about the EU referendum, of course. He was looking very pleased with himself.'

'Not an absolutely new experience for him,' I said.

'So what's the dirt on him, Dave?' Ken said.

'I don't have any, really,' I said, and half stood up to refill their glasses. 'I was always much closer to his parents.'

'The enlightened plutocrats,' said Ken.

'That's right,' I said, and hoped we weren't going to argue about them.

'So what are you writing about, love, in your book?' Edie said.

'I'm writing about my early life mainly – teens and twenties. That and my mother, you know. It's really since she died,' I said, 'and going through all her stuff . . .'

'Oh, that's so touching,' she said, 'it must bring memories flooding back.'

'Yes and no,' I said, not ready to go into it.

'She sounds such a remarkable person.'

'She really was,' I said.

'I wonder how much you actually remember, from so long ago,' Edie said.

'David's got an amazing memory,' said Richard, 'as you know.'

'Well,' I said, 'I've been thinking about all this. The teenage stuff is more like writing a novel. I remember places, and experiences, very clearly, but they're stills, you know, rather than clips. Or GIFs perhaps, sometimes – a head turns, a hand comes down, but you never see what comes next, it just does it again. Besides that, of course, there's anecdotes, things I've been told, that I know I did, even if I can't really remember them. And no one recalls more than a few words anyone actually said fifty years ago. You just have to make that up.'

'A bit of improv,' said Ken.

'Because you did write about your acting career, didn't you, in your first book?' Edie said, holding my eye to conceal her uncertainty.

'Well, that was a more general book, about experimental theatre in the Seventies and Eighties – I don't want to go there ever again. What I'm writing now is more about my personal life – things I really didn't want to talk about before. I want to write about falling in love.'

'Oh, yes?' said Ken, and Richard gave us an interesting smile as he absorbed the idea.

'And I want to write about being like I am, but never knowing much about where I came from.'

Edie said cautiously, 'I mean, you've never been to Burma, have you – or Myanmar, don't we say now?'

'No,' I said, 'though we might go, mightn't we, Richard?'

'No, we might,' said Richard, as if anything was possible.

'Now things are a bit easier there. People always assume I've been, for obvious reasons, and because of *Wingate's War*, but as you know that was all shot in the Philippines.'

'Anyway,' said Ken, 'you're only half Burmese.'

'Well, quite,' I said. 'I only half need to go there.'

'I mean I've always I meant to ask you,' Edie said, in the resolute manner she adopts around racial questions, 'what kind of support you've ever had, you know, from the Burmese community?'

There's a strict but forbearing tone I use at times with

students, and I fell back on it now. 'Show me the Burmese community, darling,' I said, 'and I'll get on to them first thing tomorrow about giving me support.'

'Oh . . . really . . . isn't there . . .'

'I believe there's a street in Gosport, where a number of Burmese people live. And it's true,' I said relentingly, 'there were some refugees, weren't there, a few years ago, who settled in Hounslow, I think, mainly. But they don't amount to much more than a village, all told. I think if you added them all up, it would be about the same population as Foxleigh.'

'What, where you grew up, you mean.'

'Exactly, just a little market town in the middle of nowhere.'

'What a vision that is,' said Richard.

'There must be other Burmese actors?'

I rattled off Richard Beckinsale, if one can be said to rattle off one name. 'Though he was only quarter-Burmese. And very sadly he's dead. People often think I'm Ken Danby, you know, the half-Chinese actor.'

'You don't look like him at all.'

'I'm glad you say that. He's much smaller than me, and five years older. I once asked him and he said no one had ever mistaken him for Dave Win. He seemed rather offended by the idea.'

Edie bit her lip. 'So it's just you . . .'

'Oh, I'm so niche, Edie darling,' I said, and we all laughed, and I saw she was glad to find we could joke about it.

When they'd gone and we were clearing up, Richard said, 'Do you have a title for this new book of yours?'

I slid the roasting tin into the sudsy water in front of him. 'I thought of calling it "Our Evenings",' I said.

'Ah . . .' He met my eye in our reflections in the window, and I could see he was touched, though many of the evenings

448

described will be those I spent with other men, and in theatres long before he'd even heard of me. When we first met, the phrase was our term for the teasingly rationed three or four times a week we saw each other, both of us still wary at having found so exactly what we wanted. Then the caution seemed absurd and the evenings joined up into one unguarded time together.

It's tricky, though, being the partner of an actor, and being effectively partnerless night after night. I remember a conversation right at the start, eight years ago now, when he was still moving his things into this house, and I had rehearsals starting for a new play by Jem Crane at the Donmar. There was a nude scene in it, negotiable, and anyway very short, where my character, a Cambodian soldier, talks to a journalist while getting dressed. 'Well, you like getting your kit off,' Richard said.

'A myth,' I said, 'I just happen to have been directed decades ago by a series of perverts who liked the look of me naked in one play, and thought they'd try it in the next.'

'Oh,' said Richard, 'is *that* it?'

'It is.'

He carried on dusting and shelving the books. 'Well, you should count yourself lucky. I don't know if you saw dear old Rob Borthwick in the back of the *Times* magazine?'

'Oh, Robin's a marvellous actor.'

'Advertising stairlifts.'

'Christ,' I said.

'Fully clothed, I should add.'

A bit later I said, 'Do you mind me doing this nude scene?'

'Not at all,' he said.

'It's unseemly, a sixty-year-old man – I know that. It never happens.'

'I shall picture it each night at eight-thirty,' he said, 'over my solitary omelette.' I knew what he minded more about the play was the loss of our evenings – that I would be laughing and shouting and swigging brown water with strangers on stage when I might have been home chopping parsley and sipping a lovely unmooring negroni with him. 'I like evenings best,' he said to me, right at the start, when a portion of our chat was questionnaires. 'A drink and good company wipe out the worries of the morning and afternoon, hard fact gives way to a happy feeling.' 'That's all very well,' I said, 'unless you're a waiter – or actor, indeed.' 'Darling, I do know that millions of people work at night: but I've never had to do it myself' – and I saw a tiny worry, that he might be beginning to nag, sweep his features clean before he gave me a kiss: 'I'm very glad you're in this play,' he said. 'And after all, what they're seeing is hardly a secret.' I gave him a rather tart look. A little later I remembered my old love Hector, and the modelling he used to do for Molleson's life class – the awful feeling of exclusion I'd had when I met the students who drew and painted my boyfriend naked once a week.

One of the boxes we brought here from Mum's house is full of Bampton things, exam papers, fixture cards, end-of-term reports, every letter I wrote her. The weight of the box comes from multiple back-numbers of *The Hive* – dark red wrappers, staples rusted . . . and inside, the ghostly posturing of Fosdyke's editorials, facetious short stories, callow well-argued essays on apartheid or Modern Art, and pages of poems, by Alec Adams ('Hungary 1956'), by Tony Bales ('To Anne-Marie, Again'), by me (a desperate sonnet, 'Rangoon Dawn'), even and uniquely a poem by Giles Hadlow, 'The Old Farmer', ten lines, simple but touching, the unexpected first showing of a boy's hand and heart any schoolmaster thrills to, which turned out to be copied, with two small changes, from a poem by Quasimodo in the previous week's *Listener*.

Each issue has a central gathering of photos, winners of the

Camera Club competition back to back with victorious hockey teams and Speech Day visitors handing out silverware – the gleam of prizes all round. The Field Day events were covered each year, and in Summer '65 there's a photo of our one-off threesome, Giles in the centre, with his right hand on my shoulder, as if decently commending one of his staff, Andrew Cousins apart to his left, ignoring the camera but winning our interest and even, somehow, winning the picture, a little cream and gold confection of luminous Englishness. His smile, at a spot just out of view, has a mixture of shyness and disdain which strikes me as very English too. Perhaps it was no more than embarrassment, and teenage dissent from the day and the task he'd successfully performed. If he seems to look out slyly to the world beyond school, he knows nothing exact about what waits for him there. Andrew declared himself early, I stayed years longer in disguise – the clever but involuntary disguise of being already conspicuous for something else.

Giles in the photo is taller and broader than Cousins and me, with no hint in his winning stare that he's dented the off-side wing of the Wincroft van, and returned it with a nearly empty tank – no sense of the agonizing conversation to follow between Mum and Mark, Mark paying, of course, and Mum feeling once again, quite illogically, in his debt. He is still good-looking – round chin, straight nose, his boyhood fineness lightly roughed up but not ruined by adolescence. Three years earlier, up at the trig point, I'd seen, and resisted, something handsome in him, the bigger boy's aura and power that I was still waiting to come into; but the photograph shows that by seventeen the larger change had begun. He had started on the shift, through his twenties and thirties, into the broad indeterminate margin of the vaguely good-looking. He put on weight, grew his hair, vain and careless in equal measure. Soon he would be one of those thousands of men, in suits and offices, bossing others around with a barely conscious reliance on vanishing good looks, a deep-seated assumption of their right to be fancied and followed.

I spent a whole evening with those copies of *The Hive*, on the trail of the teenage Dave Win. On black-and-white film my face reads in varying depths of grey; it stands out in these photos even as it blurs into shadowed panelling or the darkness of bushes. Sometimes I'm echoed by Manji or, earlier on, by the senior much darker figure of Tafawa Balewa. In the Poetry Club, I'm enthroned, at the heart of things; in the 3rd XV I'm at the end, on the wing, floating away, still smiling. The other boys seem to show that they know I'm there; I feel I'm displayed, as something unusual they have in their lives, which they could explain to their parents, if asked, and are almost proud of. But I have no memory of the picture being taken. I found myself wondering, 'What is that smiling Burmese boy doing there? Am I related to him in some way? What was he thinking?'

32

In rehearsals for *Space*, a new play by Eva Lehmann-Holst at the Almeida, starring Annick Lafeu, the red-haired French star of *Contretemps* who finds herself suddenly a well-known figure in England, or at least in Islington, where shoppers turn in the street and the staff at our lunchtime cafe ask to have selfies with her. I modestly lean back, till the manager says, 'Kenneth, isn't it, we want you in it too.' Annick reminds me at moments of Elise Pleynet, who transfixed and alarmed me as a teenager longing to act. Offstage, she makes me feel thirteen again. She has the same hauteur, and sense of her own distinction, intercut with tiny and intoxicating moments of intimacy; though today of course stardom comes with numerous demeaning requirements, her Twitter feed, her Instagram and so on. Also she is on the way up, where Elise, when I met her, was already (as I didn't quite apprehend) in a long decline, her grand Gallic style already slipping out of date. Stars exert their own forcefield, on the audience and on the other actors, but Annick is generous in rehearsal, and eager for experiment, perhaps to break out from her long-running TV role. The feeling, after a week, is extremely positive, and unexpectedly defiant, with a French star, a Danish designer and a play translated from German.

Appalled, at the end of the run-through today – 'Have you voted?' Thea said, very confidently, and those of us who had yet to do so looked glad of the reminder. 'I'm so sorry, Annick,' she said, 'that you should have to witness this squalid business. Very soon it will be over, and then I hope we can get back to normal.'

'I don't take it personally,' said Annick, 'and anyway, it is so stupid, they shoot themselves in the head. They can never win.'

I said that the young (among whom, in some unexamined part of my mind, I still counted myself) were overwhelmingly against it, and old-age pensioners the keenest for it.

'You must be a pensioner, Dave, aren't you, by now?' said old Ted York.

'Yes . . . just,' I said. 'Of course I voted with the young.' Ted was fixing up the wide-brimmed hat and blue silk scarf with which in the street he likes to disguise and announce himself. A mad idea occurred to me. 'And you?' I said.

'I've not voted yet,' he said rather primly, 'but I shall go to the polling station on my way home, where I shall not, I'm afraid, cast my vote for Remain.'

There was a short and complicated silence after this, in which good manners, friendship, professional respect &c tried in each of us to hold back the question, 'Why, Ted? Why?', while I at least was thinking tactically that there was time to change his mind, or take him next door to the pub and get him so pissed he forgot when the polling station closed. 'Why, Ted?' Thea said at last. 'Why?'

'Oh, I love Europe, love France,' said Ted, gathering up his briefcase.

'Of course you love France,' said Thea, 'you've performed at the Avignon Festival for years. You starred in *The Caretaker* in Aix-en-Provence last summer. They love you. But they won't love you if you vote to leave.'

'No, we won't,' said Annick.

'In fact I doubt very much,' said Thea, 'that you'd even be allowed to work there.'

'It's the immigration, really. It's out of control. I'm sorry, Dave,' he said, as if I were an immigrant myself. 'I don't like being bossed around – except by you, my dear, of course,' and with a fractional raising of his hat to Thea he went out. 'Silly old fool,' said Julia, Thea had a hard and disillusioned look, and all of us must have had similar thoughts about quite what we were going to be saying tomorrow morning.

And then, the cast coming in next day for rehearsal – ten o'clock, the bleary actor's 'first thing', the grim mood of defeat, and the prophetic gloom. Hopkins got it just right, of an earlier disaster: hope had mourning on; hope was twelve hours gone. We'd known it ourselves, some of us, in '83, worse in '87, but those were defeats that took immediate effect, which was to carry on as before. Last night's vote was for action in the future, a devastation due to hang menacingly over us for years. Long enough to count the time, make plans, as under the death sentence of a disease. It was something as personal as this that I'd felt last night, watching TV, and watching again this morning first thing in cognitive shock: that Giles had won. He was on every channel, interviewed at home, in the studio, in the street. He was very pleased, he was delighted, but he didn't smile, not quite – what he let us see was his chilling impatience to get on at once with the job.

When Ted came in, the talk fell silent, as if we were the guilty ones. 'Good morning, all,' he said soberly, and hung up his hat and went to the coffee machine. Victory must have hung rather heavy on him. And he seemed, as he joined our loose circle and sat down, to mask the glint of success with a hunch of apology, elbows on knees, mug held in both hands.

'We'll start straight in on Act Two,' said Thea: 'five minutes?' She was entirely professional, we looked about, shook ourselves out of the trance of our shock, got up and went past

Ted to the toilets, did our own little stretches, no organized warm-up today. I chattered through my words in my usual way as I walked around, as if on my phone in the street. Act Two opens with a brief exchange between me and Annick, tech-savvy adviser to visionary new leader; then Ted comes in, and they have a storming ten minutes together, the ebb and flow, wiles and force, of two strong personalities of different generations locked together. The play is set in a near future somewhat brighter than the one we'd been picturing just before; and, as so often with acting, it meshes here and there, but not completely, with matters in our other lives. I suspect I let these offstage ironies colour my performance today – Thea frowned a little but let it run. I made way, with a simpering flourish, for Ted as he entered the room, then I sat to watch them, and the almost unbearable thing, from ten seconds in, was his brilliance: his complete command, week two of rehearsals, first thing in the morning, of colour and timing, the voice like an orchestra, so often mimicked you forget it's unique, his odd agile way, for an overweight elderly man, of taking up the bare white space of the room and shaping it. It was stuffy today, a fan sweeping with its own quiet ripple across the scene and back again, the striplights bright; but Ted was already in a theatre. He is (I'm sure he very much wanted to remind us) a great actor, soaked in experience, lifting a scene in which Annick's star-power is quite different, that of beauty and the future – and of being French. And for now the play itself demands that we get on with each other – two or three of the cast confessed they had been in tears last night, but we must work for a semblance of unity through our first shock of grief.

The next weekend, our last but one visit to Crackers, to deal with the sale of the contents – that sounds too grand, I mean we'd stuck everything we didn't want to keep in Morlands' monthly auction. For once Richard drove and I was the passenger, and mildly astonished by the things I noticed, farm buildings and big houses and far-off church towers that I'd missed on the two or three hundred times I've driven there myself. We had *Record Review* on the radio – mostly unscripted chat now instead of the concise and unanswerable lectures I grew up on. 'Too many "you knows" and "sort ofs",' said Richard, and I gruffly agreed. It was the *Tallis Fantasia* on 'Building a Library' and that took me back, even so: a great drench of Englishness, in different versions, wistful, defiant, driven or dawdling, as the autumn countryside swept by. Several, of course, not English, but French, German, Italian visions of what Englishness might be, now walls of sound, now veils. We weren't at all sure ourselves which one we thought best.

The sale was on view for two days in Morlands' barnlike room, with a dung and beast smell from the nearby yard where the livestock sales took place. 'And this, I suppose, is the dead-stock,' said Richard. 'Oh, look,' I said excitedly, 'there's the standard lamp.' The dining table glowed hospitably, the old bleachings and stains from knocked-over wine glasses barely showing. I'd had fairly high hopes for it, and the chairs, and Esme's posh antiques, the Regency card-table, the Welsh dresser; but Morlands warned me that all such furniture has been massively devalued – young people don't want these old things now. The cardboard box of corroded aluminium pans, the mincer, the mixer, I couldn't see anyone wanting; then there were the deckchairs and the bird-bath from the garden, and the sundial with the legend SENSIM SINE SENSU, known since adolescence – 'Though I've never known exactly what it means,' I said; 'just a bit of nonsense, according to Esme.' Richard peered at it, it's not easy to read. 'Oh, well it's Cicero, isn't it,' he said, a little too promptly: '*De Senectute*. I suppose, sort of . . . "slowly, without sensing it, we grow old".'

'Sort of?' I said.

'I mean it's an approximate translation,' he said, and slapped me on the wrist.

Back at the house there were just the unsaleable things, the flammable three-piece suite and the five beds. And in Mum's bedroom, the task left till last, out of sentiment and indecision, the two built-in wardrobes filled with her clothes. I went up to the room by myself. She was eight months dead and her ashes buried with Esme's, but I still felt an intruder – I had a stupid unstoppable habit of knocking as I pushed the door open, against the thick shabby pile of the carpet. The stripped mattress was the most horrible thing, hospital signal of a patient gone. Mild summer sunshine waned across the old green carpet, stained and worn, but fresh as new in squares where the two bedside cupboards had stood. It was the room of Mum's old age, where she'd slept alone for her last fourteen years – the early nights, the sleeping pills and still the early waking. It was hard now to recall it in its pomp, to colour it in as the scene of her most passionate life.

In her last year I used to hear her moving around at three or four a.m. 'It's dawn when you can see the veins on your hands,' she said, when I brought in her tea. 'That's one of the few things I can remember your father saying.'

'Oh, really?' I said, indifferently, so as not to make her clam up, indeed to make her feel she might work a bit harder to bring out the interest of her point.

'You can tell he was quite poetical. Or observant, perhaps I mean.'

'I'm going to test it myself, when the birds wake me up. There's a blackbird here that goes off like a car alarm.' She smiled, and of course what I couldn't help picturing was his hands and hers in the very first light, with its warning they must separate. It was, in its quiet way, the revelation of a life. 'What other poetical things did he say?'

Mum blinked and shook her head. 'I wish I could remember,' she said. And I wondered if she had only now, at ninety-two, remembered my father's remark about the dawn light, or if she'd thought of it on and off for seventy years, but kept it to herself. On each visit I trimmed her fast-growing fingernails for her, and felt as I had all my life the heat of her hands, just the same, though they were twisted now, she couldn't sew, did the crossword in ill-fitting letters, and the veins indeed stood out thick and blue in her spotted skin.

Now I closed the door quietly behind me and was crossing the room with heavy resolve just as the doorbell rang. Richard didn't answer so I went down. It was Jane Mew. 'I saw your car,' she said, 'and I couldn't pass by without saying hello. And also, I suppose, goodbye.'

'Oh, Jane!' I said, and smiled at her ruefully – I didn't think she'd want to be hugged. 'That's very sweet of you. In fact you're just in time for a sherry' – which I felt was what had drawn her, by unerased habit, to call at exactly this time.

'If you've got some,' she said.

'There's half a bottle we keep for emergencies.'

'Well . . .' said Jane, stamping her boots on the mat and looking quickly past me, as she came in, to nerve herself for the empty house.

'Actually you've come at a very good time – we're just about to go through Mum's clothes.'

'Richard's with you, good.'

'I've put it off and put it off. You might have ideas about what to do with some of them.'

'I don't know . . . I could have a look, I suppose.'

'And of course,' I said, going into the kitchen, 'if there's anything you'd like yourself . . .'

'Kind thought, Dave,' she said. 'We were rather different shapes, though, your mother and me.'

'Well . . .' I said. There was no point denying this, Mum

always lean, Jane short and now extremely stout; brown corduroy trousers were her normal wear, never I think made by her old friend. 'There might be a scarf or something?' She seemed worried by the thought of the clothes, but didn't want to shirk the task. When she'd knocked back her first sherry she made her way upstairs with me while Richard started on the lunch.

This time I was conscious as I opened the bedroom door of the shock the bare room would be to her – I went in first to screen it from her. 'Ah, yes,' she said, glancing round.

'You must have been in here before?'

'I think once or twice.'

'Let me show you the problem,' I said, and I crossed the room quickly now and flung open the doors of the first built-in wardrobe, and then, with a flourish, of the second. She stood and looked at the extraordinary spectacle, dresses and skirts hung so tight on the rail that with the opening of the doors they seemed to let out a breath and expand into the room in a rustle of scarlet and mustard and purple, the old bold colours. Jane stared, lips pressed tight for ten seconds in self-control. Then she said, 'Oh, dear,' and gave me a brief shy smile.

'If you'd rather not,' I said – I could feel her setting me off.

'No, no, Dave – let's do it. We're doing it for her. It's her life's work.'

So Jane was a great help, in her way, but as a good friend of Mum's for over half a century she was more upset than Richard would had been. I'd always been fond of her, as one of the girls, but after I left home our chats when we did meet were all about what I was doing, and I'd thought of her almost as a woman with no life of her own. Now we were abruptly intimate – I felt, just a little, that I was intruding on her. 'I remember this one,' she said, and reached in to pull out a red dress, and spread it over her arm, for us both to admire. 'She looked a million dollars in this.'

'It's gorgeous, that one,' I said, 'I remember it too. She made it for the party, when we moved in here. I mean, what do you think we should do with them, Jane, the best ones especially?' I took down another, a summer frock, green and blue leaves. 'I remember her wearing this.'

'Yes, indeed,' said Jane. 'And then' – her dumpy figure groping, almost smothered, between two flouncy dresses – 'there's this one, her slinky number!'

'Did she wear that?' I said.

'Did she ever!'

'Well, I'm glad . . .' I said, and we found ourselves grinning at each other. We had reached rather quickly, with the sherry perhaps, that state of excited fascination with a dead person's things that can coexist with grief. We went through the lot then, laughing and wincing and Jane sometimes blowing her nose. The skirts and the frocks were parties, and weddings, and ordinary weekdays, much-worn successes and one or two bold items even Jane had never seen her try on. I was ever so slightly mistrusting the speed of the whole thing, after an eight-month wait. It was like casting off mourning.

'I think what I'd do, Dave,' she said, when we'd sorted the clothes into slithering heaps on the bed, 'have you got a big suitcase? Then pack up everything you'd like to survive, two suitcases perhaps, and drop them off at a Nearly New shop. Not the one here, you don't want to see strangers walking around in them, or I don't anyway – and not one anywhere near you in London. Drop them off somewhere in between.'

'High Wycombe?' I said.

'I believe they'd find excellent homes in High Wycombe,' said Jane, so judiciously that I burst out laughing.

A few of the trousers and jackets were stained and Jane said to put them in a bin-bag. I felt I was a child who needed to be told these things, and given permission. When I came back upstairs with a bag she was kneeling on the floor, with the deep drawer at the bottom of the cupboard, meant for shoes, I think, pulled open. 'Have you seen this?' she said. She reached up as she turned to me, with a light bolt of red tartan silk across her arms, like a vestment, the colours vivid as if new. 'It was in here, under these old jerseys.'

'Her longyi,' I said, 'I haven't seen it for fifty years.' Then I watched as she unfolded from a sheath of tissue paper the beautiful yards-long gaung-baung that Mum had wrapped round her head and round mine on rare reckless evenings when I was a child. Jane passed this to me too, it felt known and not quite known, because it was what it had always been, not what I remembered, though now as it ran through my hands it brought with it the shadows and gleams of days I had utterly forgotten, and which were lost again four or five seconds later.

'These,' said Jane, 'you must keep always.'

'Oh, I will,' I said, and gave them back to her to wrap. Then I helped her up. 'Did Mum ever talk to you about Burma, I wonder, and what happened?' I felt awkward at once, admitting my own ignorance and asking her perhaps to break a confidence.

'Well, it was the terrible loneliness, Dave, wasn't it, she talked about that sometimes.'

'Oh, did she?'

'She'd gone all that way for some reason, and then wondered what the reason was. If that makes any sense.'

I saw now, at last, that I really must ask Mum directly about it – well, it was one of a number of things. 'Did she ever speak about my father?'

Jane thought for a bit, which was unnerving. 'I mean, she wasn't in love with him or anything – sorry, Dave . . .'

'No, heavens, Jane, you don't have to spare my feelings – I mean, my feelings aren't remotely involved.'

'Well . . .' she said, and looked at me, as if to say this itself was a subject worth going into, but she went on, 'and she was lonely, as I say, and twenty-four, wasn't it? You remember what that's like . . .' with a curious smile, and I said,

'Oh, I certainly do . . .'

'And there she was on the far side of the world . . .'

I still wondered about Mum – she was an effective actress because everyone thought acting was beyond her. In games like Contraband and Cheat she shocked us with her bare-faced winning lies, when she'd seemed barely to have grasped the rules. 'Really, Avril,' Esme used to say, 'I'd no idea I was living with a hardened deceiver.' Mum's quiet, hurried manner seemed to leave no time for planning a deception, or suggest any aptitude for bringing it off. I said, 'Jane, she wasn't a spy, was she? Esme used to tease her and say she must have been – I can see it makes sense in a way, but I don't believe she was, do you?'

'Well,' said Jane, blinking out of the window as if taken aback by the question, then looking narrowly at me, 'well, *she* wasn't, no.'

She went on for a bit, about how she didn't know the details, situation pretty complex in Rangoon, but she might have been talking outside, beyond the window, only faint sounds, her lips moving. The funny thing was that it was one of my own early stories, explaining in a dorm or on a private walk in the woods with a friend the unaccountable absence of Dad, the secret agent, the Burmese Bond. 'Yes, I see,' I said.

'The reason she never told us about him was she didn't know anything about him herself. I think she only saw him two or three times.'

I said, 'But she said—' and laughed straight away at the pointlessness of protest.

'As soon as their little affair was discovered the bloke simply disappeared' – Jane jerked her head with a disillusioned look as if to say both *good riddance* and *what do you expect?*

I wanted to put in a plea for my mother, for it all to have

been a bit better than that. 'But she had the photograph,' I said, 'in the fancy frame. That must have meant something.'

'Yes, I imagine that's him,' said Jane.

It wasn't a moment to be short with Mum's grief-stricken friend, but I said fairly firmly, 'Well, it's written on the back, Jane.'

She looked down, looked up, she caught my tone. 'Oh, I think it may well be your father, Dave,' she said, 'but I very much doubt that's his name.'

For the house itself, multiple offers came in on the day it was put on the market, and the price climbed up for a fortnight in a welcome but abstract way. The estate agent's calls had a note of excitement I couldn't match. I had never much liked the house, although it had been 'home' for most of my life, and I knew every cupboard and stuck door and clicking bit of parquet in the place. Without my mother in it, and the things she'd made, it seemed more than ever a house to get out of completely.

'Will we ever come here again?' I said. When the deal was done and the time had exactly run out I pushed the keys of Crackanthorpe Lodge through Knight Frank's letterbox and stood looking at the envelope where it lay on the mat inside their locked glass door. In the window, held by nearly invisible wires, colour photos of two dozen houses to buy and to rent hung gleaming in the air. For the first time in my life I had nowhere in this town to let myself into. 'I'm homeless,' I said, when I got back in the car.

'Mm,' said Richard, 'though, unlike most homeless people, you also own a three-bedroom house in Kentish Town. And you've just had £845,700 paid into your bank account.'

I felt for the consolation in this, but as we swung through the empty square and up London Street, with the prospect of two hours' drive ahead of us, I caught glimpses here and there through windows and closing front doors of people I would never know beginning their evenings, just as they had before and still do now.

33

The following March Cara organized a Memorial Gathering (not a *service*, she insisted, and not a *meeting*, something Mark had had quite enough of in his long life). She asked me if I would read a poem, and we texted ideas back and forth for a week before agreeing on Yeats – grand, grim and rather discomfiting, I felt, to many who were likely to be there. 'Surely among a rich man's flowering lawns . . .' Mark, like me, had his inner anthology, I remembered him reciting these lines to me thirty years earlier – we had chanted along together, nearly in step, and holding each other's eye.

> What if those things the greatest of mankind
> Consider most to magnify, or to bless,
> But take our greatness with our bitterness?

The Gathering took place in the Cadogan Hall, where I was part of a huge crowd of people almost all unknown to me. I recognized the directors of the Tate, of the British Museum, Glyndebourne . . . The speakers sat in the reserved front row, some with their spouses and partners; Richard alas was interlocuting in King's Lynn. I was next to John Constable, the famous painter; as we waited we talked in a surprisingly heartfelt way about Lydia, whom he'd seen a lot of when he lived in New York in the 1980s. We agreed that Cara must be missing her especially today. Behind us row on row of people were talking too, at an uncertain pitch brought on by that room, somewhere between theatre and chapel. The printed order was headed 'Mark André Hadlow 1922–2016, A Celebration', but it had something of the funeral we'd all missed.

Everyone must have wondered if Giles would be speaking, but he'd got an unavoidable meeting in Brussels at the exact same time. He was very involved now, as we knew all too well, in insulting pretences at negotiation with heads of the EU. Charles Pearson, who emceed the event, allowed himself a quiet joke about this, which drew a rather bitter and impressively unanimous laugh in the echoing space. Giles had, however, written a short greeting, as he called it, which Pearson read to us – I drummed up a loud masking rumble in my head and blocked it out. And Laura Hadlow had come, bringing their son and daughter, whom I'd only seen before on television, as anxious-looking adolescents whirled along behind their father at Brighton or Blackpool; now they were in their late twenties, the girl fair like Laura, the boy hauntingly like Mark. They sat with Cara, in the front on the right, and made up a little for the obvious absence of her own two children.

I learned quite a lot from the first two speakers, one a colleague of Mark's from early on, who described the family background, the businessman father and the glamorous and difficult French mother with her own career on the stage: not a happy marriage, or a long-lived one, but filling Mark with his lifelong conviction of belonging to both cultures. Eric Hadlow had set up the Hadlow Exhibition at his son's public school – for a moment to my own surprise I coloured up, as if everyone were aware of me. Next was a woman I'd sometimes seen on TV, demolishing the government's economic arguments with laconic severity. Today she was more expansive, evoked Mark's business genius, and his ever-growing work as a philanthropist, which alone had justified, to his mind, the making of such large amounts of money. The impression of something close to sainthood felt more credible coming from so fierce a source. After her a young string quartet Mark had sponsored played some Haydn, which in its vigour and inventiveness and sanity seemed to confirm what the previous two speakers had said about Mark himself. I think we all saw how impossible it would have been for Giles to be here.

When it came to my turn I saw people checking the order of service and blinking at me, some of them, in a disoriented way, turning their heads as if I might be hard to hear. (I have never been hard to hear.) And no doubt there was also recognition, and a sense of some of them knowing a bit about my part in the story, and even being pleased at hearing and accepting this racially distinct person. I had memorized the poem, to make it more immediate, but to some people this is always confusing, it makes them self-conscious and they barely take in what you say. So I held my *Collected Yeats* open in my hand to anchor and formalize their experience. The book itself when I glanced at it seemed to me a gathering of memorials, of the shadowy years beyond years through which I'd owned it and read it and slipped dog-eared markers between its pages.

> Surely among a rich man's flowering lawns,
> Amid the rustle of his planted hills,
> Life overflows without ambitious pains;
> And rains down life until the basin spills . . .

I looked up and out at the raked rows of faces, blots of red plush here and there in the pattern of dark suits and dresses, with a question in my mind as to what part I had played in a life that had been full of these hundreds of other people. I felt I was an intimate, as well as being way out on the periphery – I was a special case, for Mark and Cara, with privileges others who knew them much better and saw them all the time never had. And I had the old feeling, from fifty years back, that Mark himself was caring and just but aloof, and Cara the one with available and changeable emotions.

> But when the master's buried, mice can play,
> And may be the great-grandson of that house,
> For all its bronze and marble, 's but a mouse.

Well, they took it, the grandees, as they had to, and in honour of Mark and of art.

Afterwards we went into a bleak hospitality room with white iron pillars and fire doors, but it was well-staffed and quickly filled up with our noise and activity. I slid a glass of champagne from its slot in the tray, and looked around, unsure where I'd find my level. I wished very much that Richard was with me. Various people congratulated me as they passed by, various others didn't. A nice enough old couple who'd seen me in *Bajazet* came past, and we talked for a couple of minutes. 'Well, we mustn't keep you from your admirers!' they said, and went off to the buffet, leaving me all alone. I noticed Giles's son, as he glanced over his shoulder, and a moment later he broke away from the group he was with. 'Hello, Mr Win!' he said. 'Thank you so much for your words today.'

'Not really my words,' I said.

'But you read them so beautifully.'

'Well, thank you,' I said, as he kept looking and smiling at me. I felt I had the interest for him of someone who has just performed, and might with a bit of luck do so again. 'And you must be . . . Mark's grandson – you're so like him.' He was really the same as Mark in the eyes and brow, but with a fuller mouth, and something flinching mixed in with the charm, reflex perhaps of having Giles as a father.

We shook hands and he said, 'I am, I'm David Hadlow.' For a topsy-turvy second or two I imagined Giles had paid me the most touching compliment – very shyly, and shamingly, somehow.

'I didn't know you were David . . .'

'Oh, after my godfather, David Harris . . . you know?'

'Well, of course, I know who you mean,' I said. It still seemed preposterous to me that Fash had not only a Christian name, but my own.

'We saw you in *Space* at the Almeida last summer, you were brilliant.'

'Oh, thank you – it was great fun to do.'

'We thought it was bound to transfer to the West End.'

'We hoped so too,' I said discreetly, 'but Annick wasn't able to commit to it.'

'Ah, yes, of course . . .'

'Do you see much theatre?' I sounded for a moment like the Queen Mother, cut off from the behaviours of the young.

'Yes, quite a lot. Actually my partner's a designer—' and he looked round and laid his hand on the arm of a young man with dyed blond hair who was talking to the group behind him. 'Babes,' he said, 'this is David Win.'

Babes gasped as he joined us. 'Hello, I'm Jonny,' he said, 'so thrilled to meet you!' and he dodged my extended hand and flung an arm round me and kissed me on the neck. Perhaps he was already drunk. 'David says you were at school with his dad!'

'I know . . .' I said. 'Extraordinary, isn't it.' He still had his hand on my waist. I was trying to picture Giles's relations with his son, and his son's boyfriend: perhaps cordial, though just as possibly brutal. I knew he had abstained in the vote on gay marriage under Cameron – 'Not my place,' he had said on *Question Time*, 'to decide on such a private matter': his pompous shifty way of saying no.

'What was he like?' said Jonny, bright-eyed.

I looked at David, who seemed tensely curious about my answer. 'I'll tell you some other time, perhaps,' I said, which was tactful and carried after all the idea of some future fun with these young people, dinner after a show. There was a dim sense of justice to it, or revenge.

'Ooh, all right, then,' said Jonny.

'I don't know how much you saw of your grandfather,' I said to David.

'Well . . .' he said, and now he was hovering himself at the threshold of a large subject. 'Well, quite a lot, in fact. We used to go and stay with them in the holidays – my Mum took us.'

'Oh, I'm so glad.'

'Yes, they were wonderful – obviously! It was just – you know . . .'

'Yes, I know,' I said.

'Aah, sweetheart!' said Jonny, and kissed him on the cheek. It occurred to me that Jonny might be on something a bit stronger than champagne.

'Anyway, we mustn't keep you,' said David, happy but a little embarrassed by this affection. 'We'd love to have you round some time – you and your husband. If you'd like that.'

For a second I was back in the long red-tiled hallway at Woolpeck, shaking Mark's hand for the very first time, when the words that his grandson had just spoken were as unimaginable as walking on the Moon. 'I know we'd both be delighted,' I said. They smiled and nodded and went back through the crowd of much older people they barely knew.

I stood by the buffet and coaxed the cautious waitress into piling a decent-sized meal on a plate. The seats were taken by the many who needed them, so I tucked into my potato salad standing up. After ten seconds an old boy, very old, but pink-faced and handsome, was wheeled up in his chair by his haggard but enthusiastic wife. 'Hello, hello,' he said. I felt he was a man who liked a party. 'I liked what you read.'

'Thank you,' I said.

'Very good. Very *clearly* read.' He smiled up at me. '*Keats*,' he said.

'I think in fact . . . wasn't it Yeats?' said his wife.

'Yes, it was Yeats,' I said.

'It was Yeats, Mike' – and she gave his wheelchair a shake.

'It was a favourite poem of Mark's,' I said.

'You're an actor, aren't you, I'm sure we've seen you in things.'

'I am,' I said, 'David Win,' with a quick drop of the head, having both hands full.

'What was it you were in?'

'*Well* . . . I was in *Wingate's War*?'

'That must be it. Terrific. Well, how exciting!'

'And you are?' I said apologetically.

'Oh . . .' – he shook his head, as if his name were so unimportant he could barely remember it himself, then muttered, 'I'm . . . I'm Mike . . . Mike Kidstow.'

'Aha!' I said, smiling over the quick large adjustment, the revealed importance of this groomed and self-consciously charming old man, with his napkin and plate and his accumulated power – accumulated but now perhaps largely formal and on the wane. 'I know you were an old friend of Mark's.'

'I was at *school* with Mark,' he said, smiling again now, at the inner prospect of a hoard of stories which at last might find their moment.

'Do you mean at Bampton?'

'That's right . . .'

'Oh, I was there too.'

Now he beamed through his own surprise. 'So we're all of us BOBs,' he said, 'what fun. Well, I'm ninety-one, so I was two or three years younger than Mark, but we became great pals – really very close.'

'Oh, yes . . .' I said.

His wife jogged his chair again. 'Don't go on about all that, Mike,' she said.

'Now you've really got me interested!' I said.

'Can't I say . . .?' said Mike Kidstow, bemusedly. 'It was, what was it? seventy-eight years ago . . .'

'No, you say what you like, dear. I'm getting another drink.' And she set off towards the buffet, draining her glass as she went.

'Well . . .' said Mike, and I squatted down with my plate beside his chair to keep whatever it was between ourselves; we were the closest of friends. 'You probably wouldn't know this, but dear old Mark – ah, Cara, Cara . . . !'

I looked round to see Cara, with her stick, and a glass of champagne in her other hand. 'Oh, you're having a drink,' I said half-guiltily, 'good!'

'I bloody well am,' she said.

'I was telling him how well he read that poem,' said Mike.

'You couldn't help me for a minute, Dave, could you?' Cara said.

I straightened up. 'Of course I could. I'm so sorry,' I said, and I went off after her, leaving Lord Kidstow smiling and alone in his chair at the end of the room. I still wonder what it was that he wanted to tell me.

34

We were driving back from Wales and a faint idea swelled in a matter of two or three miles into a chance that mustn't be lost. It was a fine windy day – for weeks the wind had been tearing, rushing autumn forward across fields and gardens and stripping the trees which in calmer days might have made a longer showing. I slowed at the junction after Swindon, and turned off and soon we were into the narrow lanes that lead over towards Shrivenham and Woolpeck. The Downs in their dreamlike mutable way lay low at first, like a failure of memory. I said, 'If I live as long as my mother, I've got twenty-three springs ahead of me.' It was the way I'd reassured myself years ago as middle age set in – that there was as much time ahead as behind, and the charm still perilously held as the proportion dwindled.

'By that measure,' Richard said, 'I've got one. Which way are we going?'

'I thought we might get up on the hill for a bit, I don't think you've ever seen that view.' And in four or five minutes the Downs began to rise and occupy the lower sky, sublimely far off yet close at hand, with everything under them, farms and woods and folds in the land, shown to a new scale. The Byre was falling into shadow, the lone thornbush still a marker halfway down the slope, the crown of the hill radiant above in the late sun; the notch in the circuit of the Rings showed clear against the blue. It was more or less the view Cara had captured in the painting we have, and Richard said simply, 'Ah, yes, I see . . .'

We came into Woolpeck on a lane that threaded through from the west and brought us to a T-junction by a row of thirties semis, the old council houses, gardens gravelled for cars now, roofs an up-to-date sheen of solar panels. I turned right out of instinct, unhappy for a moment at not knowing where I was. Then the road bore round steadily to the left and past the end of a barn and there across the meadow on Richard's side was the farmhouse, the three gables and ten staring windows, the old bareness to it, and a feeling something further had been stripped away. My mind was absorbed in impressions beyond words, and I pulled up on the verge where the hedge was low enough for us to see across. 'Yes . . .' I said, staring and nodding, 'my god . . . well, they seem to have got rid of the tennis court, and there was a huge hedge beyond it, and then the shed Cara used as a studio – that's all gone.' 'Right . . .' said Richard, 'well, perhaps we should get out': so we did, and as I gazed at the house I had a weird sense that we ourselves were being watched. I felt I had a somehow inadmissible purpose in being there, and when a woman came past with a dog and said, 'Hello!' in the country way I'd grown up with but abandoned in London I smiled and walked on as if we weren't concerned with the house at all. But of course it was spellbinding, it stood off in the present as it possessed me from the past. If its setting looked bleaker and barer, at least to the right the picture was framed by the double line of beeches flanking the drive, the last leaves clinging on, heads as high as the roof of the barn beyond. 'Those trees had just been planted when I first came here,' I said.

'Well, that was nearly fifty years ago, love,' Richard said.

All trace of the Pollitts had gone – I felt this very clearly. Giles had let the farm, on a long lease, and the house had the ordinary unhaunted look of a place where a family get on with their busy lives, not thinking of the family who lived there before. We came to the gateway and looked in for a minute.

There was a sense of order, of the proud but unsentimental use of a serious property. I felt the mystery of its self-containment, practical but private, engaged as it always had been in its own business, which was no business of ours. As we went back to the car and then drove on and up as far as we could, to the hikers' car park, I tried to explain the presence of the place in my mind, its function, so habitual as to seem instinctive, visited innumerable times, little mental occasions, glimpse more than word, though particular words bring it back: chickenwire, Clytemnestra, plutocracy. When I hear even now of a *coup d'état* it is Ernest the Hereford bull that I see. The house itself is where any novel I'm reading is instantly set, the stage-set of sofa, rugs, table I'm crossing and speaking in has, in my mind alone, a view of the sunlit Downs from the window, a boot room unimaginable to the audience, and a high-fenced tennis court, like a further stage, waiting.

We were up at the Rings for the sunset – leaning on the wind, thrilling and awesomely accelerated from the strong winds of childhood – a breathless feeling of alarm at our new weather, whatever its episodic splendour. It was bleak, after a lifetime of fears defied, to face these further challenges, which after our death will be inescapable to others as death itself. I thought randomly, mere images of clever David Hadlow, radiant Nina Adeleke – in their middle years, as the whole globe combusts. Still, for now, the last sunlight, edging upwards across the Vale, lit the woods and hedgerows, ancient churches, cars on sidelights tiny in the far-off lanes, and turning homewards. 'We'd better go down,' said Richard, 'before we get blown down.' I took his arm, and we made our way, cautious then scuttling, off the steep grassy bank, and then on towards the car.

I've seen it once, and I'll see it for ever, though I shall never watch it again. The angle is high, and the light is a hazy-edged pool where walking figures enter, swell and cast shadows before melting steeply away. I don't know about the speed of the recording, but there's a jerkiness to it, the tiniest time-lapse, which gives the movements of ordinary passers-by an atmosphere of threat, thrown out or feared. Any figure who comes back into the light again a short time after leaving it has the air of a criminal, just before or just after committing a crime. The high vantage-point makes the faces of hooded or hatted pedestrians hard to make out. It's all in colour, of a sort, though the effect on the screen is small-hours black-and-white, and the sound too is vague and fragmented, delayed hiss of tyres of a passing van, raised voices in broken barks if heard at all.

Our man is not hooded, he moves fast, but with a sense of purpose and direction which keeps changing, because he is drunk, three times over the driving limit, and he's taken in more than a gram of cocaine in the past half-hour. Police cameras mean nothing to him, nor do government warnings about not meeting other people, or going out. There is very little traffic. He passes through the field of view from top to bottom, a pale burly figure in jeans and a tank-top, despite the cold night; thirty-eight seconds later by the ever-running ticker at the top of the screen he comes back, crosses the street and pisses in the small front garden of a house with lit but curtained windows. He's just done himself up when he notices the man with a shopping bag who is walking through briskly from the top of the picture, and shouts something the police determine later is simply 'Oi! Cunt!' The smaller figure is in a dark pea-coat and white trousers, with a blue mask under his chin, that he must have pulled down from his face after leaving the Sainsbury's Local. He is quick and elegant in his movements, East Asian, perhaps, in appearance. The encounter lasts twelve seconds, not to be described, and incoherently noisy, so that the curtains of the pissed-on house are flung open, a woman who's arrived on the far side of the street stops dead and watches for a horrified moment before running off. The assailant steps back into the road to stare at what he's done, and think about doing some more. Analysis of the recording suggests he shouts, 'Fucking Chink poof cunt,' before he draws himself up, staggers and strides and jogs off out of shot. All this happened 130 yards from this house, on the 28th of March 2020.

Edie and Ken came round the next day – we stood yards apart in the hall and I said, 'Oh, for fucksake,' and Ken gave me a hug that went on for ten seconds or more, then Edie did the same, gasping behind her mask. He was angry and bewildered, she was anxious for me, and frightened, too, as if the same unimpeded violence could break in here. I saw I had to comfort her, and reassure her. She started making tea, but the Scotch was out before the kettle had boiled, and we went into the living room. David's seat was left empty in such a respectful way that I got up and sat in it myself.

They wanted to talk about it, 'if you do, Rich'. What had happened? What did we know? Where was it again that he was? The Royal Free, the Whittington, UCLH were overwhelmed with patients struggling and nearly dying and dying for real. It was Cara Hadlow who'd come through, frail on the phone, unable to go out if she'd wanted to, at ninety-seven. She had him transferred by private ambulance to a small private hospital in Marylebone – Ken raised his eyebrows and let out a heavy sigh when I told him this. 'Well, thank god for that,' he said.

'And have they got him,' said Edie, 'the man who did it?'

'They picked him up within an hour. He's a well-known local villain. We've seen him around, drinking outside the Castle. He's shouted stuff at David and me before now.'

'GBH is it then?' said Ken.

'At least,' I said, 'or could it be attempted murder? – I should know, I edited a book about all this years ago.' We didn't know yet what the police would work out – about how what was said expressed motive.

'It's only because of that camera outside the recycling centre that we know what happened at all. You know, people climb in and nick stuff their neighbours have thrown away—' I gaped at them.

'Dave doesn't remember . . . ?'

'Oh, nothing, as yet, but he's still very drugged, you know, and confused.'

The first cases in the country had been in late January, Chinese nationals in York. China was the source, no doubt of it, and over the next two months police figures showed hate crimes against Chinese people tripling, online hate speech towards East Asian people in general increasing by 900 per cent. In official and government records non-Chinese East Asian people were conflated as 'Asian: Other'. In a few weeks history went backwards by a century.

On 16 March over-seventies were urged to stay home, and later the same day the theatres were closed. David was a week into *Burmese Days* at the Dorfman, playing U Po Kyin, a small part he was having fun with, and felt born to play. Each night the audiences were thinner, punters with tickets not showing up. 'It's like during the fucking Protectorate,' he said, when the message confirmed there would be no show at all the next night, and maybe not for weeks.

'Just look forward to the Restoration,' I said. 'Remember, all that raunch.'

'Despite appearances, lovey,' he said, 'I wasn't even *born* in 1660.'

We were due to have David Hadlow and Jonny for supper the following Sunday, but they texted and said they didn't want to expose us to any risk. 'So it's not just the government who think I'm geriatric,' David said, 'but David and Jonny too! I'm seventy-one, not ninety-one!' A bit later we went upstairs for an hour and he made this point in another way, very persuasively.

In the first week in hospital he was sedated, and in a very bad state. The left side of his face was so beaten that the eye wouldn't open, and his right wrist was broken. There were complicated internal injuries, a ruptured spleen that had been operated on at once, and several other matters being monitored. I got used to driving out of our silent street, down through locked-up Camden Town, with masked figures in a long line, yards apart, outside Tesco for food, then crossing the empty Marylebone Road and parking where I liked outside the hospital. The throat swab extended by a visored nurse, the wait for clearance, and a sense almost of privilege at having a problem other than Covid, as I was asked to go upstairs.

The second week he was brighter, and wrote notes – tapped notes, on his phone with his left thumb (the right hand still bandaged and splinted). He still had no memory at all of the attack, and was puzzled, above all, by the morphinated present: 'This morning', he wrote, on his fourth day, 'Mr Marchant the consultant and the two lesser doctors with him were fish – standing up, of course, like the Fish Footman in *Alice*, or the fish St Antony preached to, upright in the water. Perhaps their masks and face-shields enriched the illusion. It was both normal and delightful – as that one night at Turnmills, on god knows what, when I said to Joey how sweet it was that the dancers had all dressed up as trees, and he smiled and squeezed the back of my neck. The fish-doctors were like the dancers, lovely, not frightening at all.'

When I went in he would tell me about his other visitors, Esme had been in, John Gielgud; his mother was coming later. Last night he'd been taken to a party at Sandringham. 'Very grand,' I said, 'did you meet Her Majesty?' 'You bet I did, we chatted for hours, she's not at all grand once you get to know her.'

In clearer hours, when he didn't need to squeeze the morphine button on his drip, he dropped, 'like a pearl-diver', he said, into a deep past clear beneath the currents. These jottings have the quality of dreams, random and blatant and cryptic at the same time. 'You mustn't mind,' he said – there were quite a lot of sex things, memories of people like Chris Canvey who seemed to be as live and exciting to him now as they had been forty or fifty years ago. And there were bits of plays and poems, Hopkins sonnets, 'Felix Randal', 'Spelt from Sybil's Leaves', almost perfect, that came up not as a test of memory but spontaneously, he said: they were part of him, and always had been. We downloaded the Shakespeare app on his phone, and when he was sitting up I perched on the bed with him and gave him cues from it and he went through parts he'd played, Jaques, Fabian, his very first role: 'Good madam, hear me speak'. 'It's my famous old memory, darling,' he said, though even he seemed a little surprised by how good it was. Mr Marchant, who plays the 'cello in a string quartet and translates from Italian in his spare time, was interested by this, and warily encouraged, though other matters under constant and discreet observation caused him deep concern. 'It's good to keep his mind occupied,' he said. They operated on him again that night, and he was sleeping when I went in first thing the next morning. At some point he had made more notes on his phone.

'Are these things for the book?' I said, when he was conscious again.

'Well, I'll have to get on with it when I'm home,' he said. 'Which I hope won't be too long. Not this week, I think.'

He died the next morning – an unstoppable haemorrhage.

Then it was in the news, and David was famous, not only for having been attacked, but in a new retrospective way: to optimize its interest, the story required him to be a bit more famous than he was – 'celebrated mixed-race actor', 'theatrical veteran David Win'. I stood at the front door and spoke to a journalist standing by the front gate. I could tell the word husband was difficult for him, from the smooth way he brought it out, eyebrows raised. I told him I couldn't say anything. 'Read his book if you want to know about his work,' I said. I shouldered the cliché and asked the press to 'respect my privacy'; and such was the deluge of death in the coming weeks, and so dismembered the normal ways of meeting and speaking, that David's story quickly lost purchase. There was a four-week gap before the funeral, no risk now of the actor's send-off at St Paul's, Covent Garden that he'd joked about and just possibly hoped for. Ten mourners maximum allowed, household members and close family. Well, close family David didn't have, or not that he ever knew of. His favourite student Calvin Leung came and stayed at the house, and we made meals together: it was unexpected but comforting, and we talked a lot about him, and I saw more clearly how Calvin had adored him. I kept David's phone charged as I went day by day through a bit more of his notes and messages, downloading photos which I hungered for and shrank from at the same time. Across the room I saw its black screen under the lamp, the kisses and smudges of my fingertips laid over his on the glass – which came alive, as bright as the lamp, when someone called for him, unknowing.

Calvin was there, at the crem up in Finchley, and Ken and Edie were supporting me. David Hadlow asked to come, representing his grandmother, and something else, we all felt: continuity after the great hiatus. We sat masked in alternate rows in the lofty brick chapel, as music was played over the speakers: Vaughan Williams seemed right. No hymns or readings during the brief godless service, though as the curtains closed on the coffin a recording of David himself from his Radio 3 *Tempest*, 'Our revels now are ended', which had me pressing the black fabric of my mask into my mouth to stop the noise.

I've been researching David dead, as he claimed I did when he was alive – seeking traces of him in the record. There are very few photos of Terra productions and I've only found him in two of them: in the famous *Troilus and Cressida*, in warpaint and a jock-strap, and also a play I can't identify, where he's merely shirtless, and carrying a rifle. TV, too, has melted away, though he'd salvaged a miraculous VHS transfer of episode one of *Hibiscus Hotel*, in which of course he's the receptionist. With freeze-frame you can follow this first screen appearance, the ten seconds in which he walks away from the camera, turns, and an obliging smile spreads across his face. He looks much younger than his twenty-two years, and beautiful, on a different level from anyone else in the show, and I can't be the only person who has longed for him to stay in the room. I click and click the button to freeze each moment of the dawning and then dwindling smile; then I trot him quickly backwards and he does it all again. The simple gesture dilates into an epic event, a sequence of tiny muscular changes prolonged over silent minutes. At normal speed, with its heartbreaking brevity, a man off-camera says, 'I want to see the manager,' the banal accidental with which this mythic saunter, turn and smile will be paired for ever.

The Granada *Jack and Jackie* was all wiped, apart from one episode, which you can watch on YouTube, in wobbly-edged black-and-white: the Madges go on holiday and find that David's character, whom they know from the cafe where he works back home, has booked into the same boarding-house. Jack Madge calls him 'Thai Pot', and the script abounds in genially delivered racism that is lapped up by the studio audience. There's also a brief outdoor sequence, shot on the beach at Bournemouth – the earliest proof I've found on film of directors' compulsion to make David undress. You can see he enjoys it, there's something almost indecent about it, which no one at the time admits they've registered. As the men change under towels, Jackie's glance wanders from the shyly emerging bulk of her husband, played by Trevor Downs, to the sleek dark figure of David in his swimming-trunks, and the freeze-frame again gets the nearly invisible comedy of her suspicion and interest, the furtive dilation of her eye.

In the reports of his murder on national news they used a nine-second clip from *Burmese Days* and on the local news channel a longer segment from his appearance on *Newsnight Review*, ten years ago, talking about race and theatre with Bonnie Greer and Kwame Kwei-Armah. He said he was optimistic about recent developments, 'I think we've seen a

484

large deep change in attitudes across the country. The next generation will look back with disbelief at the racial prejudice we grew up with.' The other panellists accord him the respect due to someone with a long track-record as an actor, but I still have the feeling that the public didn't know his work, they hadn't really taken him in.

I have all his diaries, kept in the diminutive hand which turns everyone who sees it into a smug graphologist: David was anal, secretive, perfectionist, 'it all makes sense'. Later on, the neatness is mainly a visual effect, of minuteness and order, and the words can be nearly impossible to make out. He was consulting the diaries as he wrote his memoir, and there are hundreds of Post-its, with more tiny writing on, frilling the pages of the small blue books. He once said the work involved a continuous traffic between 'confident memory' and 'honourable invention'. Any bit of dialogue from fifty years back must be an invention, except a few salient phrases (which time and repetition may have chiselled into greater salience still). The most the diaries themselves contain is phrases such as, 'H said there was "no point in being with me" if I was going to "ignore him and lay down the law about everything"': to which nearly forty years later David could still no doubt conjure up a reply.

So I've edited (salvaged, not savaged) what I seem years ago to have called his magnum opus – the unfinished counterpart to the one book he actually published. I've hardly touched what he wrote, from fear of hurting it, some further violence to him. I hesitate for once to do my job: to pull his text into a shape that I've imagined myself, or imagine (knowing him so well) that he'd imagined. He wrote a lot, but these are only fragments of what he could have said.

It's been strange to read my husband's detailed accounts of

his long-ago lovers; strange to think of him in his room above mine, writing them up. Striking that he remembered them in such detail, that they weren't just the embarrassing barely believable episodes most people rarely think of and never mention. Terra was a free space for gays and lesbians, however nerve-racking it may have been in other ways: there was solidarity. But I sense something else in David's stories of Chris Canvey and Hector Bishop, a feeling of surprise, and gratitude, even decades later, that they had loved him and wanted him.

When the new lockdown loomed in late October, the prospect of being alone again in this house as the nights closed in was a terrible one. I asked Calvin if he'd like to move in to David's room, and make a bubble with me, a baby family unit. The libraries were closed, and this house seemed a reasonable place for him to get on with his work on queer theatre.

He does what he can to console me – in the depths of the night, when goods trains rattle miles-long past the house and bring me up into unwelcome wakefulness. He is warm and cool equally – sleeps soundlessly, unmoving. Are we an odd couple, brought together by a shared love of a third person we can neither of us now have? The truth is we have little else in common. Old friends who come in on Zoom are nice to him, and wave and call out when they see him cross the room behind me; they take him as a symptom of my grief, and wait for the time when I'm over the worst of it, and the rules are relaxed, and things get back to a version of how they were. Calvin is both solid and substanceless: he takes up space in a room or a bed, but to me he is mainly a comforter. I think this is true, at the moment.

If you lose your husband when you're sixty-two, it's a poor look-out. You feel this, and you know others feel it about you. Then I think that David was sixty when he met me, and what he sometimes called the best years of his life were all ahead of him. Crude survivor's thoughts, at odds with both the heartbreak and decorum of grief.

David hadn't settled finally on a title for his book – but I remembered the idea he had mentioned when I asked him, the little phrase he uses half a dozen times, and which seems latent in the text much more often. I'm not sure yet if the possessive pronoun is a solace or an ambush.

Alan Hollinghurst is the author of six previous novels, *The Swimming-Pool Library*, *The Folding Star*, *The Spell*, *The Line of Beauty* (winner of the 2004 Man Booker Prize), *The Stranger's Child* and *The Sparsholt Affair*. He lives in London.